Lucy King spent her adolescence lost in the glamorous and exciting world of Mills & Boon when she really ought to have been paying attention to her teachers. As she couldn't live in a dream world for ever, she eventually acquired a degree in languages and an eclectic collection of jobs. After a decade in southwest Spain, Lucy now lives with her young family in Wiltshire, England. When not writing, or trying to think up new and innovative things to do with mince, she spends her time reading, failing to finish cryptic crosswords and dreaming of the golden beaches of Andalusia.

Growing up near the beach, **Annie West** spent lots of time observing tall, burnished lifeguards—early research! Now she spends her days fantasising about gorgeous men and their love-lives. Annie has been a reader all her life. She also loves travel, long walks, good company and great food. You can contact her at annie@annie-west.com or via PO Box 1041, Warners Bay, NSW 2282, Australia.

THE FLAW IN HIS RIO REVENGE

LUCY KING

A PREGNANCY BOMBSHELL TO BIND THEM

ANNIE WEST

MILLS & BOON

First published in Great Britain 2024
by Mills & Boon, an imprint of HarperCollins*Publishers* Ltd,
1 London Bridge Street, London, SE1 9GF

www.harpercollins.co.uk

HarperCollins*Publishers*, Macken House, 39/40 Mayor Street Upper,
Dublin 1, D01 C9W8, Ireland

The Flaw in His Rio Revenge © 2024 Lucy King

A Pregnancy Bombshell to Bind Them © 2024 Annie West

ISBN: 978-0-263-32005-3

04/24

This book contains FSC™ certified paper
and other controlled sources to ensure responsible forest management.

For more information visit www.harpercollins.co.uk/green.

Printed and Bound in the UK using 100% Renewable Electricity
at CPI Group (UK) Ltd, Croydon, CR0 4YY

THE FLAW IN HIS RIO REVENGE

LUCY KING

MILLS & BOON

CHAPTER ONE

AT ELEVEN P.M. on a Saturday night in September, in the gilded ballroom of a seven-star Athens hotel, the charity auction at the Stanhope Kallis Foundation gala was drawing to a close. A sumptuous six-course dinner accompanied by the finest wines had preceded it, and as a result, over the last hour, millions of euros had been thrown at luxury villas, questionable art and cases of claret by well-fed, well-oiled guests determined to outdo each other.

Santiago Ferreira, however, who was lounging in the seat for which he'd paid a five-figure sum, had eaten little, drunk less and was saving his money for the last lot on the list.

Stone-cold sober, biding his time and ignoring the puerile one-upmanship that was going on around him, he slowly turned his coffee this way and that. He watched as up on the stage Thalia Stanhope, the foundation's CEO, hovered in the wings. Her dark hair was swept up into an elegant pile on the top of her head. The pearls dangling from her earlobes and circling her throat gleamed white against her olive skin. The full-length dress encasing her pneumatic body was cherry-red and tight.

She was more beautiful than he remembered, he

thought, letting his gaze drift over her dispassionately. So cool and composed, despite the sultry sensuality. She—the daughter of an aristocratic British banking mogul and a Greek shipping socialite, who'd been brought up with immense privilege and educated at the world's finest institutions—was the epitome of class, sophistication and inherited wealth.

He, on the other hand, was the now-orphan son of an impoverished single mother and a wealthy father who'd refused to acknowledge him—and whom he'd therefore never met—and had grown up in a shack in a drugs-and-guns-ridden favela on the outskirts of Rio de Janeiro. He'd received very little in the way of formal education and hadn't even learned to read and write until he was fourteen. He was brash not subtle, rough not elegant, and *his* wealth was newly acquired.

He was everything she wasn't, as she'd once so brutally reminded him. But that hadn't stopped them embarking on a blazing affair the evening they'd met on Naxos, at the wedding of a former colleague of his to Thalia's twin brother, sixteen months ago. One look across the bar was all it had taken to detonate an explosion of heat between them and instinctively propel him towards her, even though his mother's experiences of the rich and privileged had taught him that getting involved with someone like her would be madness.

'Dance with me,' he'd murmured, in the faintly accented yet flawless English he'd vowed to master the minute he'd realised it was the language of technology.

'Yes,' she'd replied breathlessly, her English polished to perfection by a Swiss finishing school that had been followed by Oxford.

He could recall nothing of the music they'd swayed to. Nothing of their surroundings. All he'd been aware of was the soft warmth of her body pressed up against his, the thundering of his pulse and the dizzying wildness of their kisses. Later, they'd tumbled into bed, setting fire to the sheets until dawn, and had subsequently met up whenever they were on the same continent at the same time, which, as the weeks had gone by, had occurred with increasing frequency.

Any misgivings had been dazzled into submission. That cool, cultured exterior of hers had concealed a volcano of passion the likes of which he'd never encountered before, all the more mind-blowing for its unexpectedness. And she'd seemed equally hooked on him. The minute the door to whichever hotel room they'd booked closed, she'd cast off her reserve, along with her clothes, and she'd launch herself at him, overwhelming him with a scorching blast of passion and need that without fail took out his knees and obliterated his brain. Their chemistry had been off the scale, their desire for each other insatiable. Their X-rated video calls had been so blisteringly hot it had always surprised him afterwards that their devices hadn't incinerated.

And then, twelve weeks later, thirteen months ago, she'd ended it. She'd just told him one day that they needed to talk—which, as everyone knew, meant only one thing—and once they were done, she'd coolly picked up her things and left. Which had never happened to him before because *he* was the one to terminate a relationship. *He* was the one who called the shots. Always. He *never* checked his phone for missed calls and messages that didn't come. He never *dwelt*. He moved on with no looking back and zero regrets.

That was why the abrupt end to their affair still irritated him so much, like a splinter lodged so deep it couldn't be prised out. Why it still dogged his thoughts day and night. Why he was stuck, unable to move on. He had not been ready to let her go. He'd been caught off guard. Humiliated. Stunned by the icy hauteur he'd never encountered in her before. She'd robbed him of his control and his strength and riddled him with doubt and confusion for the first time in years.

This disruption to his personal life could not be allowed to continue, he'd realised after months of wallowing in bitterness and self-pity. It had gone on for far too long already and enough was enough. Where he came from, weakness and uncertainty could get you killed. Obsession with the opposite sex, he learned at an early age, led to powerlessness, misery and despair. An absence of control could easily lead to unwise decision-making and impulsivity.

And so he'd come here tonight. Not just to secure the advice he sought but also to right a wrong. Several wrongs in fact, because he was not some plaything of the rich, to be picked up and discarded on a whim like his mother. He was not Thalia's inferior, despite what she'd intimated shortly before turning her back on him and walking out of that Paris hotel room. And no one rejected him these days.

Closure was what he wanted. Retribution. And to that end he intended to decimate her objections to him and rekindle their affair. To reel her in slowly and surely and to finish what they'd started. When the time was right, when the attraction had faded and he was ready, he'd let *her* go. And then, with the record set straight, the bewilderment and humiliation all hers, the power and invincibility once again all his, he'd finally be able to move on.

It was a simple but effective plan. He didn't doubt it would work. He was exceptionally single-minded and could be very persuasive when he chose to be. He'd had to put things on hold in order to focus on the recent sale of his software business, but that had been finalised and signed off six weeks ago. Having been catapulted from millionaire to billionaire, he now had a bank balance to rival hers, and all the time in the world to pursue other objectives.

'And lastly, to our final lot,' intoned the auctioneer, as every muscle Santi possessed tightened and adrenalin surged through his system. 'If you want to set up a foundation, expand your charity or organise a fundraiser and need a little help, this one's for you. Our CEO, Thalia Stanhope, is offering one hundred hours of her valuable time to consult and advise on any aspect of your enterprise. With a decade of experience in the sector, what she doesn't know isn't worth knowing. She is the ultimate expert. The best in the business. Who'll start me at fifty thousand?'

Silver paddles started flashing up and down almost instantly and within minutes the price for the lot had reached a quarter of a million.

Who'd have thought there'd be so much charitable feeling in the room? Santi reflected wryly, impervious to the growing buzz, his pulse beating steadily as the bidding continued apace, but pointlessly. Or was it the idea of spending one hundred hours in Thalia's company that was so appealing? He could understand that, on a superficial level. It had been double that amount of time before she'd shown him her true colours. Six weeks into their affair, he'd still been in her thrall, completely taken in by her exquisite façade and fiery passion.

But the motives of others were irrelevant. No one was going to win her but him, and his rivals had had their fun. It was time to close this lot down and activate the plan.

'Fifty million euros,' he said in an uncompromising tone that cut through the proceedings and warned everyone else to back the hell off.

A stunned silence descended over room, then the auctioneer found his voice and a minute later, with the bang of the gavel and a rush of triumphant satisfaction that was unexpectedly intense, given the fact that the outcome of the lot had never been in any doubt, Thalia was his.

CHAPTER TWO

FIFTY MILLION EUROS? What on earth was Santi Ferreira playing at? Who paid five hundred thousand euros an hour for *advice*? Why would he even want to? Was he *mad*?

Suppressing her shock and stamping out a sharp flare of emotion, Thalia somehow managed to deliver her speech, thanking everyone for their donations and support. Then she coolly stepped off the stage as if she hadn't just experienced an upset of cataclysmic proportions.

So much for assuming his presence here this evening was a benign coincidence, she thought darkly, as she batted aside a claim for her attention and made a beeline for him instead, no longer remotely interested in keeping her distance but intent now on finding out what he was up to.

Despite the attendance of six hundred guests, she'd clocked him the minute he'd walked in. With his towering height, powerful build and knee-trembling looks, he didn't exactly blend in. But even though she'd been irritatingly aware of where he was and who he was speaking to virtually every single second of every single minute, she'd steered well clear. The last time they'd seen each other had not been pretty, and she'd had zero desire to make an approach. Neither had he, she'd assumed with increasing relief as the time had passed without contact. But clearly she'd been labouring under a false sense of security. Because, since one presumably didn't spend fifty million euros in the heat of the moment, he must have had this move up his sleeve all along.

Behind her, up on the stage, a swing band consisting of ten sharp-suited musicians with vintage instruments got going, but all her attention was focused on the man who'd upturned her evening so dramatically.

With every inch of progress towards him her heart thudded faster and the odd fluttering in her stomach intensified. There were so many unknowns to the situation she thought, her nerves twisting tighter. She was at such a disadvantage. She'd have to establish control right from the off and set him straight on a few things because, whatever the reasons behind his winning bid, she couldn't work with him. She just couldn't. He was too overwhelming, too much of a distraction, too *everything*. That was why she'd had to end their affair all those months ago, even though it had been the last thing she'd wanted to do.

She could recall the moment they'd met as if it were yesterday. Her twin brother's wedding had been an event that, to her shame, she'd been dreading, and it had turned out to be every bit as difficult as she'd anticipated. She'd been sitting at the bar, nursing a glass of ouzo and struggling to untangle her complicated feelings about Atticus marrying Zoe—and killing off their ultra-close thirty-year twinship for good—when some sixth sense had prickled her skin and tightened her chest.

Her mouth dry, her pulse pounding in the most peculiar way, she'd looked up and around, and there he had been. The best looking, sexiest man she'd ever laid eyes on staring at her from the other end of the bar. Tall, broad-shouldered, his shaggy sun-streaked hair tousled as if he'd just rolled out of bed. And his eyes... Somehow, they'd seemed to smoulder. Dark and intense, they'd fixed on hers so intently that, for one long heart-stopping moment, she hadn't been able to breathe, let alone look away.

The guests, the music, her turbulent feelings, everything else had simply dissolved. All she'd been able to see was him. All she'd been able to hear was the thundering of her blood in her ears. Then he'd lowered his glass, his mouth curving into one slow devastating smile of pure temptation, and the burst of heat that had swept through her body had nearly burned her to a crisp where she sat.

This man could be exactly what she needed, she'd thought dazedly, desire pummelling away inside her as he'd headed in her direction, his compelling gaze unwavering, his intentions thrillingly obvious. A delicious distraction. A gorgeous, sexy pick-me-up who could grant her the oblivion she craved.

And that night he'd been everything she'd hoped for. In his arms on the dance floor everything but the feel of his hard body plastered against hers and his intoxicatingly masculine scent had fled her head. Afterwards, up in her room, he'd made her forget her own name so skilfully and so often that when he had enquired about her schedule and they'd discovered that they would both be in Italy the following week, she hadn't thought twice about agreeing to his suggestion that they meet up again.

For three giddy months she'd indulged the insane chemistry that burned between them, thinking about him constantly, almost to the point of obsession, until the voice in her head became too loud and insistent to ignore any longer. How could she figure out who she was without her twin brother if she didn't allow herself the time and the headspace to work on it? it persisted. How could she learn to forge her own path in life if she remained tangled up with someone else?

Atticus was the only person in this world who'd ever truly understood her, who'd been there for her no matter what. She'd always had him to turn to and rely on. Together, they'd survived the childhood trauma of appallingly neglectful parenting. But now she had to discover how to stand on her own two feet. And that couldn't happen if she kept falling back on Santi, who had swept her off into a different world, where she didn't have to think about anything but them every time they met.

Deep down she'd known that terminating their fling was the right thing to do, but the thought of it had nevertheless kept her awake at night and nauseated her by day. Having to explain to him the reason for doing so when she could barely articulate it herself had tightened the knots in her stomach even further. But in the end, with his shockingly unexpected and profoundly hurtful accusations of arrogance and snobbery in response to her announcement that they needed to talk, he'd made it very easy for her.

Thalia's heart thudded frantically as she neared and Santi rose from the seat in which he'd been lounging so carelessly, all gorgeously untamed six foot three inches of him clad in a perfectly fitting black dinner suit. His eyes were locked onto hers. A lazy smile played at his beautiful mouth. He wore his hair shorter now, she noticed distractedly. She thought she preferred it longer, even though the newly exposed cowlick was quirkily attractive. Then he slowly tugged free his bow tie and undid the top two buttons of his snowy white dress shirt, revealing a tantalising wedge of tanned skin, and a torrent of memories that she'd fought so hard to erase cascaded into her head. Of her undressing him. Of him undressing her. And then the touching and the heat and the uncontrollable need...

A burst of bittersweet longing swept through her and she was filled with the clamouring urge to grab his hand and haul him off upstairs, into the nearest available bedroom, in order to establish just how reliable her memories were.

But that was not going to happen, she told herself, ruthlessly obliterating the unwelcome desire and straightening her spine. Their bridges were well and truly burned and she was making great progress on her journey of self-discovery. She was successfully navigating solo relationships with her scandalous, self-centred mother and her four other siblings. Careerwise, she was breaking free from the safety net of the foundation and branching out on her own. She was being brave and taking risks and she would allow absolutely nothing to jeopardise any of it.

'Good evening,' he said in sexily accented English,

his deep voice skating over her nerve endings, sending shivers down her spine and, appallingly, tightening her nipples.

It wasn't a good evening at all, she thought, gritting her teeth against the unwanted response of her body to his, hugely grateful for the thick fabric of her dress that concealed the evidence. In fact, thanks to him, it was quite possibly the most stressful evening she'd had in months and, given the emotional rollercoaster of the last year, that was saying something.

'That's debatable,' she said with a cool smile, drawing on the diplomatic skills she'd picked up at finishing school, designed to hide all true thoughts and feelings. 'But fifty million euros is quite a sum. It will be appreciated by many.'

'You're welcome.'

'However, it does come as something of a surprise.'

His dark eyes glinted with—what was that? Triumph?—and a strange sense of wariness rippled through her. 'It's been a long time.'

One year, four weeks and three days. Not that she'd been counting. 'It has indeed.'

'How have you been?'

There was a question. In the aftermath of their breakup she'd been a hurt, soggy mess—for longer than she cared to acknowledge. Having eventually got over him, she'd then had to deal with the fallout of her brother's marriage, which had been, and still was, very emotional and stressful. Now, tonight, she wasn't quite sure how she was. Unsettled, baffled and faintly dizzy from the effects of his head-spinning scent might just about cover it.

'Couldn't be better,' she lied smoothly, wishing the band weren't quite so loud, so they didn't have to be standing quite so close. 'You?'

'Exceptionally well.'

'I'm so pleased.'

'You've been avoiding me all evening.'

He'd noticed? How? Had he been as aware of her as she had of him? Surely pique couldn't be the reason for his outrageous bid. 'If you wanted my attention, Santi, all you had to do was call.'

'Would you have picked up the phone?'

She would have last August. For days after they'd parted company in Paris she'd waited for an apology that had never come. It was mortifying to recall how pathetically weak she'd been when the whole point of splitting up had been so she could find her inner strength. 'I guess we'll never know.'

'Would you like a drink?'

'No, thank you.'

'Then let's dance.'

As the memory of what had happened the last time they'd hit the dance floor flashed through her head, her heart skipped a beat and then began to race. 'Absolutely not,' she said, determinedly not thinking about the hot, wild kisses that had practically blown the top of her head off that night.

'For old times' sake.'

A shudder ran through her. 'I see no need to recall those.'

'What are you afraid of?'

Nothing she was going to admit to him. It pained

her to admit to herself how strongly he still appeared to affect her. 'Tripping over my dress.'

'I won't let that happen.'

He planted a hand at the base of her spine, his touch burning her like a brand. But even though she nearly jumped out of her skin with shock, and every instinct urged her to pull away, she did not. She would not let him see what he was doing to her. Nor would she cause a scene. They were attracting enough attention as it was. So she pulled herself together and went with him to the dance floor. And when he took her hand in his, his arm around her waist to hold her close, she did not think about how much she'd missed the heat and strength of his body or the feel of his skin against hers.

'So let's talk terms,' he said, beginning to move her skilfully around the space, while she resisted the temptation to stare at his mouth or tuck her head into the perfectly positioned spot where his neck met his shoulder and assured herself that this torture couldn't last for long.

'Do you really want my advice?'

'What else would I want?'

'I have no idea.' That was the trouble. He was as unreadable as a blank page and she couldn't work out quite what was going on. 'But we have history and you paid well over the odds for my time.'

He tutted. 'So suspicious.'

'Can you blame me?'

'Not for that.'

Thalia frowned. What was he talking about? What else could he blame her for? If anyone had the right to be aggrieved it was her. He was the one who'd been bru-

tal when she'd hoped they'd be able to part as friends.
'I'm not sure I follow.'

'I sold my business.'

'So I read. In a record-breaking deal. Congratulations.'

'Thank you.'

'You must be very proud.'

Something unidentifiable flickered in the depths of
his dark gaze. 'It's just money,' he said with a faint
shrug of the muscled shoulder she had a hand on.

'It's a lot of money. In fact, you might now be even
richer than me.'

'Quite possibly. We'll have to compare bank balances some time.'

Hmm. 'So what are you going to do with it?'

'I intend to channel a significant chunk into philanthropy. However, I have no idea how to go about doing
that, and even less inclination to devote hours to finding out, hence my need for your expertise.'

'I'm flattered.'

'I hear you're the best in the business.'

She was.

Or at least she'd thought she was.

She'd worked for the sixty-year-old family foundation
for a decade, helping it to fulfil its mission to improve
the lives of millions of people around the world. It tackled complex social problems, established educational
and health programmes and supported entrepreneurial
and empowerment initiatives. It built communities and
changed outcomes.

Joining the organisation straight from university,
Thalia had thrown herself into the work. She'd started

at the bottom, learning from the ground up, and had been appointed CEO five years ago. In this position, she oversaw fundraising ventures and the allocation of those funds.

She'd loved every minute of all of it.

Until recently.

She'd always known that her surname and the status it inferred had fast-tracked her career. Her connections were unparalleled, her wealth unimaginable. Because of who she was—a member of the glamorous Stanhope Kallis clan—she was invited to the most prestigious events and had access to the richest, most beneficent people in the world. She'd never minded that. With privilege came responsibility, she'd always felt.

But ever since Atticus had met Zoe, and she'd had to reassess her life, it had begun to bother her. Was she genuinely good at what she did or was she merely a convenient figurehead? Did she command real respect or was she just being indulged? As the doubts had settled in she'd begun to question every decision she'd ever made and every conversation with the board she'd ever had, until she'd no longer been certain of anything.

The morning of the eleventh day in a row that she'd woken up dreading going into work she'd decided that the only way to find out what she was truly capable of was to take the plunge and branch out on her own. Setting up a consultancy service to provide charitable advice and support to others might backfire but, on the other hand, it might not. She'd never know if she didn't try. And that was what her lot this evening had been about—not just to raise money for good causes but also to land a high-profile client with whom she could launch her new business with a bang.

Well, she'd certainly achieved that, she thought as Santi twirled her out, round and back into him again. Right now, with his mega-bucks deal still reverberating through the business world, he was as high-profile as they came. If they hadn't had a past he'd have been the ideal candidate. So she had to ignore her misgivings and get a grip. What she was trying to achieve both personally and professionally was too important to be scuppered by a handful of historic hurt feelings and irritatingly persistent chemistry. She had to be mature and rational about this, because it sounded as though he did genuinely need her help, and a deal was a deal.

'I'll set up a call,' she said, accepting the fait accompli with as much grace as she could muster. 'Does this coming Wednesday suit?'

'This coming Wednesday doesn't suit at all.'

'What about the following week?'

'I'd prefer to conduct our discussions face to face,' he said, his cool smile hinting at implacability. 'With maximum privacy and minimal distraction.'

How irritating. 'My office here in Athens, then.'

'Or my home in Brazil, on the coast, west of Rio. I was thinking ten days, ten hours a day, eight to six.'

Outwardly, Thalia continued to move with him in time to the music, but inwardly she reeled. He wanted her to fly halfway across to the world to stay with him in his house for ten days? What on earth was he *thinking*? Had he completely lost his mind? On no level was it a good idea. It was unnecessary, unprofessional, unacceptable, and absolutely not going to happen. 'I'm afraid that won't be possible.'

'Why not?'

Because she didn't want to spend time with him and remember how badly he'd hurt her and how naïve and stupid he'd made her feel. Because awkwardness and tension did very much not make for an atmosphere conducive to working together. Because containing the unfortunate attraction she apparently still felt for him would be a herculean battle, and she wasn't a masochist.

And what if it got too much and she failed to resist him? The potential for mortification didn't bear thinking about. The implications of a relapse and undoing all the progress she'd made appealed even less. 'I have commitments.'

'Rearrange them.'

'As I'm sure you'll appreciate, it's not that easy.'

'Fifty million euros says it is.'

At that, she visibly stiffened. Goosebumps broke out all over her skin and her blood chilled. For a moment all she could do was stare at him in shock, frozen rigid in his arms, thinking, who was this man with his diktats and blackmail and his relentless attempts to crush her arguments to dust? Had she ever known him at all?

'Are you suggesting that if I refuse to accommodate your demands, you'll withdraw your donation?' she said, once she'd regained the power of speech.

'Would you like to put it to the test?'

No, she would not. The foundation welcomed every cent it was promised and she could not deny it such a fortune. And much as she might loathe the idea, she needed him. Reneging on the deal that had just been struck would damage her reputation for trustworthiness and reliability, and where else was she going to find a client of his calibre? Those who'd been bidding for her lot before he'd swooped in to snatch her up didn't come close.

She had no option but to yield to his outrageous terms. And it would be fine. She could bury the attraction. She'd just have to. From here on in, she'd channel indestructible resilience and Sphynx-like serenity. However deep she had to dig, whatever the provocation, she would remain cool and composed. She would battle every further attempt he made to wrestle control from her. She'd once given it up all too willingly, and she would not be that careless again.

She'd resist his charms and ignore the unwelcome effect he had on her. She'd look forward, not back. After all, theirs would be a professional relationship, and with his ten ten-hour days, a finite one at that. She would not fail. He would never know how much he'd hurt her with his cruel accusations. How devastated she'd been to discover how little he'd thought of her, when she'd thought the world of him. He'd certainly never know that he continued to have such a dramatic impact on her, despite her desperately wishing otherwise. So she lifted her chin and pulled her shoulders back and said, 'Of course not.'

'Because I'm sure there are others out there who'd welcome the opportunity to work with me.'

Well, *that* wasn't happening. 'But none with my experience and expertise.'

'Excellent,' he said with an annoying air of smug satisfaction. 'Then we're agreed. I'll see you at the airport, tomorrow morning at nine.'

CHAPTER THREE

THE REASON SANTI had boarded the plane at seven thirty this morning, a whole ninety minutes before he had arranged to meet Thalia, was because even though his body clock, still on Brazil time, should have switched him off like a light, he'd had a fitful night, thanks to unexpectedly erotic dreams in which she had had a starring role, and eventually he'd figured that he might as well head to the airport and kick up his heels there instead of in his hotel room. It had nothing whatsoever to do with the habit he'd once developed of turning up early at whichever venue they'd agreed upon so he could enjoy the anticipation of her arrival. Similarly, he'd taken up his current position—horizontally sprawled along the sofa—in order to relax and enjoy the buzz of owning a brand-new top-of-the-range plane. The fact that it afforded him a view of the door was mere coincidence.

Everything was going exactly according to plan, he thought with bone-deep contentment, as he took another quick glance at his watch, the third in as many minutes. The only thing he hadn't considered was the physical impact Thalia apparently still had on him.

Last night, he'd watched her make her approach and

his pulse rate had rocketed with every step she'd taken. It was in the expectation of the righting of wrongs, he'd told himself, easing the sudden pressure on his windpipe by loosening his bow tie and unbuttoning his collar. Although that hadn't explained the lightning strike of heat that had shot through him so unexpectedly that he'd nearly forgotten where they were and everything that had happened, and pulled her in for a kiss.

Instead, he'd opted for a dance, to remind her of how hot they'd been together. He hadn't expected to remember how perfectly she fitted him or how in synch they moved. And he certainly hadn't anticipated responding to her quite so powerfully, until he'd forced himself to recall what this was all about so he could refocus. But intense chemistry was hardly a problem. On the contrary, it would make the job of seducing her into his bed when the time came quite literally a pleasure.

A shift in the air and a tingling of his skin indicated Thalia's embarkation, and a moment later she entered the cabin. This morning she was wearing a navy trouser suit over a white shirt. Her dark glossy hair was tied up and back, but her effect was no less potent now than it had been the night before. When her gaze landed on him, slowly travelling from his bare feet up the length of his body to the top of his head, it left a scorching trail of fire in its wake.

'Good morning,' he said gruffly, ablaze yet unable to tell from her inscrutable expression whether her perusal of him had affected her in any way. Not that it mattered particularly. Her frosty demeanour last night suggested that, for her, the attraction had dimmed—but he'd soon relight it. Combustible chemistry like theirs didn't disappear completely. All he had to do was switch on the charm and let nature take its course.

'Nice plane,' she said, smoothly turning her attention to the well-appointed space as she advanced into it.

'Thank you.'

'Yours?'

'As of a month ago, yes.'

'It's immaculate.'

The wood was polished to a gleam he could see his reflection in. The carpet was thick, cream coloured and unmarked. It was everything he'd specified, far surpassing his expectations, and the first time he'd flown in it, he'd thought, *Not bad for a kid from the favela.*

'It's brand new.'

'Ours could do with an upgrade.'

'How many do you have?'

'The company has three. The family has one, which is usually commandeered by my mother. All of them are ancient and none of them is the size of this.'

'This is the biggest there is.'

'Naturally,' she said with a dryness that made him frown briefly, because what was she implying? That new money bought the shiniest and best while old made do and mended? Well, so what if it did? At least he'd earned his billions. In his view, it was those who hadn't who merited derision.

'Who else are we expecting?'

'No one.' He sat up, swung his legs down and round, and rose to his feet. 'But it's a twelve-hour flight, so the crew outnumber us by six to one.'

She paused mid-step, a flicker of alarm skittering across her face. 'Won't we be stopping for a refuel?'

'No need. The distance we're travelling is well within range.'

'I see.'

'Is that a problem?'

'Not at all,' she said, heading for the table by the window and settling herself into a seat with a quick smile that didn't quite reach her eyes.

'Are you sure?'

'Quite sure.'

'You seem a little put out by the thought.'

'I'm fine.'

Clearly she wasn't, Santi reflected as he folded himself into the seat opposite her, and watched lazily as she set her bag on the floor and extracted her laptop. But that suited him just fine, because a twitchy Thalia was a vulnerable Thalia, and with any luck that would make her even more susceptible to seduction.

'So let's get started,' she said briskly, placing the device on the table between them and opening the lid.

'With what?'

'Work.'

He arched an eyebrow. 'Now?'

'Yes.'

'We haven't even taken off yet,' he observed, making himself comfortable and loosely fastening his seatbelt. 'What's the hurry?'

'We're busy people.'

'I'm not. I have no demands at all on my time at the moment. Apart from breakfast.' And the plans he had for her.

'Well, I am, I do, and I've already had breakfast,' she said. 'And as you pointed out earlier, this is a twelve-hour flight. We might as well make use of it and knock off one day of the ten. What else are we going to do with the time?'

Santi could think of many things they could do with the time. At the rear of the plane was a cabin that had a super-king-size bed in it and a lockable door. He could keep her busy in there for hours, proving to her over and over again how much she'd once liked his swagger and his brash, uncouth ways.

Alternatively, she could continue to try and control the situation he'd put her in and he could amuse himself by indulging her. Last night, she'd attempted to dictate terms. This morning, she was having a crack at manipulating them. At no point was she going to succeed, of course, but she was welcome to carry on if she wished. The greater the battle, the sweeter her surrender. And surrender she would. Because, interestingly, she wasn't as immune to him as her no-nonsense approach would suggest. Now that she was in his direct line of sight he noted that her cheeks were stained with a faint flush. The pulse at the base of her neck was fluttering madly. She was sitting bolt upright, as if terrified of any part of her body bumping into any part of his, and she was taking great pains not to look at him.

She was nothing but a fraud, he thought with satisfaction as the engines fired up and they started to taxi to the runway. Seducing her would be the easiest thing he'd ever done. Revenge would be his in no time at all. And so he sat back, stretched out his legs beneath the table in deliberate provocation, and said with a smouldering smile, 'I'm sure we'll think of something.'

* * *

The trouble, Thalia reflected half an hour into the flight, was that despite her best intentions to ignore Santi's irritating effect on her, she could only think of one thing. And that one thing was, unfortunately, sex.

It had started the minute she'd stepped aboard and seen him reclining on the sofa, barefoot, dishevelled and louchely gorgeous. His arms had been raised, his hands behind his head. His black polo shirt had ridden up to reveal a thin band of tanned skin just above the waistband of his jeans. Her mouth had instantly dried, her pulse had spiked and then begun to thunder, and the bolt of desire that had shot through her had wiped her head of almost all rational thought. To her absolute horror, she'd wanted to throw herself on top of him and kiss him until neither of them could think straight, which had once been her wont.

As if that hadn't been unsettling enough, he'd then mentioned the size of his plane. To anyone other than him, she might have made a sly remark about anatomical over-compensation. But she knew from experience that he had absolutely nothing to worry about in that area, and God, why had she even been *thinking* about that area when it bore no relevance to anything?

Now, as they climbed to forty-five thousand feet, he was eating the breakfast that had been brought to the table by an obliging member of the cabin crew, and even that was a torturous event to witness.

'So what have you been up to since we last saw each other?' he asked while she tried to keep her eyes off his big strong hands and insanely sexy mouth as he devoured a plate of fruit and bread and downed endless cups of black coffee.

Nothing that she was going to tell him about, she thought, with a shudder of something that could have been recoil at the idea of spilling her innermost angst, but could equally have been longing. 'Work, mainly. You?'

'Same. Until six weeks ago.'

'What made you sell your business?'

'The offer I was made was too good to refuse.'

'Do you miss it?'

'No. I'd taken it as far as I could. I know when to pull out.'

She disagreed. It had always been far too soon for her liking. Panting against each other, limbs trembling and hearts thundering while they put themselves back together, she hadn't been able to tell where she stopped and he started, and if she'd had her way he'd have stayed lodged deep inside her for ever. But, dammit, these were wholly inappropriate and utterly atrocious thoughts to be having, so she ruthlessly scrubbed them from her head and vowed to keep her mind out of the gutter.

'What are you going to do next?' she said, recalling with effort what they'd been discussing and willing the heat raging through her to subside. 'Apart from your philanthropic endeavours, I mean.'

'I thought I'd invest in startups,' he said, directing a killer smile at the attendant who'd materialised to remove his now empty plate and cup. 'Mentor young entrepreneurs. Dabble with an app or two. I don't yet have a firm plan. I've had other things on my mind.'

'Such as?'

'There's a project I'm working on.' He turned the smile on her, a wicked glint sparking in the dark depths of his eyes, and for a moment she felt as dazzled as if she were staring into the sun. 'A mergers and acquisitions type of affair.'

She blinked and forced herself to focus. 'Going well?'

'It's in the early stages of development, but I have no doubt it'll be successful.'

'Good luck with it.'

'Thank you.'

See? This is the way forward. Polite small talk.

'Have you had much time for dating?'

His eyebrows rose at her question, but he could not be more surprised by it than she was—because what the hell? Since when did his dating habits constitute small talk? 'I've had no time for it at all.'

Why that came as a such a relief she really couldn't fathom. She didn't even know why she'd asked. She wasn't remotely interested. He could date the entire world if he felt like it, and now she had to act like it was no big deal that she'd asked. 'I've had loads of time for it myself.'

'I'm sure you're leaving a trail of broken hearts wherever you go,' he said dryly, as if he could somehow tell she was lying. Which was annoying, because the last thing she wanted was him reading her mind when it was in such chaos. 'How's the family?'

Currently causing her a whole lot of grief, although she welcomed the change of subject, because discussing hearts in any shape or form with him felt unwise in the extreme. And besides, if anyone was in danger of breaking hearts, it was him. Not that their relationship had lasted long enough to get to that stage, of course.

'Very well indeed.'

'Did I read that your mother has just relieved the eleventh Duchess of Swinburne of her husband?'

'Quite possibly,' she said, wincing a little on the inside. 'I don't keep track of her antics but it does sound like something she'd do. That marriage has been on the rocks for years but that's no excuse. She's mad, bad and dangerous to know.'

'Like mother, like daughter.'

What? Was he serious? 'That's a terrible thing to say,' she said, outraged. 'I'm none of those things. I've certainly never broken up a marriage. Thanks to her behaviour, I'm not remotely scandalous.'

'It was meant to be a compliment.'

For a moment, she just stared at him. 'In what world would that be considered a compliment?'

'You have certain skills that could make a man lose his head.'

She was not going to enquire. His eyes were almost black and his smile was smouldering and she knew perfectly well what skills he was referring to, although he was the only man to ever bring them out in her. With him, she'd done things she'd never done before. She'd trusted him implicitly. Only heaven knew why. And why had he even brought it up?

'Don't be ridiculous,' she said, but she couldn't deny it did send a certain frisson through her to know that he thought of her that way. 'You didn't lose yours.'

'Didn't I?'

Of course he hadn't. She hadn't lost hers either. Their

fling had lasted only three months and it had been almost entirely about sex. They'd known every inch of each other's bodies, but of each other's minds...? Not quite so much. 'Don't think I don't know what you're doing,' she said, narrowing her eyes at him.

'What's that?'

'For some inexplicable reason, you're taking great delight in trying to unsettle me. But it won't work. I'm not interested in a trip down memory lane, Santi. I'm here to work, and that's it.'

'Noted.'

Reminding herself that she did not care what he thought of her in any way other than the professional, Thalia pulled herself together and sat a little more upright. But at the same time Santi shifted in his seat, his knee bumping against hers, and if she hadn't still had her seatbelt fastened she'd have jumped a foot in the air. Every nerve-ending she possessed jolted. Her entire body flushed with heat, and she could not have been more appalled.

'My apologies,' he said, seemingly unaware of the effect the contact had had on her, thank God. 'I should have specified a larger table.'

'You could always move to another one.'

'I'm enjoying the view at this one.'

Yes, well, she wasn't. She was finding this whole experience very uncomfortable indeed. The conversation was both excruciating and baffling, and the thought of having to endure another eleven hours of it, and him, filled her with despair. 'I could do with stretching my legs.'

'Why don't I show you around?'

Show her around? Luxurious as the space was, it wasn't exactly palatial. She didn't need a tour. She just needed to get away from his penetrating gaze and regroup. But within a nanosecond of her getting up, he had too, and a moment later, he'd taken her elbow—completely unnecessarily—and propelled her down the plane to the cabin at the rear, which she hadn't realised existed until he opened the door and ushered her in.

'The bed is custom made,' he said, while she made appreciative noises and battled images of the two of them writhing around on top of it. 'The sheets have a three hundred thread count and the blankets are made from vicuna wool. The wet room can comfortably fit two and there's enough water for four twenty-minute showers. More importantly, the door is soundproofed.'

Why was he telling her this? she wondered dazedly, trying and failing to not think about all the beds and showers they'd once shared and the noise they might have made while doing so. The level of detail and the lingering felt deliberate, but was he simply proud of his new toy or was he still messing with her? She was feeling so lightheaded in the confined quarters that she couldn't begin to work it out. All she knew was that she had to vacate the room before she pushed him onto the bed and got him out of his clothes.

Thalia returned to her seat, hot and shivery and in even greater discomfort than before, and as she'd suspected the flight went downhill from then on. Santi kept looking at her when there was no need and smiling at her as if he knew something she didn't. He constantly invaded her space and filled her vision, and if he accidentally touched her one more time, a brush here, a bump there, she would not be responsible for her actions.

Over a lunch of prawns, salmon and the prettiest arrangement of tropical fruit she'd ever seen, all she'd been able to focus on were his hands and mouth, both of which she wanted on her again. In the afternoon, she tried to send some emails—a suitable replacement for her at the foundation still needed to be found, after all—and to engage in the conversation he initiated, but it was impossible to concentrate. Her imagination, sparked by the earlier tour and the distressingly appealing notion of being mad, bad and dangerous to know, had gone into overdrive. It was unhelpfully creating scenarios in which sudden turbulence tumbled them to the sofa or he simply reached for her hand and bore her off to the bed in the cabin, while she put up not one iota of resistance.

If only there was a need to refuel, she thought desperately, closing her eyes in the hope of a much-needed nap and a break from the scalding looks and the stomach-flipping smiles. She could really have done with a midway stop. It was unbelievably hot in here, there seemed to be a problem with the oxygen supply and she hated being so affected by someone who had once had—and might still have—such a low opinion of her.

But there wasn't. And there was little point regretting that she hadn't had the wherewithal last night to tell him in no uncertain terms that she'd make her own way to Brazil, so she'd have to get through what was left of the nightmare by gritting her teeth, steeling her nerves and counting down the minutes.

At least she'd get some respite on landing. She'd ordered a car to meet her at the airport and booked herself into the Bellavista, a hotel near his house, the address of which she already knew because they'd once had a conversation about where he lived and she'd later looked it up on Google Earth.

Once there, she intended to spend the evening reminding herself of why she could not and would not surrender to the attraction and giving herself a stern talking-to about resolve and inner strength. She would develop tactics to stop wondering if his hair was as soft as she remembered and his mouth as clever. She would train herself to recall the way they'd ended and how sad and hurt she'd felt in the aftermath instead.

Come tomorrow, she was sure, after a good night's sleep and some distance, her defences would be fortified, work would start and everything would be back on track.

To Santi's surprise, two cars waited on the tarmac that shimmered in the uncharacteristically sizzling heat of a mid-September afternoon. One he recognised, the other he did not. At the bottom of the steps, Thalia said, 'As it's nine p.m. Greek time, I'll head to my hotel now. See you tomorrow morning at eight,' and by the time he'd recovered from his shock enough to figure out what was going on, she'd collected her suitcase, climbed into her car and driven off.

Up until that moment he'd been congratulating himself on a flight well spent. He hadn't missed an opportunity to push his agenda and, judging by the skittishness that had intensified with every smile he'd flashed at her, he definitely had her rattled. She'd been frequently distracted. More than once he'd caught her staring at him with a darkening gaze and a hitch to her breathing when she thought he wasn't looking, and it was clear that she was halfway into his bed already.

This move of hers with the convertible and the hotel was an unanticipated development, he was perfectly willing to admit, as he donned a pair of sunglasses and watched her disappear into the dusty distance, but it didn't present a problem. There was only one hotel in the vicinity and it was in dire need of a new roof.

Striding towards the low-slung sports car the colour of anthracite, Santi pulled out his phone and made a call. Twenty minutes later and several hundreds of thousands of Brazilian reals poorer, he arrived home. Half an hour after that, as expected, so did Thalia.

'My hotel has had to close suddenly,' she announced, getting out of the car and slamming the door shut behind her, her jaw tight and her colour high. 'For two whole weeks.'

Standing in the entrance, leaning nonchalantly against the doorframe, Santi rubbed a hand over his bare chest and feigned concern. 'Oh?'

'A fire in the kitchen.'

'That is unfortunate.'

'Extremely.'

'Was anyone hurt?'

'No.'

'A relief.'

'For whom?' She stalked to the back of the vehicle and jabbed at the key to pop the boot. 'I did explain I don't need to be fed, but apparently the establishment now poses a health and safety risk. I was told the nearest open hotel is over a hundred kilometres away, which is inconvenient to say the least. I can hardly sleep in the car for the next ten days so I'm going to have to stay with you.'

Of course she was. That had never been in doubt. She was not and never would be in control of anything that was happening here. But it wouldn't hurt to let her think she was. To lull her into a false sense of security and then sweep the rug from under her feet. And besides, he wanted her to come to his bed happily and willingly, not furiously and grudgingly. So he'd let her recover tonight and up the ante tomorrow. 'I'll take your case.'

'I can manage.'

'Follow me.'

Well, this was just *great*, Thalia thought as she followed Santi, who'd completely ignored her point about managing and had lifted her case out of the car as if it was filled with air instead of ten days' worth of belongings, into the house. First, there'd been the shock of his dramatic reappearance in her life, and his wholly outrageous blackmail that had upended her weekend. Then she'd had to contend with uncontrollable, disruptive lust, which would not leave her alone. And now, to top it all off, the fiasco of a fire had landed her here, his house, for the next ten days.

What a twenty-four hours. The entire world seemed to be conspiring against her. So much for respite and a pep talk. So much for fortifying her defences and everything being on track. She felt utterly defeated. So exhausted that even her bones ached. She'd barely slept a wink last night. Her earlier attempt at napping had not been a success. As a result of the excruciatingly stressful and long flight, her ankles and feet were swollen and her skin felt like sandpaper. She couldn't work out what time it was where, and to add insult to injury, while she'd been desperately begging the hotel receptionist to let her stay, Santi had apparently showered and changed into khaki shorts and a loose white shirt of which he hadn't bothered to do up even one button. He looked cool and refreshed and unfairly gorgeous; she looked a mess. And it really shouldn't matter, but somehow it did.

'Dinner will be ready in an hour,' he said, setting her suitcase down beside the bed, which stood in the centre of a large room that had white walls and polished dark wood floors.

'I'm not hungry.'

'Are you sure about that?'

She wasn't sure about anything. Least of all the knowing gleam in his eye. Something about this whole situation didn't feel quite right, but she couldn't put her finger on what was amiss. Her brain was frazzled. She was dead on her feet. Keeping her eyes and hands off his bare chest was taking up her last few drops of energy. She just wanted to clean up, take care of the throbbing ache between her legs and pass out. 'Quite sure.'

'If you need anything, my room is just across the hall.'

'Goodnight, Santi.'

'It's only half past six.'

'Not back home it isn't,' she said and shoved him out of the room.

CHAPTER FOUR

THE TROUBLE WITH crashing out early and forgetting about jetlag was that it could lead to a person spending much of the night awake. And so when Thalia's alarm went off at seven the following morning, all she wanted to do was roll over and go back to sleep. But, as she had important work to do, she levered herself out of bed, showered and dressed and then, armed with her laptop, went in search of the kitchen and a much-needed coffee.

She'd been too weary and dejected yesterday to take in any of her surroundings. But now, despite still feeling gritty-eyed and groggy today, she was able to observe that beyond the first-floor bedroom wing, much of the house didn't appear to have any walls. Mostly it seemed to be built around trees, multi-levelled platforms on stilts, thick gnarled branches pushing through the thatched roof. Here, there was a vast decked open-air living space with views over the sparkling sea. There, a wide staircase swept round and down to verdant gardens and the golden beach beyond. She'd been to some spectacular properties over the years—her ultra-wealthy family owned a number of them across the globe, in fact—but she'd never seen anything quite like this. Rustic and sprawling, it seemed to emerge from the lush vegetation as if having grown from seed. Every inch revealed some new architectural or natural curiosity.

The clink of crockery and the heavenly scent of brewed coffee led her down the stairs and, unexpectedly, outside. Bracing herself for a renewed assault on her fragile senses from her host, on the defences she hadn't yet found the energy to strengthen, Thalia took a deep breath and pulled her shoulders back.

But she was still unprepared for the sharp punch to the chest she experienced when she saw Santi lounging at a table beneath a huge parasol by the pool, facing in her direction. He was wearing nothing but a pair of black board shorts and mirrored sunglasses. His tan was deep and his muscles were as defined as she remembered. He looked like a model, posing solely for her entertainment, and God, how on earth was she supposed to concentrate with all this physical perfection on display?

Swallowing hard and reminding herself that in ten minutes, at precisely eight a.m., work would begin—because she would *not* be thwarted again—Thalia willed her racing pulse to slow, dug deep for composure and forced herself to move forwards.

'You have a very interesting home,' she said, inanely grasping onto the only thought in her head that wasn't revolving around the appallingly inappropriate urge to straddle his lap, plant her hands on his chest and crush her mouth to his.

'I like it.'

'Have you lived here for long?'

'Eight years. I bought the land and built the house with the first million I made.'

'Its design must be pretty unique.'

'It affords me privacy and space and I appreciate nature.'

She appreciated nature too. Especially when it looked like him. Maybe keeping her eyes on the distant hills across the water instead of the ridges and bumps of his abs would help with her concentration.

'Come and take a seat,' he said, indicating the chair next to him, the only chair in sight.

'Thanks.' Thalia pulled it out, dragged it as far from his as possible without being obvious and sat down, facing the sea.

'Coffee?'

'Yes, please.'

'Help yourself to breakfast.'

'It all looks delicious,' she said, piling a plate with guava, papaya and pastries to make up for her missed supper the evening before, while he filled a cup and pushed it in her direction.

'Did you sleep well?'

No. 'Yes, thank you.'

'I trust you were comfortable in your room.'

She should have been because it was airy, cool, simply furnished and in theory very restful. She could touch the trees from the generous balcony. The voile curtains that fluttered at the wide-open doors added to the whimsical serenity. Before falling into bed last night she'd spent a good hour in the ensuite bathroom with its huge, high-pressure rain showerhead that made her think of the Iguazu Falls, not that she'd ever been. The only problem with the room was its location, across the hall from his—so he'd said—and not in a hotel five kilometres away. 'It's charming.'

'Mine is similar but double the size.'

'How lovely,' she replied, determinedly not envisaging his gorgeous, bronzed body tangled up in snowy white sheets, but instead drinking deeply of the coffee he had made— just the way she liked it—and taking strength from the hit of super-strong caffeine.

Their sleeping arrangements were irrelevant, she told herself firmly. The *only* thing that mattered for the next ten days was making a success of this situation. Proving to herself that she had talent and ability in the field she loved and that she was able to survive perfectly well on her own. She'd get used to the way he made her feel. Over time it might even diminish so as to be undetectable. It was simply a question of mind over matter. Finding her inner strength and focusing on the long-term goal, which was not going to be obstructed by anything or anyone.

'So I've identified a good spot for a workstation,' she said, setting down her cup and stabbing a fork into a piece of papaya. 'Upstairs on the deck. A big table, plenty of space. It's ideal.'

'I see no reason to move.'

Her eyebrows shot up and she stared at him for a moment, fork hovering in mid-air. 'Are you suggesting we stay here by the pool?'

'Is that a problem?'

Yes, it was. She wasn't on holiday. 'Well, it's not very professional, is it?'

'I can work in a variety of locations.'

'I prefer to stick to an office.'

'It seems a shame to waste the weather.'

She glanced up at the cloudless blue sky from which beat down the morning sun, already hot and intense, and frowned. 'Isn't the weather always like this at this time of year? I thought this was the dry season.'

'Sometimes it rains.'

'All the more reason for proper shelter.'

'My house, my rules, Thalia,' he said, pausing in his slathering of butter over a slice of bread to lift his sunglasses. He ran his hot dark gaze over her smart white shirt, taupe trouser combo. 'You might want to reconsider your outfit.'

'Ditto.'

'I anticipate needing to cool off.'

That announcement was accompanied by an unnecessarily wolfish smile, and she thought that if anyone was going to need to cool off it was her. Despite the early hour she could feel a bead of sweat trickling between her breasts. Her skin was prickling and her blood was boiling. And all because of a scorcher of a look. 'Can't you at least put a T-shirt on in the meantime?'

'Do I bother you?'

He did. Very much. Was it his intention to wander around semi-naked the entire time she was here? How was she supposed to handle that? Had he no sense of decency? Professionalism? And how would he feel if she wafted about in nothing more than a bikini? Perhaps she should try it and see.

'Not at all,' she lied smoothly. 'I'm merely thinking of sunburn.'

'Are you offering to rub sunscreen into me?'

Thalia ignored the strong temptation to say yes and stifled a sigh. What on earth was he was he playing at? First the plane, now this. Was he flirting with her? Why? And, more importantly, how could she get him to stop?

'Why don't you tell me more about your philanthropic plans?' she said, despairing of him, herself and this whole massively inconvenient situation as she picked up a knife and sharply sliced a tiny custard tart in two. 'What sort of thing do you have in mind?'

'I'll take that as a no to the sunscreen.'

'It's eight on the dot and I won't tolerate another delay.'

Santi shifted in his seat, sending a wave of deliciously masculine scent in her direction, which she ruthlessly repelled.

'I'd like to focus on Brazil,' he said, angling his body and stretching out his long, muscled legs, which didn't help her composure at all when she could remember as if it were yesterday how they'd felt rubbing up and down against hers in various beds across the globe. 'Specifically, the underprivileged and the disadvantaged, of which there are many. I want to improve literacy. To show young kids in the favelas and elsewhere that there are ways out, and to create the opportunities to enable that.'

'These are causes that are personal to you,' she said with an understanding nod, finally in her comfort zone, thank God.

His eyebrows rose. 'How do you know that?'

'I Googled you.'

It had been one of the first things she'd done after

he'd left her room the morning after her brother's wedding. She'd wanted to know everything about the man who'd repeatedly rocked her world. And she hadn't been disappointed, because information on him abounded.

He'd grown up in Rio's most dangerous favela, she'd discovered. At the time, it had been headquarters of one of the largest gangs in the city. There'd been frequent clashes among the police, local drug cartels and rival gangs. Violence and gun battles had been a regular occurrence. His schooling had been chaotic and, along with the majority of his friends, he'd dropped out for good at thirteen. With no qualifications, and therefore limited job options, most of his peers had turned to drug dealers for work, and a life of crime. He'd been one of the lucky ones, finding salvation in a library that had been running a course in coding.

She'd read for hours about how his tough, precarious upbringing had driven him to succeed, and had pored over articles detailing the stellar growth of his tech business. He'd overcome such hurdles with such enviable strength and determination it was no wonder she'd been smitten from the off.

'Background knowledge on a project is always useful,' she said sagely, as if she'd done her research for professional purposes this morning instead of over the course of many weeks, long ago, for personal ones.

'I agree.'

'Did you Google me?'

'I did,' he said with a nod. 'It took quite a while to wade through all the photos of you at various society events, but eventually I found what I was looking for.'

'And what was that?'

'Your suitability for my requirements.'

Oh.

'One article I read said you became interested in the idea of charity after watching a programme on global poverty as a kid and being deeply affected by it. You rounded up unwanted toys and clothes at home and found ways of putting them to good use. At school you ran an annual designer clothing sale and raised thousands for good causes. You have a masters in charity management and went straight from university to work at the family foundation where you've been ever since.'

Every word of what he said was true, she thought, reminding herself sternly that she didn't *want* him to be interested in her personally. She even recalled the interview—one of the few she'd ever given, since the foundation had a PR department for that sort of thing.

What she hadn't revealed at the time or at any moment since, however, was where those unwanted toys and clothes had come from. They certainly hadn't come from her parents, as might have naturally been expected. Before he'd died from a heart attack when she was a teenager, her stern, aristocratic father had only had time for her eldest brother, Leo, who'd been destined to take over the family empire since birth. Her mother had always been too busy jetting around the world and causing scandals to acknowledge any of her children's existence unless it suited her. It was the nannies who'd overcompensated for this criminal lack of parental attention by showering her and her siblings with material possessions, as if those could *ever* make up for bewilderingly wilful neglect.

She'd only emerged relatively unscathed because

she'd had Atticus to cling to. While the others had floundered, each in their own way, she'd turned to him to celebrate her successes and lament her failures. He was the one who'd talked her through friendship dramas and teenage angst when there'd been no one else. He'd been her rock, and she'd always believed that she'd been his.

But she didn't want to think about her twin right now, about everything she'd had and all she'd now lost. She wasn't even sure any more what that was. Lately she'd been wondering if perhaps their bond hadn't been as strong for him as it had for her, if the need for support and security had been hers alone. She'd had a smattering of boyfriends, but she'd never managed to find the same depth of connection with any of them. Yet Atticus had met and married Zoe with no trouble at all. He hadn't thought twice about sacrificing their closeness and casting her aside. Could he have found her a nuisance all these years? Could he too have been indulging her while sighing on the inside? The possibility of that being the case was too much to bear.

'I've had every privilege going,' she said, swallowing down the sudden lump in her throat and yanking herself out of the painful past and back to the present, 'and I've always felt that that comes with enormous responsibility. But more than that, it was simply always what I've wanted to do.'

'Your resume is impressive.'

'That's what you paid for. And speaking of which, have you had any thoughts about fundraising?'

He shook his head. 'Not yet.'

'Any idea who you'd like on the board?'

'None.'

'Do you even have a name for your venture?'

'No.'

'We *are* going to be busy.'

Thalia clearly wanted to get underway, in order to be done as quickly as possible, but Santi felt no such urge. He was quite content to draw things out for as long as it pleased him, and screwing with her attempts to engage him in the details of his project would satisfy his need for control. So every time she tried to drill down into the minutiae of what he wanted to achieve, or brainstorm mission statements, he found he had a phone call to make or a swim to take. A drink to fetch or food to prepare. These pronouncements were met by frowns and sighs and much gritting of the teeth, but he was not remotely deterred, even though by mid-afternoon the frustration was rolling off her in waves and he could practically see the steam coming from her ears.

'You look hot,' he observed from the far end of the pool, because riling her was fun and somehow it appeased his sense of injustice. 'Come and join me. The water's great.'

Evidently that was one provocation too far, because in response to his invitation Thalia slammed down the lid of her laptop and jumped to her feet.

'You're not taking this remotely seriously, are you?' she said, marching towards him, arms folded across her chest, which did interesting things to her cleavage. 'You're ruining everything we're trying to achieve. You have the attention span of a gnat. You're driving me mad. How you managed to build a billion-dollar business I have no clue.'

Grit and determination and a great idea was how he'd done it. A talent for coding, a driving need to get out of the slums after one of his friends had been shot in the chest, and sixteen-hour days spent hustling for deals. But he was not going to go into that with her. And anyway, that information, unlike some, was already in the public domain. 'What's the hurry?'

'In ten days' time I'll be gone and we won't have nailed down a thing. Your philanthropic endeavours will be dead in the water and your money completely wasted. That's the hurry.'

'You're making the mistake of assuming the days are to run consecutively.'

She stared at him, speechless for a moment, wide-eyed and open-mouthed, as if shock had rooted her to the spot. 'What?'

'You really should have been more specific with the details of your lot.'

Her brows snapped together, her jaw clenched and a flush hit her cheeks. 'I never anticipated blackmail.'

'I always get what I want.'

'Are you implying that I'll be here for as long as it suits you?'

'In a nutshell.'

She thought about that for a moment—he could almost see her brain overheating with the effort—and then she began to radiate such ire and frustration she blazed.

'This may be some sort of bizarre power trip of a game to you, but it isn't to me,' she said, her hands now on her hips as she glared down at him in glorious passionate fury, any semblance of cool long gone. 'I didn't just decide to offer up my services at the auction on a whim. My entire future career is at stake here.'

That piqued his interest. 'What do you mean?'

'I'm about to step down from the foundation,' she said hotly. 'I'm setting up a consultancy service, to help others to help others. You're my first client. You're supposed to be my success story.'

Ah. 'So that's why you turned your nose up at the thought of me hiring someone else at the gala the other night.'

'Yes,' she said through clenched teeth.

'I could make or break you.'

'In theory.'

'Interesting.'

'The only interesting thing about anything is why you're intent on sabotaging my efforts.'

Well, he wasn't telling her *that*. 'You need to keep me sweet.'

'This is impossible,' she said, throwing her hands up in utter exasperation. '*You're* impossible. We're making no progress whatsoever and you don't even seem to want to, despite claiming to be desperate for my advice and paying handsomely for it. There's absolutely no point in me being here. I'd be better off cutting my losses and starting again. Anyone who's ever tried to work with you would understand, I'm sure.'

There was every point in her being here, she was not starting again and he'd been going about seducing her in entirely the wrong way, he was beginning to realise. No wonder she was resisting the obvious chemistry. Focusing on establishing her new business clearly trumped it. So much so that he would have admired her strength of character had it not been in direct competition with his objectives.

He had to amend his tactics and appeal to her brain as well as her body. He had to show that he respected what she was trying to achieve and flatter her talents, while also continuing to fuel the attraction. His goals hadn't changed. And he *did* want her advice. For years he'd relied on the charity of others, and he'd made himself a promise long ago that as soon as he was in a position to pay that back, he would. That was why, despite allowing her to think otherwise on Saturday night, he would never have withdrawn his fifty-million-euro donation to her foundation.

'All right,' he said, adjusting his strategy to incorporate all these new revelations and heaving himself out of the pool. 'I can see this is important to you. And it is to me, too. So let's get to work.'

CHAPTER FIVE

NOW THAT SANTI had decided to cooperate—and what a blessed relief that was—they made excellent progress. He finally came up with a name and a mission statement. Thalia enlightened him about jurisdictions and structures, lawyers and accountants and PR, and then tasked him over the next few days with researching literacy programmes, building a potential board of trustees and outlining a launch event.

His brain worked dizzyingly fast, he was focused and engaged, and unlike earlier she could totally see how he'd achieved everything he had. She admired his ambition for his charity. A cause obviously close to his heart, he was taking it very seriously indeed, which made his earlier behaviour all the more incomprehensible.

'So are you going to tell me what on earth this morning was about?' she asked when they finally wrapped up at six.

Stretching the kinks out of his muscles, Santi looked at her, a picture of innocence that she didn't believe for a moment. 'What do you mean?'

'The phone calls and the swims and the constant provision of snacks,' she said, reflecting that all of those distractions had been a trial, although the swims had been particularly wearing.

Every time he'd dived into the pool she'd had to stop what she was doing and watch. The power with which he completed length after length had reminded her of the strength with which he'd once held her, and she'd almost fainted with longing. Their hotel-room affair had been conducted mainly indoors, occasionally on a balcony, and she feared the sight of him climbing out of the pool, with the water sluicing off his magnificent body, glistening in the sunlight, would be permanently etched into her retinas. None of it had made for an easy day. 'Does it give you a thrill to toy with me?'

'That would depend on the type of toying you're talking about,' he said with an unhelpful glint in his eye.

Well, she certainly wasn't talking about the type of toying that involved tying her to a four-poster bed in New York, working her into frenzy and then leaving her there throbbing and panting and cursing him for an hour, even if the eventual multiple orgasms had been worth it. 'How about ten days that could turn out to be twenty, thirty or whatever you decide?' she said, gritting her teeth against the unwelcome onslaught of memories and focusing.

'There's no need to be quite so dramatic. I'm merely factoring in the weekend and the odd half-day break.'

'I don't like being manipulated.'

'Who does? But perhaps you'd like to join me for supper.'

She wouldn't particularly. She'd spent much of the day on edge and she could do with some time out of his disturbing orbit. But she'd refused the snacks on principle, hard work always gave her an appetite and her culinary skills were virtually non-existent, so pettily cutting off her nose to spite her face held little appeal.

'That would be nice,' she said grudgingly and packed up her things.

On the upstairs terrace, which had large squishy chairs and a fabulous panoramic view of the sparkling sea and the forest-covered hills of the islands beyond, Santi furnished Thalia with a glass of deliciously cold white wine and then lit the grill—a machine that came with levers and wheels like something out of the Industrial Revolution.

Within moments, the scent of woodsmoke filled the warm evening air, and it made her think of the hotel she should have been staying at, where there'd been no such smell, which was odd because surely a fire significant enough to close down the entire establishment would have left some trace. There hadn't even been any visible smoke, now she thought about it. Had it been windy? She couldn't remember.

'You really love what you do, don't you?'

Setting that particular conundrum to one side, Thalia switched her attention to the man sprinkling salt over churrasco like a pro with one hand and tossing a green salad with the other. 'I do,' she said, taking a moment to admire yet another of his talents.

'You're very good at it.'

'Thank you.'

'Very passionate.'

Ah. She should have known that allowing her frustration to boil over and telling him why she needed this project would come back to haunt her. 'Yes, well, I'm as determined to get what I want as you are and, as I said, there's a lot at stake for me.'

'So why leave the foundation to set up on your own?'

'It's a long and complicated story.'

'The night is young.'

'I wouldn't even know here to start.'

'Try the beginning.'

No, thanks.

'Why are you so interested?'

'We have to talk about something.'

'There are plenty of other topics of conversation.' Such as running a successful business. This country of his, which she'd never visited before despite having a girlfriend who lived in Rio. Destruction of the rain forest. That was a good one. 'I hear there are whales to be found around these parts at this time of year. That could be a fascinating discussion. I like whales.'

'We never bothered much with small talk.'

That was true, she supposed. Even their attempts on the plane had failed one way or another. But did they have to chat about *her*? She wasn't even sure she wanted to discuss the last couple of years. She never had before. She wouldn't have had anyone to share her woes with even if she did. Her mother had little time for anyone other than herself. Atticus was at the centre of her existential crisis, so he wasn't an option, and her other siblings, with whom she was trying to establish new relationships after stupidly believing for thirty years that because they didn't get her like her twin did she didn't really need them, were busy with their own lives.

Leo was wrapped up in his wife, Willow, and baby

daughter, and building boats on Santorini. Zander was running the family empire from London and working his way through the world's female population. Daphne, who'd once had cancer and therefore chemotherapy, was undergoing stressful and emotional fertility treatment, and who knew where wild child Olympia was or what she was doing?

Thalia was on her own on this journey of self-discovery of hers, but that was fine. That was the whole point, and it wasn't as if she needed advice or support. She knew what she was doing, even if it did feel like a struggle sometimes. Besides, some sixth sense was warning her that it might be unwise to open up to Santi. She'd seen how ruthless he could be when he wanted something. Any hint of emotion or vulnerability and he might well weaponize it. In fact, it wouldn't surprise her in the slightest if, at some point, he used her earlier admission that she was relying on him for her future success as leverage to strong-arm her into doing what he wanted.

'We could talk about you instead,' she said with a pointed lift of her eyebrows.

'You first.'

Well, that wasn't an outright no, which was encouraging, because she found she was beginning to have questions that hadn't been answered by any article she'd ever read. About his mother, his father and how he'd handled not having one. Whether he had any advice about launching a business and what this mergers and acquisitions project he was working on entailed. Nothing too intimate, of course. She had no interest in knowing *why* he hadn't dated anyone over the last thirteen months.

Still, a quid pro quo could be the way forward. Perhaps the relentless desire she felt for him and her inability to control it were down to the fact she'd never had closure. Their breakup had been unexpectedly brutal and she'd carried the wounds of it for months. Quite possibly she still did. Maybe clearing the air—explaining where she'd been at the time and, in return, finding out why he'd thought her arrogant and shallow, and whether he continued to do so—would somehow rid her of her infatuation with him. She could only hope.

'All right,' she said, taking a fortifying mouthful of wine and bracing herself. Even though she owned her behaviour and feelings now, she wasn't proud of them, and discussing it wasn't going to be pleasant. 'You don't have siblings, do you?'

Raking the embers with a poker, Santi didn't answer immediately. But after a moment he gave his head a faint shake and said, 'No.'

'Well, as you know, I have a twin. And having a twin—even a non-identical one—isn't like having a regular sibling. The bond is unique. It's like having a built-in best friend. Or at least that was how it was between Atticus and me. For years we knew what the other was thinking without having to say a word. We were consistently there for each other, whatever the circumstances. It was always us against the world.'

'That sounds intense.'

'It was,' she agreed with a nod. 'Very. We weren't together all the time obviously. Eventually I went to university in the UK, and he studied law in the States, and then we embarked on our respective careers. But we spoke every week. He was my go-to person for almost everything. Our connection always seemed unbreakable.'

Santi put down the poker, topped up her glass and then sank into the chair next to hers. 'Seemed?'

'When he met Zoe, everything changed,' she confessed, stifling a sigh. 'She's lovely and she makes him insanely happy, but for me it's been a difficult adjustment. I had him all to myself for thirty years. Of course he'd had girlfriends in the past but never anything serious. Then she came along and it was as if—' She shrugged. 'I don't know—she somehow stepped in and took my place. It felt like betrayal. Rejection. Loss. And it was horrible. Deep down, I hoped the relationship wouldn't last, which is awful.'

'Did you speak to him about it?'

'I considered it briefly, but what could I have said? That I was jealous? How pathetic would that have sounded?' She shook her head. 'No. I didn't want to ruin things for him. He was really happy. So I kind of avoided them, which I guess was pretty cowardly but I was so confused and upset I didn't know what else to do. When they got engaged, I couldn't kid myself any more that it was just a fling. I realised I had to figure out how to exist without him being my constant support and always at the end of the phone, and that made me assess everything else. Family. My identity. Work. I've had it so easy in my career. I didn't even question my appointment as CEO of the foundation. But then I found myself wondering why I ended up in that position and what I'm genuinely capable of. That's why I need to branch out and set up my own business. To see if I can make a success of things independently. I know it's not a real test since I'm not going to be destitute if it fails but it's the best shot I've got.'

'You won't fail.'

'I hope not.'

'The auctioneer on Saturday night was right,' said Santi. 'You *do* know what you're talking about. You *are* the ultimate expert and, from my point of view at least, there *is* nothing you don't know.'

'Yes, well, we'll see,' she said, doing her best to ignore the pride that shimmied through her at his praise and recall the purpose of this conversation. 'But in the meantime I can't allow any distractions.'

'Am I a distraction?'

He was the ultimate distraction, but he already held way too much power in this situation, so she was not going to admit how much he still affected her. 'When we met,' she said, not quite answering the question instead, 'you were just what I needed.'

'And what was that?'

'An analeptic.'

'In what way?'

'Even though I was so pleased for them, I found Atticus and Zoe's wedding incredibly tough, and I know that makes me a not very nice person, but that's how it was. It was as if his life was suddenly going off in a completely different direction and I was being left behind, alone and adrift. I was miserable that evening and just wanted something else to think about.'

'Me.'

She nodded. 'You.'

'I had no idea you were feeling that way,' he said

with a frown that suggested he was faintly offended by the knowledge.

'I hope no one did. I tried hard to hide it. But you made all those ugly shameful emotions disappear,' she said, remembering with the ghost of a smile how completely bowled over she'd been by him. 'You made *everything* disappear. I'd never experienced attraction like it. You were supposed to be a one-night stand but the sex was so mind-blowing I couldn't help but want more and so it became an affair. You were a wonderful escape from reality. When I was with you I didn't have to think about anything else. And when I wasn't with you I didn't have to think about anything else either, because you and what we were doing together were in my head pretty much all the time. Normally my relationships fizzle out pretty quickly—not that there've been that many of them—but ours didn't and the longer it went on the more I began to realise that it had to stop. I'd switched one dependency for another. How could I work out who I was on my own if I wasn't ever *on* my own? I needed space and time to work on myself. I still do. I had planned to tell you all this. That morning in Paris I was going to explain everything. But before I could, you said all those horrible things and I went into shock and after that I didn't think you deserved the truth.'

Finally at the end of her confession, Thalia stopped and drained the last of her wine, her heart pounding and her mouth dry. But actually, voicing that truth hadn't been so bad. Perhaps she'd spent so long analysing what she'd thought and how she'd felt, she'd become inured to it. Santi looked a bit shellshocked, though, which was understandable because it was a lot to take in. But at least she'd got it off her chest. At least she'd told him about Paris and clarified in no uncertain terms why she could not give in to the chemistry again. Now she could switch the focus to him and drill down into how he'd ever got the idea that she thought she was better than him.

'I see,' he said, although he probably didn't see at all because he didn't have siblings, let alone a twin, so how could he?

'I told you it was complicated.'

'You were right.'

Muttering something about the grill being ready for the meat, Santi got to his feet and thought that 'complicated' had to be the understatement of the century. Never in a million years would he have guessed that Thalia had had all that going on. At no point in any of the conversations they'd had while in the throes of their affair had she said anything about her relationship with Atticus or how she felt about it. But then they hadn't really talked about much apart from logistics. There'd been little inclination to chat when they'd met up in person. Mostly they'd communicated with their bodies.

He picked up a pair of tongs and transferred the churrasco to the grill, and as it began to sizzle he wondered what to make of her many astonishing revelations, some of which could have the potential to blow the assumptions he'd been living with for months to smithereens.

Did they have any implications for his pursuit of vengeance?

Had they put a different spin on things?

No. Nothing had changed. Her explanation for why she'd ended their relationship made a certain sort of sense, and bravely holding her hands up to everything she'd thought and felt at the time was admirable, but he could never forget the chilly disdain and sheer disgust with which she'd looked at him in that Parisian hotel room, and the need to get the upper hand with her and restore control still burned deep within him.

Sentimentality had no place in this scheme of his, he reminded himself grimly, and he had no intention of quitting it, so he wouldn't think about how tough the last couple of years must have been for her. He wouldn't envisage her miserable and confused and made increasingly wretched by her brother's happiness. That her mind had been equally blown by the sex they'd had together was of no interest to him at all. How into him she'd been was as irrelevant as how into her he'd been. None of it mattered. Not her previous relationships, not her insecurities and how she was overcoming them, not the oddly jarring discovery that she'd been using him.

Above all, he would not dwell on the fact that he'd lied about having siblings because that can of worms did not need opening. In any case, these days he hardly ever thought of the father who'd disowned him before he was born or the socialite supermodel half-sister he'd never met. The one time, years ago, when he'd dared to venture into the exclusive neighbourhood in which he'd discovered they lived—so very different from the shack in the favela he called home—barely crossed his mind any more.

He would tell Thalia anything she wanted to know

about his life now—and he had no doubt that she would be imminently holding him to account and pressing him for details—but that particular part of his past, with the dangerous anger and resentment it had provoked and the unsettling intrusion it could make into the present if he let it, would never be up for discussion.

'So what was your upbringing like?' she asked predictably the minute he put the sliced churrasco on the table she'd moved to and sat down.

'The diametric opposite of yours, I imagine.'

Her eyebrows rose, her expression cool. 'You know nothing about mine.'

'I can guess.' Opportunity, security, everything money could buy...

'I very much doubt it.'

He handed her the tongs. 'Then enlighten me.'

'My father was stern and authoritarian and believed that children should be seen and not heard,' she said as she helped herself to some meat. 'My mother embarked on a string of affairs virtually the minute the ink was dry on the marriage certificate. She was—and is—so busy gallivanting across the world she was rarely around. Parental affection and support were non-existent. We were all basically brought up by nannies. Materially, we wanted for nothing but the money just meant that the neglect and dysfunction were easier to hide.'

Santi reeled. She was right. He couldn't have guessed. 'None of that appeared in any of the articles I read,' he said, having to reassess his assumptions once again, which was not a particularly comfortable experience, since he was rarely wrong and didn't much like it.

'I know.' She put down the tongs and added some salad to her plate. 'Selene's affairs and scandalous behaviour are well-documented but the rest of it is our little secret. I don't know how I'd have coped with it all without Atticus. Who do you have to face the challenges of life with?'

He had no one, and that was fine with him. Allowing people to get close raised the possibility of rejection, and all the wild emotions that came with it, and who needed that? 'Friends,' he said, although the people he hung out with were really more acquaintances.

'How did you feel about not having a father?'

'It was nothing unique,' he said easily as he served himself, giving her the answer he'd given to so many so often before. 'You can't miss what you don't have.'

'I would say that's a shame but sometimes fathers aren't all they're cracked up to be.'

It was on the tip of his tongue to agree but he bit back the words. Just because she too had suffered rejection at the hands of hers did not mean that his experience had to be shared. It wasn't as if he was after understanding or catharsis. He'd come to terms with his past years ago, so he had no need to talk about anything. The mere thought of where such a conversation might lead—exposure, vulnerability, weakness—turned his stomach and chilled his blood.

'Although I do feel that family is important, however rubbish,' she added. 'I wouldn't be without any of mine.'

'I wouldn't know.'

'What was your mother like?'

Desperate. Helpless. Fragile. Everything he'd determined not to be. 'She died fifteen years ago.' Three years before he'd had the money to pluck her out of the favela, which was something he'd always regret.

'That wasn't what I asked.'

'She was typical of her environment.'

'Which was?'

Wretched. Filled with such danger and threat that he did his best not to think about it, let alone talk about it. 'You must have read up on it,' he said in an effort to deflect her as he spooned some chimichurri onto his plate.

'I'm after the story behind the headlines.'

A faint shudder ran through him. 'There is no story.'

'There must be.'

Well, she wasn't getting it. 'Let's eat.'

Thalia was not remotely surprised when Santi called it a night shortly after they'd cleared their plates. She'd spilled her guts and she'd felt it only fair that he did the same. He, however, had evidently thought otherwise. He'd shut down all further attempts to converse along the lines of anything except business, and even that topic had run dry after a while. If she hadn't been so annoyed by it she'd have been impressed by his skill at avoiding answering her more personal questions with anything other than lines that sounded as though he'd delivered them a thousand times before.

But she wasn't convinced you couldn't miss what you didn't have and she didn't buy his story about there not being a story behind the story. Despite the outwardly relaxed pose, a tiny muscle had visibly throbbed in his cheek and his smile had tightened, which suggested that he definitely had something to hide. Would she ever find out what that was? Who knew?

There was one thing, however, she did know. The quid pro quo she'd tried to make happen had not materialised, and therefore she was not telling him anything else. She was through with talking. She'd revealed too much already without getting anything in return, and enough was enough. On more than one front, come to think of it, because she was fed up with being constantly on the back foot and having to scrabble about for control.

So that was it for conversation and compliance. Santi could count the days whichever way he chose. She was counting them consecutively, and if she decided to start at seven and end at eight so she could finish earlier there was nothing he could do to stop her. They were her hours as much as his, so from here on in she'd be making no further attempt to clear up the past. She'd find some other way to draw a line under them and move on. In the meantime, all she'd be focusing on was work.

CHAPTER SIX

ONE UNINTENDED CONSEQUENCE of shutting down the conversation when it cut a little too close to the bone, Santi came to realise the following morning, was a cool and clipped Thalia who could barely bring herself to look at him, which was immensely irritating since it presented a major setback in his plans to seduce her.

Unfortunately, this state of affairs did not improve with the passage of time. He upped the wattage of his smiles but they failed to pierce her frostiness. Every attempt he made to engage her in conversation fell on stony ground, and by lunchtime he'd decided that the situation could not be allowed to continue. He *would* get her into his bed, she *would* end up falling for him and he *would* then leave her high and dry. And so, as he had no intention of opening up to her as she'd tried so hard to get him to do at supper, he figured he was just going to have to thaw her another way.

'We're taking the afternoon off,' he announced, once lunch had been cleared from the poolside table by the housekeeper, who came in three times a week to restore order to the place and restock his fridge.

'I'm not,' Thalia countered with a chilly smile as she returned her attention to her laptop.

'I feel we could do with a break. The last forty-eight hours have been pretty intense. And it is very hot.'

'You can do whatever you wish but I'm expecting an important call.'

She'd have to mount a far better objection than that to deter him. 'Phones are mobile these days,' he said dryly.

'Very amusing,' she said, clearly not in the slightest bit amused.

'I've had reports that a pod of whales has been sighted nearby. I thought we could take a look.'

A flicker of interest skittered across her face—there and gone in a flash, but evidence enough that he'd found a weak spot to exploit. 'You go and fill me in when you get back.'

'There'd be no need to make up the hours, if that's what's concerning you.'

'That's not concerning me at all.'

'The boat has Wi-Fi.'

'I'd expect nothing less.'

'Perfect for phone calls.'

'And yet I find I'm still able to resist.'

Not for much longer. 'The whales are travelling with calves.'

As he'd anticipated, that did give her pause for thought. She went still, a faint frown creasing her brow, her beautiful brown eyes narrowing minutely. 'Calves?'

'Lots of them,' he said, sensing victory and closing in on it. 'It's a rare thing to see. A once-in-a-lifetime experience, I'm told.'

'How far away are they?'

'About four miles off the coast.'

Her frown deepened, as if she were waging some internal battle, and then she said, 'So we could be there and back in, say, a couple of hours?'

Well, in theory, they could, he thought with a mental air punch of triumph. But in practice they weren't returning until she'd lost the attitude and the seduction was back on track. 'Perhaps even less if we get going now.'

'I'll fetch my things.'

Having made some calculations with regards to distance, time and speed—for both the boat and the whales—Santi took the scenic route and he took it slow. He motored them between uninhabited islands, into the sparkling turquoise shallows of forested coves fringed with golden sands and around jagged rocks that jutted into the sea, before heading out into open water and speeding across the ocean to their ultimate destination.

Initially, and quite probably deliberately, Thalia positioned herself at the bow of the boat, as far from him as it was possible to get. But, as he'd anticipated, the heat of the afternoon sun and the spectacular scenery eventually melted her enough to join him on the flybridge, where he warmed her up further with idle and non-threatening conversation—which was how he came to learn that she loved swimming and loathed coriander.

On arrival at the recommended spot some fifty minutes after they'd departed, he switched off the motor yacht's engine. As they bobbed about on the sea in the vicinity of the few other boats that had heard the news and gathered there, he opened the hamper of drinks and snacks his housekeeper had prepared, then handed her a bottle of chilled sparkling water and extracted one for himself.

'So this is a pleasant way to spend a Tuesday afternoon, don't you think?' he said, sitting down beside her and stretching out his legs.

'I'd rather be getting on with our project,' she replied dryly. But she was smiling faintly as she cracked open the lid, and she didn't edge away, which was encouraging. 'However, it is rather lovely to be on the water. I've always found it very relaxing. I can't remember the last time I was out on a boat. Ironic really when half the family fortune comes from shipping, but I've been so busy lately there hasn't been much time for relaxation.'

'I know what you mean.'

She took a long sip of water, which was more arresting an action than he'd ever considered before, and then set the bottle on the table. 'How long have you had it?'

He cleared his throat and scrubbed his head of the urge to set his lips to her neck, which would no doubt earn him a shove into the table. 'Seven years,' he said, just about managing to recall her question. 'I acquired it as soon as I had a jetty to moor it to.'

'It doesn't look as though it's simply for show.'

It wasn't, which was why it could probably do with a repaint. 'Why would I have a boat simply for show?'

'It can happen when one has billions in the bank.'

'You'd know about that better than me.'

'I've never really seen the point of trophies.'

'Neither have I, despite having been bombarded with offers the second the sale of my company hit the press. The plane is purely practical.'

'Where do you go?'

'In this?' She nodded. 'Up and down the coast. The furthest I've been so far is Natal, just over a thousand nautical miles north of here. It's the easternmost point of the country. Do you know it?'

She shook her head, the sun glinting off her shades. 'This is the first time I've been to Brazil. I have a friend in Rio, who I've been meaning to visit for ages, but somehow I've never got round to it. That now seems a shame. I messaged her to see if she'd like to meet up when I'm done here but I haven't heard back yet.'

The offer to take her into the city and show her around was on the tip of his tongue, an urge insisting it be voiced, but with a flicker of alarm Santi bit it back. He tended to avoid Rio if he could, since it held few good memories, and acting as a tour guide wasn't what these ten days were about. He didn't know why he'd even thought of it when, this trip aside, he had no intention of taking her anywhere other than his bed.

'It's a vast country to explore,' he said, rubbing away the bead of sweat that he could suddenly feel at his temple.

'What made you choose to live on the coast?'

'I like being able to look out into nothing but blue sky, space and endless possibilities.'

'Quite the contrast to the favela, I imagine.'

His eyebrows lifted. 'How very perceptive of you.'

'I can be.'

Not if he had any say in the matter. He didn't want her poking around in his psyche. Even he tried not to go there if he could help it. And he was supposed to be quizzing and mellowing her, not the other way round. 'Where does your interest in whales come from?' he asked, vaguely wondering where the hell the sea breeze was.

'When I was ten, I saw a documentary on them and

was hooked,' she said. 'They're an extremely social and caring species. They protect each other and nurture their young. I found that novel yet appealing, even back then. I still do.'

'With your upbringing, I'm not surprised.'

'I see I'm not the only perceptive one here.'

But the difference was, he had an ulterior motive. Revenge was the only reason he was expressing an interest in her. It wasn't as if he *wanted* to create a connection. In fact, it was the very last thing he intended to do. He'd probably find it easier to breathe and cool down if he stopped staring at her.

'I wonder where this pod is,' he mused, purposefully sliding his gaze from hers to look out to sea, even though it was a wrench.

'I hope we don't capsize when it comes along.'

'Why would we?' he said with a slight frown. 'This vessel is twenty metres long and five metres wide.'

'There's no need to be defensive. All I meant is that a blue whale can grow to more than that, certainly in length. The waves they generate from surfacing can be huge.'

'These are humpbacks.'

'Ah,' she said knowingly. 'They tend to be shorter, but they're restless and have a habit of investigating vessels. Let's hope they give us a wide berth.'

'Let's hope so.'

'So what do you find novel and appealing?' she asked, shifting slightly to face him, which dragged his gaze back to hers, as if their eyes were magnets.

Her. Sitting on his boat in the sunshine, looking as if she belonged there. But she didn't, no one did, so he scrubbed that thought from his head and drummed up a different answer. 'Swimming in new waters. Meta- phorically speaking.'

'I thought you said it was just money.'

'It is. But having so much of it still requires some getting used to. Perhaps you could give me some tips.'

'I doubt it. The only thing I own personally is my flat in Athens and you've never needed any tips about anything, from what I recall.'

'Neither did you,' he said, thinking with a surge of heat about the way she'd instinctively known what turned him on most, right from the start. 'You always read me like a book. Remember Seville?'

She flushed. The pulse at the base of her neck flut- tered madly. For a moment she appeared struck dumb. Was she doing as he suggested and remembering the weekend they'd taken things to another level? But then she swallowed hard and gave herself a quick shake. 'I was referring to your business and the articles I found on it.'

Oh. Right. 'Were you?'

'Absolutely,' she said coolly. 'Why on earth would you think otherwise?'

He didn't know. And come to think of it, that wasn't the only question he couldn't answer. Why did he feel as though he could sit here and talk to her for hours? Why did he want to grab her by the hand, take her down below and keep her there until neither of them could think straight? And why was he worried about the state of his boat and fascinated with the idea of sharing common ground with her when all that mattered was seducing and then abandoning her?

This expedition was not going the way he'd anticipated, he thought, his stomach churning with unease.
He hadn't thought it through properly, or at all, if he was
being honest. He was more on edge and less in control
than he'd have liked. He had the horrible feeling that if
he wasn't extremely careful he could wind up revealing more than he'd ever intended, which was less than
zero, so he could not have been more relieved to suddenly spot a plume of water shooting up from the sea.

'Turn around,' he said, twisting abruptly to rummage
in the hamper for the binoculars.

'Why?'

'Because we have company.'

Pacing up and down her balcony that night, not remotely soothed by the serenity of her room or the gentle
sounds emanating from the tropical vegetation, Thalia
reflected darkly that this afternoon's trip had been an
extremely bad idea.

Not the actual whale-watching bit of it, of course.
That had been incredible. She'd counted twelve ani-
mals in total. Eight adults, four calves. She'd never seen
such magnificent creatures. They'd surfaced and hung
around for over ten minutes before moving on, and she
didn't mind admitting that the sight of the pod playing
about in the water had stolen her breath and brought a
tear to her eye.

Nor was Santi the cause of her woes. All he'd done
was suggest an afternoon off, even if he had been irritatingly insistent about it.

No. What was really troubling her was, well, *her*. Or
more precisely, her complete abandonment of common

sense and resolve. She was the one who'd given in to temptation and agreed to go with him to see the whales, when she should have been stronger and resisted. She was the one who'd relaxed and lowered her guard, despite vowing to do precisely the opposite.

Why had she done all that? Had she gone mad? Honestly, she was hopeless. And she knew now that the whole adventure had been one colossal mistake because she was wound more tightly than the spring of the Rolex that circled her wrist.

If she'd been stronger and stayed behind, or even kept to the bow, as would have been sensible, she wouldn't have had a fascinating insight into his character or caught an intriguing glimpse of a possible inferiority complex, true. But nor would she have been plagued ever since with memories of their affair, thanks to his shocking and unexpected reference to it.

Seville.

How could she ever forget those two days, six weeks after they'd met? She'd been working in Madrid, he in Lisbon. They'd stayed in the marble-floored and stucco-walled presidential suite that occupied the entire top floor of the city's finest hotel. Through tall French doors, dressed with crisp white curtains, countless historic monuments beckoned, but they'd been ignored. In the master bedroom with its beige silk walls and subtle sense of glamour, he'd encouraged her out of her comfort zone for the first time. And, after taking to the new and exciting like a duck to water, she'd then pushed him out of his. Vanilla with a hint of chilli, was how she'd described the earth-shattering experience that had turned out to be not a one-off.

The arrival of the pod had provided a brief and stunning distraction but it had been over all too soon. And then, as Santi fired up the engine and motored them back—without dawdling, thank God—the memories had descended thick and fast and now she couldn't push them back into their box where they'd been kept under lock and key.

She couldn't help remembering the sex—how instinctively they'd moved together, how willingly they'd trusted each other and how white hot and intense the pleasure had been, whatever the spice. She couldn't stop thinking about what might have happened this afternoon had the wash of a whale rocked the boat and landed her in his arms. Nor could she forget how thrilling she'd found it when he'd sparked up a conversation with their fellow whale watchers in Portuguese, a language she didn't speak but perhaps ought to learn because it was so incredibly sexy, at least it was when he spoke it.

In his own environment, Santi was even more attractive than he was out of it. The desire that had been simmering away inside her for days was heating, which was a concern she'd feared even as far back as Saturday night, and she couldn't even find peace in sleep because jetlag was still keeping her awake. Her muscles ached. Her nerves were at snapping point. Her cortisol levels had to be stratospheric and, quite frankly, she didn't know how much more of it she could take.

Perhaps a swim and some exercise would provide the relief she needed, she thought in faint desperation, flapping a hand to dispatch a whining mosquito. Not here to relax, she hadn't packed a bikini, but she was hot and sticky and tingling all over. More importantly, it was the middle of the night and, while she might be wide awake, her infuriating host most likely was not.

Returning inside, Thalia grabbed a towel from the bathroom, carefully opened the bedroom door and peered into the soft darkness. She waited for a moment, ears pricked, then, encouraged by the silence, tiptoed out. She stealthily descended the floating staircase and headed to the pool, which shimmered enticingly beneath the silvery light of the moon that hung low and large in the inky sky.

Keen to feel the glide of cool water over her hot, sensitised skin, and yearning for the soothing of her turbulent thoughts, she dropped her towel on a lounger and quickly stripped off her camisole and shorts. She padded to the edge and was just about to slip silently in when from behind her came a dry, 'Nice evening for a dip.'

With a yelp of shock she lost her balance and her dignity and toppled in headfirst instead.

'What the hell do you think you're doing?' she spluttered once she'd surfaced, her heart thundering as she pushed her hair back, dashed water from her eyes and glared up at the man who was standing there looking tousled and disorientated. He wore nothing but a pair of close-fitting white shorts that left little to the imagination—not that she needed to use her imagination, because she knew exactly what lay beneath. 'You scared the living daylights out of me.'

'I could ask you the same thing,' he said gruffly. 'It's two-fifteen in the morning.'

'I still have jetlag.' And a bad case of Santi-itis to which she was *not* going to admit. 'I thought a swim might help. I had no idea you were awake.'

'I wasn't.'

'Then how did you know I was here? I was so quiet.'

'You set off the alarm.'

That would explain it. 'I wasn't aware there was one.'

'It's silent.'

'Sorry.'

'It's fine,' he said, shoving his hands through his hair and then rubbing them over his face in an obvious attempt to rouse himself properly.

But it wasn't fine, Thalia thought despairingly, the sight of his muscles doing their thing drawing her attention to his hard, hair-smattered torso and dissolving her stomach into a puddle of lust. Nothing about this situation was fine. In fact, it felt oddly intimate and decidedly dangerous and why, oh, why hadn't she just stayed upstairs and had a shower instead? 'Please turn around so I can get out.'

'I've seen you naked many times before.'

'That's completely irrelevant,' she said, flushing from head to toe despite the coolness of the water.

'Your rear view is as appealing as it ever was.'

Agh. He was utterly impossible. 'Are you going to do as I ask?'

'Why don't I join you instead?'

What? No. Absolutely not.

With the way she was feeling, who knew where skinny dipping with him might lead? The only solution was a speedy exit so she could recover and regroup and figure out how she was going to face him in the morning. If she was going to have to give him a full frontal now to achieve that, so be it.

Before she could question the wisdom of her decision, she pulled herself out of the pool, reached for the towel and wrapped it around her body. She picked up her sleepwear and was about to make a dash for the stairs, but then she made the mistake of casting him a quick glance. She instantly froze, because he was standing unexpectedly close, and something about the intensity with which he was looking at her switched every cell in her body to high alert.

She couldn't avert her gaze. She couldn't move. She just stood there, frozen, enveloped by the heat emanating off him and his intoxicating scent and drenched in pool water and want.

'I should go up,' she said, her voice so hoarse it was barely audible. 'I don't know what I was thinking. I apologise again for disturbing you. Goodnight.'

'Wait.'

Before she could take even one tiny step, his arm shot out and he wrapped his hand round her wrist, rooting her to the spot. Her skin burned where he touched her. The move closed the distance between them and altered the angle of their bodies. Now they stood almost chest to chest, and she could barely breathe.

His gaze dipped to her mouth and a bolt of desire shot through her, pooling low in her abdomen and firing heat through her veins. Time slowed right down and the world shrank. The air between them was heavy and crackling, as if a storm were about to break. She knew she ought to take a step back, shake him off and kill the buzz that she really didn't need, but she was gripped with such a strong urge to touch and taste that she could feel herself swaying towards him instead.

'What do you want?'

'You know what I want.' His voice was low, rough and scraped over her nerve endings.

'No,' she said, but her protest was weak.

'I've missed us, Thalia. It's been over a year since we broke up and despite how things ended, I still dream of you every night.'

Her head swam. She'd missed them and dreamed of him too. But she wasn't going to admit it. She'd already told him far too much. 'I don't.'

'I don't believe you.'

'Stop.'

'I can't. I don't how it's possible but you're more beautiful and sexier than ever. I look at you and I can remember every single extraordinary thing we did together as if it were yesterday. I want to pick up where we left off. Feel what you do to me.'

He gave her a gentle tug so their bodies were flush against each other. The hard length of his erection pressed into her abdomen and her heart crashed violently against her ribs. His mouth was mere inches from hers. She wanted to kiss it more than she'd ever wanted anything, to be instantly transported into a world where there was nothing but ecstasy.

'I can certainly feel what I do to you,' he murmured, stroking his thumb over the delicate skin of her wrist and the pulse there that was pounding wildly.

Denying it was pointless. Despite her words, her body was giving her away. Suddenly she couldn't remember why being with him here like this, now, wasn't a good idea, why she shouldn't be lifting her chin and setting her lips to his or sinking into a kiss with a soft sigh of longing and pleasure.

His mouth moved on hers slowly, thoroughly, and her head emptied of everything but him. Tiny flickering flames licked along her veins and desire swelled, an achingly sweet build-up of heat and need that robbed her of breath and liquefied her bones. Helplessly, she pressed herself closer, shifting against him to find some kind of relief for the aching throb between her legs, and the tempo of the kiss changed as it so often had in the past. He wrapped an arm around her waist—a band of steel that clamped her tight against him and prevented escape. Her free hand found its way to his neck and she dug her fingers into his hair, equally disinclined to let him go. The more he demanded from her, the hotter the fire in her belly burned. She wanted his hands all over her. She wanted him inside her with frenzied desperation.

'Come upstairs with me,' he murmured raggedly when he finally lifted his mouth from hers, and she was on the point of saying yes, yes, yes, when her conscience suddenly woke up and demanded to know what on earth she thought she was doing.

She froze. She gasped. Had she completely lost her mind? she wondered, appalled at her lapse of control, pulverised by excoriating heat and rampaging desire. However tempted she was, she could not go upstairs and make everything she'd dreamed of come true. She wouldn't succumb again. She would resist and reject him with everything she had, because her life right now had no space for any man, let alone one as wholly consuming and potentially damaging as him. She had to face reality, not escape it.

So she swallowed hard, took a deep breath and

inched back to put some air between them. 'No,' she said, more breathlessly than she'd have liked.

'Why not?'

'Nothing can happen between us again. You know that. I even told you why.'

His eyes glittered in the low light. A muscle ticked in his jaw and his frown was deep. 'Do you still think you're better than me?'

What?

'Of course not,' she said with feeling. 'I never did. *You* thought that, and I have no idea where you got the idea from because what did I ever do to give you that impression?'

'You didn't correct it.'

'That you could think that of me hurt. Badly. I just wanted to leave to lick my wounds in private. I was referring to what I told you last night. But I have no wish to rehash the past, Santi, either the recent or the distant, even if you do. I'm here to work, and that's it.'

'Don't be naïve.'

'What do you mean?'

'You know as well as I do that you'll be in my bed before the week is out.'

Her breath caught and her heart lurched. She could see it. She wanted it. She didn't even find his arrogant presumption offensive. But he was wrong. Dead wrong. The kiss they'd just shared had been a moment of madness in the moonlight. Hell would freeze over before she fell back into his arms again. She was not as weak and vulnerable as she had been at the time of their affair. If, for some unfathomable reason, rekindling it had been his aim—with the flirting and the wander-

ing about with very little on—he could forget it. She
was never going to yield, and it was beyond time that
he realised that.

'Sex isn't part of our deal,' she said, finally pulling
herself free from his hold and ruthlessly stamping out
the part of her that desperately wished it was. 'Your
fifty million euros buy my time and expertise only. So
if you think that sleeping with you is how I ought to be
keeping you sweet, you can think again.'

CHAPTER SEVEN

SANTI WATCHED THALIA disappear back into the house for a moment, then spun round and dived into the pool. To clear his head. To rid his body of the desire that throbbed in every fibre of his being. To work out what the hell the last quarter of an hour had been about, because the one thing it *hadn't* been about was retribution.

Abruptly roused from a deep sleep, he had not been firing on all cylinders when he'd gone to investigate the security breach. He'd been hot, discombobulated and barely awake. Then he'd stumbled across Thalia in all her naked, beautiful, perfect glory and he'd instantly lost what little reason he had possessed.

She'd shimmered in the moonlight like some sort of nymph, all soft curves and long dark wavy hair. Every other memory of their short-lived affair—not just Seville, which had occupied his thoughts far too much this afternoon, and which he should never have brought up in the first place—had slammed into his head, one hot on the heels of the other, and instinct had taken over. He'd spoken nothing but the truth. He had dreamed of her. He did still want her, with a need that bordered on desperation.

But not for a single second had his plan for getting

revenge and restoring control crossed his mind. He'd kissed her because after her bold and breathtaking exit from the pool he simply couldn't *not*. He'd invited her upstairs with no other thought in his head than getting her beneath him and sinking into her soft welcoming heat.

He should have kept his mouth shut. He knew from experience that if he'd focused on intensifying the kiss instead of suggesting they move things inside, he'd have had her flat on her back on a sun lounger within moments.

So why hadn't he? And why, when he could have easily salvaged the situation by kissing her again and relighting the fire, had he demanded an explanation for her refusal instead?

That had been an error. Demanding to know whether she still considered herself above him and exposing to her a vulnerability he barely admitted to himself had been another. And, come to think of it, why had his heart nearly leapt out of his chest when she'd fallen in the water in the first place?

He was more susceptible to her than he'd ever imagined, he thought grimly as he hit the end of the pool, turned and powered back down it. Physical involvement with her was obviously a must. Emotional involvement was very much a must not. Yet now, with her rejection of him smarting as if he'd been stung by a hornet, he was beginning to realise that ever since he'd laid eyes on her the night of the gala he was thinking and feeling things he shouldn't.

Take the strength of his reaction to events merely going his way. The triumph he'd felt when her lot had closed and he'd won. The relief when she'd showed up at the airport at nine a.m. on Sunday morning. The pleasure that had ripped through him at finally having her on his territory when she'd turned up here in a cloud of dust, irate and tired but still the most desirable woman he'd ever met. None of these outcomes had been a surprise, so why had he felt them so intensely?

Then there was the absurd and wholly unnecessary compulsion to impress her. When she'd boarded his plane and begun to question him about it he'd barely been able to stop himself from bragging. When she'd admired his house, he'd puffed up with pride. Asking for her opinion of her room had had him waiting for her answer with bated breath and, ridiculously, he had actually cared what she thought of the size of his boat. The moment he'd been turned away from his father's house without even the chance to show him what he'd made of himself he'd sworn never to try and impress anyone ever again. Yet when it came to Thalia he hadn't thought twice.

Not for a second since he'd switched tactics and knuckled down to work with her had he thought about using the fact that she badly needed his project to redress the balance of power between them. A word in the right ear and he could have destroyed her business before she even launched it. But instead, he'd immersed himself in the experience, basking in her enthusiasm and admiring her confidence. He'd looked forward to eight a.m. and willed the minutes to slow as six p.m. approached, and—his own discomfort and confusion aside—he'd enjoyed her excitement over the whales this afternoon far too much.

Lastly, and perhaps of the greatest concern, was how much he *did* dwell on everything she'd told him at supper the night before, despite his every intention not to. He wanted to have a word with Zoe about how Thalia felt, even though he didn't know her well enough for that level of intimacy and it was absolutely none of his business. He found himself contemplating sibling relationships, making unhelpful comparisons between his, which were non-existent, and hers, which were tricky but at least there, and then having to manage the resulting emotions. He was frequently preoccupied with the subject of her previous boyfriends, and he couldn't squash the annoyance that for her their affair had been nothing more than a displacement activity.

It couldn't continue. He had the sickening feeling that if he wasn't careful he could fall under her spell again and this time, instead of merely denting his pride and threatening his track record, she could do him serious damage.

He would not put himself in that position. He had no interest in emotions of a romantic nature. For years he'd been witness to the harm they could do. How often had he come home to find his mother in tears because his selfish, cruel father had casually cancelled a date? How much had he despised the way she rushed off to put on her best dress and a slash of red lipstick the minute she was summoned? Love was toxic, he'd come to realise. One party held all the cards, the other, none. It was a weakness that destroyed self-esteem and obscured reality.

It was now becoming blindingly clear that he'd been playing a dangerous game with Thalia. He'd allowed himself to be influenced by the past and had totally overreacted. Since when had he been so melodramatic? This wasn't some telenovela in which he had a starring role that demanded he avenge his mother's treatment at the hands of his father by taking it out on someone else. And how was he going to proceed anyway? Thalia's parting shot indicated a will that dominated chemistry, and that blew his plan to bits. Because how could he break up with her if he couldn't get her in the first place?

He'd been an idiot for thinking he had to resort to revenge to achieve his goals. Ejecting her from his life and drawing a line under the last sixteen months would be ample indication of the power and control he sought. That would be the act of a man ruled by cold calculation, not adolescent hot-headedness. And why did he care what she thought of him? What was so special about her? Nothing. Plenty of other people were glad of his company. Some were so desperate for it they didn't care where he and his money had come from.

His philanthropic intentions remained unchanged, but that posed no problem. He'd find another adviser somewhere at some point. Right now, however, the number one item on his agenda for the morning was sending his current adviser home.

CHAPTER EIGHT

'YOU'RE FIRING ME?'

Thalia stared at Santi from across her room just before eight the following morning, scarcely able to believe her ears. It had taken a lot of guts to answer his knock on the door. She couldn't think about the events of the night before without burning up with embarrassment and desire, but with so much at stake for her professionally, hiding beneath the sheets simply wasn't an option.

She'd brazen her way through the day by pretending it hadn't happened, she had figured as she'd showered and dressed. If at any point he referred to her nakedness or the kiss that had kept her awake for hours, she would take a leaf out of his book by simply ignoring it and changing the subject. She'd draw on all the deportment skills she'd learned at that ridiculous finishing school in Switzerland—which her mother had insisted she attend in a rare moment of maternal interest in her eldest daughter, but in hindsight hadn't been a complete waste of time—and focus on the work.

Not once had she envisaged that work being snatched away.

'Technically, I didn't hire you,' he said, standing in

the doorway as still as a statue, his handsome face completely devoid of expression, his body language utterly unreadable, although the fact that he was fully dressed for once—in shorts, a buttoned-up shirt and deck shoes—didn't bode well. 'But essentially you are correct. I no longer require your services. The plane is still at the airfield. It will take you wherever you wish to go. It shouldn't take you long to pack.'

She stared at him, for a moment unable to convert her stunned thoughts into speech. *What on earth is going on?* she wondered, her head spinning like a top. He'd been so insistent she come here. He'd ruthlessly crushed her every attempt to push back, so a volte face like this made no sense at all. Unless the timing wasn't a coincidence and it was a direct response to their moonlit poolside encounter.

'Is this because I won't sleep with you?' she asked, chin up, eyes narrowed.

His jaw clenched, the tiniest indication that he wasn't quite as calm as he was trying to make out. 'Of course not.'

'Are you unhappy with my professional performance?'

'On the contrary.'

'Then why the sudden change of plan?'

His gaze dropped to her mouth and darkened. 'You mess with my head.'

'Yes, well, you mess with mine too,' she said, her lips tingling while a shiver rippled down her spine. 'But for the sake of my career I'm prepared to rise above it.'

'Your career won't suffer,' he said flatly. 'I'll find you another project.'

'I don't want another project,' she shot back, equally prepared to dig her heels in. Because whatever he thought, she was not leaving. 'I'm already invested in yours and I'm enjoying it immensely. I've never started anything from scratch. This work is super-important to me and I intend to see it through to the end.'

'Too bad.'

It was for him. 'And let's not forget, you blackmailed me into coming here,' she felt obliged to point out. 'I rescheduled meetings and cancelled engagements to make this work. I've suffered swollen ankles and jet-lag to accommodate your demands. I've danced to your tune for the last four days, and I will not risk my reputation and my future just because you can't control your response to me.'

'Leave and I'll donate another fifty million to the foundation.'

Ooh, that was a low blow. First blackmail, now bribery. It was a lot of money—and for a nanosecond she was torn—but she'd come this far and she was not for turning. And besides, she could match his offer any day of the week if she felt like it. 'I'm going nowhere and you can't make me.'

His dark eyes flashed. 'Then *I'll* go.'

She blinked in shock. *What?* 'Where?'

'Anywhere.'

'Am I that much of a problem?'

'Yes.'

Wow. She didn't know whether she was flattered or outraged. 'You'd really leave me here on my own?'

'Absolutely,' he confirmed with a sharp nod. 'The kitchen is very well stocked and my housekeeper can be put on standby if needs be. You have a car and you're not without other resources.'

All of that was true, yet he clearly wasn't thinking straight because this was completely nuts. 'You're overreacting.'

'The situation as it stands is untenable. It has to come to an end. But don't worry, I'll give you an excellent reference.'

She didn't care about the reference. Well, not right now she didn't. She cared about improving literacy and helping kids out of the favelas and launching his charity and her business with a bang. But more than that, she and Santi weren't done. Not by a long shot. Quite why this was the case when she had no intention of kissing him again she had no idea, but she felt it in her bones. By hook or by crook she would resolve this situation to her satisfaction, which was why, when he spun on his heel and strode out of the room, she scooted round the bed in hot pursuit of him.

'Now hang on a minute,' she said, hurrying to catch him up as he crossed the deck as if he had the hounds of hell snapping at his feet. 'Why is the situation untenable? I'm sure we can find a suitable compromise. Wait. Santi. This simply isn't—'

But she didn't get to finish her sentence because the next second she'd tripped over a low-level branch, her ankle had twisted and given way and she was crashing to the floor. On landing, she let out a howl of pain and cursed loudly and fluently the architectural oddities of this house that meant it had trees growing inside it.

Santi stopped abruptly, whipped round and stalked back to her. 'Did you do that deliberately?'

Now she *was* outraged. 'Of course I didn't,' she snapped as she sat up, gingerly prodded her ankle and gritted her teeth against the sharp pain that shot up her leg. 'You need to get an arborist in here. This whole place is ridiculous.'

'When you grow up in the sort of place I did, green-ery matters.'

'That's what a garden's for.'

'Let me take a look.'

'I'm fine.'

Ignoring her, he bent down, scooped her up into his arms and dumped her on the chair in which, thirty-six hours earlier, she'd stupidly revealed her issues with her brother and her identity. While she fought for breath and control of her spinning head, he dropped to a squat, lifted her foot onto his knee and slid off her shoe.

'Does that hurt?' he asked, pressing his fingers against the tender bump that was rapidly swelling around the bone.

'Ouch,' she muttered with a wince. 'Yes.'

'What about this?'

He gently rotated her foot and brought tears to her eyes. 'On a scale of one to ten, it's an eleven.'

'I'll sort out some ice and then get the first aid kit.'

'I thought you had a plane to catch.'

His jaw was tight. His mouth was set in a flat line, frustration radiating off him in waves. And even though she really hadn't tripped on purpose, she was glad his plans had been thwarted. Now he knew what it felt like.

'Evidently not any more.'

Santi vented his feelings about this infuriating turn of events by filling the air with muttered expletives while he rummaged around in the bathroom for a tubular support bandage and painkillers. He'd had it all mapped out. All sorted. But Fate had clearly had other ideas and what the hell else could he do? He could hardly leave Thalia here on her own with an ankle that was swollen and sore but thankfully appeared to be sprained rather than broken. Yes, he was keen to remove himself from her head-wrecking orbit so he could forget about her and the damn kiss that had kept him up all night, but he wasn't completely without empathy.

He should have waited until she appeared downstairs at eight before confronting her, he thought grimly, finally finding what he was looking for. That would have been a root-free event. But it would also have meant firing her by the pool, the scene of the crime, and the last thing he'd wanted was to recall the unacceptable madness that had happened there beneath the moonlight. Besides, regret was pointless. Grudgingly admitting she was right about the need to hire a tree surgeon served no purpose at all. A solution to the situation was what was required.

As he stalked off in search of a pair of crutches—souvenirs of a broken tibia he'd suffered while skiing in St Moritz a couple of years ago—he figured he'd just have to follow her example and rise above the attraction. He didn't have any other choice. He'd immerse himself in the tasks he'd set her and keep face-to-face interaction to a minimum. As much as he was able to he would steer clear of her, and when he couldn't he'd simply ignore her scent, her gaze, her presence, her everything. It needn't be for long. It had once amused and suited him to keep her around indefinitely but that was very much not the case now. He wanted her out of his house as soon as was practicably possible, and he'd do everything in his power to facilitate that.

Laden with medical equipment, Santi headed back to his inconvenient patient. He set the crutches to one side, braced himself, then resumed his position at her feet.

'You wanted the ten days to run consecutively?' he muttered, removing the ice he'd packed around the swelling and observing with some relief that at least it hadn't got any bigger. 'You have them. In fact, why don't we take the day we flew here as day one? We've completed two more since then, so another week and we'll be done. Your ankle should be healed by then. And on that note we'll revert to your original idea of working up here. No need to navigate the stairs and risk further injury.'

And no unnecessary torment caused by memories of last night by the pool either.

'Oh,' she said dully. 'OK.'

Expecting more enthusiasm for the idea and not a little gloating, due to the fact that he was giving her her way on a number of fronts, Santi glanced up at her and frowned. She looked shaken and distressed, he noted with a sudden skip of his pulse and a sharp squeeze of his chest. Was she in a lot of pain? Could she be going into shock? How on earth would he treat that? He raked his gaze over her a little more intently and saw with alarm that she was trembling.

'Is everything all right?' he said, concerned that the painkillers and a stretchy bandage might not cut it and vaguely wondering where the nearest hospital might be. 'You're very pale. Do you need to lie down?'

Thalia blinked slowly, as if coming out of a trance, and gave herself a quick shake. 'What? No. I'm fine,' she said with the flash of a smile that didn't quite reach her eyes and did little to reassure him. 'Everything's fine.'

'Are you sure?'

'Absolutely.'

She sounded adamant even if she looked anything but. He'd have to take her word for it and keep a close watch over her. 'Let me know immediately if that changes.'

'Of course.'

But while Santi had been fetching the first aid kit and crutches, Thalia had received a phone call from Atticus, and as a result of it, nothing was fine at all.

When she'd seen his name flash up on the screen she'd thought, with an absurd little bubble of hope and delight, that perhaps he'd telepathically felt her pain and was ringing to see if she was all right. He wasn't, of course. He hadn't felt her pain for many months now.

'Hey, sis,' he'd said in Greek from down the other end of the line—in Naxos, she'd presumed, although the days of him letting her know where he was all the time were long gone. 'I have some news. Zoe's pregnant.'

It was a good thing she'd been sitting down because she'd suddenly felt as if she were falling from a great height. A lead weight had seemed to settle on her chest, compressing her lungs and making it hard to breathe. 'Oh, wow,' she'd managed brightly, her throat tight, her heart thumping oddly fast. 'Congratulations.'

'It's three months now. All's going well.'

'I'm so pleased.'

'Would you like me to send you a copy of the ultra-sound?'

Not particularly. She didn't need physical proof that their lives were spinning off in even more divergent directions. But what sort of a sister would she be to say thanks but no thanks? Envy and resentment were terrible emotions to experience at such a happy announcement, and very few sets of twins celebrated life's milestones at the same time. So she'd taken a deep steadying breath, fixed a smile to her face in the hope that it would be reflected in her voice and said, 'Very much.'

'I'll email it over now.'

'Do the others know?'

'You're the first I've told.'

Some consolation…

'But Willow guessed a couple of weeks ago,' Atticus had continued, killing that tiny buzz stone dead. 'The four of us went for dinner and she noticed that Zoe wasn't drinking or eating shellfish. She teased out the truth.'

Oh.

'I'm so pleased,' she'd said again, finding it hard to speak around the hot tight lump in her throat. 'Please say hi to Zoe and pass on my congratulations.'

'I will.'

At the other end of the line, she'd heard a muffled voice and then Atticus had said, 'I'd better go,' and cut the call, leaving her awash with emotion and floundering until Santi had returned with the supplies to fix her ankle.

Thalia tried not to mind that her brother hadn't even

asked how she was, let alone where she was, what she was doing and who she was doing it with. It might have been nice to have been the first to know about the baby beyond their little unit of two, but just because she was Atticus's twin it wasn't her *right*. And it was natural that he and Zoe would meet up with Leo, their eldest brother, and his wife. Why wouldn't they double date? They were the perfect foursome.

She was thrilled for her brother and sister-in-law. Of course she was. But God she was lonely. She'd attended so many weddings recently. Three of them had involved her siblings. Everyone seemed to be coupling up but her. She was thirty-one. She'd always wanted to get married and have a family of her own, despite the train wreck of her parents' union and the terrible example they'd set. Sometimes she yearned for it so much her heart physically ached, even though she'd had to put men on pause while she completed this journey of self-discovery.

So why couldn't she find her soulmate? Was it simply that not knowing who she was doomed a relationship from the start? Or did she expect too much? Was she so used to the close connection she'd had with Atticus that she subconsciously sought a similarly intense and instant connection with the men she dated? Could that also be why they failed? Because she had little time for superficiality and small talk and threw in the towel too soon?

She'd certainly had an intense and instant connection with Santi, she thought, watching him stretch the bandage over her foot with his lovely, big, capable hands, the pain of the sprain lessening as she began to suffuse with heat. And not just a physical one. They hadn't talked all that much or all that deeply during their torrid twelve-week affair, but it was uncanny how often, when they were apart, she'd be daydreaming about him and a message would arrive in her inbox or on her phone a second or two later. Whatever the content—a logistical arrangement, an amusing anecdote about work, a spot of sexting—they'd always perked her up, she recalled.

So maybe he could perk her up now.

And maybe she should let him.

Because, actually, why *was* she fighting the attraction? Did giving in to it and losing herself in the blissful pleasure that only he could give her *really* have to be a problem? The circumstances of this situation didn't remotely resemble that of their affair. For one thing, now he'd agreed to the consecutiveness of their workdays— an unexpected yet satisfying solution to the stalemate they been stuck at before she'd tripped—her stay here had a deadline. So there simply wouldn't be time for things to get complicated. And she was so much stronger now. The chances of being blown off course again were virtually non-existent.

She wanted him desperately. Instead of constantly battling the desire, she longed to embrace it and let it flow. She wanted more of the kisses that led to long hot nights of fireworks and oblivion. It would be beneficial to rid herself of the unbearable tension that was causing her so much stress, she told herself. She would be more productive and better able to do her job. And would it not give her a form of closure?

'Why are you looking at me like that?' Santi muttered, jolting her out of her thrilling, tumbling thoughts.

'How am I looking at you?'

'As if you're thinking about kissing me.'

Her gaze dropped to his gorgeous mouth and lingered. Her pulse rate accelerated as shivers began to race up and down her spine. 'What if I am?'

His hands stilled on her foot. 'Did you bang your head when you tripped?' he said with a frown.

'No.'

'Then why?'

'Because I'm tired of fighting the attraction I feel for you,' she confessed, lifting her eyes to his, but finding nothing to read in their dark unfathomable depths. 'I don't think I can stand another seven days of it. I accused you of overreacting before, but it's entirely possible I've been guilty of the same.'

'I understood I'd be an unwelcome distraction.'

'You wouldn't be unwelcome any more. Why don't you kiss me again and see?'

He shook his head and returned his attention to his doctoring. 'It's not going to happen.'

'Why not?'

'You might have changed your mind, but I haven't. If you hadn't sprained your ankle, I'd be long gone.'

'But surely if we want each other the situation is no longer untenable.'

'I don't want you.'

She didn't believe that for a second. He might not want to want her, but he had last night. Very much. 'It would be just sex,' she said, focusing on getting what she needed instead of the turmoil in her head and the trouble in her heart. 'For six nights. That's all I ask.'

'You're not having it. Think of the damage sleeping with a client would do to your reputation.'

'Who needs to know?' He wouldn't tell. He hadn't said a word about their affair. 'You even said I'd be in your bed before the week was out.'

'I was mistaken.'

'Do you really think you'll be able to resist me?'

'Without a shadow of a doubt.'

'You couldn't before.'

'That was then.'

Yes, well, they'd soon see about that.

CHAPTER NINE

ONCE HER ANKLE was securely bound, Santi left Thalia to make her own way to the workspace that she'd identified as suitable the morning after she'd arrived. To help her there he'd have to touch her in places that were more tantalising and dangerous than a lower leg—the handling of which had been a tough test of his will-power as it was—and she had the crutches. Arranging a stool with a cushion upon which to rest her foot was as far as he was prepared to go and, having done that, he removed to the kitchen to prepare breakfast. He took his time over it, because eggs and fruit should not be rushed, he felt, then delivered the tray to the table at which she now sat and stalked off.

'Wait. Where are you going?' she called after him, sounding faintly startled and not a little aggrieved.

Anywhere she wasn't, he thought darkly. Just because the out-of-sight-out-of-mind theory hadn't worked thirteen months ago, it didn't mean it wouldn't now. 'Downstairs.'

'What if I need something?'

'Call me.'

He descended the stairs two at a time and strode into his ground floor study, resolutely not thinking about kissing her or her shockingly tempting proposal. But he'd barely had time to fire up his laptop before his phone rang.

'So sorry to disturb you so soon,' she said, practically purring down the line, 'but would you be an angel and bring me some sparkling water?'

Gritting his teeth, Santi told himself that it was his own damn fault he was in this position. Thalia had injured herself at his home and was in pain because of him—again. Although physically this time rather than emotionally, and at least that could be alleviated with medication. Therefore he'd fetch her her water.

Ten minutes later, he was summoned to adjust the stool. A quarter of an hour after that, he had to go and check that the bandage wasn't too tight because she couldn't feel her toes, and five minutes after *that* he brought his laptop back upstairs and plonked it down at the other end of the table because all this toing and froing was driving him nuts.

The rest of the morning passed achingly slowly. Ostensibly he researched literacy programmes, but in reality he was so distracted that he achieved very little. Her gaze kept sliding in his direction and lingering—as intense, as focused and as sizzling as a laser. She claimed his attention on the most spurious of pretexts and, once she had it, she batted her eyelashes at him and smiled winningly, all wide-eyed innocence and sultry seductiveness, which was a truly mind-boggling combination.

'It's fascinating to see you in your natural habitat,' she mused at one point as if he were a wild animal, which was apt, given how he was beginning to feel.

'Is it?' he replied, feigning a complete lack of interest in her observation and keeping his focus on the screen of his laptop.

'You suit this environment far more than any one of the hotels rooms we frequented.'

'Are you implying I lack elegance and sophistication?'

She was silent for a moment as if she was considering that, and then she said, 'Not exactly. Although those wouldn't be the adjectives I'd use to describe you.'

'Which ones would you use?'

'Untamed. Unpredictable. Unbelievably exciting.'

The first two certainly applied to him now. She'd mentioned the hotel rooms and all he could think was the heat they'd found in them, the passion and then, God, the boundary pushing that she'd embraced with an enthusiasm that he suspected had destroyed him for anyone else. 'You never seemed to mind that.'

'Oh, I don't mind at all.'

She clearly saw his refusal to engage in a six-night fling with her as a challenge, the irony of which did not escape him. But he could handle a few smouldering looks, a smattering of barely-there touches that nevertheless set him on fire, and the occasional reference to their affair, he assured himself as he did his utmost to ignore her. He couldn't control her behaviour, but he could most certainly control his. He would not forget the danger she presented and he would not take her up on her proposition, no matter how great the attack on his defences, which she upped after lunch.

She was on the phone, rattling away in French to a lawyer who apparently specialised in global charities, when a parcel with her name on it was delivered to the

house. Refusing his offer of help, she hobbled with it
to her room. Twenty minutes later she emerged, having swapped her usual uniform of smart trousers and
demure top for a skimpy black bikini and a pink and
gold sarong. Her hair was down, instead of up, flow-
ing loose over her shoulders, and at the shocking, gorgeous sight of her Santi nearly swallowed his tongue.

But he did not comment. Not when she made her way
back across the deck, her barely confined breasts jig-
gling with every hop of the crutches. Not when she sat
down and adjusted her bikini top, which surely didn't
need to take nearly as long as it apparently did. Not even
when she shot him a heat-filled glance and fluffed out
her hair—just as she'd used to after they'd had sex—
did he react.

He would not give her the satisfaction of knowing
how much she affected him. How very un-angelic the
thoughts stampeding through his head were. She would
not win this battle of attrition she'd decided to wage.
All he had to do was stay strong, maintain his grip on
his control and count down the minutes until he could
put her on a plane.

But in the event, despite his very best efforts, her assault on him proved so effective that his defences didn't
even make it past seven before collapsing into rubble.

'I'm clocking off,' she said on the dot of six p.m.
'Would you mind carrying me down to the pool? I could
really do with a swim.'

Yes, he did mind, he thought, his jaw tight, every
muscle in his body tensing. Very much. It had been
bad enough picking her up when she'd tripped, but at
least then she'd been clothed. All that soft warm semi-

naked flesh in his arms now might just undo him as it had done last night.

'The bandage isn't waterproof,' he said, sounding as though he'd swallowed rocks.

'Then I'll take it off.'

That made him envisage her taking everything else off too, and he remembered how she'd looked in the moonlight until he ruthlessly obliterated the images from his head. 'If you so wish.'

'Please?'

The bat of the eyelashes and the tremulous smile bounced straight off his armour. They didn't suit her anyway. 'No.'

'I'm not sure trying to make it down the stairs with crutches on my own would be a good idea. As you pointed out earlier, there might be a risk of further injury.'

And *she'd* accused *him* of manipulation? 'That's why there's a handrail,' he said flatly. 'One on each side. Take it slowly. You'll be fine.'

She gave a deep sigh of resignation. 'All right,' she said with overly dramatic despondency. 'I guess I can manage.'

She got up awkwardly and made her way with apparent difficulty to the stairs. Abandoning the crutches, she grasped the handrail and took a step. She immediately went rigid, and her breath hissed through her teeth, and with a clatter of his chair Santi sprang to his feet.

'Oh, for God's sake,' he muttered, very nearly at the end of his tether as he strode towards her. Whether or not she was faking it, he couldn't let this continue. What if she fell? Did he want that on his conscience too? And why the bloody hell hadn't he had a lift installed?

He grabbed her free arm and wound it round his neck with one hand and planted the other on her waist. 'Lean on me.'

'Thank you.'

Together they made their way down the stairs, and as he huffed and grunted he wondered if she really needed to lean into him quite so closely? He could smell the shampoo she used, and memories of all the showers and baths they'd shared slammed into his head. The minimalist slate bathroom that had a panoramic view of the Tokyo skyline and a bath that comfortably fit two… The South African game reserve treehouse with its open-air bedroom and the glassed-in shower around which a thunderstorm had raged… The smooth softness of her skin beneath his fingers made him think of the endless hours he'd spent exploring her body with his hands and his mouth in all four corners of the globe and he ached to do it again.

At the bottom of the stairs, in order to put a swifter end to his torment, Santi swept Thalia up into his arms once more and strode across the grass to the pool area, avoiding with determination the pool itself and targeting a double sun lounger instead. He deposited her in the centre of it, wondering if he would ever be able to scrub from his head the feel of all that warmth and softness plastered up against him. He was about to spin round and make a bid for freedom, for air, for sanity, when she suddenly whipped off her bikini top and all the blood shot from his head to his groin.

'I thought you were going for a swim,' he growled,

frozen to the spot, his scowl so fierce he suspected it might well turn permanent.

'I think I'll sunbathe for a bit first.' She looked up at him, her eyes lit with a wicked gleam that triggered a surge of desire so overwhelming it threated to swamp him. She waved a hand in the direction of her chest. 'You aren't bothered by a bit of toplessness, are you? You did say you'd seen it all before.'

He had said that and he had seen it all before. But this was different. Now he didn't want to see anything. Except, he did. *Por Deus*, he *did*. He wanted to look at her for hours and touch her and taste her so badly he was in agony, and when she wriggled back to make herself comfortable, what remained of his control evaporated.

What was his problem? he wondered as the final strand of his stretched-to-the-limit patience snapped. Why was he making such a mountain out of this molehill? He hadn't slept with anyone in the thirteen months since they'd split up—even the thought of it had made him recoil with distaste—so he should be biting her hand off. It was just sex, until she left. Six nights of the extraordinarily intense pleasure he'd only experienced with her.

What damage could she possibly do in that time? There'd be no risk of emotional involvement. The only thing they'd be sharing was the incredible passion that burned between them, which ought to be indulged because it was so staggeringly rare. He would never be lured from the purely physical. Of that he was absolutely certain. So what was he worried about? And did it really matter who was in control right now?

'I give up,' he said, lowering himself to the lounger,

his pulse hammering and his entire body racked with anticipation. 'You win.'

'I don't know what you're talking about.'

'Yes, you do.'

'You're right,' she said, an almost beatific smile curving her beautiful mouth as he leaned in, planting his hands either side of her, and she fell back. 'I absolutely do.'

Oh, thank God for that, Thalia thought, wrapping her arms around Santi's neck and almost weeping with relief as his mouth came down on hers. He'd put up quite a fight. She'd had to pull out all the stops. For one heart-stuttering moment she'd thought she'd failed, and the rejection that had sliced through her had been twice as sharp as anything she'd felt this morning on the phone to Atticus. But then his resistance had visibly disintegrated and now he was kissing her with a thousand times more heat and passion than he had done last night.

Losing herself in the electrifying sensations shooting through her, from the top of her head to the tips of her toes, she moaned and tangled her fingers in his hair. The kiss turned harder and wilder, and with what few functioning brain cells she had left she wondered whether he sought to punish her for her games. But if he did, he was failing. She wanted it all, whatever he had in mind for her.

She tightened her hold on him, just in case he had any intention of pulling away—which would be punishment indeed—and with a harsh groan, he moved a hand to her hip. He slid it up her side until he reached her breast and she instinctively arched her back in encouragement, craving the full contact that she knew from experience would be thrilling, but to her frustration he refused to comply.

'Touch me properly,' she panted, wrenching her mouth from his to catch her breath, willing to beg if she had to.

'When I'm ready,' he said roughly, his voice gravelly and low. 'I'm the one in control now.'

'Tease.'

'You're one to talk.'

Her head spinning, her heart pummelling her ribs, she pressed on his shoulders to urge him lower. But all he did in response was reach for her wrists and trap them in one hand above her head against the lounger. The other he skimmed over her body with featherlight caresses that made her whimper and shiver and writhe.

The torment was relentless, the tension unbearable. He trailed kisses all over her neck and finally gave her what she needed by cupping her breast with one big warm hand. Within moments she couldn't take any more. She was burning up, needing release, and she drew in a ragged breath to plead with him when he deftly undid the knot tying her sarong. Then he dipped his hand beneath the band of her bikini bottoms and the words dried up in her throat. He captured her achingly tight nipple in his mouth and eased his fingers into her slick wet heat, and she had to bite on her lip to stop herself from crying out at the intensity of the pleasure that whirled through her.

He knew exactly what drove her wild. He'd once dedicated hours to finding out and he hadn't forgotten a thing. He showed her no mercy. He wound her tighter and drove her higher and he didn't stop until she was trembling and moaning and shattering beneath him as fireworks exploded behind her eyelids and wave upon wave of ecstasy thundered over her.

'Are you still on the pill?' he said hoarsely some minutes later.

His words were muffled by the fog in her head and the pounding of her pulse as she floated down to earth. All she could manage was a weak shake of the head and a soft, breathless, 'No need.'

'So you haven't been dating all that much, then?'

'No.'

'Don't go anywhere.'

There was no chance of that. She couldn't have moved even if she'd wanted to. Her limbs had lost all strength. Her bones had dissolved. She was still seeing stars. Had it always been that intense? Or had the build-up of tension over the last four days after such a long absence added a dimension that hadn't existed before?

Tiny aftershocks of pleasure rippled through her. She touched the tips of her fingers to her abdomen and the muscles beneath her skin twitched. Incredibly, she could feel desire stirring again. She closed her eyes, flattening her hand and inching it down her body, imagining his mouth there, on her, as he—

'Stop that.'

Her eyes flew open and her hand stilled, her entire being flooding with heat at being caught in the act—even though it was nothing she hadn't done before with him. 'What took you so long?'

His mouth quirked. 'How's the sprain?'

'What sprain?'

'Very funny.'

'I can't feel a thing.'

'That'll be the endorphins.'

'I think I need more.'

'I'll see what I can do.'

He took care removing her bikini bottoms. Less so tossing them to the ground. He pulled his T-shirt over his head and that joined them. His shorts and underwear followed a second later but she didn't have time to ogle the magnificence of his body because, barely before she had time to think—*hello!*—he'd rolled on a condom with more dexterity than she could have managed, given how badly she was shaking, and settled himself between her thighs.

He kissed her deeply and lengthily, until the world faded away and there was only this. Only him. She ran her hands over his shoulders, loving the feel of his muscles flexing, and then over his hot smooth back and lower.

They'd done this so many times, she thought giddily, yet each time had been a revelation. Now was no different. She could sense an urgency in him she'd never felt before. And a restraint. Because of her ankle? It genuinely didn't hurt. She raised the leg in question and wrapped it around his hips, bending the knee of the other, instinctively lifting her pelvis to hurry him along. As ever he read her body beautifully. In one easy move he pushed into her, and the feel of him hard and deep inside her was so achingly familiar—as if it had been days since he'd been there, not months—that she found she had to swallow down a tiny lump in her throat.

Santi swore gutturally, suggesting he was equally

affected. Then he began to move, his breath hot and harsh on her neck, his delicious weight pressing her down, and she could do no more than just close her eyes and go with it.

While he transported her to a place where there was nothing but the promise of explosions and oblivion she dug her fingers into his hair and clung on. She pressed hot kisses to his neck and nipped his earlobe and felt the shudders rip through him. He cupped a breast and rubbed a thumb over her nipple. Her heart nearly leapt out of her chest. And all the while, he thrust in and out of her, the thrillingly exciting friction there and everywhere else obliterating her reason, her thoughts, everything but her senses.

The tension spiralling inside her was maddening. She was prickling all over, hurtling towards a destination she knew from experience was star-filled and wondrous, and she wanted to get there. She wanted to get there so desperately. Her blood was boiling. Her nerve endings were on fire. Murmured words flowed from her mouth in broken incoherent bursts, about how good he was making her feel, what she wanted him to do to her and what she was going to do to him later.

In response, he quickened and deepened his movements, and crushed his mouth to hers in an earth-shattering kiss that propelled the tingling in her toes up through her body, spreading into every inch of her with ever increasing intensity, until it split her apart, drenching her in pleasure and wrenching his name from her lips.

While she trembled and gasped, he held her tight and then buried himself in her one last time, so deep it was as if he wanted to fuse himself to her. With a muffled roar, he climaxed, pulsing into her so fiercely that it detonated another mini explosion, and then he collapsed on top of her.

And as their breathing evened, and their heartbeats slowed, Thalia lay beneath him, slightly squashed, slightly sweaty, her ankle now beginning to throb a little. But her head was blissfully empty and her troubling feelings were soothed, and there really was no place she'd rather be.

CHAPTER TEN

SEVERAL HOURS LATER, in his bed, to which he'd carried Thalia when the sun had set and a chill had tinged the air, Santi peeled himself away from her and flopped onto his back in order to recover from the latest in a long line of mind-blowing orgasms. He was boneless, blissed out and overcome with lassitude. He might have lost today's battle down there by the pool, he thought woozily, as his body cooled and his surroundings swam back into focus, but it didn't feel much like defeat.

'Why did we ever stop doing this?' he murmured absently once he'd regained the power of speech, rolling onto his side and propping himself up on an elbow.

Evidently less affected than he was by the sex marathon they'd just undergone, Thalia sat up abruptly, clasping the sheet to her chest, and stared at him wide-eyed and open-mouthed. 'Are you serious?' she said with a quick fluff of her gloriously tousled hair. 'You broke us up.'

'You did that,' he corrected. 'I just got there first.'

'With wholly unfounded and hurtful accusations,' she said, looking still ever so slightly upset about it. 'I'll never forget them. You called me a pampered princess. You said my nose was stuck so high in the air it was a wonder I could see where I was going. That I wouldn't know real life even if I were stripped of everything I had and dumped right in the middle of it. Why did you even *say* those things?'

Santi winced, his gut churning with self-recrimination as he remembered the conversation. Her question was one he didn't particularly want to answer. At least, not with the truth. His burning need for control and where it stemmed from was a rabbit hole down which he would never venture with her. He rarely went down it himself. He didn't like to recall the teenage rage and resentment he'd felt at his father's rejection and his mother's despair, or how hard he'd found it to contain those emotions and stay on track. If it hadn't been for the intervention and mentorship of a charity-organised youth worker—who'd met him when he was fourteen soon after his friend had been killed, and had introduced him to literacy, computers and coding—he could have easily gone down an altogether different path.

He should never have brought the matter up, he thought regretfully. If Thalia hadn't rendered him so weak and befuddled he'd have been more circumspect. He'd have to take more care going forward.

But perhaps he ought to apologise for the things he'd said to her that morning. She'd had the courage to explain where she'd been at the time and he'd reluctantly come to realise that he could have been wrong about the icy disdain she'd bestowed on him. It might not have been a reaction to him but rather to what he'd said. And this was the second time she'd sought clarification. Even if he had had the energy to distract her by kissing her until she couldn't think about anything other than him, continued avoidance did rather smack of cowardice.

'You caught me by surprise and I don't take rejection well,' he said, as if it had really been that simple.

'Who does?' she observed with a frown. 'But all I'd said was that we needed to talk.'

'Everyone knows what that means, and I was right, wasn't I?'

'That's still no excuse for lashing out the way you did.'

'I know. I handled it badly. I apologise.'

She tilted her beautiful head and regarded him quizzically. 'Was I ever arrogant or condescending towards you?'

'No.'

'I don't even know why you thought I would be. I mean, I'm not generally. I'm acutely aware of how lucky I've been and how privileged I am. And why on earth would anyone look down on you with everything you've achieved?'

Which was what, exactly? A stuffed bank account and a private jet? A formidable reputation in the business world and stellar success? It would never have been enough.

He could still recall turning up at his father's sprawling villa in Copacabana, shortly after he'd set up his software business and sold his first licence, thinking that finally he'd done something to make the old man proud enough to recognise him and welcome him into his life. Only to have the housekeeper shut the door in his face. Now the guy had been dead for eight years and he'd never be impressed.

'I wasn't ready for us to be over,' he said, stifling the troublesome memories and the unpleasant emotions that they stirred up. 'It was a cheap shot to save face. I'm sorry I hurt you. That was never my intention.'

'You should have let me explain.'

Perhaps she was right, but ultimately there'd have been little point. It wouldn't have changed anything. It wasn't as if he'd have offered to help her with what she'd been going through. He didn't have the necessary resources, and emotional support had never been—and never would be—his thing. Although if he had heard her out he could have avoided hurting her, he supposed. 'The result would have been the same.'

'But not the fallout. Thanks to you I spent weeks fretting over everyone I'd ever met and everything I'd ever said to them. What with all the other angst I had going on at the time, my confidence had already taken a battering. You demolished what was left of it. It's been hard work getting it back.'

Great shafts of guilt swiped at his conscience. He hadn't thought about her at all. That morning had been all about him. If only he hadn't fallen into old bad habits the repercussions would have been different for him too. He could have avoided the strange ache he'd felt deep inside in the days after their breakup. He wouldn't have stewed in a swamp of familiar resentment and perceived injustice these last thirteen months. He'd have had no need for retribution. She wouldn't be here now.

Something twanged in his chest and he rubbed it away. 'How can I make it up to you?' he said, not wanting to analyse quite how he felt about her not being here and instead switching his focus from the past to the present.

'You can start by making me something to eat.'

While Santi took himself off to heat up some delicious-sounding fish stew that his housekeeper had prepared earlier, Thalia downed two painkillers, arranged a cushion to support her ankle and contemplated his recent confession.

Obviously she was delighted they'd finally cleared up the Paris misunderstanding, but she did get the feeling that there had to be more to his explanation than met the eye. Such impulsivity didn't fit with the man who'd built a successful business from scratch and sold it for billions at the relatively young age of thirty-four. He couldn't have done that with a thin skin. He'd have failed at the first hurdle. So he must have developed inches-thick armour plating. He must also have faced rejection many times over.

But perhaps not on a personal level, it occurred to her as she settled back against a pile of pillows and awaited his return. Because who in their right mind would ever voluntarily ditch a gorgeous, successful man like him? If she hadn't had an exceptionally good reason for doing so, she certainly wouldn't have. She'd never met anyone who'd got her quite so well quite so quickly. They might not have talked in much depth during their affair, but the messages they'd sent each other had been frequent—dozens of mini conversations that had kept her going when they'd been apart—and excitement had leapt inside her on receipt of every single one. There'd been no thoughts of throwing in the towel with him.

The three months they'd dated was the longest she'd ever been out with anyone. Who knew what might have happened if they'd met at another time?

No doubt, when it came to relationships, he was used to being the dumper rather than the dumpee, and it was his fragile male ego that had pushed him to jump in before she could say anything. But now she was wondering why he remained single despite having everything going for him. Did he have commitment issues? His father had never featured in his life. He hadn't even known who he was, she'd read. So could that be it? He had no example to follow? It didn't seem the most likely explanation. Her parents' marriage had been deeply dysfunctional—how they managed to produce six children she had no idea—but that didn't stop her from wanting a partner and family of her own.

So maybe he just hadn't met the right woman. In fact, who *would* be the right woman? The dates he'd had in the past, according to photos in the press—and she'd cast only a very casual eye over them—suggested he didn't have a type. Not that she was interested or anything. All she wanted from him was a successful outcome for his project and mind-blowing sex for a week. She didn't have the time or the head space for anything more.

But maybe she ought to investigate a little deeper and push a little harder when she ventured into more personal waters and he inevitably changed the subject. She ought to know more about the man she was going to be sleeping with for the next six nights. She was no longer prepared to let him get away with shutting her down the minute she got too close.

She knew it wouldn't be easy. He was harder to crack than the most sophisticated of safes. But by his own admission he owed her and she would prevail. Somehow, she would lull him into a false sense of security with so much sex it would turn his brain to mush and then—bam!—she'd unlock all his secrets and have him right where she wanted him.

The following morning, citing expediency—easy elevation of her still slightly swollen ankle, a convenient location to indulge the attraction whenever it overtook them—Santi convinced Thalia to work from the bed. She needed no persuasion and twenty-four hours later he'd been proven right on both fronts. The swelling had thankfully subsided and being in close proximity to a bed had indeed been most convenient.

The downside of such a plan, however, was that at some point during one such lust-filled occasion her laptop must have got in the way because when she returned to it half an hour later—still breathless, still dizzy—she found that the operating system had somehow disappeared.

'I'm seriously impressed,' she said, lying back against a pile of pillows and watching as, beside her, a naked-from-the-waist-up Santi applied his programming magic to the device.

'By this? Compared to some of the things I've worked on, this is child's play.'

For a moment, she admired the way his long, tanned fingers flew over the keyboard and thought, with a delicious shiver, of the way they'd skimmed over her. 'What's been the most complicated?'

'The global online payment system was a challenge,' he said as pages of incomprehensible data started flashing up on the black screen. 'It took years to develop. Coding isn't always logic and predictability. One tiny glitch can bring the whole thing crashing down. Luckily we were able to identify the bugs and iron them out before going live but it was extremely stressful for months.'

She knew all about stress. Although he was doing a pretty good job of relieving some of hers, he still clammed up whenever she tried to talk to him about anything in his past. He was monosyllabic on pretty much any topic other than sex and work and it was becoming increasingly frustrating. So much for his wanting to make things up to her. And so much for turning his brain to soup.

Perhaps it would do them good to get away for a bit, she mused while he continued to fiddle with her laptop—out of this room, out of the house and leave all this behind for a while. Perhaps getting out and into nature was the way to find out more about the man she was sleeping with. She hadn't been the only one to let her guard down the afternoon they'd gone whale watching, and she wanted to see more of the country that he clearly loved so much, beyond these four walls and views of the south Atlantic.

'How far away are the Iguazu Falls?' she asked as he hit a button that to her relief turned the screen back to an interface she recognised.

'A couple of hours by plane. Why?'

'I've heard they're spectacular. One of the seven wonders of the natural world, I read.'

'They are.'

'I'd like to see them. Will you take me?'

He slid her a glance, his expression oddly unreadable. 'When?'

'No time like the present.'

'I'm not a tour guide,' he said with a slow shake of his head, 'and you have a sprained ankle.'

That? Pah.

'It's had plenty of rest. It's as good as new.'

'We're here to work.'

'I'll stay an extra day in lieu.'

'No.'

'Please?'

'Borrow my plane and go on your own when we're done.'

What would be the point of that? 'I feel we could do with a break,' she said, more than happy to use his own arguments against him while her laptop's operating system steadily updated. 'We've barely left this room in thirty-six hours. We could do with fresh air and a different view. I went whale watching and survived.'

'That was one afternoon.'

'It's still early. We could be back by this evening. And just think of all that nature you like so much. All that untamed wildness. I imagine there's no place like it on earth.'

'There isn't.'

'When were you last there?'

'Two years ago.' The look he gave her was pointed. 'But if you're about to tell me it's time for a revisit you'll be wasting your breath.'

Desperate times called for desperate measures, and

she had every intention of getting what she wanted, so she fluttered her eyelids and lowered her voice. 'I'll make it worth your while.'

He stilled. A flicker of heat flared in the depths of his eyes and a thrilling little wave of satisfaction rippled through her. 'How?'

She leaned over and whispered in his ear, taking care not to dislodge her laptop, most gratified to hear his breathing shallow and to feel his jaw clench as she explained in great detail exactly how she'd be expressing her appreciation.

'Fine,' he muttered when she'd finished, thrusting the device at her—which now showed the familiar login box, the clever man—and flinging back the sheets. 'Pack a change of clothes and your passport. I'll alert the crew.'

Santi didn't want to analyse how swiftly he'd caved into Thalia's demands—or why. However much she might intimate that he still owed her for what he'd said in Paris, accommodating her wishes wasn't what was required here. But then she'd whispered those sweet nothings into his ear and he'd surrendered in a heartbeat, justifying the move by telling himself that she clearly wasn't going to let it go and he'd run out of excuses anyway.

But there was still the opportunity to snatch victory from the jaws of defeat, he thought darkly as they pulled up at the airport twenty minutes after they'd left the house. He'd made a whole raft of arrangements that meant he could hang out in a nearby hotel and leave her to it for the day. He'd already viewed the falls from a multitude of angles and taken a boat up the river. He could still vividly recall the fascinating hike through the forest and the swim beneath a waterfall that had come at the end of it. He didn't need to do any of that again and she didn't need a chaperone.

What he *did* need was to prevent any further attempts she made at profound conversation by getting her to make good on her promises. So the minute they boarded his plane he took her hand and chivvied her down the aisle to the cabin at the rear.

'Are you planning on calling in my debt now?' she said, a little breathless as he pushed open the door and ushered her in.

'Is that a problem?'

'No. But it's a good thing it's not a zero-sum game.'

He closed the door and flipped the lock. 'Everyone's a winner.'

'I had very distracting thoughts the last time we were in here.'

'Show me.'

Dark eyes gleaming with heat and excitement, Thalia planted one hand on his chest and pushed. He fell back onto the bed and she straddled him, her hands making swift work of his belt and fly. Heart thundering, desire throbbing in every cell of his being, he lifted his hips and she shifted to pull down his trousers and shorts. Then she wrapped her hand around his achingly hard length and dipped her head. He closed his eyes and gave himself up to sensation.

When she took him in her mouth he groaned and shook. Within moments, he was tangling his fingers in her hair, muttering incoherent words in Portuguese even he didn't understand. She upped the pressure and he shuddered, the exquisite tension building, and he was soon so close he could feel the familiar waves of pleasure surging, so close he was losing the ability to think, and so when she stopped, abruptly lifting herself off him and taking her velvety wet warmth with her, he could have wept.

He opened his eyes, prepared to beg if he had to, but a second later she was back, naked from the waist down. She deftly rolled on protection—he gritted his teeth so hard they nearly shattered—and then with his assistance and a thick hoarse moan sank down onto him.

His head spun. His pulse pounded. She leaned forwards, sealing her mouth to his in a crushing kiss, moved—once, twice, a third time—and then she was shaking and juddering and panting so wildly it tipped him over the edge. Gripping her hips, he thrust up hard and exploded, pulsating into her so powerfully and for so long it hollowed him out.

'That was something else,' he said, once he'd caught his breath and his head had stopped spinning.

'I promised you membership of the mile-high club,' she said with a blinding smile that whipped the air from his lungs and made his chest contract. 'And I always keep my promises.'

So did he, he thought as he rolled her onto her back. And buried his face in her neck so he could not get caught up in the wicked merriment dancing in her eyes and lose what was left of his mind. Especially those promises he made to himself.

Rendered dazed and weak-limbed by their antics in the cabin, which had only got wilder with the soaring altitude, Thalia briefly considered it a shame they had to land. But her disappointment vanished the instant they transferred to the helicopter that Santi had arranged to ferry them to their destination. They took off, veered to the right, and almost instantly they were flying over the thick dark green forest of the vast national park, which stretched out to the horizon as far as the eye could see in all directions. In the distance, a cloud of spray rose up over the trees into the azure sky. A sliver of river came into view and grew into a wide murky brown ribbon that cut a winding swathe through the flat landscape.

With every passing moment, the anticipation rushing through her swelled. This approach allowed for a build-up, which was almost unbearable. And then there were the falls, down on her right, at the point where the river curved into the shape of a horseshoe—hundreds of cataracts of varying heights and widths, a roaring, tumbling force of nature, so awe-inspiring and magnificent that she found she was pressing her nose up against the glass, her breath catching in her throat.

'This is the largest waterfall system in the world,' Santi shouted, leaning in close so she could hear him over the whirring of the helicopter's blades, the buffeting wind and the extraordinary thunder of water below. 'It's nearly three kilometres wide. There are two hundred and seventy-five individual falls that drop eighty metres into the river below. Only twenty percent are on this side. The rest are in Argentina. The border runs right through the middle of the Garganta del Diablo.'

'What's that?'

'The Devil's Throat. That one there.'

Leaning around her, he pointed to the largest fall,

down which water crashed powerfully into a creamy white pool. It was almost indistinguishable, thanks to the mist it must have been generating for millions of years.

'Can we get any closer?'

'On foot and by boat you can. See that walkway? It takes you right on top of it.'

'Will we be doing that?'

'If you'd like.'

She flashed him a grin. 'I truly cannot wait.'

The helicopter landed a short time later on the helipad at the Hotel das Cataratas, where they grabbed a quick sandwich and, in response to her stream of questions about the local area, Santi revealed an extensive knowledge of the local flora and fauna.

'Because of the spray, the micro-climate of the rainforest here is subtropical,' he said, resting his elbows on the railing of the terrace beyond which the waterfalls roared and coated them in droplets. 'It's home to all sorts of wildlife.'

'Such as?'

'Tapirs, giant anteaters, howler monkeys, ocelots, caimans. The last time I was here, I spotted a jaguar. That was a moment. If you're lucky you'll see some of them this afternoon. I've ordered a car to take you across the border into Argentina. From there you can cross the walkway above the falls and hike through the forest. There are many trails to choose from. None of them is particularly challenging.'

Thalia stared out at the view, not caring about getting drenched, only thinking she could listen to him for hours. The passion in his voice... The depth of his knowledge… But then his words registered and she turned to him, frowning. 'Are you not coming with me?'

'I wasn't planning on it,' he said with a quick apologetic smile. 'Thanks to you, I have work to do.'

'Oh.' Her shoulders dropped. Her stomach plummeted. That was disappointing. And not because she wouldn't be able to quiz him further and learn more about him. She was enjoying his company. She'd never had it quite like this before, and she wanted more. 'That's a shame. I was looking forward to an insider's guide. Your expertise. What if I get lost? What if I fall in?'

'You won't.'

'It won't be the same without you.'

He studied her for a moment, a faint frown creasing his brow as if he were battling with himself, then he gave a shrug and said, 'I guess work can wait.'

CHAPTER ELEVEN

THALIA COULD NOT have been more delighted that Santi had shelved his plans to accommodate hers. She could easily have gone alone and hired a guide of her own if she'd felt the need, but if she'd had, she'd have missed out on the tales he'd told her of his travels around the country. She wouldn't have learned about the wildlife of the Pantanal, the boat trip he'd once taken down a piranha-infested tributary of the Amazon, or riding a beach buggy among the dunes of the northeast coast, one of the last places left on the planet with hundreds of miles of unobstructed sand.

She would never forget the thrill of standing above the falls, hearing and feeling the powerful rush of cascading water beneath her feet. The sheer jaw-dropping magnificence of the sight had blown her mind and yet she hadn't been able to keep from sliding glances in Santi's direction. She hadn't been able to stop thinking that he was pretty jaw-dropping and magnificent too.

After returning to the riverbank, they trekked along a trail that led deep into the forest. He pointed out an ocelot and she spied an eagle. Being so far off the beaten track, they didn't come across any other visitors. So when they arrived at a set of stairs that descended into a wooded area they didn't think twice about stripping off and diving into the large deep crystal-clear pool into which poured more frothing water.

'I don't think I've ever seen anything so stagger- ingly beautiful,' said Thalia, floating lazily on her back and gazing up at the sky and around her at the forested sides of the pool.

'Neither have I,' muttered Santi as he pulled her squealing with shock and delight into his arms and shut her up with his mouth and his hands, at which point she thought there might be something of her ex- hibitionist mother in her after all.

By the time they returned from the boat trip that had given her another equally exciting experience— although at that point she'd run out of superlatives to describe what she saw and how she felt about it—it was too late to go anywhere else, so he booked them into a suite at the hotel and ordered dinner to be sent up to the room.

'Thank you for today,' she said over coffee, feeling replete, molten-hearted and completely overwhelmed by everything she'd seen and heard. 'It's been amaz- ing. I can't remember the last time anyone other than a paid employee organised anything for me. I've spent a decade devoting my time to helping others. It's been lovely to be on the receiving end of such attention for a change, even if I did coerce you into it.'

'You're welcome.'

'Your knowledge of the area is seriously impressive.'

'As I may have mentioned once or twice, I like na- ture.' He swung his gaze from the view to hers, a smile hovering at his mouth, and she couldn't help swooning a little. 'It's not just that I grew up with very little of it. It's also that while it can be organised, systematic and comprehensive, unlike coding, it's not at all logical.'

'Isn't it?' She had no clue. She was just enjoying the way his mouth moved.

'Logic is a human intellectual construction,' he said as he lifted his coffee cup to his lips. 'Nature is the opposite of that. I find the dichotomy fascinating.'

She found *him* fascinating, she thought dreamily. He was tough and dominant yet could also be caring and thoughtful, even when it went against his better judgement. If she wasn't careful, she could be in danger of becoming smitten all over again. 'Why on earth have you never married?'

It was unfortunate that at that moment he'd taken a mouthful of coffee because it clearly went down the wrong way. He coughed. He spluttered. He put the cup down with a clatter and gave his chest a thump. 'That's a very personal question,' he said a little hoarsely as he dabbed his eyes with a napkin.

It was. No doubt about it. But she'd been pussyfooting around topics that were personal to him for long enough and now she wanted answers. 'You're thirty-four and highly eligible. It's curious.'

'It's also none of your business.'

That was true too, but that didn't mean she had any intention of giving up. 'Have you never met anyone special?'

'We're not discussing this.'

Oh, yes, they were. 'Do you have a problem with commitment?'

A flare of heat flickered in the dark depths of his

eyes, as if he truly believed he could detract her that way. 'Whatever happened to just sex?'

'To echo what you once said, we have to talk about something.'

'No, we don't. If you're finished here we can go back to bed where I'll show you how very much we do not have to talk about anything.'

Thalia ignored the wave of desire that spread through her at that darkly delivered promise, and focused. 'Do you mind not having anyone to share your success with?'

Evidently realising she had no intention of quitting this conversation, Santi gave a deep sigh of what was clearly exasperation and said, 'No.'

'Don't you get lonely?'

'No.'

'Lucky you. I do.'

'Then sort out your issues with your brother.'

Thalia frowned. That wasn't what she'd meant, but she was hardly going to confess to him that the source of her loneliness was a lack of romance caused by her many hangups, so she went with his interpretation. 'It's not that easy.'

'It might be. For all you know he might be finding things as difficult as you are.'

'That's highly doubtful,' she said, trying not to sound morose but failing. 'He has other things to keep him occupied, like a wife, and in six months' time a baby. Zoe's pregnant.'

'Oh? I must send her my congratulations.'

'There'll be even less time for me once he or she arrives.'

'You might find the opposite thing happens and your relationship gets stronger.'

She stared at him, the majestic backdrop of the falls momentarily forgotten, the previous dreaminess history. 'How on earth do you figure that?'

'You'll have to cram more into less time. That would be pretty intense, I imagine.'

'You're mad.'

'I might be right. Have you ever considered that it can't be easy for Zoe either, having to share Atticus with you?'

No, she hadn't, but that wasn't the point. 'What would you know about it?'

'Not a lot, I admit.'

'Well, then.'

'I'm just thinking logically.'

Thalia bristled. 'Are you implying that I'm not?'

'You could be being blinded by emotion.'

'Blinded by emotion?' she echoed in indignation.

'I get that the apple cart's been upset,' he said while she wondered if he was even aware of the dangerous path he was treading. 'But you have had months to deal with it.'

The *apple cart*? It was an entire bloody orchard that had been uprooted. 'I'm aware of that.'

'Has it occurred to you that you might be squandering a perfectly good sibling out of obstinacy?'

What? For a moment, she had no words. Did he think she wanted to be this conflicted? That she didn't want to find a way through the mess she'd been in for close to two years? 'That is *not* what I'm doing.'

'Then why don't you just talk to him?'

He had no idea. It wasn't that simple. How could she explain to Atticus how she felt? What would she say? Would he even listen? And what if she somehow ended up losing him for good? After all, he did have someone else to share his life with now. Soon he'd have two someone-elses, and probably more in the future. He didn't need her. He might never have needed her. It was all just so hard, like stumbling around on uncharted territory at night without a torch or a compass, and by suggesting it was her fault she was in this mess Santi wasn't helping. 'You don't have siblings so I don't expect you to understand.'

He tensed. Frowned as if lost in thought for a moment. Then gave a shrug. 'My mistake.'

Much later, while Thalia slumbered beside him in the moonlight, Santi stared up at the ceiling of the hotel room, his head pounding, his stomach roiling, and thought that that was just one of many mistakes he'd made today.

The first was agreeing to bring her here when there'd been absolutely no reason to. The second was throwing aside his plans to leave her to explore the waterfalls on her own and accompanying her around the site instead. The latest was bringing the topic of her brother up over coffee in the first place.

He should never have done that. He should never have allowed the simmering envy and resentment he'd suddenly felt to get the better of him. He'd been so close to confessing that she was wrong and he *did* have a sibling that he could scarcely believe it.

Why on earth would he want to *do* that? It made no

sense at all. If he hadn't stopped himself at the last minute, biting back the words piling up in his head, he'd have had to admit that he'd never met his half-sister, despite knowing perfectly well who she was. At which point Thalia would have probably—and rightly—called him a hypocrite and accused him of very much not practising what he preached. Following that, no doubt, she'd have continued to prod around his psyche until she'd uncovered all his secrets, all his complexes, and he could never allow that.

He'd been unsettled by the day, that was the trouble. He'd assumed that he'd have everything under control, but once again he could not have been more wrong. The minute he'd glimpsed Thalia's disappointment when he'd told her to go it alone, the promise he'd made to himself to keep emotion out of what they were doing vaporised. He hadn't liked the disappearance of her smile or the dimming of her enthusiasm. He'd liked even less knowing that he was the one who'd crushed both. He'd compensated by deciding to show her everything and then oversharing his fascination with nature, so captivated by her engagement with what he was saying he'd overshared some more.

And then, as if that hadn't been worrying enough, she'd started firing questions at him over coffee about marriage and commitment and loneliness. He didn't generally dwell much on such things. He was fine with his life as it was. He never analysed the decisions he made when it came to relationships, until he'd had one with her, which had ended, at which point he'd then seemed to do nothing but. Why was she even interested in such things? She'd better not have changed her mind about the purely carnal nature of what they were doing.

Whatever had been behind that conversation, she had the potential to be as dangerous as he'd feared. She battered his defences and threatened his inhibitions and had him abandoning the promises he'd made to himself left right and centre. He enjoyed spending time with her way too much, and if he wasn't extremely careful he might well find himself spilling his guts to her and questioning every value he lived by, and that simply could not happen. He would not give her that power. He would never be in her thrall again.

He didn't want to contemplate what might have happened if they hadn't split up last August. Or how long it had taken him to get over her. And he definitely didn't want to think about why he'd really lashed out in Paris, which he suspected deep down had had nothing to do with hurt pride and a dent in his track record and everything to do with his bone-deep fear of rejection. All that was going on here was work and sex for another four days—back at the house to which they'd be heading first thing in the morning and from which they would not move again—and that was the way it would stay.

CHAPTER TWELVE

WHEN THALIA'S FRIEND in Rio messaged her at ten on Sunday morning to invite her to lunch later that day, she had no hesitation in saying yes. Her irritation with Santi for providing an unsolicited, uninformed opinion on her relationship with her brother hadn't dampened her desire for him one iota—if anything, tinged with a certain edginess, the sex had been even hotter—but instead of lessening since they'd returned from Iguazu at the crack of dawn yesterday, her frustration had intensified.

She did not appreciate the implication that she was being immature and petulant. Alone in the world for the last fifteen years, he knew absolutely nothing about anything when it came to family. Or her. If he did, he'd know that obstinacy was not behind her reluctance to speak to her brother. Fear was. She feared rejection, she'd forced herself to acknowledge, because—annoyingly—she had found herself mulling over his observation and wondering if it had some merit. She feared discovering that everything she'd believed to be true about their relationship was a lie and that her entire life was built on sand. That was why she hadn't called him in months and kept the conversations short when he rang her. Ignorance and denial were way more appealing than the truth and potential devastation.

Nevertheless, part of her wished she hadn't pushed the conversation into such sensitive territory the night before last. She hadn't learned anything new about Santi and the lovely day they'd spent together was now stained with sourness. Breakfast on the hotel terrace had been an exercise in excruciating politeness, the tension as thick and cold as the tropical fruit smoothies they'd been served, and the atmosphere since then had only become more strained.

She didn't know how to fix it. Or quite what there was to fix. All she did know was that she could do with some time and space away from him to regain perspective and regroup. The last week had been a huge upheaval and insanely intense, and lately the pressure had been compounded by a severe lack of sleep.

So, with the details of lunch arranged, she made a call to her family's personal private office in Athens and then abruptly closed her laptop.

'I'm going to the city,' she announced, gathering up her things up from the table and getting to her feet.

Santi whipped his head round, his dark simmering gaze colliding with hers, and she had to steel herself not to respond to the inevitable wave of heat that swept through her. 'I'm sorry?'

'I'm meeting that friend of mine in Rio for lunch. She lives in Ipanema. I haven't seen her for years. It'll be good to catch up. And don't worry, I'm not playing hooky. She's on the board of a number of South America based charities. She'd be an excellent addition to yours. I can't imagine she'll take much persuading. She's like me—has had a lot, keen to pay it back.'

He sat back, all broad strong shoulders and loose powerful limbs, and frowned. 'Ipanema is a three-hour drive.'

'Which is why I've ordered a helicopter. I noticed the day I arrived here that you had a helipad,' she said in response to the sharp raise of his eyebrows, 'and as you once pointed out I have resources. It'll be here in half an hour.'

'That's quick.'

'My family are very good customers.'

'When will you be back?'

'I'm not sure. I may stay overnight. Don't wait up.'

Santi was now beginning to look at her as though she'd slapped him round the face with a wet fish, but he'd get over it. He might even find the time apart useful. Perhaps he could sort out whatever was on his mind that had him scowling about the place. She understood that she'd fired some uncomfortable questions at him in Iguazu but they hadn't been that bad. It wasn't as if she'd asked him for commitment or anything. She'd merely been curious. So if that *was* why he was being all chilly and aloof—rather an overreaction, she felt— then no doubt he'd welcome some space as much as she did.

But in all honesty, she didn't much care what he was thinking right now. She just wanted to escape, catch up with her friend and stop feeling so conflicted about everything for a while.

'Have a great day,' she said, and, with the tight flash of a smile, left.

* * *

The trip to Rio turned out to be exactly what Thalia needed, although far more surprising than she could ever have anticipated.

The minute the helicopter rose into the air the weight lifted from her chest and she felt as though she could breathe for the first time in days. The tension gripping her muscles melted clean away. The bubbling desire and sensory overload that were ever present when she was in Santi's vicinity vanished. She hadn't realised she'd been in such danger of once again becoming wholly encompassed by him. What they were doing would come to an end on Wednesday, and the opportunity to reset could not have come at a better time.

The route east took her over the sparkling sea of the south Atlantic. Below, on her left, tree-covered hills became villages that grew into suburbs that turned into the sprawl of city itself, built around the beautiful Guanabara Bay and overlooked by the iconic statue of Cristo Redentor.

On landing, she took a taxi from the heliport through the streets of the city to the beach bar in Ipanema. She found her friend sitting at a table on the sand with a pair of caipirinhas in front of her and Sugarloaf Mountain behind.

She'd met Gaby, an internationally renowned supermodel from Copacabana, five years ago at a fundraiser in Marrakech, which she'd organised in aid of cancer research. They'd been introduced, had immediately hit it off and had stayed in touch. She hadn't seen her for a couple of years now, but as Thalia embraced her friend and sat down, somehow it felt like yesterday.

'I can't believe you're working and staying with Santiago Ferreira,' said Gaby, still clearly gobsmacked by the revelation one hour, a lot of conversation and a large platter of seafood later.

Thalia broke off a chunk of soft cheese bread and dipped it into a bowl of fragrant aioli. 'I can't quite believe it myself.'

'What's he like?'

Ruthless, aggravating, sexy as hell. 'Impressive,' she said, knowing Gaby well but not quite well enough to go into explicit detail. 'Very good at getting what he wants and beyond handsome in an untamed kind of a way.'

'Nice?'

Nice was far too anodyne a word for a man like him, but he'd fed her well, shown her some incredible sites and taken good care of her ankle, so when he wasn't being domineering or moody or challenging or single-mindedly giving her more pleasure than she thought she could bear, she supposed he was rather nice. 'I take it you haven't met him.'

'I haven't, but I very much want to.'

'Oh?' Thalia glanced over at her lovely, stunning friend with her short white-blonde hair, her willowy height and perfect figure. The shaft of jealousy that whipped the air from her lungs caught her by surprise. 'Why?'

'Because he looks exactly like my father.'

The jealousy evaporated. Her eyebrows shot up. She nearly choked on the piece of bread she'd just put into her mouth. 'Seriously?'

'The resemblance is uncanny,' said Gaby, taking a

sip of her soda water. 'They share the same features. Eyes, nose, mouth. Even the cowlick. When he hit the news with that deal it was such a fascinating rag to riches tale that the press couldn't get enough of him. His photo started popping up everywhere.'

'I know.' She'd been doing a pretty good job of forgetting all about him until then.

'I was on a lilo the first time I saw one. It was such a shock I nearly fell into the pool.'

'He can have that effect on people,' said Thalia, thinking with a shiver of her own unplanned midnight dip the other night. 'So what are you saying? Do you think your father could also be his?'

'It's possible,' said Gaby with a faint shrug. 'I read that he didn't know who his was and mine wasn't the nicest of men. He had multiple affairs. That was why my mother eventually divorced him. I do hope he is. Or if not a half-brother, a cousin or something. I'm disappointingly devoid of relatives.'

'What does your mother say about it?'

'She's as in the dark as I am, but she did remark that nothing would surprise her when it comes to my father.'

Well. This was an intriguing turn of events. If by some chance, Gaby's father was also Santi's—and now she was looking, she could see that her friend and Santi shared a jawline, which was quite possibly why she'd felt as though she'd last seen Gaby way more recently than two years ago—then it meant that he wasn't all alone on this planet, after all. And that was such a relief because no one should be, in her opinion. Her family regularly bewildered, confused and distressed her in different ways—especially over the last year or so—

but she couldn't imagine life without them. Deep down, she could now admit, it had been bothering her that Santi had no one.

'What are your plans for the rest of the day?' she said, the seed of a plan taking root in her head even while the excitement drumming through her drowned out the voice of her conscience that warned her not to interfere—that it wasn't her place to manage any-thing, especially a potential bombshell like this, that this wasn't the way to fix the simmering awkwardness, and, above all, she could not make up for the strained relations between her and her brother by fixing those between Gaby and hers.

'Not a lot. I'm between jobs. Why?'

'Why don't you come back with me this evening and meet him?'

'Are you sure that would be wise?'

'Of course,' she said, so determined to make it hap-pen that nothing else mattered. 'Not only has he ac-quired an experienced and enthusiastic trustee, but he might also have gained a sister. A great one. Who wouldn't be thrilled by that?'

'Maybe we should call ahead first.'

'And spoil the surprise?'

'All right,' said Gaby with a flash of the megawatt grin that had made her famous. 'Let's do it.'

Once he'd got over his shock at Thalia's abrupt de-parture, Santi had initially been delighted at the pros-pect of her lunch in the city. Her off his property and out of his hair was exactly what he'd been after before she'd tripped and sprained her ankle and scuppered the idea of either putting her on his plane or getting on it himself.

Things between them had been frosty since they'd returned from Iguazu. He hadn't been able to shake the feeling that he was hurtling along a perilous road that he couldn't get off, and worse, possibly didn't even *want* to get off.

He told himself that without her distracting presence he could work on obliterating the thoughts of his father and half-sister, which kept bothering him with irritating persistence. He could knuckle down to completing the tasks she'd set him, with which he hadn't yet got very far. He could catch up on some much-needed sleep.

But to his immense frustration, none of that happened. Disappointingly, once again, out of sight was not out of mind, and his concentration remained shot. The scent of her lingered in his bed, rendering sleep impossible. He prowled round the house, trying and failing to find something to take his mind off the fact that she wasn't there, and achieving nothing.

He kept wondering where she was, what she was doing and whether she was all right. Rio could be dangerous for the uninitiated. Regardless of the tense state of affairs, he should have insisted on going with her, even though the city held few good memories and he avoided it where possible. He lost count of the number of times he grabbed his phone to call her before tossing it away in disgust.

When she walked through the door, just after six, the relief that spun through him nearly took out his knees. She'd obviously decided against staying overnight. Because she couldn't wait to get back to him? He could not afford to let his thoughts head in that direction. So instead, with effort, he contemplated the bemusing absence of whirring helicopter blades sounds—she must have driven back—and strode into the hall to greet her.

The plan was to apologise profusely for his recent moodiness—it wasn't her fault his past was trying to muscle in on his present—and then throw her over his shoulder and cart her off to bed. But she wasn't alone, and when he saw who she was with he slammed to a sudden halt, the breath whipping from his lungs, the floor tilting violently beneath his feet, his head draining of every thought he'd ever had.

'Santi,' Thalia said with a breezy smile, as if she wasn't blasting apart his carefully constructed lie of thirty-four years and shattering his entire existence by bringing this woman here. 'This is my friend, Gabriela Cardoso.'

A cold sweat broke out all over his skin. His stomach churned. He knew who she was. He'd seen her face staring out of countless billboards, magazines, newspapers. It had haunted his dreams more often than he liked to admit. He'd never expected to see it right in front of him. Could he even begin to hope that her being here, with Thalia, in his house, was nothing more than some kind of horrific coincidence?

'Prazer em te conocer,' he said thickly as he held out his hand for Gabriela to shake, even though he wasn't pleased to meet her at all. He was, in fact, shocked and petrified—as he'd always been. Because what if the truth came out about their shared parentage and she too slammed a metaphorical door in his face?

His pulse hammering, his head pounding, he

wrenched his gaze from his half-sister and turned it on Thalia. 'What's this all about?'

'Firstly, she's agreed to be on the board of your charity and, secondly, she suspects you might be related. Isn't that great?'

Thalia was beaming, as if delighted with her cleverness in bringing this about, but there was no 'might' and nothing 'great' about any of it. He was burning up. He felt light-headed. He was going to vomit. Pass out. Quite possibly both.

'You had no right.'

Her smile vanished and she frowned. 'What?'

He couldn't handle this. He was totally unprepared. Emotion was surging through him in great rolling waves and his control was unravelling so fast that it was going to be history within seconds.

'Excuse me,' he said, backing away as if both women were brandishing weapons at him, which, in a way, they were. 'I have some calls to make.'

Well, that was not the reaction she'd been expecting, thought Thalia, eyes wide, jaw on the floor as Santi spun on his heel and stalked off as if being chased by a prowl of hungry jaguars.

If she'd allowed herself to give it much thought, which stupidly—she now realised—she hadn't, she'd would have said she'd anticipated surprise, yes, but also joy, a tear and a hug or two, and perhaps even a little gratitude. She would never have expected thunderclouds and retreat, even though things between them lately had been fraught. So what on earth was going on?

'I think we can safely say he's not overjoyed to meet

me,' came the dry observation from her right. 'I told you we should have called.'

She turned to Gaby, swallowing hard. 'I'm so sorry,' she said, mortified and appalled in equal measure. 'I had no idea he was going to do that. He must have gone into shock.'

'I suspect it's more than that,' said her friend, her expression thoughtful, though she had paled a little. 'Did you see the look on his face when he first laid eyes on me? It was as if he'd seen a ghost. He knew who I was before you suggested it.'

Thalia frowned. Santi had never known who his father was, so how could he know about Gaby? It didn't make sense. 'That's impossible.'

'It's unlikely, I admit, but it's not impossible.'

'But that would mean he's been lying to the world. And why would he deny knowing you?'

'You'd have to ask him.'

'I don't think I dare,' she said with a wince. 'I don't think I've ever seen anyone quite so angry.'

'Look, I'm going to head off,' said Gaby, hitching her bag higher on her shoulder and turning to walk out the way she'd just come in. 'It's a long drive back to the city.'

Thalia followed her out to her car, every step she took as heavy as a lead weight. 'I'm really sorry,' she said, her voice tight and small. 'This is all my doing. I feel terrible.'

'Don't worry about. Really. I'm glad to have met him, even if it was for a nanosecond. It's a start. I hope. Give him my number and tell him he can call me any time if he wants to. Let me know about the trusteeship. I'd be really interested in it but not if it's going to be difficult. Good luck.'

Thalia waved her friend off, her head spinning, her entire body trembling. Somehow, without intending to, she'd messed up badly. She'd presumed. She'd overstepped. She'd been arrogant and unthinking and not just with regards to Santi. Despite Gaby's reassurances, her friend *wasn't* all right with what had happened. She'd caught the searing disappointment that had flashed across her face, and it piled guilt onto the remorse. She did not deserve to be let off as lightly as she had been. She'd call her tomorrow to check she'd got home safely and find out how she genuinely was about this. But in the meantime, she had to track Santi down. She owed him an apology too.

She found him sitting on the terrace necking a bottle of rum and she paused for a second, her heart hammering and her breath short. She felt a bit sick, thanks to the regret knotting her stomach, but she could not run off to the hotel that was currently closed for business and she could not leave things this way. She stepped forward and cleared her throat, preparing to apologise, grovel if she had to, but he got in first.

'How dare you ambush me like that in my own home?'

She flinched at the quiet cold fury she could hear in his voice and swallowed down the hot lump in her throat. 'I'm so sorry,' she said, rubbing her hands down her trousers as she came to a stop in front of him. 'It was never my intention to cause you distress. I thought you'd be pleased.'

His expression was darker and harder than she'd ever

seen it and her chest tightened. 'Whatever gave you that idea?'

'I don't know.' She shook her head, unable to work out quite what she'd been thinking at the time. 'When Gaby told me that she suspected her father could be yours, I just got overexcited by the thought of you finding out you had a long-lost half-sister. I might have been projecting my issues with my brother onto you and her. But I was way out of line. It's none of my business.'

'Precisely.'

'I should never have interfered.'

'No. You shouldn't.'

'I should have given you her number and let you deal with it in your own way.'

'You should.'

She bit her lip, desperate to make up for her mistakes. 'But if there was anything you wanted to talk about, I'm very good at listening.'

The silence that fell then was deafening. He appeared to be utterly speechless. He just glared at her, incredulity written all over his darkly handsome face, before he eventually snapped, 'Are you joking?'

'You might find sharing whatever it is you're thinking cathartic.'

'You have no idea what you've done.'

Her cheeks burned. Her eyes stung. 'Tell me so I can fix it.'

'Leave me alone.'

CHAPTER THIRTEEN

AT THE BOTTOM of the bottle, Santi had to admit defeat. He had hoped that copious quantities of rum would obliterate the emotions that had broken free of their bonds and were now rampaging through him, but they hadn't. He was stone-cold sober, still in turmoil, still unable to get a grip on anything. The past and the present had collided, the resulting compound had imploded, and all the old feelings he thought he'd successfully buried—the rejection, the bewilderment, the anger and resentment—were thundering through him like a tornado.

And all because Thalia had gone for lunch.

His head was pounding. His pulse was racing and the air pressure seemed to have dropped. He was finding it hard to breathe. How was he to find peace? That was the question ricocheting around his brain as he rubbed his chest and forced some warm evening air into his lungs before he passed out. Shoving everything back in the box from which it had escaped felt like a Sisyphean task. Rum clearly wasn't the answer. Nor was gazing up and out into the dark starry sky, which had always filled him with a sense of serenity, but tonight was having no effect on him at all.

Perhaps the solution, then, was escape. There was

nothing keeping him here. Thalia's ankle was fine. He could leave right this minute, put as much distance between himself and the two women who were causing him the kind of torment he hadn't been subjected to for years. Then he could throw himself into mentoring budding entrepreneurs in a place far, far away.

But would that actually solve anything?

Wouldn't the maelstrom follow him wherever he went?

Contrary to what he'd always assumed, he evidently hadn't dealt with the past. He hadn't buried anything. It had all just lurked in the recesses of his mind until Thalia had blithely come along and shone a spotlight on it, turning his entire world to chaos.

Maybe he should seek professional help instead. He'd never really considered it before, but that was how other people seemed to vanquish their demons. The thought of discussing his with Thalia, as she'd suggested, made him want to throw up. The exposure... The vulnerability... The surrender of power... Just imagining it raised the hairs at the back of his neck and covered his skin in goosebumps. And how could she help anyway? Just because she'd spent months of working through her own issues with family didn't mean she'd be any good at unravelling his. Their situations were entirely different.

Although, were they?

Both stemmed from the sort of dysfunction that should have led to state involvement but, for very different reasons, hadn't. Both aroused emotions of the negative kind—jealousy and resentment in her, anger and bitterness in him. Both had lain dormant until an external force had made them erupt.

So might she understand the feelings he was experiencing and the causes of them? Might she have some insight into how to handle them? He certainly wasn't making much progress on his own, and it was her fault he was in this mess. She'd stirred the hornet's nest, so maybe he *should* task her with fixing it. Quite frankly, however tough it might be to open up to her, things couldn't get much worse.

Before he could think better of it, Santi slammed the bottle down and surged to his feet. He strode to her room, knocked once on the door, and then, without waiting for an answer, barged in.

'What are you doing?' he said, coming to an abrupt halt, his brows snapping together in a deep frown at the sight of her clothes strewn all over the bed.

'Packing. I'll go in the morning.'

Well, *that* wasn't happening. Not now he'd decided to seek her advice. Not at all, in fact. 'No. Stop. I want to talk to you. About Gabriela.'

She stilled. Her gaze flew to his. 'Oh. No. Really. You don't have to do that.'

'You were the one who suggested it,' he said, stalking to the chair in the corner and throwing himself into it. 'You said you could fix this and you owe me.'

Looking pale and contrite, Thalia swallowed hard and gave a nod. 'All right,' she said, putting down the pair of trousers she'd been folding and sinking down onto the edge of the bed. 'I'll do my best.'

With a shove of his hands through his hair and a clench of his jaw, Santi braced himself and ground out, 'Her father *is* my father and she *is* my half-sister.'

'How long have you known?'

'About him, ever since I can remember,' he said, fighting to keep his heartrate down and his breathing even. 'He met my mother in the bar where she used to sing in the evenings. They had an affair that resulted in me. He wanted her to terminate the pregnancy. She didn't.'

Eyes widening, Thalia emitted a tiny gasp. 'That's awful.'

Yes, well, it didn't stop there. 'He was an extremely successful businessman,' he went on gruffly. 'She tried to get financial support out of him but he maintained that it was her choice to have me and refused. He strung her along for another decade before discarding her. He'd married a debutante. My mother was nothing more than his bit of rough.'

Thalia winced and he wished he could have put it a different way, but the truth could be ugly. 'And he never met you?'

'Not once.'

Her expression hardened, as if she was outraged on his behalf, which he found oddly comforting. 'What a bastard. I'm not surprised you've always claimed not to know anything about him.'

'It was just easier to pretend he never existed.'

'I completely get that. The situation sounds beyond painful. You must have been so angry and hurt.'

'I was,' he agreed, marvelling at her ability to get straight to the heart of it. 'Living where I did didn't help. There were many outlets for that anger, none of them good. When I was fourteen, one of my friends was killed in fight over gang territory. I wanted vengeance so badly it burned me up inside and it would have been very easy to get it. But in the nick of time I was scooped up by a charity who worked in the neighbourhood. They gave me a mentor who showed me another way out.'

She tilted her head. 'Coding?'

'Right,' he confirmed with a nod. 'Aside from challenging my brain, it calmed me down and gave me the space and peace to think. I realised that getting a grip on the anger and all the other emotions I was struggling to deal with was simply a question of control. There was so much I couldn't do anything about. My response to it all, I could. It became a way of life.' Until he'd met her, at which point that life had gone to hell in a handcart.

'That makes sense. So when did you find out about Gaby?'

'I was twenty when I set up my software business,' he said. 'Twenty-two when I sold my first licence. I found out where my father lived and went to his house. I figured he'd be proud.' He sighed and rubbed his hands over his face. 'God only knows why. I didn't get beyond the front gate. But I did see a girl swinging in a hammock beneath a tree in the garden.'

Her gaze softened. 'That must have been a shock.'

Shock was an understatement. He'd felt as if a neutron bomb had gone off inside him. 'I'll never forget it,' he said, recalling the power of his reaction as if it were yesterday. 'The sun was shining down on her like she was the chosen one. It was as if she'd been gilded. I couldn't stop staring. Initially in awe and then in growing resentment. It was impossible not to feel envy and rage at the injustice.'

'I'm not sure that anything in that house was gilded.'

'What do you mean?' he asked with a frown.

'You'd have to talk to her.'

His pulse skipped a beat and then began to race. 'I don't think I can.'

'Why not?'

'As I told you before, I don't like rejection.'

'Which is understandable. But Gaby came here to meet you,' Thalia pointed out. 'That's acceptance, not rejection.'

'What if I don't live up to her expectations?' he muttered with an inward wince.

'I'm not sure she has any, but I have her number if you want it.'

He sighed and shifted in the chair, but it did nothing to ease his discomfort. 'I don't know what I want. I don't know how to handle any of this. I was hoping you'd tell me. You're an expert in family dysfunction.'

'Unfortunately, I have no advice,' she said, shaking her head ruefully. 'I've been trying to find a way through my issues for months and have got nowhere, mainly, I suspect, because I'm terrified of discovering that my relationship with my brother has been a lie all these years. I don't think I could bear it if it was. But I know that the situation can't continue. You were wrong about me putting it off because of stubbornness, but you were right about how long it's been dragging on. It probably isn't a very healthy state of affairs, and I guess it is just about possible that Atticus is as unhappy as I am with the way things are. I've yet to find the courage to find out.'

'You and me both.'

'You have a far greater excuse than I do,' she said. 'What you went through must have been deeply traumatic. I'm just a poor little rich girl. There's no need to feel sorry for me. But it's no wonder you have such a problem with privilege. Your father abused it in the worst possible way.'

'My mother made it worse.'

'How?'

'She somehow drilled it into me that we were inadequate,' he said, recalling the many times she'd been let down and poured out her despair and unhappiness to him. 'For years I believed it was my fault that we were where we were. I swore to do better, and I have, materially, but sometimes, deep down, I'm still that angry kid who doesn't feel good enough.'

'None of it was your fault and you're more than good enough.'

Was he? For her? Why was he even thinking about that when on Wednesday she'd be gone? 'She's also the reason I'm still single,' he said, not wanting to think about Thursday and beyond. 'She never got over my father. She died of a broken heart when I was nineteen, which I just couldn't understand when he'd been so cruel. You were right to question my ability to commit. From her, I learned that love is toxic, for the weak, and that with relationships come an imbalance of power.'

'Not always,' she said after a moment's consideration. 'Great examples of love abound. Spend some time with Atticus and Zoe if you need proof. And there wasn't an imbalance of power between us.'

Wasn't there? 'You walked away.'

'Not because I wanted to,' she said. 'Because I had to. For weeks afterwards I felt bereft. I'd thought the world of you. I couldn't eat. I couldn't sleep. Breaking up with you affected me more than I ever thought it would.'

For a second, he could barely breathe. His heart felt too big for his chest. 'Me too,' he confessed gruffly. 'You once claimed I didn't lose my head when we were together, but I did. I thought of you constantly. Whenever we arranged to meet, I used to count down the hours. I saved all the messages you sent and the voice-mails you left and still have them. Afterwards, I wanted to call you. I wanted you to call me.'

'What do you think would have happened if we hadn't split up?'

'I don't know.'

But he knew what he'd dreamed of, he knew what deep down he'd craved but hadn't thought he deserved, and it was too much. Too overwhelming and terrifying. He didn't want to talk any more. Or think. Or remember. He was wrung out. All he wanted right now was to lose himself in her until everything swirling around inside him settled.

'I don't want you to go,' he said, giving free rein to the desire that was beginning to sweep through his body, erasing the memories and the emotions as it did so.

Her gaze darkened and her breath caught. 'All right, I won't.'

'But I don't want to talk any more either.'

'Then what do you want?'

'You.'

It was late when Thalia woke to a disappointingly empty bed, but that was no surprise. She and Santi had talked long into the night. About his life in the Rio favela and hers in the Athens mansion, the differences and the similarities of their upbringings, and about family. When she thought about how hard life had been for him her heart ached. He'd overcome virtually all the odds there were to make a success of himself. With the lawlessness and the violence of his youth, so many where he came from never got that chance.

He was complex, astounding and endlessly compelling. She understood him and his need for control so much better now. She felt closer to him than she ever had before, and while that would have alarmed her greatly a week ago, now she was wondering whether it might not be worth pursuing.

According to his revised schedule, she had only another three days here, but she felt it only fair that she offered to extend her stay. She disagreed that they take the day they'd flown out as day one because no work had been done and they'd had quite a few breaks since then. When the one hundred hours were up—and in all honesty she'd rather lost count—maybe they could continue to date. They lived on different continents, and had different demands on their time, but they'd made it work before.

His charity project had a long way to go yet, and she could still self-improve while exploring a new and exciting relationship with a man she was falling hard and fast for. She didn't know why she'd ever believed that those two things were mutually exclusive. She'd made excellent progress in so many areas—Atticus-related issues notwithstanding, although thanks to Santi's support she was going to take the bull by the horns and call him in the next day or two—and she was in a much better place now than she had been thirteen months ago. She was beginning to figure out who she was. Her confidence was returning. She was ready for a proper relationship, with him. The only question was, was he ready for one with her?

Last night's conversations were certainly encouraging. He'd opened up to her in a way that she'd lost all hope of ever experiencing. He'd sought her advice. He'd told her things he admitted he'd never shared with another living soul. They'd connected on a level that went far deeper than anything they'd shared to date.

It thrilled her to know that he'd once been as equally into her as she'd been into him. Could she begin to hope that was the case now? She was head over heels in love with him, but how did he feel? Last night she'd asked him what he wanted and he'd told her he wanted her. But *how* did he want her? Just physically, or for more?

She would have to tread carefully. The last twenty-four hours had to have been incredibly draining for him and she didn't want to subject him to any more emotional stress. So she would start by drumming up some of that courage she'd mentioned and ask him what he thought of continuing their fling. After all, nothing ventured, nothing gained, and she was ninety-nine percent sure he'd agree. Why wouldn't he? The sex was out of this world. She would keep things light. She would subtly show him he was definitely good enough for her, and try to be good enough for him, and see how things went from there. He'd soon discover that a relationship was nothing to fear. He might even come to learn that love didn't need to be toxic, and when that happened—

well, her heart was practically bursting out of her chest just at the thought of it.

But first she had to call Gaby and apologise for last night. She couldn't possibly indulge in giddy dreams about the future when fully deserved guilt was still stabbing at her conscience. So she rolled over, picked up her phone from the bedside table and brought up the number.

'Hi,' she said when her friend answered. 'How are you?'

'Couldn't be better,' said Gaby, who, it sounded, was in a café somewhere. 'How are you?'

Thalia was on cloud nine. She was in love and brimming with excitement about where her relationship with Santi might be heading. But that probably wasn't what Gaby wanted to hear. 'I'm fine,' she said, forcing herself to calm down and focus. 'I just wanted to say again how sorry I am about yesterday evening. I should have listened to you. I made a lot of presumptions that were wholly unfounded. I can't think what came over me.'

'Truly, don't worry about it,' said her very generous-hearted friend. 'How's Santi?'

'OK, I think.'

'What happened after I left?'

'I apologised and we talked. You were right about your father being his.'

There was a brief pause, and then Gaby said wonderingly, 'So he *is* my brother.'

'He is.'

'Will he call me?'

'I think so,' said Thalia, mentally crossing her fingers. 'But maybe not just yet.'

'I can wait. Whenever he's ready. I'm not going anywhere.'

Talking of which… 'Did you get home OK?'

'Not exactly.'

Oh? 'What happened?'

'Nothing,' said Gaby. 'It was just getting late so I decided to spend the night at the hotel.'

Thalia frowned. 'Which hotel?'

'The only one in the area. The Bellavista. I got the last free room.'

What? Her frown deepened. 'That's odd.'

'Why?'

'It's meant to be closed.'

'What for?'

'The fire that happened last weekend,' she said, a strange chill rippling through her. 'I was told it would be shut for a fortnight.'

'It's very much not shut. It doesn't feel as though it ever was. Hang on a moment.' There followed a muffled conversation in Portuguese and then Gaby was back. 'There was no fire,' she said.

'Are you sure?'

'Definitely. Could you have misunderstood?'

It was possible. It wouldn't be the first time. 'Maybe.'

'I'd better get back to breakfast, which, by the way, is excellent.'

'Let's not leave it so long next time. Have a safe trip home.'

'*Adeus.*'

The call ended and Thalia sat up, deeply confused. What was going on? Could Gaby be right? Had she misunderstood the situation at the hotel? She thought back to last Sunday afternoon, following the satnav from the airport, arriving, trying to check in and then being taken into the office where the situation was explained, and... No, she hadn't. She'd been tired and overwrought, and she didn't speak Portuguese, but she'd managed pretty well with a combination of Italian, Spanish and English, and the conversation she'd had with the receptionist had definitely been about a fire in the restaurant.

But why would she have been told there was one when there wasn't? It didn't make sense, although it did explain why she'd felt something was amiss at the time. The cars in the driveway. The absence of any smoke-related evidence. And then, having had no choice but to drive here, pulling up to find Santi already standing in the doorway, as if he and his fully made-up guest suite had been expecting her.

Surely he couldn't have been behind this mysterious fire? she thought, more bewildered than ever. He'd thwarted her every attempt to control the situation she'd found herself in, but to manipulate her like that seemed extreme. Why would he do something of that nature anyway? And what would it mean if, for some unfathomable reason, he *had* been pulling her strings?

There was only one way to find out.

CHAPTER FOURTEEN

DECIDING TO TALK to Thalia had been the best decision he'd ever made, Santi reflected as he pressed some coffee grounds into the filter of a stove-top coffee maker and screwed on the top.

Once he'd started he hadn't been able to stop, and he'd held very little back of the darkness and torment that had consumed him as a teenager.

But she hadn't been put off. She'd been encouraging and sympathetic. She hadn't judged him at any point, even when he told her about the dangerous ways in which he'd channelled his anger—the fights he'd started, the odd jobs he'd done that had taken him onto the wrong side of the law—before finding tranquillity in the soothing logic of coding and problem solving.

Her understanding had loosened the knot of anguish he'd carried with him for so long, and the crushing pressure he'd felt recently was easing. The exposure, the vulnerability and the surrender of power that he'd dreaded had not materialised. On the contrary he felt stronger and more invincible than he ever had before.

She was good for him. In fact, they were good for each other, and he could no longer remember quite why they'd limited what they were doing to Wednesday. He saw no reason why they shouldn't carry on. He wasn't as hopeless at giving emotional support as he'd always thought. He wanted her more than just physically. He wanted everything she was, for ever. He was head over heels in love with her and it didn't feel toxic at all. It felt thrilling and wonderful. The future—if he could persuade her to be in it—didn't seem nearly as bleak as it once had. Instead, it was full of possibility and hope.

'Good morning,' he said, his heart turning over when she wandered into the kitchen looking both ravished and ravishing, with dishevelled hair, skin that bore the marks of his stubble and the shorts and camisole that made him think of the warm silky softness that he couldn't get enough of.

'It was when I woke up.'

Her tone was unexpectedly cool, and in response to it a sharp flare of alarm leapt in his chest. 'What's happened since then?'

Could she have reflected on everything he'd told her and now be horrified at how screwed up he was? Was she about to tell him she didn't want to have anything more to do with him? The thought of it chilled his blood and drained the strength from his limbs.

'I just spoke to Gaby.'

His vision cleared. The world righted. That was a relief. But why would that turn Thalia's morning from good to bad? 'I thought I might call her later,' he said, in case she was still upset at the way he'd behaved towards her friend and his half-sister. 'Introduce myself properly. Explain last night and make an arrangement to meet.'

'She didn't drive home.'

'Oh?' He set the coffee pot on the stove and lit the ring beneath it.

'She stayed at the hotel.'

'Well, it's a long way to Ipanema.'

'The one that was supposedly shut for health and safety reasons following a restaurant fire,' she said. 'Only it turns out there was no fire. It never closed. But I suspect you already knew that, didn't you?'

Santi stilled. His heart gave a great crash against his ribs and the air whooshed from his lungs. He'd forgotten all about the call he'd made and the instructions he'd issued. So much had happened and changed since then. He could scarcely believe it had been little more than a week.

The instinct to defend and deflect—as he'd done so often before when backed into a corner—sprang to life. For half a second he considered it, but then he stamped it out. There was no point in denying what he'd done when she'd evidently worked out the truth. He had no defence and he didn't want to lie to her ever again. 'Yes.'

'How much did it cost you?'

He flinched at the cold accusation he could hear in her voice. 'A new roof.'

'Why did you do it?'

Why *had* he done it? He must have been mad. He deserved every inch of her stony expression and the simmering condemnation that was rolling off her in waves. All he could do was try and explain and hope that in light of everything they'd talked about last night she forgave him.

'I'd planned all along for you to stay here, with me,' he said, willing her to listen to him and give him a chance. 'I didn't appreciate you going off-piste. It was infuriating.'

'So you manipulated the situation. You manipulated me.'

Regret thumped through him, churning up his stomach and tightening his throat. 'I'm sorry,' he said roughly.

'You had no right to do that. I understand your need for control and where it comes from. And I get that you fear chaos ensuing without it. But that's no excuse.'

'I know.'

'What you did makes me question everything else that's happened since Saturday night. It makes me wonder what else you might be manipulating.'

Outwardly, Santi didn't move a muscle. Inwardly, however, every cell of his body was recoiling in icy panic. Under no circumstances must she wonder that. If she got wind of his insane plan for revenge, even though he'd abandoned it days ago, this fledgling relationship of theirs could well lie in ruins.

'I'm not manipulating anything,' he said, his heart pounding so hard it hurt. 'How ever this started, trust what we have now.'

'How on earth can I? And what is that anyway?'

'I don't know,' he had to admit. This was all so new, and he hadn't had a chance to properly figure it out. 'But it's more than just sex.'

Her eyebrows lifted. 'Is it?'

He went cold. His head spun. 'Don't you think so?'

'I did last night,' she said. 'Yesterday—and even this morning—I thought we could see where this went. I thought we had a shot at something great.'

'We do.'

'I'm not so sure now.'

'I screwed up,' he said, feeling as though he was standing on the edge of a giant steep cliff, beneath which lay nothing of the future he'd been tentatively imagining, but instead all of his snarling, snapping fears. 'Forgive me. It won't happen again.'

Thalia wanted to believe Santi. She did understand why he'd done what he'd done and she wished she could make the necessary allowances, brush it aside and move on. But however hard she tried, she couldn't. He'd lied to her. He hadn't given her wishes a second thought before bulldozing them. She'd refused to fall into line and been punished for it. How could she forgive him for that? How could she trust that it was a one-off?

She went through the motions of breakfast and work, struggling to find a way through the chaos in her head, but she couldn't shake the feeling that the sands beneath her feet were shifting. Whereas once she'd thought she had him all figured out, she was now longer certain of anything. He wasn't the man she'd thought he was. The bright, hopeful future she'd dreamed of was now blurry and grey.

The morning dragged by and the sense of unease she felt swelled. She couldn't stop analysing everything else he'd said and done since he'd swooped back into her life, so much of which had bothered her at the time. The determined flirting in the beginning, when at that point their relationship had been purely professional. All that touching on the plane, the innuendo, the knowing smiles, and his subsequent wandering around the house semi-naked. He'd smouldered at her endlessly and had provoked her whenever the opportunity arose. It was as if he'd been trying to seduce her, right from the start, but why would he have suddenly wanted her back in his bed when they'd parted on such bad terms over a year earlier?

On the night of the gala she'd questioned why he had been so determined to secure her services, and that question was now rearing its head again. He could have sought help for his charity endeavours anywhere, and she was good, but so were many others with whom he did not have history. She didn't understand why he'd insisted on bringing her to Brazil when the options she'd presented him with had been perfectly reasonable, even allowing for his need for control. It hadn't been an on-the-spur-of-the-moment sort of a thing. It had been premeditated. He'd even admitted earlier that the plan *all along* had been to have her stay with him.

So just how far back had that plan gone?

How *had* this all started?

And why did she get the feeling that something was still badly wrong?

By lunchtime, Santi couldn't bear the suspicion and wariness with which Thalia kept looking at him any longer. The blood in his veins flowed sluggishly. He was sweating in a way that had nothing to do with the heat of the day. A lead weight had settled on his chest, crushing him with a terrible combination of guilt, remorse, panic and dread.

He could tell that his earlier confession was festering within her. She evidently wasn't able to forgive him as he'd hoped. He was losing her, he sensed with a plummeting stomach. He was falling off that cliff edge and tumbling headlong into the desolation that lay below, and it was every bit as sickening as he'd feared.

He desperately wanted to fix the situation but couldn't figure out the right way to go about it, or even if it was possible. He could give her more time and space but she might never find her way back to him. He could come clean and tell her the truth about everything, but he knew that if he went down that route he risked losing her for good.

However, that was happening anyway, he'd eventually forced himself to acknowledge, cold fingers of fear clawing at his gut as he contemplated the options and their outcomes. And he'd never been any good at passivity. If this relationship stood any chance of survival—and it was too promising to throw away out of cowardice—he had to try and rebuild her trust in him, even if it meant destroying it further first. Even if with the stakes so stratospherically high, the chances of everything he longed for crashing down around him were immense.

He'd faced his demons and survived. Whatever the result of the conversation he had to have with her, however devastating the potential fallout, he'd survive that too. He couldn't do nothing, and he would not go down without a fight.

'Come and sit down,' he said when she returned to the poolside table bearing two tall glasses of fruit juice. 'We need to talk.'

Thalia set the glasses on the table, her hands trembling slightly and her heart thudding way too fast. She thought about the last time that phrase had been uttered—by her, then, though, not him. They'd been over shortly afterwards.

So was that what was going on here? Was Santi going to tell her he'd had a rethink and now wasn't interested in taking their relationship any further? How would she feel if he did? Relieved? Cheated? Or devastated?

Part of her wanted to run away and hide so she didn't have to face whatever it was he wanted to talk about, but that had never solved anything. For *two years* she'd been struggling with her feelings regarding her brother and Zoe mainly by sticking her head in the sand, so she sat down and braced herself.

'First of all,' he said, his expression more serious than she'd ever seen it before, 'you need to know that I'm in love with you. You are the most incredible woman I've ever met and I want to marry you and spend the rest of my life with you.'

At his unexpected declaration, her heart soared with joy. A tsunami of relief crashed through her. He wasn't putting an end to their affair. Maybe all was not lost. Maybe they could work through her doubts and her worries together.

'I'm in love with you, too,' she said, her voice thick with emotion, 'and I'll marry you any day of the week.'

'Good,' he said, letting out a ragged breath. A light briefly flickered in the dark depths of his eyes before disappearing. 'Remember that.'

'Why?'

'Because you might forget it when you hear what I have to tell you.'

She couldn't imagine forgetting something as momentous as that ever. What could possibly be so bad that she would? 'All right.'

He shoved his hands through his hair and swallowed hard. 'It was no coincidence that I was at the gala on Saturday night.'

Ah. The questions rampaging through her head were finally going to be answered. It was as if he'd read her mind. Again. 'I gathered that,' she said cautiously.

'I always intended to win your lot.'

'I gathered that, too.' She leaned forwards, pulled one of the glasses of guava and pineapple juice towards her and took a sip before setting it back down. 'What I don't understand is why?'

For a moment, Santi didn't respond. Across his face skated a flurry of emotions that she just couldn't identify. Then he took a deep breath and said, 'Revenge.'

She blinked and sat back. 'What?'

'I was out for revenge.'

'On who?'

'You.'

The word hit her like a blow, and for a second she couldn't breathe. She felt as if he'd punched her in the gut. The juice curdled in her stomach. 'Why?'

'Ever since I can remember I've been in control of the relationships I've had,' he said while she fought for composure, for her brain, which had suddenly gone MIA. 'I start them. I finish them. Then you came along and ended ours before I was ready and suddenly I was in control of nothing. You confused the hell out of me. You made me doubt myself for the first time in years and that filled me with anger and resentment, emotions I thought I'd buried long ago. It went on for months, eating me up inside, until I realised I couldn't let it continue. So I came up with a plan.'

Her heart slowed right down. She went very cold. She could never have anticipated this to be his explanation. 'What was it?'

'To take back the power and restore control.'

'How?'

'By seducing you,' he said, his voice cracking, although his steady gaze did not leave hers. 'By getting you to fall for me and then ending it.'

The silence that fell then was thick and deafening. Thalia couldn't speak. She was struggling to process what he was saying. She didn't even know where to start. All she could hear was the thundering of her blood in her ears. 'Was *I* your merger and acquisitions project?'

'Yes,' he admitted gruffly. 'But the night we kissed by the pool, I abandoned it. I realised it was a terrible thing to have done.'

'Because I wasn't complying.'

'You weren't,' he said. 'And that made me reassess. The strength of your will highlighted just how plain wrong I'd been to pursue it. I should never have allowed my insecurities to get the better of me. If I could wind back time and do things differently I would. In a heartbeat. I never expected to fall in love with you again. But I don't think I ever fell *out* of love with you. That was the real reason why I lashed out in Paris. I'd fallen for you—quite possibly the minute I laid eyes on you—and you broke up with me. It wasn't just the rejection that hurt so badly. It was my heart.'

He carried on explaining how he'd felt about her then

and how he felt about her now, but to Thalia they were just words, words and more words. All she could think was that this whole thing had just been one big game to him. For her, these last eight days had been a brave leap of faith both professionally and personally. For him, it had been payback for something she hadn't even done.

The relentless flirting and the attention that she'd lapped up now made perfect sense. She'd made it so easy for him. The kisses, the sex, the conversation. She'd shared with him her innermost angst. She hadn't known how right she'd been when she suspected he'd use it against her. She felt like the biggest fool in the history of the world. And the pain of it was so excruciating she had to switch herself off before she burst into tears.

'Say something,' he urged.

'What do you want me to say?' she said numbly, her eyes nevertheless stinging, her throat tight. 'That what you did is OK just because your guilty conscience has forced you to confess? It's very much not OK.'

'I know that. If you let me I'll spend the rest of my life making it up to you. Remember that I love you and you love me.'

Hah. 'I fell in love with a fantasy,' she said bitterly. 'That man doesn't exist.'

'Yes, he does. You're the only person on the planet to know the real me. You've changed me. You've opened my eyes and shown me what love can be. Who I can be with you.'

He reached to take her hand but she whipped it away before he could. 'You've proven yourself to be ruthlessness over and over again, Santi. For all I know, your plan is in full swing, even now, and this is all part of it. You say you love me but how can I believe that? How do I know it's not just a line? How can I ever trust you again?'

'Because I could have got even so many times,' he said, looking and sounding faintly desperate. 'I could have ruined you professionally the minute you revealed what was at stake for you. I could have used our kiss to further my agenda. But I didn't. And it wasn't a conscious decision that I made on either of those occasions. It just never crossed my mind. The truth is I gave up on revenge before I even got going. I love you and I will be sorry for what I tried to do till the day I die.'

Santi stopped, and clearly it was her turn to respond but her head was buzzing. She was sure there was logic to what he said, but she couldn't see it. She still felt so very stupid. So naïve. He'd been right all along about the imbalance of power in a relationship. He'd had it all. She'd had none. But she could redress that. She had some pride left. It was pretty much all she *did* have left.

'I wouldn't worry about it too much,' she said with a brittle smile.

'What do you mean?'

'I've been using you, too.'

He frowned. 'What?'

'Remember the morning I twisted my ankle?'

'Yes.'

'While you were off getting the bandage and the crutches, Atticus rang. He told me Zoe was pregnant. It sent me into a spin. I just wanted to forget that he was drifting even further away from me and, as we both know, you're very good at making that happen.'

With effort she mustered up a pitying look. 'You were so easy to seduce. Ironic, now I think about it.'

He paled. He stared at her, as if struck dumb. 'Are you serious?' he managed eventually.

'Why wouldn't I be?'

'I don't believe you.'

Now he knew what it felt like. 'You're not the only one who gets what they want, Santi.' She got up. Her legs were so weak they barely held her up, but they just had to carry her to her room because she couldn't bear to look at him any more. He'd shattered her heart, her hopes and her dreams, and she was on the point of collapse. 'I think we're done here, don't you?'

CHAPTER FIFTEEN

FOR SEVERAL MINUTES after Thalia got up and walked off Santi just sat there, staring at the space she'd occupied, reeling as if she'd physically struck him, the shocking revelation that she'd been using him scything through him and dicing his heart to pieces. Not that he could feel it—he was frozen in shock. Then the shock subsided and in flooded every insecurity he'd ever had, blitzing his brain and battering him on all sides.

Of course she'd been using him, insisted the inferiority complex he'd naïvely assumed that, with her help, he'd conquered. What else could he have expected? He'd been an idiot to think that someone like her would genuinely fall for someone like him. Nothing he did would ever be good enough to impress her.

As he'd always feared, love had made him weak and needy and desperate. He'd handed her his heart and she'd stomped all over it. And as a result he was bleeding as if she'd stabbed him with a thousand knives. He'd all but begged her to believe him, to trust him, but to no avail, and the emotions swirling though him like a hurricane made him want to howl.

He'd taken the biggest risk of his life and he'd lost. So he was glad she was leaving. He was far better off alone. He always had been. Alone, he couldn't be hurt or rejected, and being rid of her was what he'd originally planned. Only he had no power right now, no control. He felt no satisfaction, just a gaping great hole in his chest where she'd been and utter misery.

He'd told her everything. He'd basked in the warmth of her smiles and their conversations. And that had been reciprocated, he was sure. When he thought of all they'd shared, how generous and thoughtful she'd been, how keen she'd been to find out who he was and how she'd let him into her world in return, he couldn't believe that all she'd sought was escape. She'd been as tangled up in him as he had been in her, emotionally as well as physically. No one was that skilled an actor.

So what if with that retaliating shot of hers she'd simply been protecting herself? He could understand that. He'd deployed that defend-and-deflect strategy often enough. She'd been badly bruised by what he'd done. He'd seen it in her eyes and on her face. Why wouldn't she want to cause him as much pain as he'd caused her? Wasn't that exactly what he'd done in Paris?

So what the hell was he doing sitting here pondering the frailty of human nature while she packed up her things? Was he really going to let her walk out of here? If she slipped through his fingers he might never get her back again, and that was something he did *not* want to have to contemplate.

The front door slammed, the sound reverberating through every cell of his being, and he sprang to his feet. This was all wrong. He was in love with her, she was in love with him, and he would make her believe it if it was the last thing he did.

* * *

Thalia's eyes stung madly as she threw her suitcase into the boot of the red hired convertible. But she would not let the tears fall. Not until she was back home and on her own. Then she could spend a month crying into her pillow. She knew how this went. She'd done it before. Only this time the pain was so much worse. It was crucifying.

She should never have put him on such a pedestal, she thought heartbrokenly as she climbed into the driver's seat and plugged Rio's main airport into the satnav. He was only ever going to fall off it. No one was flawless. Everyone made mistakes. She could be making one right now. She could be making the biggest mistake of her life…

But no. She wasn't. There was nothing left for her here. Even if she could persuade herself to believe that Santi did love her, that he did regret what he'd done, it was worthless without trust. By destroying that, he'd wrecked anything they might have had.

With a stifled sob, she fired up the engine and was just about to switch the car into gear when the front door flew open. Santi strode out of the house and planted himself an inch in front of the bonnet.

'Stop,' he said, feet wide apart, arms folded over his chest.

Her heart lurched and then began to race. But she'd been distracted by him for the last time. She would never succumb to such lunacy again. 'Move out of the way.'

'No.'

She revved the engine. 'Don't make me run you over.'

His eyes were dark, his expression fierce. 'Do what you need to do, Thalia. I'm staying put.'

And so was she, obviously, because behind her was a wall and, despite everything, she couldn't mow him down. 'What do you want?' she said, taking her foot off the accelerator, killing the engine and glaring at him over the windscreen instead.

'I am not letting you go.'

Her head spun for a second before she hauled it back under control. 'I'm not yours to keep.'

'I love you and you love me. We belong together.'

'You could not be more wrong.'

'We still have work to do.'

'Find someone else. That's what I'm going to do.'

His gaze drilled into hers, so intense, so penetrating, it was as if he was trying to get a glimpse of her very soul. 'Were you really using me?'

She jutted up her chin. 'As much as you were using me.'

'That'll be a no, then, thank God,' he said, his relief visibly immense.

Her strength and fury drained away along with most of her defences. She was tired and sad and trying to figure it all out was so very hard.

'Consider everything we've done together, Thalia. Everything we've talked about, everything we've shared.'

'What do you think I was doing while shoving my things into my suitcase?' she said helplessly. 'I've thought about nothing but that. It didn't work. It only made me more confused.'

'It was all real. Every second of it. You must believe that. You have to trust me.'

'I want to,' she said, her voice raw with the emotion that she simply couldn't hide any more. 'So much. But I can't.'

'You can. Please. I need you.'

It was the crack in his voice and the sheer desperation etched into his features that smashed the last of her weakening defences to pieces, striking her right in the heart. Her chest ached and her vision blurred. Was she *really* going to throw what they had away? Up until this morning, it had been so good. Santi was the only man—her brother aside—who'd ever truly understood her. He had an uncanny ability to read her mind and he'd forced her to confront some difficult truths. He challenged her. He made her laugh. She wanted to spend the rest of her life with him. That hadn't changed.

Perhaps trust was a choice, she thought, her blood pumping faster as the possibility of that hit her. She could choose to believe him when he said he'd given up on his plan for revenge the night they'd kissed by the pool, and that he deeply regretted coming up with the idea in the first place—or she could choose not to believe him. The evidence that their relationship had been genuine was all there. She didn't even have to look very hard. It was in every smile he'd ever given her, every look, every touch.

So maybe what was holding her back from making the choice she desperately wanted to make were *her* insecurities. The fear of it all going wrong again. Of not being enough for him. Of the connection they shared disappearing.

But that was no way to live.

Not when he'd shown her how wonderful the alternative could be.

And why wouldn't she be enough for him? Why would their connection disappear and their relationship implode?

This last year had been all about being brave and taking risks. Was she really going to stop now, at this most crucial moment in her life, when her happiness, her hopes and dreams and her entire future were at stake?

No, she was not. She was going to shake off her doubts and worries and choose to put her faith in him, in them.

'I need you, too,' she said a little giddily, as the gloom and misery lifted to reveal a future that once again looked bright and exciting.

He went very still. His gaze bore into hers. 'What are you saying?'

'That I do believe you and I do trust you. I know you. You know me. Everyone makes mistakes.'

'Not quite like mine.'

'That's true. But I choose to let it go.'

A muscled ticked in his jaw. 'Are you sure?'

'I've never been surer of anything,' she said, her heart beginning to swell. 'I just got a little lost for a while back there.'

'I am sorrier than you will ever know.'

'Enough to come over here and show me how very sorry you are?'

'If I wasn't slightly concerned you might still drive off.'

'Then I will come to you.'

She got out of the car and walked unhesitatingly into

his arms. His mouth came down on hers and she lost track of all time and place as he held her tight, as if he couldn't bear to let her go, and kissed her so deeply she didn't ever want to come up for air.

'I love you very much,' she said when they eventually had to break apart.

He smiled and swept her up into his arms. 'I will love you for ever,' he said, and carried her into the house.

EPILOGUE

One year later

AT ELEVEN P.M. on a Saturday night the following September, in the gilded ballroom of a seven-star Rio hotel, the fundraising auction at a gala being held to launch the brand-new Fundação Ferreira was drawing to a close. A sumptuous six-course dinner accompanied by the finest wines had preceded it, and as a result, over the last hour, millions of dollars had been thrown at luxury villas, questionable art and cases of claret, by well-fed, well-oiled guests determined to outdo each other.

Santi lounged at a table in the centre of the room and reflected that the last time he'd attended a charity auction, he'd wound up acquiring a wife. Tonight, however, he was not bidding on any of the lots. Tonight, he was celebrating the culmination of many months of hard work.

He truly did not think he could be happier or prouder of everything he and Thalia had achieved in the past twelve months. They divided their time between Greece and Brazil. Her business was flourishing. The charities he'd set up beneath the umbrella of his foundation were already changing lives in the favelas.

Perhaps most importantly, the sibling troubles that had caused them both so much grief were history. His relationship with Gaby, tentative at first, had gone from strength to strength. Thalia and Atticus had talked and reshaped their thirty-two-year twinship. They were all here tonight, in fact. Atticus and Zoe were across the table. On his left was his sister and to his right was the woman with whom he was more in love with every day that passed.

'You did it,' she murmured, her eyes shining with warmth, love and pride as the gavel came down on the last lot and the band struck up a tune.

'*We* did it,' he replied, resting a protective hand on her seven-month bump and feeling their baby kick.

'Want to dance?'

'Always.'

* * * * *

A PREGNANCY BOMBSHELL TO BIND THEM

ANNIE WEST

MILLS & BOON

This book is dedicated to some special friends
who all had a hand in getting this story over the line.

A big thank you to Anna Campbell,
Michelle Douglas, Judy Griffiths, Cathryn Hein
and Efthalia Pegios.

CHAPTER ONE

VASSILI LAY ON his side, head resting on his folded arm. The pillows had long since disappeared and he didn't have the energy to roll over and search for one.

Yet, heavy as his limbs were, the view before him, lit by a spill of early morning light, compelled him to touch. He lifted a heavy arm to trace the perfect work of art. The long, elegant sweep from nape to narrow waist and further, between those enticing dimples at her pelvis and lower to the taut rise of firm buttocks.

She shivered, silky skin warm against his fingers, as if even that feathering touch was too much for a woman so thoroughly sated.

He knew the feeling. Their passion had been explosive. It had been more intense, more powerful, just plain *more* in so many ways.

The first time they'd shared their bodies had been a revelation. He'd got the sort of high he associated with skydiving or reaching the peak of Everest. The second time should have been less momentous. So should the third, fourth and so on.

Yet each time she undid him so that when he managed to pull himself together afterwards, everything, himself included, felt for a short while new and unfamiliar.

He flattened his palm to the curve of her buttock, stroking down to the apex of her thighs.

'Really?' Her voice was muffled and raspy from lack of

sleep and even that was arousing. Despite the fact he couldn't possibly be ready for her again. Her face pressed against the bedding, honey-brown hair tangling around her shoulders. 'It's too soon.'

Vassili knew it was too soon, but he couldn't resist. Leaning closer, he discovered hot, slick skin and downy curls. He cupped her there, feeling her tremor of response.

Something shot through him. An unfamiliar sensation. Not just physical this time. More than sexual interest. More than satisfaction.

Possessiveness?

He frowned, rejecting the inconceivable idea. He was many things but possessive wasn't one of them.

She twisted her head. Slumbrous eyes snared his.

He felt the pulse of something heavy in the air, unseen but no less real for all that. That same pulse reverberated through his exhausted body.

A few days ago, even last night when they'd fallen into bed before sunset, he'd have called it desire. Now he wasn't sure it was anything so simple. This was desire on steroids. Just as climaxes with her were stronger, longer and more intense than any orgasm he could remember.

'Aren't you worn out?' she murmured.

'Shattered.'

One dark eyebrow arched. 'And yet…?'

She shifted her weight, her thighs trapping his hand. Vassili felt a jolt of energy straight to his groin. He inhaled sharply and saw her eyes widen.

'You can't be. Not after…'

He shrugged.

After the ecstasy they'd shared, too many times to keep count, they should be totally wasted. Yet he felt the tiny, shuffling movement of her pelvis against his hand and the weighted surge of heat in his groin.

Death by sex. Was it possible?

Surely their bodies would surrender soon to exhaustion. Yet already he was imagining straddling her thighs, lifting her hips and driving into her lush, velvety warmth. Feeling her convulse around him, her spasms drawing him to completion as she gasped his name.

He loved the way she whispered his name as ecstasy took her. As if he were some precious, wondrous secret instead of an ordinary man.

Yes. Absolutely yes.

Deliberately Vassili moved his hand, questing, and she gasped, shaking her hair off her face. The morning light revealed high cheekbones, the endearing couple of freckles across her nose and stunned hazel eyes.

And dark shadows under those eyes.

Because neither of them had slept a full night for five days.

Because they'd been insatiable for each other.

But while he'd been here at the resort relaxing before that, she'd been working right up to the night he'd brought her back here to his private bungalow. From what she'd said she'd worked long hours in the busy weeks prior to that.

Guilt smote him and he dragged his hand away from her delicious heat.

'Sorry. I couldn't resist, but you're right, it's not possible.'

Except it was. But fortunately his stirring penis was hidden from her view by his raised thigh.

Vassili watched the swift play of emotions across her features. Was that disappointment? Nevertheless it was time to stop being self-indulgent. There'd be plenty of time when she'd rested.

'Sleep now, *kopela mou*. Let's conserve our strength for later.'

He leaned across and brushed his lips across hers as tenderness rose, competing with his selfish libido.

As ever, she shaped her mouth to his, returning his kiss with a sweet directness that seemed both innocent and extraordinarily appealing. 'Is that a promise?'

Her hand cupped his cheek, making him aware of his abrasive stubble. For the first time he noticed the reddened patch at the base of her neck and her breast. No doubt there were more elsewhere.

He should have shaved.

Dismay filled him.

First at the idea of hurting her.

And then, shockingly, at the twist of satisfaction deep in his belly at the idea of her wearing his mark.

More possessiveness?

It was so out of character he put it down to severe lack of sleep.

'I've marked your skin.' He rubbed his knuckle gently across the reddened patch at her neck. 'I didn't mean to hurt you. I'm sorry.'

Something gleamed in those green-gold eyes that turned his regret to molten need. 'No need to apologise. I rather like it when you're not so suave.'

Suave! He'd stopped off here on the Great Barrier Reef after three weeks adventuring in Australia. His only concession to suavity was shaving and getting his hair cut the afternoon he'd seen her, being filmed on the beach. Because he hadn't wanted to scare her off by looking like a shaggy vagabond when he invited her for a drink.

Vassili captured her hand and lifted it to his mouth. She smelled of sated woman and the tropics. He was growing addicted to the scent of coconut lime body wash. It was more attractive than any designer perfume.

'Nevertheless, I'll shave now, ready for later.' Unable to resist, he pressed another quick kiss to her lips then pulled back. 'Get some rest.'

He waited until she closed her eyes and her breathing slowed before getting out of bed, then walked stiff-legged to the bathroom for a cold shower.

* * *

Laura woke slowly, aware of a decadent lassitude as if her bones had turned liquid.

Perhaps they had. Through the night, time and again, she'd melted under Vassili's touch.

If someone had told her that she'd ever meet a man whose laughing dark eyes, sexual charisma and surprisingly considerate nature would tempt her into a week of lovemaking, with a virtual stranger, she'd never have believed them.

She pulled the sheet over her body.

When it came to men, Laura was the poster girl for caution. For distrust.

Not with all men, of course. Jake was her best friend but he was the exception that proved the rule. At twenty-five she'd learned enough to know it would be a snowy day in hell before she took any man at face value.

Yet Vassili had tempted her with a mix of sexual allure and devastating honesty. It was the honesty that had undone her—what she'd always wanted from a man, and learned never to expect.

'I want you,' he'd said. 'I want your beautiful body and your smile that's pure sunshine. I want to spend time getting to know you and I think, hope, you might enjoy being with me too.'

If any other man had said that she'd have turned her shoulder and walked away. Except her body sent another message. *Yes, yes, yes!*

It had never happened before, this instant sexual connection.

She'd met his eyes and felt a throb of hunger such as she'd never known. He'd shrugged his broad, bronzed shoulders and his mouth had curved up in a self-deprecating smile and he'd laughed. *At himself.* 'Forgive the lack of subtlety. But I prefer plain speaking.'

That had stopped her in her tracks.

He didn't take himself too seriously, he'd explained, and

he'd got in the habit of being direct. Then he'd apologised for possibly offending her and asked about the photo shoot she'd just finished.

Laura had found herself taking a seat at the poolside bar beside him and accepting a mocktail so bedecked with tropical fruit it had left them both laughing.

For the next hour he'd asked about her modelling work. He hadn't made the usual flippant or suggestive comments about swimwear shoots and whether she posed naked. His questions had been about the business. He'd been insightful, probing and apparently genuinely interested.

When asked, he'd explained he was visiting from Greece on holiday then switched the subject back to her, to the Great Barrier Reef and the gorgeous, tropical paradise here around Port Douglas.

How many men would give up the opportunity to talk about themselves? Laura knew she was biased, yet in her experience the answer was not many.

Somehow she'd found herself agreeing to dinner and spent it laughing over his misconceptions of what he'd expected in coming to Australia. From there they'd moved to tales of travel misadventures.

And all the while the pulse of attraction between them had grown heavier and stronger, like the throbbing beat of a drum, low in her body.

Even then she could have resisted temptation. Except he'd treated her to the one thing she'd never had from any man except Jake. Unabashed honesty. Vassili had admitted that he wasn't looking for a relationship. He'd be moving on soon. All he could offer was fun and sex and as much pleasure as she wanted.

Still he hadn't touched her. Not by so much as the brush of the finger. Yet she'd been preternaturally aware of his body so close to hers right through the evening. His gaze had been as heavy as a touch. She'd felt it stroking her body, igniting fires of longing.

So that when, finally, they kissed, it had felt inevitable and right.

So right that after one night together she'd deferred her plans to leave and Vassili had extended his booking to be with her. He'd admitted there was work waiting for him at home but added he could keep on top of it online. Not that she'd seen much evidence of him working apart from the odd phone call. As for her, she had a break between jobs but should be using the time on her own business project.

But how long since you've taken a break? You're always working on one project or another. Surely you deserve some downtime.

Maybe that was why this time with Vassili felt so wonderful. Since the trauma of her teens, Laura had craved certainty and safety. She'd worked as hard as anyone she knew, built a reputation for reliability and professionalism and saved methodically. She'd needed stability and a safety net.

Her spur-of-the-moment decision to take time off and devote herself to pure pleasure was out of character.

Yet the way she felt with Vassili—freer, happier, more *alive*—she wouldn't have missed this for the world.

A few days ago they'd swapped numbers. Vassili had invited her to visit Greece and look him up. Meanwhile, he'd decided he needed to see more of Australia and was already planning a return visit later this year.

His expression had told her it wasn't Uluru or Tasmania he wanted to see when he came back. That look, the velvet invitation in his voice, made it clear *she* was the drawcard for his return.

Not that he tried to suggest they were at the beginning of a serious, committed relationship. She wouldn't have believed him if he had. She was no blind romantic who wove such dreams.

Yet her heartbeat quickened, because she knew he wasn't ready for this to end either. They might not have a permanent future but what they shared was too good to give up yet.

Laura snuggled down into the bed, smiling.

Given her past and her trust issues it was highly unlikely she'd ever marry. But occasional liaisons with a man like Vassili, who was sexy, great company, and made her feel truly appreciated, sounded mighty appealing. He'd made it clear he wasn't looking to settle down, but nor was she.

Her smile widened. The man was pretty close to perfect.

A door opened and she opened her eyes.

Laura frowned. He was dressed. Not merely in board shorts ready for a day at the beach, but in lightweight trousers and a soft shirt. His hair was damp from the shower but instead of shaving as he'd said, he'd left his angular jaw dark with a night's growth of beard.

Something eager and feminine that lived in the pit of her stomach curled in on itself. That shadowed jaw made him look even more masculine and a little dangerous. Or maybe it was the glint in his dark eyes.

Registering his expression, Laura pulled herself up against the headboard, dragging the sheet with her and tucking it under her arms. Over five days she'd learned to read Vassili's expressions. From laughter to intense concentration. From curiosity to tenderness. And at least thirty degrees of pleasure, varying from awareness to ecstatic exultation.

But she'd never seen this. Surely the banked heat in his narrowed eyes and the flat set of his mouth spoke of anger. More than anger, something deeper that she couldn't read.

'What is it, Vassili? Are you okay?' Clearly he wasn't.

He been heading to the walk-in wardrobe but stopped and turned to her, his expression gradually easing. Yet his body was rigid. Something was definitely wrong.

She shoved down the sheet and climbed out of bed, insides

churning as she finally deciphered his expression. Hurt mixed with anger.

He crossed to her in a few swift strides, capturing her hands in his and holding them against his chest. Through his shirt she felt the quick thud of his heart.

'What can I do?' she asked.

He shook his head, his smile endearingly crooked as he squeezed her hands then kissed her knuckles. 'Thank you, but there's nothing you can do.'

'It's bad news?' Her heart ached for him. Twice in her life she'd faced terrible news. Each time it had pulled her life inside out and to this day she remembered the pain in vivid detail. 'I'm so sorry, Vassili.'

'It's not what you think. No one's died.' He paused and a muscle flexed at the hinge of his jaw as if he ground his teeth. 'It's not a tragedy but… There's a family matter. An urgent family matter to be sorted out. I'm needed in Greece immediately.'

Dismay vied with sympathy. 'Of course. I understand.'

That didn't prevent her distress at the thought of him going. She wasn't ready. Nowhere near ready to go their separate ways.

'Thank you for understanding.'

Again he kissed her knuckles and her insides did that melting trick. No man had ever kissed her hand before Vassili. She'd never known how incredibly tender and sexy it was.

Her gaze fixed on his sculpted lips. They were full, sensual, and on someone different, might have looked almost too beautiful for a man. But teamed with the ultra-masculine planes and angles of his arresting face…

Laura leaned up and pressed her mouth briefly to his. She told herself it was a kiss of reassurance yet at the same time she was storing up sense memories for the future. The feel of his mouth on hers. The unique, dark taste of him. The scent of soap, cinnamon and male flesh that she found both comforting and arousing. The heavy quickening of her pulse that happened whenever they were together.

Reluctantly she eased back. 'I'll pack for you while you organise transport. Or would you prefer...?'

'No, that would be wonderful. Thank you.' He didn't move, his gaze devouring hers, then he shook his head. 'I don't want to leave like this. It's been memorable.' Then he released her hands and stepped back. 'But we'll see each other again.'

A day later Laura still remembered his tone of regret, her pulse quickening at the memory.

She should go home. She had work to do. But Vassili had booked the bungalow till Sunday and told her to make herself at home and somehow she hadn't found the energy to leave. She'd caught up on sleep but hadn't found the energy to turn on her laptop or phone. This was the first time she could remember ever switching off totally, living in the moment without thought to the future.

It felt utterly decadent and selfish and she loved every minute.

Now she discovered those feelings weren't simply the product of her liaison with Vassili. That was the biggest part, but so was time out from the bustle and rush of her life. Her modelling, fledgling business and occasional volunteer work at a family support centre were important to her. But she couldn't remember the last time she'd spent a day ignoring them all.

She'd been overdue a holiday.

Yet she feared the truth wasn't so simple. She missed Vassili. Yearned for him. She didn't want to leave this place where they'd been so happy.

That realisation finally drove her from the privacy of the bungalow. Perhaps if she were with other people it would break this strange mix of lassitude and restless energy.

She was browsing in the exclusive resort boutique when she heard her name. Not someone calling out to her but an excited whisper. Her nape prickled.

She'd been modelling for a few years and was moderately successful but not a household name. It was too soon for the prestigious tourism advertisement to have aired yet. They'd only finished shooting last week, the final segment being on this beach, with her in a bikini and sarong, extolling the joys of a holiday Down Under.

Even so, occasionally someone recognised her. It was a part of her job she didn't like. She was no longer the shy twelve-year-old who shrank from public recognition. She couldn't be, when modelling was a lucrative shortcut to launching her real career.

Even so, when the whispering intensified she had to make an effort to push her shoulders back rather than shrink down as she used to, trying to minimise her height.

The whispers followed her from the boutique and she heard Vassili's name too. That made her frown. So did the way the saleswoman was watching her so avidly.

As Laura crossed the foyer a couple she'd seen earlier in the week nudged each other, and again she caught Vassili's name. One of them lifted a phone until a member of staff hurried forward and said something that made him frown and put it back in his pocket.

But that was enough for Laura.

Moments later she was striding towards the secluded accommodation that had been her haven for the last week. Inside, she leaned against the closed door, annoyed she'd let a little public recognition unnerve her.

Everywhere she looked evoked memories of Vassili. The big, squishy lounge where they'd lain together more times than she could count. The private courtyard with its plunge pool. She shivered, muscles softening as she remembered making love there in the moonlight. The gleaming kitchen where he'd made Greek coffee for her.

She'd laughed, commenting on him carrying powdered coffee and a *briki*, the tiny coffee-making saucepan, on his travels.

Vassili had shrugged and said the resort had provided them as it provided mouth-watering baskets of fruit, cheeses, fine wine and other goodies.

Laura had frowned and asked if he was some sort of VIP. He'd replied that his uncle was a very successful businessman. Then Vassili had distracted her as only he could and she hadn't thought about it again.

She thought about it now. The women in the boutique had known not only her name but Vassili's. His full name, Vassili Thanos.

She suddenly realised that in some ways she knew very little about him. He didn't speak about work or family. But nor had Laura spoken about her family.

He'd said they were *comfortably off.* And she'd been more interested in the fact that there was no woman in his life. It was the one absolute dealbreaker for her, for she'd never enter a relationship with a man, no matter how brief, without being sure he was free.

In other ways Vassili had been so open, entertaining with stories of his childhood in Greece and his more recent adventures. He was a thrill seeker, doing things she'd never dare, like diving with sharks, jumping from aeroplanes and climbing cliffs for fun.

Laura had been fascinated hearing about places and adventures so far beyond her own experience. She had a passport but had never been out of Australia.

One day she would. Maybe she'd take Vassili up on his offer to stay with him in Greece.

Her breath snared in excitement. His invitation was more than tempting, like the man himself.

He was irresistible. She'd been mentally rejigging her schedule and her finances, dreaming of lazy days in the Aegean. No one, ever, had done that, distracting her from her plans and her work.

All the more reason to find out how those people know him.

Laura pushed off the door and crossed to where she'd left her phone.

Her search was immediately successful. Vassili Thanos was no stranger to the public eye. His daredevil adventures and his wealth made him too fascinating.

Comfortably off.

That was one way of putting it. His uncle, Constantine Pappas, ran one of the biggest logistics companies in the world and it appeared Vassili was a part of that company. Enough to make him a billionaire in his own right.

Laura felt numb. Vassili, a billionaire? It explained his ability to travel from Africa to the Andes and everywhere in between, pursuing dangerous sports from desert car rallies to caving and ice climbing.

He hadn't told her about his wealth, but she thought she understood. He was one of the most authentic, engaging people she'd met yet she guessed many people would treat him differently if they knew about his money.

Presumably some women pursued him as a result.

Laura huffed out a laugh.

At least he knows it's not his money you want, just his body.

Which made his invitation to join him in Greece, and his plans to visit her, even more significant. *He trusted her.* She'd felt the same about him though she hadn't opened up about her past either.

It was easy to forgive him for keeping his wealth secret.

But as she absently scrolled through the search her smile froze and so did her lungs. She blinked and read again, scrolled down and found another, similar headline.

She dragged in air as the world tilted. For a second she felt faint. But Laura wasn't the fainting type. Especially as the implications of the article sank in.

The family emergency that had made him rush away wasn't someone's ill-health or a crisis in the family business.

It was the announcement of his upcoming wedding to his long-term fiancée.

Laura stared, dumbstruck and disbelieving.

The whole time they'd spent together he'd been promised to another woman. They'd been engaged for years.

There was a photo of them, not a posed formal shot but an impromptu one that showed them grinning at each other, his arm around her shoulders. It wasn't their physical proximity but the absolute understanding and affection in their locked gazes that screamed intimacy.

The phone clattered to the floor as Laura ran for the bathroom, just making it in time as she brought up her breakfast.

He'd made her the other woman.

Some things were forgivable but not that. Never that.

CHAPTER TWO

Three months later

VASSILI FINISHED THE cost analysis report and sat back, mulling over the pros and cons.

Given the economic climate and challenges to supply chains, on first glance acquiring a failing shipping company seemed madness. Except it had failed because of poor decisions rather than from intrinsic weakness in the business model.

Despite his uncle's ever-cautious approach, Thanos Enterprises hadn't become phenomenally successful without taking risks.

That was one of the many differences between him and Constantine. His uncle would, left to his own devices, keep doing business the way Vassili's father and grandfather had done. He was loyal, dependable, appallingly obstinate and, right now, the bane of Vassili's life.

They both knew it was by taking carefully calculated risks, by moving quickly to seize opportunities and spin them round to their advantage, that Thanos Enterprises had transformed from a middling company to a world leader in the past decade.

The worst of it was that *because* Constantine knew it, and Vassili had a talent for identifying such opportunities, he was determined to tie Vassili to a desk on the executive floor of their Athens headquarters. Keeping him yoked to the family business by clipping his wings and trying to guilt him into settling down.

As if guilt weren't a permanent weight between his shoulder blades and deep, deep in his gut.

As if he'd ever walk away from the family.

Constantine was overreacting even more than usual. And this time he'd persuaded his sister, Vassili's mother to side with him against her own son.

Vassili rubbed a hand across his unshaven jaw and grimaced.

Why couldn't his family be happy with what he'd done for them? What he continued to do?

He might have refused the public position of CEO, leaving that to his uncle. But it was Vassili's work, his insights, his nose for success, that had transformed the company.

They had what they wanted, growth and accelerating profits. Why couldn't they stop at that and accept he didn't want to become another grey-faced, suited drone on the executive floor?

He turned his head, taking in the dark blue of the Aegean. They'd left Crete this morning, heading north-west on his yacht towards the Peloponnesus then the Ionian islands. Vassili had a hankering for a change of scene. For the past few months, since Australia, he'd been unable to settle, moving from one place to another every few days.

The idea of him five or six days a week in the Athens office was unthinkable. With an effort he turned back to the report. If those figures were right—

His phone rang. Caller ID revealed it was his assistant, Aleko, who knew he didn't want to be disturbed. He needed to concentrate.

It's not Aleko interrupting your concentration. You've had trouble focusing for months.

That knowledge turned his frown into a scowl.

He sighed and picked up the phone. 'What's Constantine done now?'

'It's not your uncle.' Vassili tensed at Aleko's tone. 'Do you know a woman called Laura Bettany?'

The wheels of Vassili's chair squealed as he shoved it back from the desk. 'Why?'

The single syllable should have conveyed no emotion yet he felt it deep inside. An inchoate tumble he refused to analyse. She was in his past. She'd made that clear and he didn't beg favours from any woman, especially one who'd written him off as a holiday fling, blanking his calls.

'I'll take that as a yes.'

'Take it any way you like. Why are you asking?'

'There's a media report—'

'I'm not interested. Now, unless there's something else—'

'You *will* be interested, Vass. If this is true, it's the first of many and you won't be able to ignore them.'

Over the heavy beat of his pulse, Vassili recognised the note of stark warning. Only bad temper had made him question Aleko's judgement. He should have known better.

'What does it say?'

Annoyance died with the thought that something had happened to her. She might be in his past but the idea of that vibrant woman no longer vibrant, perhaps no longer alive, sucked the heat from his body.

He shot to his feet, stalking to look across the deck to the sea beyond. But in his mind's eye he saw glittering hazel eyes. A welcoming smile as she lifted her arms to pull him down to her.

'I've just sent it to you. But I wanted to check first that you did know her.'

Did? Past tense.

Invisible hands clutched his throat in a death grip. He couldn't breathe. His fingers were numb as he accessed the message.

What he saw there dragged the air back into his lungs with a whoop of relief. It wasn't a death notice.

But his relief turned to something indefinable as he scanned the article. If you could call it an article rather than a piece of sly supposition and blatant intrusion.

Lovely Laura—Pregnant!

It showed Laura, the same Laura with whom he'd spent that memorable week, head down and arm protectively across her abdomen, hurrying towards a parked car. It was obvious she was trying to avoid the photographer and, despite Vassili's anger at her, his fingers twitched with the useless desire to meet the paparazzo and smash his camera.

Shaking his head, he focused on the text. It was an overblown gossip piece short on fact. 'Sources close' to Laura spoke about her inability to work recently due to morning sickness. There was a rumour she was about to lose a lucrative modelling job because once her pregnancy showed she'd no longer fit the look required for the promotion.

Then there was his name, identified as the potential mystery father along with breathless insider detail of their 'love tryst in the tropics'.

There were even photos of the resort where they'd stayed on the Queensland coast. So many photos, he wondered if the resort had supplied them along with the story.

Vassili reeled. At the possibility it might be true, despite the precautions they'd taken.

A baby? She might be having his baby?

Tension clamped his nape and spread down his spine.

But he wasn't a man to jump to conclusions. He reached the end of the piece and started again from the top. There was virtually no actual fact there but it was in his nature to check every detail.

The world knew him as a restless adventurer but that was only part of his nature. Once the cautious, methodical part of his character had been dominant. Theo used to tease him about ending his days as an accountant if he didn't change his ways. To Theo, working in an office with numbers was the equivalent of hell. He'd never been able to sit still longer than ten minutes. He'd always been the one to lead them into trouble, while Vassili got them out of it.

Vassili rubbed his chest with the heel of his hand, a gesture that had become unconscious over the years.

Drawing a calming breath, he considered the implications.

There was no reason she'd make a statement denying her pregnancy. Vassili had been the subject of enough outrageous rumours to know it would be a full-time job trying to counter the lies told about him. Instead he tended to ignore public gossip. The chances were she wasn't pregnant.

Even if she were, there was nothing to say he was responsible. It was true that, despite her enthusiasm and seductive passion, he gained the impression Laura hadn't been as sexually experienced as he. But that was conjecture.

If he'd made her pregnant...

He stopped as emotion sideswiped him. He rocked back on his heels, taking a deep breath designed to ease his racing pulse.

If he'd made her pregnant, he'd be one of the first to know. He mightn't know all the details of her life but he was a decent judge of character. She'd never hide that news from her baby's father.

Then there was the question of financial support.

Laura hadn't been interested in his fortune. She hadn't known about it. Hadn't known about his family or position and he hadn't told her, fearing she might change and treat him differently. It had been liberating to be treated as an ordinary man, not a potential financial sponsor.

A friend had been hounded by a woman with a paternity suit after a one-night stand. The baby hadn't been his but the dollar signs in her eyes had been all too real.

A harsh grunt of laughter cracked the still air.

Laura was definitely no gold-digger.

He'd called her on his return to Greece. Called and called again, unwilling to believe it until he had no choice.

She'd done the unthinkable. She'd blocked his calls, obviously viewing their liaison as a casual fling, soon forgotten.

Even now, months later, that stung.

Vassili wasn't used to women ghosting him. Women liked him. Always he'd been the one to end relationships, never his partner. Not that he was a playboy. He didn't have the time or inclination to be obsessed with sex.

Except with Laura. You were obsessive about her. You couldn't get enough of the woman. You'd been going to extend your stay in Australia a second time because of her.

Until the news from Greece forced his hand.

Even now he craved her. It had been months and he still woke in a sweat from dreaming about her.

The fact he hadn't been able to forget her when she'd so blatantly moved on was an annoying prick to his pride.

Vassili shook his head, planting his feet wide and folding his arms as he stared, unseeing, at the view.

It's not Laura specifically. It's just that you weren't ready to end the liaison. That's why you're on edge. Because it feels like unfinished business.

A crooked smile tugged his lips. An unexpected pregnancy certainly fitted the definition of unfinished business.

It couldn't be true. It was just media gossip.

Nevertheless, he needed to be sure.

He turned to his phone. 'Aleko. There are things I need you to do.'

'They're getting worse. They tried to follow me when I left your place.'

Laura read Jake's scowl as he put the bag he'd brought from her home onto the lounge beside her.

She bit her lip, contrition filling her as she wrapped her

arms around her updrawn legs. 'I'm sorry. I shouldn't have involved you. They'll be after you too now.'

His laugh washed across her in a warm wave, his smile reassuring.

'As if! I kept my helmet on and I was too quick for them to follow. Especially when I went down a one-way lane the wrong way. Plus, somehow the numberplates on my bike were accidentally obscured. Just as well no traffic police noticed.' He shrugged. 'We're mates, Laura. You'd do the same for me.'

Despite the tension crawling along her shoulder blades at the news the press was still camped outside her door, she laughed.

'What? Take you in if you found yourself hounded by photographers wanting a story about your pregnancy?'

Her gaze travelled the length of her lanky friend, from his oversized boots to his blond hair sticking up from where he'd worn his motorcycle helmet.

A grin split his face. 'Yeah, that too.' He unzipped his jacket and strolled into the kitchen area. 'Cuppa?'

'Thanks, that would be lovely. But I should make it for you. You're doing all the favours here.' She put her bare feet on the floor, moving to rise.

'Don't,' his deep voice boomed. 'It's the first time since you got here that I've seen you rest. You look haggard, like you haven't slept in weeks.'

'Gee, thanks. I really needed that boost.' Laura kept her tone light. 'You do wonders for my ego.'

One sandy eyebrow lifted as he grabbed some mugs. 'You want me to start lying to you?'

She shook her head. They'd known each other since school, bonding over their misfit status. One of the things she treasured about Jake was his uncompromising honesty. And his generous heart. Behind his scruffy exterior was a heart as big as the Harbour Bridge.

'Of course not. But there's honesty and then there's rubbing it in.'

The boiling kettle clicked off and Jake nodded, making the tea. 'You know you'll always look beautiful to me. But you really do need rest. I worry about you.'

'Oh, Jake.'

She surged to her feet and into the kitchen, wrapping her arms around him. When he tentatively patted her shoulder she gave a watery sniffle. He was a sweetie but he wasn't into physical demonstrations of affection.

'You're not crying, are you?' He sounded horrified. 'I understand though. With those vultures following your every move.'

Laura pulled back, wiping her eyes and getting milk from the fridge. 'Ignore me. You're right, I *am* tired. It's making me soppy. I'll be right in a sec.'

'Of course you will. This fuss will blow over as soon as there's some new gossip for them to get excited about.'

She nodded and took the mug he pushed towards her, though she doubted the press would leave so easily. Not now they'd made the connection between her and Vassili Thanos. He was exactly what the media loved—photogenic, sexy, rich, and with a daredevil lifestyle that set him apart from other billionaires.

Billionaires! How had she got tangled up with one?

He didn't act like one, not that she was an expert. If anyone had asked, she'd have said he was as down-to-earth as the next guy and more trustworthy than most. Apart from his phenomenal charisma and his ability to make her feel gloriously special and happy.

Which showed what a terrible judge of character she was. He'd also managed to make her feel guilty, cheap and tawdry.

Her mouth turned down and she lifted the mug to her lips, hiding her expression from Jake.

'Come on, babe.' Jake was beside her, ushering her forward. 'Sit down and take the weight off.'

She caught his eye and smiled.

It was something his grandmother used to say, the old lady who'd been half Jake's size even when he was in high school.

But she'd been a formidable woman, fierce when she needed to be but generous too. She'd taken one look at Laura that first afternoon and pulled her into the kitchen, setting hot scones and home-made jam in front of her and proceeding to make her feel as if she'd come home.

It had been a long time since anywhere had felt like home to Laura, even before her mother died. In those last couple of years her mother had been a shadow of her old self and it had been Laura looking after her instead of the other way around.

'Are you going to tell me what's up?' Jake's words cut across her maudlin thoughts, thank goodness. 'Something happened while I was gone, didn't it?'

She hadn't planned to mention it but why pretend when he'd already guessed? 'My agent called to say they'd had more calls from Greece, from Thanos Enterprises, wanting to contact me.'

Jake's mouth firmed. 'But she didn't give them your details?'

'No. She wouldn't go against my wishes like that.' But she'd counselled Laura against her decision to sever all ties, advising that if a man like Vassili Thanos really wanted to talk to her he'd eventually find a way, whether she wanted it or not. Better to talk now than make an enemy of him by playing hard to get.

Hard to get!

Bitter humour dragged Laura's mouth down at the corners. That was one thing Vassili Thanos would never accuse her of. She'd been putty in his hands. She'd been so eager for him she'd let herself be taken in by his fake niceness, his apparent honesty.

Thinking about him made her stomach churn.

She'd fallen for him like a ripe plum and she hated herself for that. She'd prided herself on her cool-headed logic. Her lack of naivety. And still…

Was that what had happened with her mum? Was that why she'd fallen for Laura's father when surely there must have been hints that he wasn't all he seemed?

But it was easy to judge in hindsight, wasn't it?

Maybe she and her mother shared a catastrophic weakness for lousy men. It was a horrifying thought.

'Whatever's going on in that brain of yours it's making you look sick.'

She jerked her head up to see Jake frowning. 'Thanks. So now I look tired *and* sick. Good to know.'

But he was right. Dwelling on what couldn't be changed wouldn't help. She'd learned that years before when her world fell apart not once but twice. First when they'd had to leave Perth and the second time when her mum died. Since then Laura had steadfastly concentrated on the present and the future.

'Thanks for getting my stuff, Jake. I really appreciate it. I'll—'

The ring of the doorbell made her jump.

It couldn't be for her. The media didn't know where she was. Even her agent didn't know. Yet her nerves jangled and her chest tightened as she struggled for breath.

'Sit tight. I'll sort it out.' Jake loped across to the tiny front hallway, closing the lounge room door behind him.

Laura made herself sip her tea, ears straining. She heard a murmur of voices, too indistinct to make out. They grew loud enough for her to identify two deep male voices.

The hairs on the back of her neck stood up. She tried to tell herself a friend of Jake had stopped by, but then why not invite him inside?

One of the voices, Jake's, grew more strident and her stomach dropped. Jake didn't do strident. He was the most laid-back guy she knew.

Could someone have followed Jake? An agent of Thanos Enterprises who'd worked out where she was? No one knew. But her hands shook. She put her mug down and got to her feet, padding across to listen at the door.

'Absolutely not! If you don't leave now I'll call the police.'

Laura didn't hear the response but recognised the answering voice.

She gasped, one hand to the wall for support, the other to her throat where her pulse hammered.

It shouldn't be possible. It really shouldn't. But as Jake's voice rose again and her skin prickled at the awareness of impending violence, she wrenched open the door.

'It's all right, Jake.'

'It's not all right. He's going now.'

Jake didn't turn, didn't shift, his wide-legged stance filling the front doorway, like a massive guard dog protecting its territory. For a second Laura imagined turning back into the lounge room letting him deal with this. But that wouldn't resolve anything.

Reluctantly she walked up behind him, putting her hand on his shoulder. 'He's here now. Let me sort this out.'

Even if it felt like facing her worst nightmare.

She'd done nothing to feel guilty about, yet her heart was heavy and her pulse skittered too fast at the prospect of what was to come.

Jake looked over his shoulder at her, then, reading her expression, stepped aside.

Beyond him, looking every bit as big and determined as her friend, was Vassili Thanos, narrowed eyes glittering and jaw set.

The man she'd hoped never to see again.

CHAPTER THREE

FURY COURSED THROUGH Vassili's blood. His vision misted as that shaggy blond giant tried to fob him off, pretending he didn't know Laura. And when that didn't work, daring to demand he leave.

The guy was dressed like a biker but the straggly hair, deep tan and coiled energy made Vassili think of a surfer. The briefing he'd received from the investigators mentioned it had been this man who'd 'discovered' Laura.

His photo of her, standing in a shallow froth of waves, laughing as she clamped a broad-brimmed hat to her head while a breeze lifted her summer dress to reveal toned legs, had launched both their careers. Hers as a model and his as a photographer.

But was he more to Laura than a professional acquaintance?

Given his bristling aggression and Laura's appearance, barefoot in a fitted tank top and filmy harem pants, it seemed all too likely.

Vassili's teeth ground so hard pain shot through his skull and his surging pulse drowned out her words.

She looked horrified to see him.

Why did that feel like a stab to the gut? She'd already rejected his attempts to reach her since his return to Greece.

No one had ever spurned him. All his life he'd been popular. Seeing Laura in the flesh, reading her dismay and instant rejection, affected him profoundly.

Especially when part of him was busy cataloguing how wonderful she looked despite the shadows under her eyes and the tension in her stiff body. She was slender, yet with those alluring curves he still dreamed about. She was supple and strong and her silky skin was softer than anything he knew.

He shouldn't want her still.

He didn't, he assured himself. He just needed to put an end to this appalling speculation.

Given the familiarity between the pair before him it was likely they *were* a couple. That was good news. It meant the pregnancy, if there was one, had nothing to do with Vassili.

He should be thanking his lucky stars.

Instead, he battled an unholy mix of emotions. A bitter brew he refused to analyse.

'You'd better come in,' she said stonily. 'Instead of making a scene out here.'

He hadn't been the one making the scene. It was her friend who'd grown agitated.

She stepped back and he entered. Her blond bodyguard folded his arms and gave him a glare that was supposed to shrivel him on the spot. Vassili ignored it. No leather-clad thug could intimidate him. In fact it would be a pleasure to teach him a lesson in manners.

But he had more important things on his mind.

He strode into the tiny flat, quickly surveying his surroundings. It looked…intimate. One long lounge, a dining table for two and on the other side of the room a small kitchen.

He heard whispers from the hallway. Laura and her friend seemed to be in disagreement. Vassili took the opportunity to investigate further, discovering a bathroom and bedroom. There was no second bedroom.

Jaw set, gut churning, he strode back to the main room. He'd come here on a fool's errand. The pair were lovers.

He paused to drag air into tight lungs.

In all probability she wasn't pregnant, or if she were, it was to her surfer boyfriend.

Why didn't that feel like a relief?

Vassili had no interest in a child that would tie him down even more. As it was he increasingly had trouble getting away to pursue his own interests. His family and the business were continually ramping up their demands. He could barely imagine the demands a baby would make.

Liar. You're not scared of a baby. You'd cope. You've coped with far worse than a surprise pregnancy.

He shoved his hands deep into his trouser pockets, trying to blot out that inner voice.

The only thing you're scared of is this feeling of losing control. These...emotions.

It had taken him years to feel as though he'd taken control of his life again but lately that restless feeling was back with a vengeance. Ever since leaving Laura.

To some he was the epitome of the privileged wastrel, permanently on holiday, pleasing himself without being tied to the burdens of responsibility. Others understood or at least suspected that he was the driving force behind Thanos Enterprises. But none of them, not even his family, realised how much self-control it had taken to build this life. To keep faith and do what he'd vowed.

The old heartache was still there, as strong as ever beneath the surface. That wasn't surprising as it was carved into his bones. Sometimes it took all his energy to ignore it or at least pretend not to be affected.

Except during that week with Laura, when all his tension had bled away. Everything kept circling back to her.

Those days in Queensland had been remarkable for many things, not least the relief he'd felt as she distracted him from the darkness inside. No effort of control had been needed. She'd filled his days and nights and all his thoughts. He'd actually been able to relax totally for the first time in years.

Was that why he felt no relief now? Instead nausea twisted inside at the idea of her with her surfer dude.

Could it be that Vassili had actually hoped she was pregnant with his own child? Because he hadn't been ready to end their liaison?

Because he still craved that unique feeling that, for a brief time at least, everything was right in the world?

Impossible. He was living the life he needed. Who could ask for more?

A door closed and Vassili sensed her enter. He turned to see her leaning back against the kitchen counter, arms crossed, the sea-green stretch fabric of her top tight across her breasts. Did they look fuller than before? His palms itched. Once they'd filled his hands perfectly. Crazy how much he wanted to touch her again.

He met her frowning stare. It was glacial.

'What are you doing here?'

He mirrored her gesture, crossing his arms and watching her attention flicker down to his chest before meeting his stare again. If she thought to intimidate him she had a lot to learn.

'Surely that's obvious. Are you pregnant?'

Hot colour washed her features before disappearing, leaving her pale. He almost regretted the need to ask. With light flooding through the balcony doors, she looked washed out, a woman who needed support, not confrontation.

But that was her fault. She'd created this situation, cutting off all contact and forcing him to come here for the truth.

'That's none of your business.' She drew a deep breath. 'Is that all? If so you can go now.'

She thought she could dismiss him? He almost laughed at her naivety. Even his uncle Constantine, the most obstinate man he knew, complained that Vassili couldn't be ordered into doing something he didn't want to.

For answer he took a seat on the lounge, palm resting on the open overnight bag beside him.

There was a bustle of movement, a waft of tropical fragrance, and Laura grabbed the bag, hauling it away before he had time to notice more than a laptop inside.

'I didn't invite you to make yourself at home.'

'No, you didn't.' Vassili shook his head. 'I call that downright unfriendly.'

'Unfriendly!' She stomped across to the kitchen, put the bag on the bench, then turned to survey him.

Instead of looking tired and stressed, her skin glowed and her eyes flashed. Suddenly she was the woman he remembered from the resort. The quicksilver, alluring woman, full of life and passion.

He'd missed her.

He hadn't admitted to himself how much he'd missed her. He felt that animal magnetism drawing him towards her. It was a sensation he'd told himself he'd imagined. But it was undeniably real. Despite his annoyance.

Vassili wanted to cut through these games and hear the truth. He wanted to find out what was wrong.

Things had been easy when they'd been together. 'Talk to me, Laura.'

'I have nothing to say to you. I want you out of my life. Why do you think I blocked your calls?'

He lifted his shoulders in an insouciant shrug that belied the tension racking his body. 'I don't know. Because your boyfriend would be upset, discovering you'd two-timed to him? Is he the jealous type?'

'He's not—' She clamped her lips shut.

He sat forward. 'Not jealous or not your boyfriend?' His guess now was both, but he had to know for sure. His pulse quickened.

'You have no role in my life. I don't want you here.'

'You've made that clear. But I'm not going until I find out the truth. Are you pregnant?'

'Even if I were, it would be *my* business, not yours.'

Never had Vassili's temper been so tested. It took every-thing he had not to react to her rudeness.

'Do you think I've travelled all the way from Greece on a whim? I need to know if you're carrying my child.'

Laura sucked in her breath, eyes rounding in dismay. Which was worse in her mind? The idea of being pregnant, or of the child being his?

Her dismay would shred a man's ego if he didn't have more important things on his mind.

'You came all the way from Greece for that?'

'Well, I certainly wasn't in the neighbourhood.' He watched her take that in. She looked more stunned than angry. He waited a beat then said softly, 'Is it just press speculation? Or are you having a child?'

Her mouth worked but she said nothing.

What was going on? It was a simple enough question.

'Surely you owe me the truth, Laura.'

That snapped her out of her funk. She straightened, hands gripping the kitchen counter behind her so tight that her knuck-les whitened.

'*I* owe *you* the truth?' Her bitter laugh held no trace of hu-mour. 'That's rich, coming from you.'

Vassili was on his feet and crossing the room in an instant. He could put up with a lot, but not someone impugning his character. He pulled up just before her, close enough to see the flecks of green and gold in her hazel eyes and to discover something other than indignation there.

Hurt? That made him pause.

When he'd left for Greece he knew Laura hadn't connected him with his well-known family. Was it possible she'd read some of the recent stories and believed them?

'I've always been straight with you, Laura. I've always told the truth.' As far as it went.

Another of those harsh laughs. It made him wince inside. He remembered Laura laughing, head back and eyes full of merriment. He remembered her soft and willing in his arms. He remembered—

'You wouldn't know the truth if it sat up and bit you. Some men are born liars.'

There was a wild look in her eyes and her breath came hard and fast. He saw the pulse jump at her throat. One of them had to de-escalate this situation.

'You shouldn't believe everything you read in the media. Most of it isn't true.'

Her eyes narrowed. 'So you didn't go back to Greece because your engagement had been announced? There was no big family party with VIPs flying in from all over Europe?'

Vassili sighed. 'It's not what it seems. Eudora and I…we're not marrying.'

'So you're not engaged?'

He paused, trying to think of a way to explain without going into detail. He'd given Eudora his word—

'You *are* engaged, then.'

Suddenly Laura sounded exhausted. He watched her colour fluctuate and knew she didn't need this stress.

'It's complicated.'

He silently cursed those complications. And the fact that he couldn't tell her about them yet. For the moment his hands were tied.

'And you think I'm incapable of understanding?' Before he could respond she shook her head, gesturing decisively with her hand. 'Actually, spare me the details, I really don't want to know. Such things are always *complicated*, aren't they?' She sneered the word as if tasting poison. 'What matters is you're engaged, yet here you are pestering me about a possible pregnancy.'

'Not a possible pregnancy.' Vassili was sure now. Laura could have given him a straight 'no' right at the start and sent him on his way. His heart beat faster. 'You're pregnant.'

That was what mattered. Not the mess his family had created of his life.

Her gaze flickered away, settling at a point beyond his shoulder. Her mouth twisted.

'Laura.' He made his voice coaxing, and watched her exhale slowly. Whatever was going on here she was severely stressed. He suspected it took all her strength to stand and face him. Regret stirred. 'Is it that you're thinking of a termination?'

'No!'

Her expression was a picture of dismay as she clamped her mouth shut. He had no doubt she meant it and equally that she hadn't meant to reveal that, since it proved she was indeed pregnant.

Something fluttered high in his chest. A feeling he had no name for. Relief?

It couldn't be excitement at the idea of having a child. He wasn't ready for children. He'd assumed he never would be.

The idea of fatherhood, continuing the family genes into another generation and being responsible for his own brood, made fear lurch through him. The notion was too entangled with the painful past, too mired in complicated emotions.

Vassili made an effort to focus. 'So you want to keep the child.' Still she didn't look at him. 'Is it mine or your boyfriend's?'

Slowly she turned, gaze locking on his, and there it was again, that sensation he'd felt so often when they'd been together. A tingling, a sense of anticipation.

In other circumstances he'd have called it delight but the look on her face, ravaged by distress, negated that. His gut curdled and he felt flummoxed, unsure how to proceed.

Was her reaction distress at being pregnant? Or solely because of him being here? Once he wouldn't have believed it but being with Laura taught him that so much he'd once considered impossible could be real.

Like the desire to be with a woman who so clearly rejected him.

Rejected *him*, or the man she thought he was after reading the news?

He raked his hand through his hair, frustrated at his inability to break through her stasis. He was used to action, quick decisions, and pivoting from a problem to a solution. But everything about this situation warned him to be cautious.

He stepped back, out of her personal space, though his instincts screamed that he should be gathering her close.

To comfort her, or himself?

Vassili frowned. Since when did he need comforting? The idea was laughable.

'Listen, Laura. You obviously need rest. I can come back later and we'll talk.'

That would give him time to gather his scattered wits. He was still processing the reality of her pregnancy.

He burned to know if the child was his as he suspected but he refused to push her so hard she collapsed.

'No. We'll talk now and then you can go. It won't take long.'

She straightened from the kitchen counter and walked to the small dining table, taking a chair. Vassili followed. She thought to dismiss him. Obviously she didn't yet have his measure.

Laura clasped her hands together on the table. 'It's true, I'm pregnant.'

'And you've moved in here because he's the father? Or for privacy?'

Vassili knew from the investigator's report that she had her own place in another Sydney suburb. It was only this morning when he'd touched down in Australia that he'd received an update that she was at this address.

She took her time responding. Long enough for him to decide she'd make a great negotiator if ever Thanos Enterprises needed one. Letting silence stretch while your counterpart hung on an answer was a tried-and-true tactic.

Yet Vassili guessed she wasn't trying to make him squirm. She looked to be battling emotions.

That tempered his blazing impatience. Badgering her wouldn't help. Nevertheless it took everything he had to wait, suppressing the turbulent feelings boiling inside.

He'd only experienced something similar once, over a decade ago, when his world had imploded and he'd learned that the unthinkable had become real. This situation had that same sense of unreality that threatened to overwhelm him.

He'd told himself it couldn't happen again. How wrong he'd been.

Laura drew a deep breath, then another, trying to use the calming techniques she'd taught herself in her teens. They didn't work. She was out of practice.

She suppressed rising laughter that felt too close to hysteria. It was years since she'd faced the stress of sudden life-changing news. She was sorely out of practice.

'Laura?'

She looked up into dark eyes and for a moment fooled herself into believing she read concern there.

Don't let him trick you. Don't trick yourself. Don't be taken in by him.

Once was understandable. After all, he was gorgeous, sexy and charming. But twice...nothing would excuse being taken in twice.

No matter how much she wanted to believe in his sincerity.

She squared her shoulders. 'Jake and I are old friends. He offered me somewhere to stay where the press couldn't find me.'

Though how long before they started hounding her friends she didn't know. Would they make that connection? Her friendship with Jake was no secret.

'Friends, not lovers?'

She hesitated, wanting, badly, to lie and say they were lovers. Anything to send Vassili Thanos packing. She despised him but even so he was dangerous. No other man had ever affected her the way he did.

Even now, when he'd made a fool of her and cheated on his fiancée, turning Laura into an unwilling third of a love triangle—make that sex triangle, since what they shared was nothing like love—she had an almost overwhelming temptation to lean into him and pretend he could make everything turn out right.

That stiffened her spine!

Never, since she'd been twelve and seen the world stripped bare of its comfortable fantasies, had she expected any man to save her.

She'd save herself if necessary.

Besides, having a baby might require all sorts of adjustments but it was hardly the end of the world.

She lifted her chin and met his eye. 'Jake and I aren't lovers.'

Laura watched Vassili's big chest rise on a deeply indrawn breath. No doubt it wasn't what he wanted to hear.

He'd come here hoping to discover there *was* no baby, or at best that it wasn't his. She couldn't imagine his glamorous fiancée in Greece being happy at the news he was expecting a child with another woman.

Yet if it didn't matter, why come himself?

Why not send some underling to buy her silence about their affair or offer child maintenance?

Laura couldn't figure him out. But there was a sure-fire way to do that. It would also achieve what she wanted—him disappearing from her life for good.

She clasped her hands over her stomach and met his eyes defiantly. 'I'm pregnant with your baby.'

CHAPTER FOUR

HE STILLED, his features turning blank and unreadable.

Vassili looked like one of those classical statues she'd seen in art books at school. The broad forehead, straight nose and high cheekbones that balanced a solid, squared-off jaw made a combination that radiated powerful masculinity. His close-cropped hair had a tendency to curl. He even had that same faraway look in his eyes as if he saw beyond her to some distant scene.

But he was no marble hero. His flesh was a warm olive tone and his pulse kicked hard at the base of his throat.

She remembered kissing him there, inhaling the exotic yet gloriously welcoming scent of his skin, feeling his powerful life force as they lay together and—

Laura sucked in a shamed breath.

There'd be no more fantasies about Vassili Thanos. He was a rich playboy who had holiday affairs while his long-suffering fiancée kept the home fires burning in Greece.

His immobility now told its own story. Despite his tale about crossing the globe to get the truth, he hadn't been prepared for it.

No doubt he'd hoped there was no baby.

Laura folded her arms protectively across her body.

Until now the only physical evidence of the baby had been missed periods and a bit of morning sickness. It was still hard to believe she was pregnant. Yet looking into his shuttered features she knew a sudden, compelling need to protect this new life. Because if she guessed right, he'd want nothing to do with it.

She was all this child had.

That knowledge sank deep into her soul, dredging up echoes of her relationship with her mother.

But she'd be stronger than her mum. No matter what, she wouldn't give up, she'd be there through thick and thin for her child. The knowledge was totally instinctive, but no less true for that.

She sat straighter, finding welcome calm. She was a fighter. She'd fight to make a bright future for herself and her baby.

Pregnancy hadn't been in her plans, at least not yet. But despite the baby's links to this man she despised, she already felt protective. Enough to know she'd be devastated if something happened to it.

'You've seen a doctor?'

His gaze was sharp. She could almost see the thoughts whipping through his head.

'Not yet.'

'But it's been months!'

'I've been busy.'

Fortunately she'd had almost back-to-back work. The money would come in useful now she was planning a future for two.

'So maybe you got a false positive to the pregnancy test?'

'That would make things a lot easier for you, wouldn't it, Vassili?' She didn't hide her contempt. 'No need for uncomfortable explanations to your fiancée would be needed then.'

If he intended telling her. Maybe he hoped to bury the news by buying Laura's silence or threatening her into it. No doubt after he insisted on a paternity test.

As if she had any interest in telling the world she'd been fool enough to fall for his dark-eyed charm! It was a momentary weakness she preferred to forget.

Vassili's eyes narrowed as if he took issue with her taunt. Laura didn't care. She carried the weight of guilt and horror after finding out she was the 'other woman' to his fiancée and wasn't in the mood to let him off easily.

'I've taken three separate pregnancy tests, all different brands. The chances of them all showing positive are slim, don't you think?'

He inclined his head. 'You still need to see a medical professional.'

Laura cocked her head to the side, surveying him. 'You really are desperate for there not to be a baby, aren't you?'

His mouth tightened. Something flickered in his eyes and was gone before she could identify it. 'Actually, I was thinking of your health, and the baby's.'

Heat scalded her throat. He'd been concerned about her well-being?

More likely he was simply a plausible liar. That fitted with her own previous experience and what she knew of him.

For that short time at the resort those old prejudices had fallen away. She'd trusted Vassili on the spur of the moment because she'd felt a powerful connection to him, the like of which she'd never known before. She hadn't been foolish enough to believe she'd found a life partner but she'd believed him to be genuine.

That was why anger as well as hurt were now so deeply embedded within her. It hurt with a freshness that belied all the defences she'd built, to be betrayed all over again. She felt ravaged by it.

'What do you *want*, Vassili? You've come all this way. What's your plan?'

The sooner she knew, the sooner she could get him out of her life.

For the first time since his arrival his mouth tucked up at one corner in a hint of a smile. Laura felt a tug of sensation deep inside, a trickle of appreciation, of response, and it shocked her to the core.

'Plan? My plan was to find out if you were okay. To find out if there was a child. That's as far as I'd got.'

She leaned back and recrossed her arms. 'You expect me to believe that? You may be a layabout but you're rich and powerful. You can't be happy about the prospect of an inconvenient, unwanted child.'

That half-smile disappeared abruptly. He sat forward. The table was so tiny she felt the ripple of energy emanating from him as he invaded her space. Because she'd called him a layabout? He'd confessed he spent a lot of the time travelling the world in search of adventure. Clearly he didn't need to work to support himself.

'Who said he'd be unwanted?'

He? He'd already decided it was a boy?

Laura was torn between indignation at his male assumption the child would have that so important Y chromosome, and surprise at the implication he'd welcome the baby. It couldn't be true, could it?

'You want children?'

Of course he wants children.

Weren't the Greeks supposed to be big on family? He probably imagined a sturdy little boy in his own image, with liquid dark eyes and a smile that would tempt the devil.

'It looks like I don't have any choice in the matter.'

So he wasn't happy about the news. Yet for a moment she'd thought she'd seen a spark of excitement in his expression.

'It must be a shock to realise some things are beyond your control.' With the sort of money he commanded Vassili was probably used to getting his way in everything.

'Oh, that's a lesson I learned a long time ago.'

Laura blinked, taking in his grim expression and harsh tone.

'So what now?' she asked. 'A paternity test? Signing some non-disclosure contract? Do you have your lawyers on speed dial?'

Whatever it took she'd do it, to get him out of her life for good.

A frown dug down between his eyebrows and his mouth

flattened. 'How about we forget the DNA test and the lawyers for now. The first thing is to get you a medical appointment.'

He pulled out his phone, as if to make one there and then. Was he trying to lull her suspicions by making her think he cared about her? Like she'd fall for that!

'*I'll* do it. I'll see my own doctor. I've been meaning to organise an appointment. I got distracted by the photographers.'

'Good. Meanwhile I'll organise better accommodation for you. This flat is cramped and anyone can get into the building. There's no security.'

Laura raised her hand. 'Stop right there. Whatever needs to be done, *I'll* do it.'

She couldn't believe she was having this conversation. Did he really believe she'd fall for his considerate act? Soon, she knew, he'd make his demands. Perhaps a gag order for her to sign, maybe he'd even threaten to fight paying child support.

Not that she wanted his money, but she was no starry-eyed innocent. She knew about the financial struggles single mothers went through.

Vassili put his phone on the table, jaw tight but expression bland, like a man determined to hide his real thoughts. She shivered.

'In the circumstances it makes sense to accept help.' When she didn't respond he went on. 'I wish you'd trust me, Laura. There are things I can't explain yet, but soon—'

'Trust!' She couldn't believe he had the temerity to say that. Not after he'd led her on, made her believe he was free to pursue their affair. Not after he'd hurt her and betrayed his fiancée. 'Absolutely not,' she said with slow deliberation, holding his stare to ensure he took in every syllable. 'That would take more time and honesty than you've got.'

His head jerked back as if she'd struck him. 'I'm all out of trust where plausible, good-looking men are concerned.'

Breath tight in her lungs, she waited for his blustering excuses. For the weasel words he'd use to try explaining away the unforgivable.

Instead he merely said softly, 'You trusted me in Queensland.'

That was a low blow. She'd been gullible in Queensland.

'That was different and you know it. I believed we were both free agents and it would be okay to indulge myself, just for once.'

His gaze sharpened as if cataloguing the admission she wasn't usually into short-term affairs. The fact she'd revealed that annoyed her. She already felt as if he'd dug deep into her soul and learned too much about her in their time together, even though she hadn't shared many details of her past.

Annoyance made her blurt out, 'In Queensland I didn't know things were so complicated.'

Laura grimaced, realising she'd used the same word Vassili had to describe his engagement. Heat seeped through her, gathering in her belly, and suddenly the toast she'd had for breakfast didn't sit so well.

'Laura, what is it? You've gone white.'

Vassili looked different. Gone was his characteristic certainty. There was no trace now of his reined-in temper or the hint of laughter that had once been so familiar. He looked… worried, the contours of his features stark and mouth taut.

Surely you're not going to be taken in so easily? Deceitful men act the part people want to see. You know that.

Abruptly she got to her feet. 'You need to go. Now.'

'Not until—'

'It's morning sickness. I'm going to vomit and I'd rather you weren't here to watch.' She paused, feeling the flesh at her hairline prickle as nausea rose. 'Please, Vassili.'

To her surprise, that was all it took.

Yet instead of speeding out of the front door, he took her elbow and led her to the bathroom, his touch solicitous, as if she were fragile.

It was the strangest feeling. One she knew she shouldn't

get used to. Fortunately, after steering her to the stool she'd placed in there, he released her. But then he surprised her by reaching for a face washer, wetting it under a tap, and wiping her face and neck.

For one glorious moment her tension eased, the dampness and his deft ministrations a blissful relief.

Until her vision blurred and nausea really took hold. 'Please, Vassili, I need to be alone.'

'We'll talk later. I'll see myself out.'

The door snicked shut and Laura was grateful there were no witnesses for what came next.

Yet as the bout of illness ended, her thoughts returned to Vassili saying they'd talk. A promise or a threat? He was a rich man determined to sort out her pregnancy to ensure the least inconvenience to him.

It was foolish to believe she'd heard warmth and caring in his tone, wasn't it?

'No, Constantine, I won't be there for the meeting.'

Walking down the street, Vassili held the phone to his ear as his uncle moved from blustering to cajoling then back again.

His patience gave way. It had been tested enough in the last couple of days since he'd arrived in Australia.

He hadn't expected a warm welcome from Laura, yet the way she'd looked at him as if he were some moustachioed villain, and her determination to keep him at arm's length, grated. He hadn't seen her since that first meeting.

Now he had important information to share, but it wasn't for a phone call. He needed a private, face-to-face meeting. But she'd refused even to let him drive her to this appointment. As if his nearness might contaminate her.

His nostrils flared in annoyance. How she'd changed from the eager lover he'd known.

No, that wasn't true. She was just as enticing, but with a haughty prickliness and steely glare that both annoyed him and made him want to seduce her back into his bed. To prove what they'd shared was real, despite what she'd read in the press.

Except seducing a woman who was tired, unwell and hounded by the paparazzi would prove him to be the selfish playboy she accused him of being.

Laura needed to hear the full truth and at last he was free to share it.

His teeth ground in frustration. Now Constantine was interfering, trying to bring him to heel. Again.

'I sent my assessment of the deal five days ago. I also provided an outline of the only circumstances in which that takeover would be worthwhile.'

Vassili had spent long days poring over the calculations, uncovering pitfalls the official figures hadn't spelled out and developing his own detailed projections.

'But the board may have questions. This is a complex negotiation, and they'd feel better if you were on hand to reassure them in person.'

Constantine would feel better, Vassili silently amended. It would give him another chance to harangue his nephew about marrying Eudora. Constantine would find an excuse to suggest an early wedding date, the earlier the better.

Because now Constantine had got it into his mind that Thanos Enterprises should stay in the family, *his* family, there'd be no let up. He'd been a loyal lieutenant to his brother-in-law, Vassili's father, and to Vassili's grandfather before that. But now he had ambitions to be more than titular head of the company. What better way to cement his role, and his family's share of future profits, than by marrying his stepdaughter to Vassili?

'If you don't trust my judgement after all this time—'

'It's not that!' Constantine said quickly.

Vassili smiled. He might avoid the day-to-day mechanics of running the business, allowing himself the freedom he needed for other things, but his uncle knew he was the brains behind the company's increasing success.

'Excellent. Then use the material I provided. If you're not confident, my assistant, Aleko, is across the details.'

Vassili looked at the number on the building before him. He'd arrived. His pulse jerked in anticipation. Or was that nerves? He hadn't allowed himself to explore his feelings too closely.

'I'm going into an appointment. If you need anything else, ask Aleko. I'll be tied up for the foreseeable future.'

'You've got a lead on a new opportunity?'

Constantine couldn't hide his interest.

At least he hadn't guessed where his nephew was or why. Vassili had been a magnet for breathless media speculation and outright lies since his teens. No one in Greece would take seriously a rumour about him fathering a child in Australia. Not yet.

'Possibly.' Vassili's mouth curved crookedly.

'Let me know if—'

'Bye, Constantine.'

He ended the call and pushed open the door to the medical facility. And discovered his heart was pounding.

Excitement or fear?

There was no time to find out for there was Laura, looking tense as she pretended to read a magazine. As he approached he saw her gaze didn't move across the pages. Did she even see them?

She bit her lip, a habit he'd only noticed since arriving in Sydney. She was nervous.

Vassili sauntered across and took the seat beside her, murmuring a compliment on her appearance.

It wasn't a lie. In a rust-red dress with a long row of buttons from neck to hem, she looked chic and sexy. He could imagine himself undoing each button, taking his time to reveal the warm flesh beneath.

His hands shook and he shoved them in his pockets because the urge to touch her was too strong.

Vassili stretched his legs out and ignored the way his nostrils quivered at the hint of lime, coconut and warm flesh from the woman beside him. He favoured her with a lazy smile as if his pulse hadn't gone haywire.

That had the desired effect. Colour rushed to her cheeks, that blank look of nerves disappearing as she focused on disliking him.

That was better. Her fragility made him uncomfortable. He wanted to chase the shadows from her eyes.

He could even grow to enjoy her dislike. Especially as he guessed it meant her passion for him wasn't completely dead. If it were, he doubted she'd be so volatile around him.

Or maybe you're just full of yourself. When was the last time any woman said no to you?

'Ms Bettany?' A smiling woman stood before them, holding a clipboard. 'I'm ready for you now.' She glanced at Vassili. 'And your partner can come too.'

He waited for Laura to say he'd come in later. After all, she hadn't invited him to her doctor's appointment, and he'd been surprised she'd suggested he attend her scan.

Could she be having a change of heart?

Hardly. Laura cast him a swift sideways look, mouth tight as if he were some necessary evil she'd decided she had to endure, then nodded.

So much for the theory that the Thanos men were irresistible to women, as Theo used to brag. But then Theo had never met a woman so determined to be unimpressed.

Ten minutes later Vassili was trying to look calm as Laura lay on her back and the technician prepared her for the ultrasound. The red dress was partly unbuttoned to reveal his ex-lover's abdomen, which had begun to swell with pregnancy.

Something shot through him, a startling blast of pride, wonder as her pregnancy became incontrovertibly real.

And more. The last time he'd seen so much of her body, they'd been naked together. Even now, in this clinical setting, he found the sight of all that silky, smooth flesh distinctly erotic.

What was wrong with him? He had a healthy sexual appetite but he'd never been obsessive.

With Laura he had a one-track mind.

Yet it wasn't that simple.

He wanted her physically. He'd been stunned to discover his need for her a constant ache since his return to Greece. Not even the ludicrous situation he'd been embroiled in there had the power to distract him from that. But he'd also missed her company. Her laughter. The warmth of her smile. The inexplicable sense of belonging that he hadn't identified until it was missing.

'There.' The technician drew their attention to the screen. 'There's your baby.'

He stared at the monitor, trying to make sense of what he saw. Why had he thought the image would be static? He watched, fascinated, as she pointed out a small, yet distinct, curved shape.

He heard Laura's breath catch and felt something snag high in his chest.

His child. Their child.

It was one thing to be told she was pregnant. It was quite another to see this new life beginning. To understand that, all being well, he'd be a father in several months.

Excitement and fear mingled as the responsibility that had seemed theoretical became real.

His gaze shifted to Laura, staring at the screen. Her dark lashes were spiky with moisture. He reached out to take her hand but stopped when the technician spoke again.

'Just let me take a better look. I'm not sure…'

'Not sure about what?' He and Laura spoke at the same time.

Tension seized his muscles. Was there something wrong with the baby? Some danger to Laura?

Vassili moved closer, trying to make sense of the shapes on the screen. Laura's breath hitched and he reached for her hand, squeezing it reassuringly.

Her fingers curled around his, making something inside him loosen and fall away. He breathed deep, seeking calm for her sake as much as his own. The pregnancy might be accidental but the link between them was real.

'Ah.' The woman looked at Laura then him. 'Everything looks normal with the pregnancy so far.'

'But?' Laura asked.

Vassili recognised the technician's carefully neutral expression. He'd spent enough time with medical professionals breaking traumatic news. His heart swooped low and his hand tightened on Laura's.

'There are two heartbeats. Two babies. You're expecting twins.' Now the woman smiled, even if her eyes looked wary.

'Twins!'

Vassili heard Laura's voice from a distance. The image on the screen blurred and so did his hearing. All he could hear was the gallop of his pulse and the stertorous sound of his breathing.

Shock, he realised vaguely as he shoved his hands in his pockets, trying to hide the effect of sudden, devastating emotions.

His lips twisted in a mirthless grimace. If he'd needed proof of paternity, this was it!

How had he not even considered the possibility of twins when Laura announced she was pregnant?

This news ripped his world in half, all over again. He stood in this sterile room with two women whose conversation came to him as distant whispers he couldn't decipher. But suddenly he was back in Greece, at another medical facility, losing the other half of himself.

Vassili struggled to swallow, the rusty taste of blood on his tongue mingling with the ancient bitterness of grief.

All he could think of was Theo. Of the things they'd shared, not just experiences and emotions but the connection others never fully understood. The unspoken communication. The prickling awareness when something was wrong with the other. The stark devastation when…

He hauled air into protesting lungs. They'd lost so much. Now Theo was gone and Vassili had never completely recovered. He'd done his best to hide his devastation, keeping busy and constantly on the move. Filling his hours so there was no time left to feel.

Except he always remembered. He always would.

Now here he was, in a country Theo had never visited, and it was the closest he'd felt to his brother in years.

Vassili hugged the sensation close, like a miser hoarding gold. Despite the pain, he didn't want it to end. For despite his efforts all these years to keep Theo's spirit alive, that sense of connection with his beloved brother had gradually faded.

Anguish reverberated through him. He felt his loss as keenly as he had a decade ago. It was so raw, a physical weight in his belly. He felt sick with grief. He wanted to turn tail and find somewhere private to grieve.

But he couldn't.

Laura and their babies were relying on him.

He looked down to find her hazel gaze fixed on him and finally remembered how to breathe.

CHAPTER FIVE

LAURA FELT VASSILI's hand fall away and turned to see him step back, his features turning first white then grey.

Her throat closed. Just as well or she would have blurted out his name, and she *didn't* want to sound needy.

Even if, right now, she felt it.

She'd never even considered the possibility of twins. The news of one child had been surprise enough, but looking after two newborns? Not just newborns. She had a mental image of herself struggling with twin toddlers. She knew people did it, knew it must be exciting as well as challenging. But in this first moment the news felt daunting.

Would she be up to it?

It was rare that Laura indulged in self-pity. But in this moment she'd give a lot to have her mother back. To have a family who'd support her. A partner who loved and cared about her.

She heard the technician murmur something about giving them time as she turned away. Vassili didn't respond. He seemed to be somewhere else, even though he stood beside her.

That's one way to get the measure of a man. Confront him with twins and see how he reacts.

Laura squeezed her eyes shut, knowing she was being unfair. She was in shock herself. Already she struggled with fear that something might go wrong in the pregnancy, plus doubts about her ability to cope when they were born.

Surely they'd be born safely, both of them.

She couldn't blame Vassili for being stunned.

But when she opened her eyes he didn't meet her look. He was staring into space, his expression...*haunted*.

As if facing his worst nightmare.

So much for his talk about supporting her and the baby. About having a role in their child's life. He hadn't been specific about how that would work, yet he'd sounded serious.

He'd backed off enough not to protest when she visited her doctor alone. Nor had he kept pushing her to leave Jake's. He'd behaved reasonably, as if he understood nagging wouldn't help either of them. Fortunately Jake had spent the last few nights at a friend's place so Laura had had space to think. Not that it had got her far. She still didn't know what to do about Vassili.

Except she'd invited him to attend this scan. Because, come what may, he was the father.

Now she regretted it. She realised that over the past couple of days he'd got under her skin again.

Again! Who do you think you're fooling? From the moment he walked in the door you felt the connection, as fresh as ever.

She'd been furious with him but even that hadn't killed the attraction she'd assured herself was dead.

How wrong she'd been.

Since his arrival Vassili had surprised her. There'd been no attempt to buy her off or deny paternity. No insistence on a DNA test. His focus seemed directed totally at keeping her safe from the press and ensuring she got medical advice.

He'd lulled her into thinking he genuinely cared about her child.

Seeing him withdraw now was a wake-up call. For all his fine words earlier, the reality of her pregnancy was too much for him.

Laura needed to be strong, for herself and the babies. She couldn't let herself trust that he'd be around to provide support.

Fleetingly she thought of her mother, struggling alone in a new city, finding work and dealing with a traumatised child without family or friends to help. Laura might not have family, but she had friends, good friends, and savings. She'd be okay. *They'd* be okay.

The technician walked back in, her gaze skating from Vassili to Laura. 'I take it there isn't a history of twins in the family? It can be a real surprise.'

'You can say that again.' Laura avoided looking at Vassili and conjured a small smile. 'And, no, there aren't any twins in the family.'

Better to say that than admit she had no idea. Her mother had never mentioned twins in her family. As for her father, he'd said he was an only child. But he'd said a lot of things and she'd learned, too late, not to believe him. He lied as easily as breathing. Perhaps he had lots of siblings she knew nothing about.

One thing was for sure, Laura wouldn't be seeking them out.

'Actually,' a gravelly voice said, 'twins run in my family.'

She turned her head to see Vassili had moved closer again. Close enough for her to see the deeper lines grooved around his mouth and something in his eyes that hadn't been there five minutes ago.

For the next little while the conversation centred around identical and fraternal twins, with Vassili displaying an in-depth knowledge.

Laura was about to question him on that when the technician suggested she might wish to have another chat with her doctor in light of the news. Not that there was anything wrong, the woman said hastily, but because expecting parents inevitably had more questions about multiple births.

After cleaning off the gel used for the ultrasound and buttoning her dress, Laura walked on wobbly legs towards the door.

Vassili reached for her but she hurried forward before he could make contact. She'd turned down the footpath towards the bus stop when his voice stopped her.

'Laura, we need to talk.'

He didn't crowd or try to touch her. He didn't try to bully

her but simply stood, tall and implacable, with an air of permanence as if no amount of force would make him leave her side.

Laura sucked in a breath, trying not to find that appealing.

Just because your dad was totally unreliable, it doesn't mean you have to go weak at the knees over a bit of masculine stubbornness and the fact he hasn't run away with his tail between his legs. He's probably too stunned to make a quick getaway. Give it time.

Yet when she met Vassili's gaze he didn't look stunned. He looked…steadfast.

A bitter laugh welled in her throat. It didn't take a psychologist to know where that wishful thinking came from. The past had marked her. Which was why the way Vassili had betrayed her and his fiancée was so untenable.

'I know the results of the scan were a surprise,' he said in a reassuring tone as if he'd seen her momentary panic earlier. 'It's a lot to take in. But there are things we need to discuss too.'

Damn him for being so reasonable. It was easier when she could be furious with him. But it was true, now more than ever there were things to sort out. Avoidance hadn't worked. It was time to confront this.

Laura inclined her head. 'Yes, there are.' The sooner they talked, the sooner he'd leave and she could breathe again. 'Shall we go to a café?'

'I'd prefer privacy. I'll drive you to the flat.'

She wanted to protest because having him in that small space had been difficult enough the first time. Despite her anger and sense of betrayal, she'd reacted to his nearness in ways that didn't bear thinking about.

But they *did* need privacy.

'Okay,' she said finally. 'Let's sort this out.'

Soon she was ensconced in a purring silver sports car, marvelling at the way he handled it so easily in the busy, unfamiliar streets. As if he were the local, not she.

Watching his hands on the wheel and his easy control of

the powerful vehicle, Laura admired his unfussy competence. She felt safe with him.

Then she remembered him saying he'd driven in races and long-distance car rallies.

Another reminder that their lives were worlds distant, barely intersecting.

Apart from the sex.

She winced and looked out the window.

'Laura, are you all right? Should I pull over?'

She hunched her shoulders, hating that he noticed her reactions. Once that had made her feel special. Now it felt intrusive.

'I'm fine.' It was a lie. She felt discombobulated by today's news, but they'd have their discussion and then he'd leave.

Is that why you've avoided discussing this properly? Because once everything is sorted you won't see him again?

Impossible! She *needed* him gone. Needed to get her life back on track.

The sound of swearing shook her from her reverie. Not that she understood the Greek words, but there was no mistaking Vassili's tone.

The car slowed and abruptly took a corner. As they turned, Laura saw a gaggle of people outside Jake's block of flats. The sun glinted off a large telephoto lens.

'Photographers.' She felt sick as the confines of the car seemed to shrink alarmingly around her. 'How did they find…?'

Any idea that he'd given away her location died when she read Vassili's scowl as he made another turn, manoeuvring through the back streets.

'It's amazing it's taken this long to locate you. They're probably going through everyone you know.'

Laura pressed a hand to her fluttering heart. None of her friends had mentioned it and she'd naïvely thought that media interest was easing. Her friends had been protecting her, not worrying her with the news. How naïve she'd been. Vassili Thanos was too big a drawcard.

She fumbled for her phone, hitting speed dial for Jake but getting a recorded message.

'If he has any sense he won't answer his phone.'

Laura turned her head, surprised that Vassili read her actions so easily.

He shrugged. 'When you grow up in the limelight you learn their ways.'

Mutely she nodded. He'd grown up rich and privileged, in the media spotlight.

'How can you bear it?'

'Mainly by ignoring it when I can.' She watched his mouth twist and felt a strange pang. 'For now I'll settle for getting you somewhere safe.'

'Any suggestions?'

She was a woman who made her own way and her own decisions. She had done since her teens. But stupefied by the news she was having twins, and vulnerable in the face of those voracious photographers, Laura wasn't too proud to accept help.

'Yes.' He changed lanes, heading towards the centre of the city. 'I just need to organise it.'

He said something in Greek and his phone, on hands-free, lit up. He spoke and after a few seconds a man answered in Greek.

Laura had no hope of following the conversation. Her knowledge of the language consisted of *moussaka*, *souvlaki* and *giros*, the few Greek dishes she knew.

Her thoughts circled uselessly, too stunned to lead anywhere useful. Finally, lulled by the movement of the car, she gave in to the exhaustion that plagued her and closed her eyes.

When she woke they'd stopped. There was no conversation in Greek. Nothing but the tick of the cooling engine. And a comforting waft of cinnamon, soap and the tang of warm male flesh.

Her nostrils quivered as she inhaled.

Suddenly aware, she opened her eyes and turned.

Vassili was in the driver's seat, his eyes locked on her.

That was what she'd felt, that tingling, heated sensation as his gaze rested on her face, her breasts, then back up to her mouth, and finally her eyes.

He said nothing, nor did he look away.

Laura felt that whoosh of ignition, as everything inside her burst into flames. In her abdomen fire swirled. Even the blood rushing through her arteries seemed hotter and faster. She saw the change in his dark eyes, the flare of something that matched her own delight.

Joy rose. Relief and exultation, that sense of everything being right again.

One of them moved closer. His lips parted and that heated stare dropped to her mouth that pouted in anticipation.

It was only as she leaned closer and felt her seat belt tighten that she came back to herself.

The pregnancy. Twins. The paparazzi. Vassili engaged to someone else.

Laura reared back, her shoulder against the door, breathing ragged as if she'd just finished her morning run instead of simply found the will to pull back from a man she knew was dangerous.

What had happened to her? Why couldn't she squash this weakness for him?

'Where are we?'

She turned to survey the cement walls and had her answer. An underground car park.

'Somewhere private,' came that deep voice. It rippled across sensitive nerve-endings like sunlight turning water into a blinding dapple of diamonds. She felt it as tiny dabs of heat warming not just her skin but other parts of her body, deep inside and vulnerable.

Her breath caught. How could two simple words do that?

Because that soft suede voice with the tantalising accent took her back to days and nights of unfettered bliss. Because she yearned for the incredible feeling of intimacy she'd shared with him, despite knowing now that it was tainted.

'Come. Let's get you somewhere comfortable.'

For a second Laura was tempted to say she wasn't going anywhere, but staying in Vassili's car wasn't an option.

Minutes later they emerged from a private lift into the most amazing apartment she'd ever seen.

The enormous living area was all windows on two sides. One side looked towards the Sydney Harbour Bridge and Circular Quay where busy yellow and green ferries chuntered in and out. That was spectacular enough. Until she turned and saw the view across the lush Botanic Gardens to the vast harbour sprawling eastwards with its inlets and promontories, all the way to the sea.

'Where are we?'

'A friend's place. He's rarely here and offered it to me. It's more private than a hotel.'

Laura nodded. She surveyed the expensive furnishings and the glimpse of a corridor that seemed to go on for ever.

'A penthouse?'

'Yes.' He gestured towards a sofa long enough to fit a netball team. 'I'll get some drinks. What would you like?'

To stretch out on those plump, pale cushions and sleep for a week.

Laura started. This was no time to rest. She had to keep her wits about her. She'd love a coffee but last time she'd tried her stomach had rebelled. 'Tea please, with a little milk.'

When he returned with a tray she was ensconced in a wing chair positioned for the view, shoes off and feet up on an ottoman.

None of her furniture was this comfortable. But then, if you had the wealth to buy a penthouse with billion-dollar views you could afford the best. The chair was probably made of some rare, expensive metal and hand-stitched upholstery stuffed with finest goose down.

'So,' she said when she'd sipped her tea and he'd settled on the sofa, 'you want to talk.'

About the babies? Or was he going to try explaining how he'd had a beautiful woman waiting in Greece to marry him, while Laura and he had their holiday romance? That thought still made her feel sick.

But she'd avoided this conversation too long. She hadn't been ready for it, had been too flabbergasted by the fact Vassili Thanos had turned up, and *stayed*, acting as if he really wanted to be an involved father.

The idea had rocked the foundations of her world. She wanted to believe it might be true because then he couldn't be as awful as she'd assumed. But hard-learned experience insisted it couldn't be. And if it were, imagine the complications of sharing a child…children with a mega-rich, married man.

'Do you feel differently now it's twins?' she blurted out. Would that test his apparent willingness to get involved?

'Differently?' He tilted his head. 'Because there's more than one?' To her amazement, his mouth kicked up in a smile that shattered some of her rigid shock. 'Of course not.' He paused, eyes narrowing. 'Do you?'

Laura shrugged. 'Yes. No.' She lifted her shoulders. 'It's made it more…overwhelming. I'm still grappling with the idea of a baby and now there are two.'

She bit her lip rather than admit she worried she might not cope. Could she manage two babies and a fledgling business? She couldn't see herself getting or holding down any modelling gigs after the births.

How far would her savings stretch? She'd earmarked them for her company. Now she'd have to re-evaluate.

Her eyes met Vassili's. He offered support but at what price?

His gaze softened and he leaned forward, elbows on his knees. 'It will be okay, Laura. You're not alone in this, remember that.'

With a deep sigh, she expelled the breath that had caught in her lungs. He was right. She was panicking instead of doing what she'd always done, make the best of the situation she found herself in and strive to make things better. Today's events, the paparazzi outside the flat and the news of the twins, had thrown her.

She breathed slowly and felt that flurry of trepidation ease.

'First things first,' he said. 'You need rest and privacy, time to come to terms with this news.'

Laura nodded. That sounded reasonable. Maybe then she'd finally be able to focus on negotiating with Vassili and planning the future.

'You can't do that in Sydney, being hounded by photographers. You need to get away.'

'That's easier said than done.'

Holidays cost and she didn't want to squander her savings when she'd need them later, even if Vassili offered to help support the twins financially.

'Actually, it's incredibly easy. It's all arranged. I sorted it out on the drive here.'

'You arranged it?'

She'd thought they were coming here for a discussion. Not for him to tell her what he'd decided.

He nodded and sat back, looking pleased. 'I know the perfect place with complete privacy, away from prying eyes. We'll need your passport, which I'm sure Jake could bring here for you.'

'My passport?'

She'd got one last year when she'd been in the running for a shoot in Fiji. But the job had fallen through and she'd never left the country.

'Yes. You'll need it to come to Greece.'

His smile widened. He looked like a magician who'd pulled a rabbit from his hat, awaiting applause.

Laura folded her arms and shook her head. Her skin crawled. 'I don't think your fiancée would approve. And I refuse to be flaunted as *the other woman*.'

CHAPTER SIX

VASSILI'S SMILE DIED.

Any objective observer would know he should have explained about that before anything else. Set the record straight for Laura. He'd felt her anger at what she believed about his behaviour but hadn't fully felt the depth of her hurt until today.

The problem was that he wasn't objective. His head, his feelings, were all over the place. He'd been caught up in the emotion of seeing their babies, and so soon afterwards, the press pack on her doorstep. Too caught up in the need to look after this woman who needed his help.

He'd simply done what he did best, take action to fix things. After years of adventurous, sometimes dangerous pursuits, he had a habit of quick decision-making and follow-through. It had saved his life, and others'. It paid off in business too, the ability to act swiftly, without hesitation.

But it's not your choice to make. It's hers.

Even if his only thought was for her well-being.

He hated that she thought the worst of him. It was natural since she didn't know the truth of his situation. Yet a foolish part of him had hoped the time they'd spent together had showed her what sort of man he *really* was. That he'd never behave in the way she believed.

'I never asked Eudora to marry me.'

He couldn't be blunter than that.

Disapproving eyes regarded him. Laura's tone was disbelieving. 'She just assumed you would?'

'It's not like that. I told you I'm not marrying.' He raked his hand through his hair.

'Yet you're engaged.'

'Look, it's a difficult situation.' Of course she didn't look convinced. 'It's a family thing...'

At the look on Laura's face he stopped. He felt a hammering in his chest where his heart beat too high and fast. Not because she was angry, but because he'd hurt her.

Of course she's hurt. She thinks you had an affair with her while committed to someone else.

Her eyes looked bruised. He hated seeing her that way.

'You don't think I've got the imagination to understand? Because I told you I have no family?' Her mouth crumpled and he felt as if he'd been stuck with a knife. 'I suppose you've got a huge family that—'

'No!'

Every muscle tensed. Every time he opened his mouth around Laura he put his foot in it. Everything came out wrong, even when he tried to explain.

It wasn't made easier by the fact he still wanted her with a potent need. Her determination to find fault hadn't diminished that. He only had to look at her and everything he'd learned about being charming flew out the window.

Usually he was fluent and persuasive, but since he'd arrived in Sydney it was one step forwards in his relationship with her and six back. He'd rarely felt at such a loss.

Instinct urged him to hold Laura close. Physically they'd always connected. But he couldn't when he was the one hurting her.

'I have a small family. Just big enough to drive me crazy.' Something glinted in her eyes. Understanding? He probably imagined it. 'If you'll let me explain?'

Perhaps he should have blurted the truth the moment he

landed in Australia. He'd wanted to, badly, but he'd given his word to keep the real situation secret, and Vassili never broke a promise.

There'd been no excuse for such stupidity on his part. Before he left Greece he should have spoken to Eudora about telling Laura everything. His only excuse had been the thorn of jealousy that lodged deep under his skin when he'd learned of her close friendship with Jake.

He'd come to Australia torn between believing Laura was carrying *his* child, and silently raging that she was now with someone else. Vassili had never been jealous before and it had thrown him.

Laura sat back. 'I'm listening.'

'Neither I nor Eudora were consulted about this engagement. Neither of us want it and there's no way we're going to marry. We're more like siblings than cousins.'

'Stranger things have happened.'

It was as if Laura was determined not to be convinced. What had made her so eager to believe the worst?

Vassili shrugged. 'Nevertheless, it's not going to happen. Especially now, with the news that we're expecting twins.'

Her eyes rounded but she said nothing.

'Come on, Laura. Do you really believe I'd marry anyone else when you're carrying my babies?'

Her face flushed then turned chalk white. He reached out to her but she shook her head.

'Don't try to change the subject!' Her eyes flashed. 'You're telling me about your engagement.'

Something was going on here that he couldn't comprehend. What had he missed? Laura's distrust was so ingrained…

No time for that now. The sooner she knew the truth, the sooner they could move ahead.

'My mother and her brother concocted the scheme. These days they see a lot of each other. Since my father's death Constantine has run Thanos Enterprises as CEO.'

'Why not you? Because you're unreliable?'

She really was eager to stick the knife in.

'Actually, no. In fact I have a knack for business.'

Theo had teased him about it, saying that Vassili would spend his life wearing a pinstriped suit, with his nose in a ledger. Meanwhile Theo would enjoy a life of freedom and excitement because the routine of nine-to-five drudgery would kill him.

Vassili's mouth dug down at the corners as a familiar shudder, like skeletal fingers playing on his vertebrae, rippled down his spine.

He exhaled gustily. 'I didn't want the CEO role. I work for the company but there are other things I want to do too.'

'Travelling the world, swimming with sharks, sledding down glaciers and having affairs.'

He shrugged. 'Life is for living.'

You never knew how long it would last. Look at his father and Theo, both gone before their time.

He refused to be drawn on the comment about affairs. She wouldn't believe him if he admitted there were far fewer than the press believed, or that what he'd shared with her had felt unique.

'And this is somehow relevant to your engagement?'

Laura's look was piercing, but he'd take that over the profound dismay he'd seen earlier.

'My mother has wanted me to settle down for years.'

She'd be ecstatic when she heard about the twins. The thought of her excitement made him both happy and nervous. Minute by minute these babies were becoming more real.

'But you don't want to marry? You enjoy your freedom too much.'

His head shot up, eyes locking on Laura's. That wasn't a question. She thought she knew him and was ready to judge. Again he picked up steely disapproval.

He didn't recall that from their time in Queensland, when

she'd seemed so positive and carefree. Was it reserved for him or did it run deeper?

Did that explain why she hadn't wanted to tell him about the pregnancy?

'It wasn't about marriage so much as being in Greece more. Not globetrotting.'

Because his mother wanted him *safe*. Theo's death still threw a long shadow.

'As for my uncle… He's CEO of the company and is rewarded extremely well for that, but he's not a majority shareholder. He's not a Thanos.' Vassili shrugged. 'Over time he's grown used to the position a bit too much. Eudora is his stepdaughter. She and I have known each other all our lives. If we were to marry then he, via her, would have a greater stake in the business empire he's nurtured these last years, and its profits.'

'He wants you to marry her for the money?'

'Don't look surprised. It's a good deal of money and Constantine has developed a taste for it.'

Vassili realised he did the man a disservice. He spread his hands. 'My uncle isn't a bad man. In fact he's been good to me. But he and my mother came from a very poor family. He's worked hard to get where he is. If he could see his stepdaughter marry into money and the safety net that provides, he'd be a happy man.'

Laura's eyes narrowed. 'I don't understand. You and your cousin are adults. You can stand up to family pressure and say no.'

'That's what we did. They'd raised the idea some time ago and we refused. The public announcement was meant to force our hands. Constantine still thinks Eudora is a little girl who will eventually do what her dad decrees.'

'She's not going to agree?'

A huff of laughter formed on his lips at the memory of Eudora last time they'd discussed this. She'd been furious and implacable.

'Never. She has plans that definitely don't include me. Which brings me to the reason I couldn't tell you the whole story when I got to Australia—'

'Because I'm not entitled to the truth?' But Laura looked more puzzled than furious. Maybe he was making progress.

'I'd promised not to tell anyone, because if news gets out it could spoil everything. But once I realised you were pregnant with my child…children…'

He was still absorbing that revelation. Was it crazy to feel this excitement? This wouldn't be straightforward. Especially as Laura didn't trust him. Was he ready for fatherhood?

But life was about making the most of what you had, whether you felt ready or not. And family was something he couldn't ignore.

Vassili caught and held Laura's gaze, trying to ignore the sizzle of response in his blood and low in his belly. He shifted his weight.

'What I have to tell you is confidential but now I have Eudora's permission to share it. I know you'll respect that confidence. I trust you, Laura.'

If only she'd trust him.

'Go on.'

'Eudora does want to marry, but not me. She's in love with someone else. But her father won't like the match.'

Laura shook her head. 'As I said before, your cousin is an adult. Surely it's her decision—'

'Try telling that to her father. He was brought up in a very traditional family with old-fashioned views. Eudora seems quiet but she has a spine of steel. He thinks, because she doesn't argue with him outright, that she'll accept his demands.'

'Is her choice so unsuitable?'

'He's head over heels in love with her. From what I've seen

he's decent, hard-working and devoted. But he's not Greek. He arrived there by boat as a refugee, leaving everything behind. He's about to study medicine with a charity scholarship. But Constantine won't see the positives. He has prejudices and the idea of Eudora marrying a foreigner...'

'If that's true she could just marry him. I don't see why the pair of you don't announce publicly that you're not engaged.'

Laura was determined not to believe him. Vassili drew a slow breath.

'Because he's applied for permanent residency. The decision will be made soon. Eudora's afraid that if her father finds out, he'll do whatever he can to stop the approval. Technically he has no authority but who knows what damage he might do if he approaches the authorities, with stories of bad character or something similar?'

He saw understanding dawn. 'We've told the family we won't marry but Constantine thinks it's just a matter of time. Meanwhile, we're not denying it publicly. The last thing Eudora needs is for Constantine to discover the truth and try to get her partner deported.'

Laura leaned back in the wing chair. Could it be true? It sounded plausible. Outlandish, but she'd never mixed with the ultra-wealthy. Perhaps arranged marriages for money were normal among them.

She gripped the chair's upholstered arms, fighting a ballooning sense of relief.

You want to believe him, don't you?

From the first she'd wanted him to be different.

If it weren't inconceivable for her to fall in love in five days, she would have said Vassili had broken her heart when she discovered he was engaged to someone else while sharing her bed.

But Laura was protected against falling in love. She wasn't sure it could ever happen and certainly didn't expect it. The idea of her, of all people, breaking her heart over a scoundrel after a mere week was laughable.

She wasn't laughing now.

She was fighting the urge to say she believed him and then move to the sofa and cuddle against Vassili, into the comfort of his embrace.

How she longed for that.

What if Vassili wasn't a love rat after all?

Laura forced herself to be cautious. She'd received a masterclass in duplicity at a young age. She'd be foolish to ignore what she'd learned.

'Does your cousin speak English? I'd like to talk with her.'

'You don't believe me.' His voice was flat, his expression tense and she had to repress a denial.

'I want to believe you, Vassili. But I'd like to hear from Eudora. These last months I thought I was the other woman in a love triangle. I can't tell you how that hurt.'

Her voice wobbled alarmingly but she didn't look away. She wasn't ashamed of her feelings, only of what she'd believed he'd done to two unsuspecting women. Now, it appeared her first instinct about him could be right, but she needed to be sure.

'You don't trust easily.'

Laura kept her chin up. 'I've learned to be careful.'

Instead of carrying anger his features revealed what looked like sadness.

'It's the middle of the night in Greece. But I'll arrange a video call later today. Meanwhile we can discuss my plan to get you away from Sydney.' He raised his hand to forestall objections. 'I'm not asking you to commit to coming until you talk to Eudora. But we need to be ready to move as soon as you've made up your mind.'

Vassili spoke with the authority of a man used to taking control.

She'd known him as a lover, charming, carefree and seductive. Now she saw someone used to wielding power. Part of it was probably the confidence of being born into money. But Laura sensed it was more and began to wonder what his role was in the uber-successful family company. His uncle might be CEO but Laura suspected Vassili's role was no sinecure.

Had her assumptions about him spending all his time in pursuit of thrills been wrong?

Whatever the truth, he was well-connected, determined and powerful. He'd make a formidable enemy.

Laura had to resist the urge to place a protective palm over her abdomen. The one thing she did know was that there'd be no termination. She wanted her babies.

After all this time on her own, the idea of having a family, a real family, meant everything.

She'd fight for that if necessary.

Vassili was talking about flights when she cut across him. His surprised expression indicated it was rare for people to interrupt him. Or maybe that was just women. They probably hung on his every word.

'Before we get onto logistics there's something I need to know.'

She sat straighter, her feet square on the floor, hands clasped in her lap.

'Go on.'

'What are your intentions, Vassili?' She winced, realising she sounded like someone out of a Victorian novel talking about a shotgun wedding. As if she expected marriage! 'I don't mean towards me. I mean towards the babies.'

'My intentions?'

He frowned, a knot of confusion on his forehead that merely added to his attractiveness.

Silently Laura cursed overactive pregnancy hormones. This was too important for her to be distracted by lust.

'I'm their father. I want the best for them. For them to grow up happy and secure. How could you doubt that?'

His words eased a little of her strain because he'd perfectly described what she wanted. And yet…

'I mean…' her hands clenched tighter '…do you see yourself being involved?'

She couldn't go to Greece, into *his* territory, without some idea of his thinking.

His dark eyebrows furrowed down. 'I see myself being their father. Of course I'll be involved. What did you think? That I'd pay a monthly stipend to cover their expenses and never see them?'

Colour flushed his cheeks and his mouth tightened. Laura saw the tic of his throbbing pulse and realised he was incensed.

Part of her rejoiced at his reaction. She had no doubt it was genuine. He cared about these unexpected babies. Warmth filled chest. Yet at the same time that only intensified her fears.

'And how do you see my role?'

He shook his head. 'I've been speaking English since childhood, Laura, but we seem to have some language barrier. I don't understand. You'll be their mother, what else?'

Her white-knuckled grip eased and her tight jaw eased. Yet she needed complete clarity. 'Their hands-on mother.'

'Of course.'

Her spine loosened as her anxiety begin to unravel.

Nebulous fear had dogged her since Vassili's arrival. Fear that, against the odds, he might try to wrest her baby—babies, she corrected—from her.

Initially she'd been convinced he'd want nothing to do with her as an engaged man. Yet at every turn he'd surprised her. His acceptance that *he* was the father. His insistence on staying. His determination to be involved. Even the way he'd respected her wishes by giving her space until today's scan.

When he'd shown such interest she'd begun to imagine a battle for custody.

'What's going through that beautiful head of yours, Laura?'

Starting, she looked up and wished she hadn't, for once

again his gleaming gaze ensnared her. Made her want things she shouldn't.

She crossed her arms. 'I thought initially you'd deny paternity. When you didn't, when you seemed so determined, I wondered…' she paused, reluctant to admit it aloud, but coyness wasn't an option '…if you might try to take sole custody.'

Any shreds of doubt disintegrated at the sight of Vassili's expression. His eyes widened and his jaw dropped.

Finally he found his voice. It grated, rough and deep.

'It's as well I know you're not *trying* to insult me.' He breathed hard through his nostrils in an obvious attempt at calm. 'I don't know the people you mix with, Laura, who'd make you even consider that. But I'd never rip children from their mother.'

Laura had thought she'd seen him angry before, but the fury in his eyes took her aback.

'Our children deserve to know both of us and we deserve that too. Don't you agree?'

She nodded, her throat closing.

An apology trembled on her lips but she dismissed it. Maybe it was the result, as he said, of mixing with people whose ideas of family were twisted. But she didn't want to get into that. It was a subject she never spoke about.

'I needed to know, Vassili.'

After a moment he inclined his head. 'Know this, then. A family of my own wasn't on my radar. But your pregnancy changes everything. I intend to be there for my children every day. Not a part-time father living on the other side of the world.'

'That will be difficult, given you live in Greece and I'm in Australia.'

He shrugged, spreading his arms wide. 'That's something we can negotiate.'

She hadn't meant to get into this much detail today, but now they'd started there seemed no point in stopping. 'I don't see there's an easy solution we can negotiate.'

The idea of shuttling her babies from one side of the world to another on a regular basis appalled her. Yet she couldn't deny Vassili's right to access.

'Don't you?' His eyebrows rose. 'Surely it's obvious. We'll marry, Laura. It's the only solution.'

CHAPTER SEVEN

'MARRY!' HER EYES looked like saucers in her suddenly flushed face. 'We can't marry. It's…impossible.'

Vassili read the dismay she didn't attempt to hide. There was no question it was real. Everything from the dazzled glint in her eyes to the short, sharp breaths that lifted her breasts reinforced it.

He'd known she was no gold-digger. The way she'd cut him off when she believed he'd cheated on his fiancée proved that. But now she knew the truth about his engagement.

And still she doesn't want you. So much for the fatal Thanos charm.

But this wasn't about his ego. It was about doing right by his children.

His children!

Yet he couldn't squash a feral mix of annoyance, bruised pride and a desire to make Laura eat her words. Especially as, despite the distance she demanded between them, she wasn't good at hiding her continued interest. Those darting sideways glances, the quick carnal flare she tried and failed to mask, gave her away.

Male pride urged him to make her eat her words.

How difficult would it be to seduce her?

He sensed she was as physically attuned to him as he was to her. Neither had been ready to end their passionate relationship and every cell in his body told him there was unfinished business between them.

But the stakes were too high. Seduction would be satisfying but he had to play a long game and win her over mentally as well as physically.

'Hardly impossible. People often marry in such circumstances.'

He stretched out his legs, crossing them at the ankles in a pose of utter ease.

Because it wouldn't do for her to read *his* emotions. Not just his response to her rejection, but his deep-seated confusion. He still couldn't believe he'd suggested marriage. The words had slipped out so easily.

In the past whenever his mother had raised it as a possibility, because she wanted him to stay safely at home, starting a family, Vassili had felt a shudder of aversion. For years, ever since Theo's death, he'd instinctively avoided any thought of creating his own family.

Yet now, with the idea out in the open, he felt no panic. When he had time, later, he'd ponder that.

'Maybe if they're in a loving, committed relationship.'

Her tone made his hackles rise. Did she believe him incapable of that? Who'd have thought the woman he'd met, with her sunny disposition and positive outlook, would be so prickly and suspicious?

With good reason, said a voice in his head that sounded remarkably like Theo's. *Even you weren't sure you could until now.*

Yet now Vassili knew exactly what he wanted.

'I know we don't have that sort of relationship at the moment,' he murmured. 'I'm not suggesting we marry immediately. But it's an option for the future.'

He'd barely stopped speaking when she shook her head. 'I can't see it working. *Marriage*, of all things!'

Vassili frowned, trying to identify her tone. Not just outrage but…repugnance?

'You have a prejudice against marriage?'

She shrugged and looked towards the harbour as if fascinated by the view. But her body betrayed her, the way her crossed legs twisted tighter and her fingers plucked at her dress until she flickered a look his way and folded her hands neatly together as if to stop them moving.

'No, I've got nothing against marriage. I—' Another shrug and a tight smile that didn't reach her eyes. 'Marriage is a commitment for life. Or it should be. It's not something to do on a whim.'

Laura's mouth twisted and something shifted hard inside Vassili. Suddenly he wanted to wrap his arms around this challenging, complicated woman and ease whatever it was that made her look so haunted.

It didn't take a genius to know something in her past had wounded her, badly. Something more than his sudden departure for Greece and her belief that he'd abused her trust.

His indignation at her rejection eased, curiosity replacing it.

'I totally agree.'

Her chin shot up, her gaze locking on his, and he felt the reverberation through his whole body. What was this? He had no name for this…receptiveness. It was as if they were linked in some way he didn't understand.

'You do?'

'Yes. My parents were very much in love and happily married until my father died.' He paused, remembering the day his father hadn't returned from work, knocked over by a car as he crossed a road near his office. Only a few years after losing Theo, it had devastated Vassili and his mother. 'We were a very happy family. I'd like our children to have that too. Security and love.'

Laura blinked. 'Marriage doesn't guarantee that. It doesn't guarantee happiness or security.'

Her stark tone jolted him. 'You speak from personal experience?'

Abruptly it occurred to Vassili that, young as she was, Laura might have been married before. The idea made his belly churn violently.

'We're not discussing my parents' relationship. This is about us, two strangers. A wedding between us would be ridiculous.'

So she was thinking of her parents. Not a failed relationship of her own. Relief was a buzz in his blood and allowed him to conjure the hint of a smile that women usually found charming.

'We're not quite strangers, Laura.' He sat straighter. 'We know each other well enough to have created those two new lives you're carrying.'

She gasped, her palm sliding to her abdomen. In that moment Vassili was hyper-aware of how precious this all was. Laura. The twins. Their relationship, fractured as it was, yet more powerful than any he'd had with other women.

His senses heightened. The red of her dress, the lush rose of her lips, deepened. The pulse of his blood grew loud in his ears. His awareness of his own body, ostensibly relaxed but actually poised and alert, intensified. He inhaled that hint of summery fragrance that was unique to Laura—tropics and lush, womanly flesh—that never failed to trigger arousal.

'I need more than an unexpected pregnancy as a reason to marry,' she said with an air that would have done an empress proud.

Slowly he nodded. He hadn't expected instant agreement, had he?

Yet Vassili knew that if she'd agreed, he'd have felt a punch of triumph greater than any he'd achieved from reaching barely attainable mountain summits or surviving killer rapids. Or devising some new success for the business for which he let his uncle take the accolades.

That knowledge killed any casual response to her words.

There was nothing casual about the situation, or, he discovered, how he felt about it. About her.

She's carrying your babies. That explains why everything feels so significant.

Another pair of twins, like him and Theo.

Vassili was surprised to register the harsh constriction of his throat and the pang deep within that combined aching loss and excitement.

'I respect that,' he said in a voice designed to reassure. 'It's not something to rush into, but something to consider carefully.'

Though now he'd lighted on the idea, it grew more appealing by the second. It was the perfect answer.

Laura still looked mutinous, her mouth tight and brow furrowed. Yet instead of being impatient at her doubt and disapproval, Vassili wanted to reassure.

'Let's forget about it for now. We have plenty of time to discuss the future. For now let's concentrate on the present. My plan to stop the press bothering you. There's a place in Greece where you can be totally private...'

In the end it hadn't taken much to persuade Laura to leave Sydney.

That evening she had a private video chat with Eudora. The Greek woman confirmed what Vassili had said about their sham engagement, asking Laura to keep that private for now. She'd been sympathetic to Laura's situation, hounded by press fascinated by her relationship with an engaged man.

Eudora had even invited her to stay in her Athens apartment, if she didn't accept Vassili's offer of accommodation.

'But you don't even know me!'

Eudora had smiled. 'I know my cousin and trust him. He's a good judge of character. Obviously he cares for you, Laura. But if you don't want to stay with him while you escape the press, my offer stands.'

Laura didn't know what affected her more, the generous offer from a woman she didn't know, or the glow inside when Eudora had said Vassili cared for her.

Laura had told herself all he'd felt for her was lust, and now a sense of duty since she was pregnant. Yet the notion of him *caring*, not just feeling responsible, was terrifyingly seductive. She tried to put it from her mind, concentrating on other things, but kept coming back to it.

Meanwhile, poor Jake was hounded whenever he went near his flat. Other friends were pestered by the press. The modelling jobs Laura had lined up in the near future were cancelled or delayed for various reasons, meaning she had no obligation to stay in Australia.

When she'd called her agent they'd had an illuminating discussion. Her agent pressed her to capitalise on public interest in her relationship with Vassili, wanting her to explore modelling opportunities with a 'sexy pregnancy' slant.

Laura, fed up and sometimes nauseous, felt anything but sexy. More, she hated the idea of using what had happened between herself and Vassili to promote her career.

Modelling had provided a decent income and allowed her to save for her business plans. But she'd never thought of it as a long-term career.

She'd been lucky getting as much work as she had. Attractive rather than beautiful, she had hips and breasts and could never compete with the women who strutted on the catwalk. Laura had done well with her girl-next-door look, especially with companies eager to show their products were used by real women of all sizes and shapes.

Now she felt her time as a model was coming to a natural end. She'd regret the income loss but not the work.

'Not long, Laura, then you can rest.'

She turned to Vassili, beside her in the back of the helicopter, his eyes glittering.

For a man who'd been travelling something like twenty-four hours, he looked ridiculously rested and energetic. Maybe being in Greece had that effect on him.

Whereas she, who'd slept most of the flight in a comfortable, wide bed, waited on by solicitous cabin staff who plied her with fine food and glossy magazines, felt decidedly second-hand.

Even the thrill of her first helicopter ride, from Athens Airport to Vassili's secret destination, wore off as tiredness weighted her bones.

'I've been resting, remember?'

She tried and failed not to sound sulky about the debilitating weariness. The last week had been a trial, sapping her energy and leaving her limp yet restless.

Laura didn't even have the comfort of being able to blame Vassili. True, the pregnancy was down to him. And wasn't that a line of thought she tried to avoid? Because it led to memories of them together, naked, and an awakening of hormonal urges she couldn't suppress.

Were other pregnant women so easily turned on?

She pressed her thighs together, determined to ignore the pulse of heat at her sex. She turned to the amazing view as the chopper left the mainland and headed over dark blue sea.

During the last week Vassili hadn't prodded or pushed. He'd simply *been* there, so reasonable it made her want to grind her teeth. Even a good argument would have relieved some of her tension.

Because she hated this sensation that her life spiralled out of her control. Disliked too the idea that it would be sensible to follow his advice and be beholden to him.

Laura had made her own way in the world since her mother died. Ceding control, even when it came in the guise of solicitous support, was tough. Especially with the future so unsure.

We'll marry, Laura. It's the only solution.

She hadn't gone an hour since without reliving those words,

feeling again that combination of amazement, rejection and the tiniest scintilla of excitement.

How was she to make decisions when she couldn't take charge of her emotions? When her feelings for this man kept undermining her. Telling herself it was just the lure of sex had made no difference. That day in the penthouse when they'd talked about the future and coming to Greece, the impulse to lean on him, physically and emotionally, had been so powerful, it had taken all her determination to resist.

Vassili spoke again, the timbre of his voice like the stroke of plush velvet, easing her tense muscles. 'Long-distance travel is notoriously taxing, even if you managed some sleep in the flight.'

Some sleep? She'd spent most of it out for the count.

She turned back to him. 'Do you suffer from jet lag?'

He had the grace to look almost abashed, as if she'd caught him out in something.

Did he think her so mean-spirited she'd prefer him to be exhausted too? Laura felt ashamed of her latent bad temper. She wasn't usually so out of sorts.

'Not often. But our circumstances are different.' He glanced at the pilot as if not wanting to mention her pregnancy when he could be overheard.

'You're right.' Both her GP, whom she'd visited again, and the obstetrician who'd miraculously found space in her diary for a consultation, had warned of increased tiredness while at the same time reassuring her that everything seemed good. 'I'm sure I'll feel better tomorrow.' She searched for some innocuous subject. 'Does this place have a beach or is the coastline all rocks?'

'Rocks?'

She shrugged. 'I've never been to Greece but I remember friends travelling in Europe talking about rocky beaches.'

Vassili laughed and the sound went through her like warm

chocolate through honeycomb, rich and delectable, turning her blood to syrup.

'Maybe elsewhere,' he said. 'Don't worry, there's a beach here that I think you'll enjoy.' He leaned across her, pointing. 'There.'

For a second Laura was aware only of his warmth, the snatch of scent in her nostrils—clean male skin and a hint of cinnamon—and the way her pulse beat suddenly hard and fast.

Reluctantly she turned her head, away from that perfectly sculpted profile, to see the long shape of an island with a sickle of white rimming one side.

Her breath caught. It looked like a tiny paradise surrounded, where the sea grew shallow around it, by water in shades of purest turquoise and aquamarine. 'It's gorgeous.'

She could imagine herself swimming in those clear depths and strolling along the pale, deserted sand.

Laura frowned. 'Where's the town?'

She could make out the cleared space of the helipad and a cluster of buildings towards one end of the beach. Was that another couple of buildings at the other end of the island?

'That's the beauty of it. Well, that and the forest my grandfather planted. Years ago it was rocky pastureland and a few olive trees.' Vassili dropped his hand but still leaned close, gaze on the view as the helicopter swooped low. 'The island is too small to support a village. It's privately owned. We'll be alone.'

He turned his head, so close she saw the tiniest variations of colour in those dark eyes, as if, deep within, fire flickered.

Her breath lodged in her throat, or maybe that was her hammering heart. Suddenly she couldn't get enough air and she felt her lungs labouring. Because last time she and Vassili had been this close…

No, no, no! Going back there was a mistake. One that had got her into this situation in the first place.

Yet she couldn't turn away. Nor did she trust herself to put a hand to his chest and press him back, away from her.

Because suddenly she was remembering the taste of him in her mouth, the gentle graze of those callused hands across her bare skin, his assured dexterity as he located and celebrated her every erogenous zone. The sound of his deep voice murmuring mixed Greek and English endearments as he fitted his body to hers and took her to the stars.

'What were you saying about being alone?'

Her voice sounded strangled and his gaze flicked to her lips. Instantly they parted as if in anticipation.

Then, suddenly, it was Vassili withdrawing, leaning back in his seat and shoving his hands into his trouser pockets.

He frowned and looked away. 'There's no village and no villagers. There's a housekeeper and her husband who maintain the place but they won't come to the house unless we want.' He swung around, his eyes locking on hers. 'We'll have absolute privacy, just what the doctor ordered.'

Vassili had never counted himself a stupid man. At school he'd excelled, especially at maths and economics. In adulthood he juggled the demands of family, his need for adventure and the intricacies of a multibillion-dollar company.

Yet it was only now, on his private island, that he realised his error in bringing Laura here, alone.

It might be a perfect spot to keep her safe, especially since, as far as the world knew, he had no interest in the place and hadn't been back here for years. Not since he was eighteen.

He pulled a dark curtain across those memories and quickly moved on.

The problem was that with just the pair of them here there was little distraction from his ever-increasing hunger for her. It gnawed at his belly, a constant distraction. And it had only grown worse since that moment on the chopper when he'd leaned close and been snared by golden-green eyes and the need he'd tried to suppress.

In Australia he'd had things to distract him on top of the news they were expecting twins. Medical appointments. Travel plans. Avoiding the press and dealing with Laura's friend Jake who'd been eager to question Vassili's motives, even if he'd waited until Laura wasn't about to confront him.

Vassili stood on the villa's terrace, feet planted wide and hands in the pockets of his jeans, and smiled grimly at the moonlight glimmering over the sea. It wasn't the water he saw but Jake's astonished face when Vassili had told him his exact intentions towards Laura.

After the Australian's astonishment had eased he'd actually wished Vassili luck.

'You'll need it,' he'd said. 'Laura's one of the strongest-minded people I know. She's had to be, given what she's been through. But if you really mean to stick by her and make her happy...' he'd paused with a hint of a threatening scowl '... I wish you luck.'

He hadn't elaborated about what Laura had been through, saying it was up to her to share.

Once more Vassili had experienced the pang of jealousy. He'd felt it first when he'd learned Laura was staying with Jake, then dismissed it, or tried to, when she assured him the Australian had never been her lover.

But Vassili had discovered his capacity for jealousy wasn't confined to her sexual partners. He envied Jake the easy intimacy he and Laura shared, that had nothing to do with sex but with trust and a shared history.

He frowned. Laura trusted him. She understood his situation now. She'd agreed to come here with him.

Not because she wanted to but because she needed to escape the limelight in Sydney. It's not the same thing.

This was a new sort of need in him.

Previously he'd had good relationships with women, especially lovers. They'd trusted and liked him, hadn't they? Yet he'd never wanted or expected to delve into their secrets or have them turn to him before anyone else, when they were in trouble.

With Laura, that was exactly what he wanted. He wished...

Abruptly light spilled from the glass doors behind him, illuminating the flagged terrace where he stood and the infinity pool beyond.

Vassili spun around and something jammed hard in his gut while his throat closed on a heavy sigh.

Laura. There was no one else it could be.

Yet that didn't stop his heart crashing against his ribs as he took in the sight of her, standing in the living room with her hand on the light switch, eyes wide as they met his through the open doors.

It was what he thought he read in her expression that rocked him. Eagerness.

And the fact she hadn't worn a robe over her pale mint sleep shorts and singlet top, despite the slight chill of this early summer night.

And the rapid rise of her chest with every shallow breath.

She was tousled and gorgeous and utterly irresistible.

Vassili told himself that wasn't desire on her face. It couldn't be. She'd headed to bed early as if determined to spend as little time with him as possible.

Because of that he tried and failed not to notice the rise and fall of her breasts.

His hands curled in on themselves, palms tingling. Synapses fired in the most primitive part of his brain, pulsing a tattoo that demanded he stride in, wrap his arm around her back and yank her to him before claiming her in the most elemental way.

Need was a clamour in his blood, a compulsion.

He searched for civilised, harmless words to break the thickening silence.

Nothing came.

The best he could do was lock his knees to stop himself stalking in there, ripping off Laura's skimpy clothes and burying himself deep inside her.

She'd made it clear she wasn't ready to resume the relationship he'd cut short when he left for Greece. He had a lot of catching up to do.

Even if it felt, to him, as if nothing had changed since those heady days in Queensland. If anything his obsession had deepened, become all-consuming.

Vassili's breath sawed in the still night air. It was the sound of desperation and a last-ditch effort not to give in to his basest instincts.

Because Laura deserved his respect. More, he needed to win her trust if he were to achieve what he wanted. Laura, and their children, in his life permanently. As a family.

He was congratulating himself on mastering himself when, instead of saying she'd only come downstairs for a glass of water and scuttling to the kitchen, Laura did the unthinkable.

She padded out on those endlessly long legs to join him.

CHAPTER EIGHT

LAURA DIDN'T KNOW why she stood there, speechless, at the sight of him. It wasn't from surprise. She'd known he was there, had watched him from her bedroom window long enough.

Yet the reality of him, and what she was doing, froze her. She waited for common sense to kick in and tell her to hurry back upstairs and lock her bedroom door behind her.

A huff of wry amusement spilled. Why lock her bedroom door when it wasn't Vassili she feared? This was *her* decision.

Though now it came to it, she couldn't help prevaricating a little. She dropped her hand from the light switch and stepped forward with a shrug of taut shoulder muscles. 'I couldn't sleep.'

That was true enough. She'd prepared for bed, had a long, luxurious soak in the bath, hoping it might make her sleepy because despite her tiredness she was suddenly wide awake. But the lap of water against her bare skin didn't calm. It elicited memories of Vassili's touch, the stroke of his capable hands, the surprising softness of his lips, and the scratchy, arousing caress of his bristled face against her skin.

He didn't move closer, just stood, features expressionless as she walked towards him, then paused in the doorway.

Had she imagined his sexual interest this week?

There was one way to find out. Come what may, she wasn't returning to her room without finding out.

For she'd just discovered the lamentable truth, that she didn't have the strength to keep her distance from Vassili when they shared the same roof.

She'd railed at her hormonal body, told herself this was a stress response, the result of tiredness fogging her brain. But the truth was that she hadn't ever stopped craving Vassili.

Was that why he'd checked into a hotel in Sydney for those two nights, leaving her in the penthouse? She'd thought he was giving her space, respecting her need for privacy. What if he just wasn't interested in her?

Then you'll know he's only talking about marriage out of duty. Not because he has any remaining interest in you.

A weight settled in her stomach. That would make it easier to say no. She had no intention of becoming unwanted baggage in a marriage of convenience.

'Laura?'

He moved closer and she stiffened. So much for her determination to see this through, to stop the torture of yearning that racked her.

'I need—'

'Can I get you—?'

They spoke at the same time. After a pause Vassili continued. 'Can I get you a drink? Warm milk to help you sleep?'

She almost laughed aloud. He didn't sound like a billionaire who owned a luxurious mansion and a private island. His offer sounded cosy and cute, almost like a parent caring for a child. He had no idea how wound up she was, of the sparking need coursing through her veins and making her feel as if her skin were too small. She wrapped her arms around her torso, trying to hold in the emotions that were too big to manage.

His offer made her realise he'd probably be a considerate father who wouldn't get angry when interrupted by young children. One who was patient and supportive.

It was a devastatingly attractive image.

She yanked her thoughts from that idea. She was in no state to think about the future now.

'No, it wouldn't help. And I'm warm enough already.' She wanted to fan herself at the sight of Vassili in pale, snug jeans that fitted his backside and powerful thighs to perfection. And the dark shirt with the sleeves rolled up... Since when had forearms been erotic?

'How about some exercise then? That might tire you enough to help you sleep. I sometimes find I'm too wired after international travel to sleep easily.'

He walked nearer, stopping only when he was so close she saw her reflection in his dark eyes. She ate him up, her mind fixed on the one sort of exercise she wanted right now. It was disappointing when he said, 'I'll turn on the pool lights if you want a swim. I don't recommend the sea at night.'

'But it would be invigorating.'

If she felt any more invigorated she'd explode. Yet breaking her stasis, committing herself to admitting her desire for him, was an enormous step. Would he use it as a bargaining point for marriage?

Even knowing he probably would didn't stop her yearning.

A shiver raced down her spine and she shuffled her bare feet on the sun-warmed paving.

'I don't advise it,' he said slowly, his gaze raking her features and settling on her mouth. Laura's chest rose in a mighty breath as she tried to grab enough oxygen to fill her suddenly starved lungs. 'You'd get out of your depth quickly—'

'I'm not worried about that.'

She was already out of her depth. But she couldn't pull back. The force that drove her was elemental, irresistible.

She'd spent months telling herself Vassili was wrong for her but she'd never felt as right as when she'd been with him. Now, with her world careering out of control, she craved to forget everything for a little while and lose herself in the maelstrom of pleasure she knew she'd find with him.

Vassili moved. Now they stood toe to toe and she watched the lines run across his forehead and knot as he frowned down at her. It had been ages since she'd had the luxury of studying him so minutely. Not since they'd shared a bed all those months ago.

The high cut of his cheekbones. The hint of dimples that grooved his cheeks when he smiled. The dark stubble that peppered his jaw, the long line of his nose and the arch of his dark eyebrows. All fascinated her and made her want to reach for him.

'Laura.' His voice dug deep inside her. 'What do you want?' She watched his Adam's apple jerk in his throat. 'Because I have to tell you—'

'You.' The word died into reverberating silence and she watched his eyebrows shoot up. 'I want you, Vassili.'

She saw the rapid flick of emotions across his features, too quick to identify. But when he opened his mouth again to question, the words spilled from her.

'I don't mean as a husband. I'm not here to talk about marriage. That's a separate thing.' It was her turn to swallow hard, throat constricting as if that simple movement had suddenly become a complex feat far beyond the capacity of her body. 'I just…want you.'

She tilted her chin high and put her restless hands together so as not to reach for him.

He had to want her too.

'But not as a spouse?'

In anyone else she might have thought she heard hurt in his tone. But Vassili stood tall, proud and arrested, as if he'd never expected her to admit her need for him.

'Can we not talk about that tonight?'

Laura brushed aside the skittering thought that she was being unfair.

Yet what about this situation was fair? Since she was twelve she'd lived every day cautiously, because she knew the terrible pitfalls that could suddenly yawn wide in an otherwise ordinary world and swallow you whole.

Her one mistake was that glorious week with Vassili when she'd discovered such tremendous joy and peace. It had been like walking into sunshine for the very first time. Now everything she knew and planned was turned topsy-turvy and she felt rudderless.

She looked into that give-nothing-away stare and realised her mistake. 'I'm sorry.'

He's interested in the babies, not you.

That old, ingrained knowledge of her own lack of importance hit her anew. She'd thought she'd sloughed it off but…

'My mistake,' she said quickly. 'I was being selfish. You've done enough, bringing me here.'

Laura did *not* want pity sex.

She swung around to go back inside when warmth shackled her. She looked down, disbelieving, to see long fingers wrapped around her wrist.

'No! Don't go.' Vassili sounded winded, as if he'd run the length of the island.

Or as if you surprised him. He's probably trying to work out a way to let you down gently so you won't be upset when it comes to discussing the babies' future.

'It's okay, Vassili. It's late and I made a mistake. Put it down to jet lag.' Laura stared at his olive-gold hand holding hers, willing him to release her. 'I'll probably have forgotten about all this in the morning.'

Liar.

'I hope not.'

Vassili's thumb moved and, to her horror, goosebumps broke out across her bare arms and her nipples budded as he caressed the sensitive skin on the inside of her wrist.

Her breath hissed and her head shot up and there he was, so close she knew he read every telltale response.

Laura felt the rush of blood up her throat to her cheeks.

'I want you too, Laura.'

His voice was smooth and rich, making a melody of her name, and her toes curled. But with the light full on him from the room behind her, she saw the crimp at the corners of his mouth and the wariness in his eyes, and knew he was thinking, not feeling.

How far would he go to persuade her into marriage and full access to his children?

A weight dropped hard and low inside her, crushing the resolve that had brought her out here and making her abruptly aware of her skimpy night gear.

From somewhere she scrounged pride. 'No, it's fine. It was a moment's madness, that's all. Everyone says pregnant women get hormonal. But it's over now. There's no need for you to…' She held his stare. 'I appreciate you getting me away from the paparazzi, Vassili. You've done enough.'

Still he didn't release her. She could have tugged her hand free but her arm refused to move, like her feet.

Slowly he shook his head. 'I'm happy to help. But to quote you, that's a separate thing. I'd have helped you even if I didn't want to make love with you.'

A tiny frisson ran through her, turning into a burst of fire low in her belly. 'Don't pretend, Vassili. There's no need for it and I've always admired your honesty.' It was one of the things that had drawn her initially.

'You think I'm lying? Why do you imagine I stayed outside tonight instead of heading inside to a comfortable bed? Why do you think I moved to a hotel in Sydney so you could have the penthouse to yourself?'

Laura stared into his proud face, searching for the amorous softening she'd seen so often when they'd been together. It wasn't there. Instead his features looked sharply honed and his eyes shone with something that was surely akin to anger. Or calculation.

'You're saying you did that to give me space?'

Despite her earlier hopes, Laura couldn't believe it. He looked so grim, not like the tender, laughing, adventurous lover she'd known.

More like a man persuading a gullible woman because it suited his purposes.

A lightning flash of memory hit her, of her father, taut and controlled, being oh-so-plausible in response to her mother's accusations.

Laura shivered and tugged her arm.

Instead of releasing her, Vassili pulled her hand towards him. Before she realised his intention her palm was pressed to the bulge straining the zip of his jeans. Her fingers automatically curled possessively and his erection twitched in her hold.

He gave a huff of bitter laughter. 'My words aren't good enough, it seems, but surely that will convince you.'

'Vassili?' Could it be she'd hurt him by not believing him? But he was right, his body proclaimed the truth. He *did* want her. In response she felt the buttery soft slide of heat down low, her body readying to take him.

Laura fought for breath, and sanity. 'I'm sorry. You seemed so different. Or maybe it's me. I couldn't be sure—'

'No apologies. We're both under stress. It's a difficult situation.'

The knuckles of his other hand brushed her cheek and she quivered as yearning rose. Now she saw it, perhaps not the same avid sexual glitter as before, but an easing in his expression, warmth in his eyes and a softening around the mouth that she took for tenderness.

It undid her.

'To be clear, Laura, I didn't sleep under the same roof as you in Sydney because resisting temptation is easier when you're not in the next room.'

'And that's why you stayed out here tonight?'

He nodded, nostrils flaring as he drew a deep breath. Even that seemed incredibly sexy. When she tested his length in her hand and saw his eyelids flicker, the last of her uncertainty fled. There was still a raft of unresolved issues between them but that could wait. It had to.

'If I don't have you soon,' she whispered, 'I'll burst.'

The hand at her cheek shifted, clamping the back of her neck in a hold that felt possessive and exciting. His other hand pressed hers against his groin. His voice when it came was a growl that edged her skin with goosebumps.

'My thoughts exactly. If you've finished talking?'

For one beat of her pulse they stood, taking the measure of each other, then Vassili walked her backwards into the room, not breaking eye contact.

The remnants of her logical brain told her to look over her shoulder and ensure they didn't trip over something. But she trusted him to know what he was doing and somehow he guided her across the space till she felt the cushioned arm of a chair or lounge behind her legs.

Vassili crowded her, his face a breath above hers. She couldn't get enough, one hand still at his groin and the other almost mirroring him, cupping the side of his strong neck, feeling the movement of muscle under hot flesh as he swallowed.

'Take your clothes off, Laura.'

The soft-voiced order made elation throb in every secret part of her body.

'I will if you do too.'

She hadn't finished speaking when he released his hold, and she swayed back before clutching him for balance. She grabbed the denim at his hips because he was already hauling his shirt over his head in an urgent movement that revealed his golden torso, pectorals dusted with dark hair that emphasised the width of his chest.

Her gaze traced that familiar body. The lean strength in the swell and dip of taut muscles that mesmerised in their movement. The silvered scars here and there that he'd acquired in his daredevil pursuits. The tiny line of dark hair that narrowed down to his groin just visible above the button of his jeans.

Laura shivered on a rush of heady excitement.

'Laura.'

His voice was gruff and she read impatience in his eyes when her gaze snapped up to his.

Elation rose. A spike of excitement as pure as any she'd known. Hands to the hem of her thin top, she pulled it up and off, letting it fall to the floor.

Arrested, he surveyed her bare breasts that grew tighter and full under his deep-browed scrutiny.

In the last weeks her breasts had become more sensitive, so she noticed even the casual brush of her crossed arms. How would it feel when he touched them? She shivered as a searing thread of excitement pulled through her body.

Standing proud before him, she felt his hot stare as a physical caress, notching her arousal impossibly higher.

Caress barely described the effect of that dark gaze. To her jangling senses it seemed she read something more like adoration in that sinfully erotic scrutiny. Heard it too in the low sound of satisfaction that emerged from deep in his throat.

Suddenly she was aware of the huge difference in size and physical power between them. The way Vassili could probably pick her up and tuck her under one arm if he wanted, despite her height.

The knowledge didn't intimidate. It titilated. Made her want to test the limits of his power with her own.

Laura hooked her thumbs in the elasticised waistband of her sleep shorts. Vassili's heavy-lidded gaze tore free from her chest, dropping to her waist. Anticipation swelled in her, making a mockery of her earlier hesitation.

Laura wanted to go slow, tease him and draw out the delicious expectation. But she couldn't. Already the soft cotton at her crotch was damp from arousal. She needed him. This minute.

Shoving down the shorts and kicking free of them, she watched Vassili free himself from his jeans. He looked even better without them. Seconds later he was naked as she, impossibly even more vital, more beautiful than she remembered.

He murmured something in Greek, in that throaty, soft voice she'd only heard when they were together like this, and it blasted any hope of control.

Laura reached for him as he lifted her into his arms. She was aware of movement, the breath-stealing slide of flesh against flesh, and then she was sinking onto a wide couch. Sensations pummelled her. The deep cushions beneath her, Vassili's crisp hair tickling her palms as she eagerly grasped his skull. The furnace heat of his long frame, the friction of their bodies and the gasps of eagerness as he nudged her legs wide and settled between her thighs. The weight of his arousal against her sex.

She inhaled the spicy clean scent that she'd associate with Vassili for ever. For months she'd dreamed of it, waking with it in her nostrils after every tortured dream. Now he was here, where she needed him.

'*Psihi mou.* I've missed you.'

Then he withdrew a little and bent his head to kiss her nipple. Sensation rocked her, exquisite, indescribable, as he took his time at her breast, then her other one. By the time he lifted his head she was hoarse from crying out, overwhelmed at the intensity of delight he evoked.

'I'm sorry, Laura,' he said. 'I want to take this slow but it's been so long that I can't.'

His breath was a mighty shudder she felt right through her being. Maybe because she was shaking too, with expectation and overwrought delight.

Unbelievably he'd brought her to the brink of crisis just with the weight of his body and his ministrations at her breasts. She didn't want slow. She was too impatient for that. But the words jammed in her throat when Vassili slid his hand down her hip and across to her sex. Long fingers sliding through slick folds made her gasp, her pelvis lifting to meet his caress.

Through slitted eyes she saw his tight smile as he confirmed how ready she was.

He moved, steadying himself, watching her watching him and, despite all she'd learned about the separation between sex and emotion, in that moment Laura felt the most profound connection. As if what they shared went deep and true, beyond the physical. She lifted clutching hands to the silky skin of his shoulders, feeling solid bone and muscle.

The next moment everything changed. He bore down in one long, slow thrust that took him, she was sure, right to her heart.

Bodies locked, eyes wide, they stared, overwhelmed by the reality of an act that transcended all that had gone before.

Laura told herself she imagined it. Yet the expression on Vassili's face matched her own astonishment. It felt like something far more than the gratification of simple physical need.

But there was no time to define the moment or hold it. Already they were moving, driven by instincts as old as time and desires as immediate and vital as the next breath.

He clamped her hips and she arched her back, hooking her ankle around his thigh to hold him close, gasping as his lips found sensitive flesh.

Then it came, the roar of conflagration as the world went up in flames. The pleasure so keen she wasn't sure she'd survive it. The amazing moment of oneness as they hung together on a thread of ecstasy before tumbling into abandoned satiation.

Afterwards came the protectiveness, the need to hold him. Keep him safe. Keep him close, his head buried in her shoulder, his strong body blanketing hers.

Laura concentrated on that and the aftershocks of delight still rippling through her body. She didn't dare think about how momentous this felt.

Because if she did she feared she'd realise she'd made an appalling mistake and opened herself up to fatal vulnerability.

CHAPTER NINE

THE MOON WASN'T FULL, yet the night sky was bright out here away from the city, full of stars. He'd left the shutters open and there was plenty of light for Vassili to study the woman in his bed.

She lay, hair sprawled across the pillow, on her side facing towards him, her palm on his chest. Yet despite that contact, as if she sought him even in sleep, there was something curiously contained about Laura. Something at odds with the woman who'd totally undone him hours before.

Her other hand was tucked under the pillow and her legs were bent, knees neatly together. She looked...self-sufficient. Not like the volatile woman who'd searched him out for the express purpose of seducing him.

Laura Bettany was a puzzle. Every time he felt he took a step closer to understanding her, she surprised him with some new insight or mystery.

Downstairs they'd shared explosive sex, different from anything he'd experienced. Even now he couldn't pinpoint exactly why it was so different.

Because you've waited so long to have Laura again? Because you haven't been able to think of any other woman since the day you met her?

No point pondering that now. Vassili had spent the last decade or so avoiding anything like emotional intimacy. This wasn't the time to mine his emotions. Especially as he suspected he'd find them discomfiting.

Far better to focus on what made Laura tick.

After that shattering orgasm he'd carried her upstairs, already planning more intimacy, slower this time and far more thorough. But after a quick visit to the bathroom Laura had fallen sound asleep with a suddenness that reminded him of an exhausted child.

Or a pregnant woman.

His conscience niggled.

He'd felt deprived, his arousal already iron-hard as she slipped into slumber. Then he'd mentally reviewed what she'd been through lately and felt ashamed of his selfishness. He'd been focused on his libido while she'd been utterly worn out.

There were other things to consider too. Like her abrupt disclaimer earlier that she didn't want him as a husband, only for sex.

Vassili frowned. He wanted to believe she'd been clarifying that sex tonight didn't mean she'd agreed to marriage *yet.*

But maybe she had no intention of ever agreeing.

That made his stomach churn and his scalp prickle.

He might have avoided the idea of marriage and children for so long that his mother had agreed to his uncle's plan to force his hand. But now everything had changed because of Laura and her pregnancy.

He'd do whatever it took to keep them, Laura and the children. To create a family.

What a turnaround for a man who'd always avoided anything like commitment.

For years he'd felt that part of himself was missing. He'd done everything he could to fill the void or at least ease the hurt by making good on his final promise to Theo. To live the life Theo couldn't, searching out the thrills and adventures that would be denied his twin for ever.

Every time Vassili had reached a summit, conquered an almost impossible trek to a pole or through a desert, or achieved something else Theo would have loved, he'd felt that he carried his beloved brother with him.

Vassili had learned at eighteen the complete devastation of loss and had no wish to go through it again, caring for someone so deeply that losing them felt like losing himself.

From then on he'd shunned the idea of searching for love or even accepting an arranged marriage with a view to having children.

But fate in the form of an attraction so strong he hadn't been able to resist, and rogue sperm that defied contraceptive precautions, had turned the tables on him. Whether he wanted it or not, he had a family on the way. There was no avoiding it.

And he realised that, despite his deep-seated fears, he didn't *want* to avoid it. He wanted these twins.

How could he not? The very thought of them made him remember himself and Theo, thick as thieves despite their differing characters.

Was that why he felt so possessive about Laura? Because she carried their babies?

It was part of it but—

Vassili wrenched his mind away from that, preferring to enjoy the view before him. Straightforward lust was easier to handle than complicated feelings.

Except that where Laura was concerned he *did* feel.

It was easier to trace the delicate dip of her collarbone, the tilt of her breasts and let desire loose. Even the indent of her navel and the rise of her hip, just hidden by the sheet, were unbearably seductive.

His mouth dried as he fought the urge to touch, easing her from sleep to arousal.

She shifted, the sheet slipping, and his breath snagged in the back of his throat, lungs atrophying, as he saw the slight swell of her once-flat abdomen. She carried his babies there and he couldn't think of anything more piercingly moving and shockingly arousing.

He cleared his throat, grappling with an upsurge of unprecedented feelings that threatened to overwhelm him. Heat washed through him. Or was it cold? He couldn't tell.

'Vassili?'

He looked up to find Laura's eyes, dark in this light, surveying him.

What had she seen in his face? Weakness? Need?

The idea was unbearable. He'd spent so long being the strong one, for Theo and then for their mother, it was ingrained in him. Now Laura needed him to look after her. And their babies. He needed to be strong for them.

'How are you feeling? Better for the sleep?'

She nodded. 'So soundly I didn't even dream.' She paused and moistened her lips. Vassili felt the pulse of hunger streak through him, settling like a pool of fire in his groin. 'I'm sorry. You probably expected more—'

He put his finger to her mouth, trying to ignore the instant thrill of arousal at the touch of her soft lips as profound tenderness welled. 'Don't apologise. You need rest.'

Which meant she didn't need him lying beside her, imagining all the things he wanted to do with her.

So instead of leaning down to kiss her lips or those delicious, pink-tipped breasts, he reached for the sheet crumpled about her hips, to pull it up. Then he'd head outside for a dip in the pool. Maybe after thirty or forty laps he'd overcome his need for her.

His fingers brushed silky skin and the soft fluff of pubic hair. He froze, all but his leaping pulse.

Make that fifty laps. Or seventy.

'Vassili…'

He jerked his hand up but instead of snatching it away, found it planted gently on her abdomen.

It hadn't been an intentional move yet he watched his fingers stop there then spread, absorbing her warmth and the incredibly fine texture of her skin.

Awe rose at the miracle that was Laura and what they'd created together.

'It's amazing, isn't it?' His voice was so husky he had to clear his throat. 'The babies, I mean. Even now it almost doesn't seem real.'

He was thinking he should move his hand, so big and rough against her delicate flesh, when her slim hand covered his.

Vassili couldn't shift even his gaze, not that he wanted to. He couldn't explain why but it had something to do with their hands together, protecting the new lives they'd sparked.

'You'd know for sure how real they are if you got morning sickness.'

'You feel nauseous now?'

He hadn't even given that a thought when he carried her up to bed.

'No. I'm good.'

Vassili turned his hand to clasp her fingers, his knuckles against the soft flesh of her abdomen.

'It's unfair you have to bear the brunt of it all.' He knew that carrying twins wasn't always easy and there could be risks. An unseen band tightened around his chest and throat. He met Laura's eyes. 'You'll have the best of medical care, I promise.'

Slowly Laura nodded. 'We have a good health system at home in Australia. But it's reassuring to hear you'll see to that while I'm here.'

How long would that be?

She was reminding him that her visit was temporary.

He'd brought her to his country on the pretext of providing a haven away from the intrusive press. Not that it was a pretext, it was completely true. Yet Vassili was looking long-term, far beyond a short break on the private island in the Ionian Sea that he'd inherited from his father.

'Naturally I will. And while you're here you must tell me if there's anything you want. Anything at all.' He lifted her hand

and kissed it, revelling in the tiny shudder of response he felt ripple through her. 'It will be my pleasure to get it for you.'

'Thanks, but there's nothing. All I want is some peace and quiet.'

Another reminder that she needed nothing else from him?

He almost wished she were the sort of person easily impressed by the things money could buy. Jewels, clothes and expensive mementos. But he knew Laura better than that.

What *he* wanted—and he saw it with crystal clarity—was for her to stay with him in Greece permanently as Kyria Thanos, his wife.

Strange how the word sat so easily in his mind when in the past his mother's hints had fallen on deaf ears.

That had been his intention when he'd ushered Laura onto the plane, to persuade her to stay. He felt it now in the very core of his being. The deep-set certainty that she belonged with him, either here in this place his family had treasured for generations or on the mainland.

Vassili wanted to keep her with him and build the sort of golden life for their children that he and Theo had shared, before their world shattered irreparably.

It was his *duty* to look after his new family.

Maybe starting a family would even help ease the ache of loss he'd never quite vanquished.

At least he'd be doing something worthwhile. Lately he'd felt his constant activity, burying himself in work or throwing himself into some new adventure, was no longer about pursing his own interests, or his promise to Theo. That maybe it was a way of hiding from the darkness inside, because if he stopped for too long the void within might envelop him totally.

His fingers tightened around Laura's. 'You're in the right place for peace and quiet. We have that in abundance.'

She knew her mind and set her own course and she had major reservations about his proposal. He had to find a way to persuade her to stay long term. To assuage her doubts.

Or undermine them by making her crave him.

Increasingly that seemed his best option.

Keep telling yourself that, Vassili, since it's exactly what you want anyway.

But this short conversation had reinforced that Laura wouldn't be easily persuaded by his wealth or status. If anything, he suspected she mistrusted those. She kept reminding him she was here short-term and that she didn't want him as a husband.

He needed a change of tactic.

He'd do whatever it took to secure his twins' future. Seducing the woman he intended to wed, showing her how very good life together would be, wouldn't just be pleasure, it was his responsibility.

The sooner he began and the more thorough he was, the better.

'What are you smiling at?'

'Hm?' He met her stare and realised he was grinning. He lifted her hand to his mouth, stroking her palm with his tongue and feeling her quiver. 'Just thinking about the joys of sharing that peace and quiet with you.'

'About that—'

'Speaking of which,' he continued before she could object, 'it's late. We should save that conversation for later. Don't you agree?'

As he spoke he tunnelled his other hand under the sheet at her hip, across to the downy hair at the apex of her thighs. She sucked in her breath as he found the pleasure point there, stroking then circling as her thighs first tensed then fell apart.

Vassili wanted, how he wanted, to accept the invitation of her sweet body. To lie between her legs and drive them both to ecstasy as he'd done earlier that night.

But the days of being driven only by his libido were gone. He'd tantalise and please Laura to the point of addiction—for him, only him—until she realised the inevitability of them together.

He'd start immediately. There was no time to lose.

Grazing the flesh at the base of her thumb with his teeth, then kissing it better, he released her hand and pulled the sheet away to settle low between her knees.

Laura made a sound in the back of her throat as if to protest, then stopped.

Vassili looked up to meet her eyes. Even in the dim light he caught their glitter and it sent excitement coursing through his blood to pool and swell low in his body.

Who was he kidding? This wasn't self-denial. Pleasing Laura had, from the beginning, been as great a joy as finding his own sexual fulfilment.

Now, meeting her gaze, feeling the warmth of her sex a breath away, there was nowhere he'd rather be. He lay encircled by the silky flesh of her trembling inner thighs, inhaling the evocative scent of her arousal.

He dipped his head, holding her stare, and tasted her. Delicious.

She jumped, her breath somewhere between a gasp and a sigh.

His body tightened on a jolt of pleasure, partly from Laura's response, but primarily from his own satisfaction.

For a second he had the clarity to wonder which of them found this more addictive. Then her fingers fluttered over his head as if not knowing where to stop, before he delved deeper, eliciting a little scream of delight as she clutched his skull.

Any thought of teasing died as Vassili lost himself in Laura. The quiver of her legs, the undulating rise of her pelvis, the glory of feasting on her essence...

He was so close to coming as she spasmed around him that afterwards he was faintly surprised to discover his erection as solid as ever as she whispered his name in that familiar, throaty voice, begging for his embrace.

No, not begging. Demanding.

His feisty lover wasn't yet enthralled enough to beg. But one day…

He smiled as he moved up her body and closed his lips around one perfect pink nipple.

'Vassili!'

Laura washed her face and rinsed her mouth, grateful for the cool water and the fresh, sea-scented breeze wafting through the bathroom's open window.

According to her doctor the morning sickness could end relatively soon. That couldn't come soon enough for Laura. Though to be fair, this morning it didn't seem quite as bad.

Or was that a case of mind over matter?

She'd woken feeling better than she could ever recall, her body humming with remembered delight and not a little anticipation. Last night Vassili had made her feel wonderful.

There'd been a glow inside her that came from his love-making. But her smile had died when she'd rolled over and discovered the other side of the vast bed empty.

It had been a struggle not to feel hurt by Vassili's absence. Until she'd checked the time and realised she'd slept half the morning away. And seen the jug of iced water and plate of delicate wafer biscuits he'd left for her.

It wasn't that he'd dismissed her, she assured herself, but that he was considerate enough to know she needed rest. And to provide something that might help settle her stomach.

Besides, last night he'd seemed far more focused on her pleasure than his own.

Laura walked back into the bedroom, collecting her glass of water and a couple of crackers, and moved to the balcony doors, drawn by the brilliant blue sky and glorious expanse of sea that filled the horizon.

How much better than the busy city and the prospect of photographers trying to snap candid pictures of her.

Leaning on the balustrade, she sipped her water then nibbled a biscuit, waiting to see if she could keep it down. It was exquisitely light with a sprinkling of sesame seeds and something she couldn't identify, awakening her taste buds. She found herself wondering if she might actually develop an appetite a little later.

Movement on the shoreline caught her attention and she saw someone emerge from the sea, diamond droplets sparkling in the sun as he shook his head.

Vassili.

Broad shouldered, long of limb, with an easy, deceptively lazy gait that belied his strength.

Her insides clenched, but not with nausea this time. With desire.

She should be completely sated after last night yet, she realised as she shifted her weight to ease the needy throb between her legs, her appetite for Vassili seemed insatiable.

Laura frowned and shoved another cracker into her mouth, almost annoyed to discover the last lingering hint of morning sickness had completely dissipated. Instead her body seemed primed to respond to the man strolling up from the beach, a beach towel wrapped around his lean hips.

A shiver ran through her.

Had she done the wrong thing, coming to Greece?

It's not Greece that's the problem, it's your reaction to him.

Last night she'd fleetingly worried that having sex with Vassili again would make her more vulnerable to him. Maybe she'd been right to worry. She only had to look at him to get turned on. Even at this distance!

They'd only been under the same roof one night and already she'd succumbed! It was unbelievable. What had happened to her determination not to let sex cloud her judgement?

For that matter how had sex become so important?

She'd spent most of her life wary of men, suspicious of their motives and reluctant to cede her autonomy in any way.

That week with Vassili at the Queensland resort had been an aberration for her.

Panic rose. How was she to hold her own while negotiating their children's future when she was under the spell of his sexuality?

It *had* to be a purely sexual craving, she assured herself. It couldn't be anything deeper. She'd never fallen for the ephemeral idea of romantic love. More, she distrusted it.

Yet as Vassili lifted his head and caught sight of her, pausing to wave, she felt a blast of something more than physical desire. Something in the region of her heart soared and she grinned as he smiled up at her.

It was a completely involuntary reaction, as natural as breathing.

But you need to be careful...very careful. He might not be a two-timing liar like your father, but it won't do to fall for him. He likes sex and he wants to be a father. That doesn't mean he cares for you. He needs to keep you sweet as the mother of his children.

That brought her back to earth with a thud and she turned away.

Vassili must have jogged up the stairs. By the time he appeared in the doorway she'd only had time to steal a T-shirt from his wardrobe to cover herself while she found her way back to her own bedroom.

'You're going somewhere?' he said as she stepped back from the doorway, hyperconscious of the fact his T-shirt skimmed her thighs and that she was naked beneath it. His gaze drifted to her breasts, which seemed suddenly fuller, puckering nipples standing proud as a shaft of heat shot to her pelvis.

Laura pressed her thighs together, trying to conquer that melting sensation low in her body.

'It's time I showered and dressed.'

Her words might be sensible but to Laura's dismay her voice had a husky resonance that made her remember the way she'd cried out his name as he took her to one incredible peak after another.

The sight of him, gloriously bare-chested, his hair wet from the sea, was too suggestive. Her skin tingled all over, drawing tight, and her breath quickened. Her fingers twitched as she imagined stroking the broad plains of his chest then down, slowly tracing the line between his muscles, past his navel to—

'You can use my en-suite bathroom to shower. Or have a soak in the bath.'

Laura blinked, yanked from her imaginings.

She remembered the bath, standing before the full-length window that looked out onto ancient olive trees and the sea beyond. It was the perfect place to relax. She'd imagined sharing it with him...

Laura stiffened. It was the reminder she needed to shore up her defences. Vassili mightn't be her enemy but it was essential she keep her wits about her. It would be too easy to be seduced by him, and not just sexually.

'How do you feel about breakfast?' he asked. 'Are you hungry?'

'I'm not sure.'

He turned back into the hallway, reappearing with a laden tray, and put it down on a table near the window.

'I prepared this earlier but when I brought it up you were asleep. I didn't like to wake you. There's fresh juice in the jug. I didn't include tea or coffee. I wasn't sure if you'd be nauseous.'

His furrowed-browed look of enquiry softened her determination to leave. 'That's very considerate.'

He shrugged. 'I've been reading up on morning sickness. I know that strong smells can sometimes be a trigger.'

He'd been reading about it? Reading about twins she would have expected, but about morning sickness?

Laura crossed her arms, unsure whether she was hugging in delight at the idea he cared enough to research what she was going through, or trying to be unimpressed.

'There's home-made yoghurt that goes well with the nuts and fruit. There's cereal and pastries. I know you're partial to almond croissants. These are freshly made.'

Laura stepped closer, drawn by fascination and sudden hunger. 'I thought there was no village on the island.'

'My housekeeper and her husband have their own house over the ridge, facing the mainland. I popped in there a few hours ago and collected the croissants. She'd promised to make some when I said how much you like them.' Vassili watched her frown and quickly reassured her. 'Don't worry, she won't come up to the house. I thought you'd prefer complete privacy. And I'll happily cook you a hot breakfast if you prefer.'

'Your skills extend to cooking?' Her voice sounded odd because her throat felt tight.

'You'd be surprised at my skills.' Vassili grinned and lifted his hands wide, drawing her attention to the play of muscles across his bare torso.

Laura snagged a rough breath and tried not to feel overwhelmed.

'What is it?' He moved closer, bombarding her senses with the sight and smell of powerful adult male in his prime, washed with seawater and glowing from the sun.

Laura tried and failed to ignore it all. Not just Vassili standing in her space, a look of concern etching his features. But the fact he'd put in so much thought to her comfort and well-being.

He hadn't been the one making the croissants. Yet he'd been considerate, letting her sleep, putting crackers and water by the bed. Bringing a breakfast designed to tempt the most jaded appetite, even reading up on her symptoms.

Her mouth crumpled at the edges and she wavered. She had good friends like Jake. But no one had cared for her like this in a long, long time. Not since the days before disaster when her father's infidelity had turned her mother into a shell of the woman she'd once been.

'Nothing,' Laura murmured. 'I'm impressed with the trouble you've gone to.'

She liked it. She could get too used to it.

And to the wonder and tenderness he'd revealed last night as he'd touched the place where their babies grew inside her. That had moved her more than anything she'd known.

It had made her realise that his feelings, for their children at least, were strong and genuine.

'It's nothing. Come, take a seat.'

He ushered her into a chair and, instead of leaving the room as planned, Laura found herself seated at the table, reaching for a heavenly scented croissant.

It wasn't just Vassili's sex appeal she had to withstand, but his consideration. She had a sinking feeling that if she weren't careful that might prove irresistible.

CHAPTER TEN

'It's absolutely stunning.'

Laura had heard Greece was beautiful, but this view caught her breath.

They stood on a rise at the south of the island. To the left, across the water, the hills of the mainland were smudged blue-grey. To the right the westering sun hung like a ripe orange, gilding the sea. Before them, in the aquamarine shallows off the point, were the pale ruins of a building.

'Surely that's a wall.' She leaned forward. 'And is that a column?'

'Steady!' Vassili's hand curled around her elbow. 'You don't want to tumble down here.'

Distracted, Laura nodded. But her interest was aroused. And maybe her distraction was a subconscious attempt not to react to his touch.

All day she'd been acutely aware of Vassili's physical presence. He only had to look at her for her pulse to leap and her nerves jangle, clamouring for more contact.

Last night had been a revelation, the passion off the scale. Yet it wasn't just a craving for physical pleasure she felt. It was a yearning simply to *be* with him. To bask in his attention and pretend his focus on her was because he was as fascinated by her as she was by him. Because he valued *her*.

As if she mattered for *herself*, not because she carried his babies.

That was a dangerous illusion she couldn't quite pull back from.

Which was why, despite the invitation in his eyes, Laura had spent the day resting alone. He, solicitous about her well-being, hadn't pushed for a renewal of intimacy. That should have pleased her, except she found herself frustrated and edgy.

This afternoon, as if sensing her mood, he'd invited her to see the island. They'd explored the beautiful gardens around the villa, venerable olive groves, the long white sand beach and the forest. The place was stunning, a pristine location mixed with the sort of luxury only significant wealth could buy.

It was a reminder that she and Vassili came from vastly different worlds.

Laura stepped back, drawing her arm from his hold, fighting the urge to lean in and rest her head on his shoulder. The more she kept her distance, the more she wanted not to.

Did he know that? Was that why he carefully gave her space? To tempt her?

Better to concentrate on the view.

'What *is* this place?' She peered at the lines of rock under the water. 'Is it an old house? A village?'

'A ruined temple.'

'A temple? You mean an *ancient* temple?'

Laura turned back to him.

How was she supposed to maintain her distance when he stood there looking like a Greek god? The late sun burnished proud, compelling features and his eyes glittered with inky intent that liquefied her insides and her resolutions.

'You like ancient ruins?'

'I've never seen any.' Something skittered in her bloodstream. Excitement? 'In Australia we don't have old buildings, not as old as in Greece. But we do have ancient rock art, thousands of years old.'

Looking down at the pale stones beneath the water, Laura felt the same awe as when she'd seen some of those amazing artworks at home. A sense of history coming alive. A fragile yet powerfully felt connection to the people who'd shared their beliefs by creating something that lasted, communicating through so many generations.

Her skin prickled and she rubbed her hand up her bare arms.

'You're cold? We should go back.'

Laura shook her head. 'Not cold. Excited. Can we explore there or is it out of bounds?'

'Not out of bounds, as long as we don't disturb the site or remove anything.' He gestured to a wooden seat she hadn't noticed, inviting her to sit. 'Here, I'll tell you about it.'

She sank down, stretching her legs and drinking in the panorama. At her feet wildflowers bloomed, the deep crimson of poppies bright against the blue water beyond. A bird called in the trees behind her and a light breeze, still warm, wafted across her skin, bringing the scent of new growth and the sea. Sydney had been damp and chill but Greece at this time of year was entrancing. Absently she rubbed her baby bump, incredulous at how vividly she could picture a picnic here with two dark-haired toddlers.

'A temple, you said?'

Vassili sat beside her. 'That's right. They believe it and the island were sacred to Aphrodite.'

Laura racked her brain. The name was familiar. 'Goddess of love?'

'Love, beauty and passion, especially sexual desire.'

She couldn't *not* meet his eyes. Vassili's voice slid across her skin like a caress. His slow smile, his suede-soft voice as he said *sexual desire*, acted like a blowtorch, melting Laura's caution. She felt it soften and disintegrate, leaving her breathless and wanting.

Last night she'd given in to lust, hoping to ease the pangs of need. Yet they'd only grown stronger. Maybe Aphrodite's influence had left a lingering magic, making Laura more susceptible to Vassili's charm.

Whatever the reason, her feelings were real and growing

stronger. Which was why sexual desire was the last thing she wanted to discuss.

'Why have a temple on an island that didn't have a village? Or was there one here?'

'That's the question. Maybe the remains of the town are yet to be found. Or maybe it was such a special place only the priests who tended the temple lived here.'

Laura turned back to the view, drinking in the peace and beauty. It *felt* like an enchanted place.

'Your family knew about this spot when they bought the island?' Even now it staggered her that a single family could own an island like this.

'The family story is that it was one of the reasons my grand-father bought it, as a love token for his wife.'

'Wow. Most men say it with flowers or chocolates.'

Her father had favoured roses, the long-stemmed ones that had no scent and drooped after a few days, but her mother had adored his occasional gifts.

Yet beneath Laura's off-hand response, she found herself responding to the idea of such a romantic gesture. 'What was your grandfather like?'

A serial philanderer maybe. A man who hoped to distract his wife from his affairs with a ridiculously romantic gesture.

'He had a gravelly, smoker's voice, a bristling moustache and piercing eyes that could read small boys as easily as books. He always knew when we were up to mischief.'

We? Vassili had never mentioned siblings. How little she really knew of his world.

'He disciplined you a lot?'

Vassili's laugh wrapped around her. 'He was more likely to join in our games. Mamá fussed that he encouraged us to get into trouble, but there was no harm in it. Adventure was al-lowed, encouraged even, but bad behaviour wasn't tolerated.'

Vassili's lingering smile tugged at something in Laura that

she hadn't felt for ages. The wish she'd had a bigger family than just her parents.

But your children will have that.

Vassili had a mother and siblings, not to mention Eudora and who knew how many other relatives. Her babies would have a family, whether she married him or not.

Warmth settled in her chest. One of the things that had worried her on learning she was pregnant was the fact that if anything happened to her, her baby—make that *babies*—would be alone.

'You've got a brother, or brothers? Any sisters?'

What would they be like? Would they welcome the twins, or shun them because Laura wasn't one of them, Greek and rich?

Vassili's silence took a few moments to penetrate. She turned to discover his smile gone, his mouth turned down.

'You didn't research me? There's a lot on the web about my family.'

'No. Once I read about your engagement I didn't have the stomach to read any more. I didn't want to know you.'

Their gazes locked. What did Vassili see? A woman too stubborn for her own good? He couldn't know how precisely his supposed betrayal had echoed the trauma that had shaped her life. How she'd felt physically ill at the prospect of reading any more about him. At least he knew now that she hadn't targeted him for his money.

'No sisters.' His voice had changed too, his tone hard to pin down. 'There was just me and Theo.'

Was.

Laura tried to read him, but apart from the downward slant of his mouth and his colourless tone, the man beside her was unreadable.

No, not unreadable.

Revelation struck as she realised Vassili's impenetrable look, the one that had so annoyed her in Sydney, was a mask to hide strong emotions.

His hand, curled around the seat between them, was white-knuckled and the pulse beating at his temple came fast and hard. His nostrils flared as he dragged in oxygen.

Regret and self-recrimination hit. How often in the past few days had she seen him wear that expression and attributed it to a sense of superiority? She'd been so wrapped up in her own fear and anger, ready to jump to negative conclusions about Vassili, because of her own experiences.

Her father had worn a mask, not because he felt too deeply, but because he didn't care enough. She'd tarred Vassili with the same brush.

'I'm sorry. It must be hard to lose a brother.'

Inane, Laura. Can't you do better than that?

But she *was* sorry. The words might be commonplace but she meant them.

She placed her palm over his hand. That connection was back, as strong as it had been last night when it had felt as if they were one being, joined in ways that far surpassed sex. It almost didn't matter whether he felt it too. The need to provide comfort ran as deep as the marrow in her bones.

'You were close.' It wasn't a question. Vassili might try to hide the depth of his emotions but his very stillness told her how much he felt.

He looked to her hand covering his. His chest rose on a deep breath.

'So close that sometimes I can't believe he's gone, though it's been thirteen years. He died just after we turned eighteen.'

Laura's eyes widened. 'You were twins!'

He'd said twins ran in his family, but not that he was one, which surely would have been natural. Unless it was a loss so deep he preferred not to speak of it.

That she could understand. She missed her mother daily, even though in their last years together Laura had been the caregiver when her mother lost heart.

'We were. Double trouble our father called us, but he'd laugh as he said it.'

An ache started up in her chest as Vassili's mouth twisted.

'I'm assuming the pair of you kept your parents on their toes.'

A huff of laughter. 'You assume right. Mamá always said we'd turn her hair white but even now it's barely grey.'

Laura squeezed his hand, glad to hear that hint of laughter. 'This place must have been paradise to two adventurous boys. A whole island to explore.'

Vassili slanted a sideways look at her, and she was relieved to see that lifeless mask had disappeared. His eyes glowed and she leaned closer, drawn by his magnetism. It, he, was irresistible.

'It was. We spent days outdoors. Climbing trees and the cliffs at the far end of the island. Swimming, yachting, wind-surfing, snorkelling, you name it.' His expression changed, became focused, and his hand turned to grasp hers. 'If you want to see the ruined temple we could snorkel there tomorrow.'

'Really? I'd love that.'

A smile curled the corners of his mouth and her toes too. A sizzle of effervescence stirred in her blood.

So much for keeping her distance. She had as much chance of doing that as of stopping the sun sinking below the horizon.

'Excellent. Tomorrow it is, then.'

Vassili felt the warmth of her hand squeezing his, read the excitement in her expression, and felt that familiar dazzle. His breath snatched, lungs expanding as he absorbed the full impact of this woman.

From the first Laura had done that to him.

She even banished the shadows that lurked whenever he stopped long enough. That was why, for years, he'd packed every hour with adventure or work, not leaving time for reflection.

But sitting with Laura, drinking in her enthusiasm, he felt…good.

Even thinking of Theo and the times they'd had together here brought pleasure not pain. For years he hadn't visited the island because of the memories, which was why he knew they'd be safe from media attention here. His rare visits over the last few years had been under the radar.

What was this magic Laura had? He wanted to define it, understand it. Understand *her*.

It was vital he do that if he were to stand a chance of persuading her to raise their children together.

'Tell me about Jake.'

'Jake? Why?'

Because he knew she, too, preferred not to speak about family. So he'd start by learning about her relationship with her devoted guard dog.

'Talking about Theo made me think of you and Jake. You're close but not related and haven't been lovers.' Vassili chose his words carefully. 'I'm curious about what bound you so closely.'

Laura surveyed him as if weighing up his words. He found himself willing her to talk, to share with him as he had with her.

She shuffled in her seat, withdrawing her hand, and disappointment flared.

But then she spoke, looking into the distance. 'We were at high school together. I was new to Sydney and didn't know anyone. He was born there but we were both misfits. We bonded over that.'

'Misfits?' He couldn't imagine it. She was bright and engaging. He imagined her as popular, with boys especially.

Again she hesitated. What was it she shared with Jake that she didn't want to share with him? Vassili tasted something metallic on his tongue. Jealousy?

'We were both slow learners, always in the lowest class together.' Laura slanted a look at him. 'We both have forms of dyslexia, which made school tough. You know kids can be unkind.'

Vassili expelled a breath he'd been holding. He wasn't sure what he'd been expecting, but it wasn't that. 'So you supported each other.'

'We did. You wouldn't believe it now, but when I met him, Jake was almost timid. His learning difficulties were more significant than mine and he'd been bullied a lot.'

Her eyes flashed and understanding dawned. 'You stood up for him. You were *his* champion.'

She shrugged. 'I couldn't sit by and do nothing. It was cruel the way some of the kids treated him. Of course I spoke up.' She smiled. 'Then over time, and with new teachers, he became more confident. Plus he grew head and shoulders taller than anyone else in the school.'

'Let me guess, no one messed with him then?'

'You've got it in one. By then we were a team. We spent a lot of time together, not just in school.'

'I'm glad you had each other.'

She didn't mention being bullied herself but he guessed from her talk of being a misfit that Laura had faced her share of discrimination.

'Me too. He's a special guy.' She shot him another look, lips twitching. 'Even if you two don't see eye to eye.'

Vassili thought of the last conversation he'd had with Jake, when he'd been frank about his desire to look after Laura and their children. 'You'd be surprised. We've buried the hatchet.'

'Have you? I'm impressed.'

He paused, not wanting to sound patronising but needing to express his feelings. 'It seems to me that for people who were labelled misfits you've both done very well in your chosen fields.'

Photography and modelling, both spheres that didn't rely on the written word.

Vassili's chest tightened. He'd had it so easy. He'd thrived at school, then walked into a job in the family firm, not to mention being born into money. He and Theo had led charmed lives until the year they turned eighteen.

'You know about Jake's work?'

'A little.' The investigators who'd located Laura had supplied a short briefing on him since she'd moved to his apartment. 'I know he's very good at what he does.'

'He's won a slew of awards.' Pride warmed her voice. 'He's one of the best around, making a name for himself and starting to earn serious money.'

'And you too. Those international tourism ads you'd just finished when we met didn't happen by accident.'

Laura shrugged. 'I fitted what they were looking for. A girl-next-door type with a wide smile, who looked good in a broad-brimmed hat.'

Vassili's brow twitched as he digested her words. She sounded off-hand about her looks. And a project that would only have been awarded to someone highly professional and experienced, not to mention pulse-stoppingly gorgeous.

'A very alluring, sexy girl next door,' he corrected. 'There must have been fierce competition.'

'You're right. I was lucky to get it and the money was very welcome.'

It was tempting to say that she needn't ever worry about money again. But he knew she wouldn't appreciate a blanket offer to support her as well as their children. Which was ridiculous, given his vast resources.

But Laura, he'd learned, was a proud woman who valued the right to make her own decisions.

'I've heard modelling is a tough, cut-throat business. You talk as if your success came from sheer luck.'

Laura tilted her head as she surveyed him, as if reading his thoughts in his features. It was disquieting. Vassili prided himself on keeping his thoughts to himself.

'You're right. But I know how fickle the industry is and

how often success hinges on being in the right place when someone wants a particular *look*. I've worked hard but it's not a permanent career. I only went into it as a stopgap to get some money, and stayed longer than expected.'

Now he was even more intrigued. 'What do you want to do instead?'

Her hesitation this time was only momentary. Vassili counted that as a gain. Not long ago she'd have refused to share anything private with him. What could be more private than her goals for the future?

'To run my own business. I've been designing beachwear since my teens when I started making clothes to sell at the markets. Sarongs, casual dresses, swimwear, even hats. I did well, but realised I needed to expand if I wanted to make a decent living. Around the same time I fell into modelling.' She spread her hands. 'It was a way to support myself and save for the business.'

'So it's on hold at the moment?'

His synapses started firing, turning over possibilities. The business she described would do well in Greece, given the influx of summer holidaymakers every year. If he gave her financial support and business advice to start up the enterprise it might be another inducement for her to stay.

Excitement burred under his skin.

'Sort of.'

A secretive smile curved the corners of her mouth and her eyes glowed. Vassili's heart thudded in response. She looked so alluring. Her enthusiasm was irresistible.

In frayed, cut-off shorts, canvas sneakers and lemon-yellow shirt tied at the waist, she looked fresh, sexy and beguiling. Not to mention bursting with an energy that reminded him abruptly of Theo.

'Go on. Don't leave me in suspense.'

The smile grew. 'After Queensland I dug out my old designs and started working. I began sourcing suppliers and updated my business plan.'

'You've already got a business plan?'

'I've had one from the start. I update it every year. Jake's gran insisted.'

'Jake's grandmother?'

'She'd worked in small business and taught me how to make a business plan over her kitchen table. She was the first person I told about my goals.'

'Not your parents?'

As soon as he asked, Vassili regretted the question. A shadow across her face. 'Sorry, I—'

Laura shook her head. 'It's okay.'

But she looked back towards the sea and crossed her arms. Defensively?

'My father wasn't around by then.'

Her clipped words revealed the man wasn't a favourite. What had he done? If he'd hurt Laura—

'And my mother...' Laura's mouth was a crimped line. 'From the time we moved to Sydney Mum wasn't doing well. She sort of faded away, even before the cancer that took her.'

'How old were you?'

'When she died? Sixteen.' Laura must have heard his sharply indrawn breath. 'But I was okay. Jake's gran took me in. I lived with them till I could support myself. I'd already got in the habit of going around there most days after school, for a while, before I had to go home to look after my mother.'

'When did you move to Sydney?'

Laura turned, her expression curiously blank. 'Piecing together my history?' Another tiny shrug. 'I was twelve when we moved to Sydney. So you see, Jake and I go way back. And his grandmother made a huge difference in my life. I wish she were still around. I'd love to show her my updated business plan over a cup of tea and home-made scones. She made the best scones.'

Vassili guessed it wasn't the scones Laura missed. He heard respect and love in her voice.

He swallowed hard, his throat surprisingly tight.

Well, you wanted to know about Laura.

Yes, but he hadn't expected this shaft of pain through his chest as he discovered what she'd been through.

She didn't seek sympathy. But she had it.

Separated under what he guessed were difficult, if not traumatic circumstances from her father, presumably at twelve when she and her mother had moved to Sydney. Was that why her mother had *faded away*? An unhappy divorce?

It seemed that from then on Laura, trying to cope in a new place and with learning difficulties, also had to shoulder the burden of caring for her mother. Then to lose her only a few years later…

It felt as if gravel lined his throat. Laura wouldn't thank him for his pity. He understood now at least part of what had made her so independent and determined. And, if her parents' divorce had been acrimonious, part of the reason she'd been so determined to think the worst of him. Because she blamed her father for breaking up the family? The man must be dead now or surely she'd have ended up back with him after her mother died.

Sympathy and admiration vied for supremacy. And something Vassili couldn't name, a vast tenderness stronger than any he'd known.

Vassili saw her watching and chose his words thoughtfully. 'I've never made scones. I'm not even sure what they are. But since your mentor's not here, if you want a sounding board for your updated business plan, I'm your man. I've picked up some experience in the corporate world over the years.'

'Really? We're talking a tiny business here.'

'You've got to start somewhere. Besides, I'm interested.'

Laura angled her head in that way she had, as if to get a better view of him. 'You're full of surprises, Vassili Thanos. I didn't think you'd like the idea of me running my own business.'

'You think I want to keep you—what's the saying? Pregnant and in the kitchen? I'm not that old-fashioned.'

Even if the thought of her permanently in his home was exactly what he wanted. If helping her achieve her career goals convinced her to stay with him, he was all for it.

'I didn't know what to think.'

'Then it's as well we've got a chance to know each other properly, isn't it?' He glanced over her shoulder at the sun sinking below the horizon. 'Let's go back to the house. I mightn't know scones but I cook a great souvlaki. You can watch and marvel at my skill.'

Her laugh sent a flurry of delight through him. He liked amusing her. Almost as much as he enjoyed knowing he'd breached another of the barriers between them.

When Vassili wanted something he always got it, no matter how much patience, planning and effort it took.

One day soon Laura would capitulate and marry him. Whatever it took.

CHAPTER ELEVEN

THE SEA WAS a drift of turquoise silk against her skin as Vassili carried her through water that was up to his beautifully sculpted chest.

Laura wrapped her arms around his neck, looking into dark eyes framed by long, spiky wet lashes. Her heart dipped and shuddered with a longing that had intensified in the month they'd been on the island.

She knew that look. Honed features taut, nostrils flared, eyes blazing. Vassili wanted to have sex with her again, and she'd let him.

Let him! She was the one who'd played provocative games, teasing and arousing him until he hauled her close.

So much for being careful not to be swept off her feet by Vassili's lovemaking, or the way he insisted on taking care of her. She'd never felt so cherished, even allowing for the fact his aim was to convince her to stay.

The days had passed in a haze of contentment and sexual bliss, especially since her morning sickness had disappeared. He'd even stopped badgering her about making decisions for the future, apparently preferring, like her, to take things one day at a time.

Laura was happy about that. She didn't want to argue continually. It was a rare delight simply to take time out and enjoy the pleasures of life with Vassili.

Even if, some time soon, they'd have to thrash out their plans for the future.

She suppressed a shudder that felt like nerves. It was easier to live in the moment, enjoying the tranquility, animal attraction and, increasingly, affection.

When it came to discussing marriage, Laura was at a disadvantage. Sensible as a marriage of convenience might be, for the sake of their children, her history made it unworkable. If there was one thing she needed from life it was to be truly valued—and loved.

She wouldn't, couldn't, accept anything less. The memory of her mother, bereft, unable to deal with the truth about her own marriage, was a harsh cautionary lesson.

Which Laura refused to think about now.

'Where are we going?' She swivelled her neck, trying to see the shore. 'The beach is back that way.'

His voice was rough, not with effort, but that masculine timbre designed solely, it seemed, to undo her. 'The beach is too far away. This is closer. And completely private.'

This turned out to be an overhang in the cliff, an almost-cave with a buttress of rock that hid them from the view of anyone on the sea, not that there was anyone.

'That's better,' he murmured as he waded into shallower water and lifted her onto a smooth rock shelf at hip height.

Laura sat facing him, their faces level, the sea up to their waists. He wore that determined look, the endearing mix of arrogance, excitement and tenderness that she'd come to know so well.

If it weren't for the fact she knew his motivations were about securing his babies and assuaging his libido, her heart might have been in real danger.

As it was, her hand went to his face, tracing the proud features she found more attractive than anything else in the world. His damp flesh was warm, his pulse thrumming against her fingertips. A reminder that for all his austere masculine beauty he was as vulnerable and flawed as herself. Well, perhaps not as vulnerable.

Vassili wasn't her enemy, even if his insistence on marriage was a recipe for disaster. A loveless marriage would destroy her, as Laura's mother had been destroyed.

Time and again Laura had thought of explaining that, only to pull back on the brink. Her fear of vulnerability had grown innate in the years since she'd learned the truth about her father, and the dangers of giving her heart to anyone.

'*Kopela mou*, where have you gone?'

Ebony eyes snared hers and her heart stuttered.

How was she going to say goodbye when the time came?

Maybe, whispered the silky voice, *you don't have to say goodbye. If you'd change your mind and say yes to a wedding.*

Scary how tempting that was.

'Nowhere important.' She spread her fingers across his shoulders then down his chest, watching him breathe deeper, eyes heavy-lidded with promise. 'How do you know about this place? Have you brought lots of lovers here?'

Laura tried to keep her voice light and failed. All that mattered was the present and the future, not the past.

'I've never brought a lover to the island. For years I avoided it. There were too many memories.' He paused, chest rising on a deep breath, as if he cleansed his lungs with it. 'Theo and I found this place when we were kids. We pretended it was a pirate's hideout.'

'Vassili.' His words jerked her out of her self-absorption. Her hands flattened against his chest where she felt the solid drumming of his lifeforce. Why did that feel as intimate as any sensual delight they'd shared? 'I'm sorry—'

His beguiling smile stole her words. 'Maybe it's time to make some new memories here. What do you say?' His hand slid around her back to grasp the tie of her bikini top.

The fact that he waited for her nod was another nail in the coffin of her resistance. Not that she'd resisted him since coming here. Instead she'd let herself be swept up in the warm tide of joy that came from Vassili's lovemaking and tenderness. She only hoped that when the time came, she could distinguish between sexual compatibility and the mirage of love.

'New memories.' She could do with some of those herself. 'I think that's a wonderful idea.'

She slid her hand below the waterline to the bulging front of his swim shorts. His arousal twitched in her hold as Vassili yanked first one then the other tie on her bikini top undone and her breasts spilled free.

His eyes grew luminous and something shifted hard inside her. The way he looked at her made her feel…

Too much. She couldn't afford to dwell on that.

But then he was bending down to cup one breast, his mouth capturing her other nipple. Her head fell back on a sigh of delight. Shivers of arousal ran from her breasts to her womb, up her spine to her scalp and right down to her toes curling in the water.

'What you do to me, *psihi mou*!'

Laura didn't understand the Greek but the longing in his words perfectly matched her own and she adored hearing it. 'Talk to me, Vassili,' she pleaded as she arched, greedily offering her breasts.

He obliged, weaving a sensuous thread of words, hoarse, admiring, beautiful words, as he played with her breasts, drawing delight with every touch, till she could stand it no more and scrabbled at his swim shorts.

'Not yet.'

She opened her eyes to see him flushed, features taut, as if he too hovered on the edge of orgasm.

Vassili took her hands and placed them on his shoulders, then he skimmed his palms over the rise of her pregnant belly in slow sweeps that felt to her aroused senses almost reverent.

All the while, glittering midnight eyes held hers. His hand dipped beneath her bikini bottom, arrowing through swollen folds while his other hand cupped her breast as he mouthed her nipple. Gently he bit down as his fingers found her pleasure point and just like that the world exploded into cascading pleasure.

The force of her climax broke her apart, like shards of bright glass catching and reflecting the sun's incandescent heat. Laura rocked against him and he gathered her close. Through her ecstasy she heard more of those sensuous Greek words, this time warm with reassurance as he wrapped one arm around her back and his other hand anchored her head against his shoulder.

Finally the trembling subsided. Slowly she came back to the present, the heat of Vassili's powerful body against hers. Salt on her lips from his skin and the smell of the sea in her nostrils, enriched by her lover's own tangy scent.

She slipped her tongue across his skin, needing to taste, and felt his shudder. It racked him from his shoulder where she rested, through his torso, right down to those powerful thighs between hers.

He was such a strong man, physically and mentally, yet she undid him.

Like he undoes you. And you love it.

Would she ever conquer this yearning for Vassili Thanos?

Was it her fate to be tied, emotionally and physically, to one man, as her mother had been tied to the man who'd betrayed her so cruelly?

For once the thought, and the fear behind it, was so fleeting, Laura banished it instantly.

Because Vassili needed her and she wanted to give him the same exquisite joy he'd given her.

Still leaning into him, she unwrapped her arms from around his shoulders and reached for the ties at the sides of her bikini bottom. They were knotted tight and she could only fumble one undone.

'Can I help?' His voice was a caress along already stretched senses. She'd swear she could *taste* the sound of Vassili's voice, like dark chocolate on the back of her tongue. He began to pull back.

'No! Don't go.'

Her focus might be on giving him pleasure, but she couldn't bear the thought of even a few centimetres' separation. She wanted his heat, the scratch of his chest hair on her skin, the solid comfort of his body against the swell of her abdomen.

But he obviously had the same idea as her, for when she reached for him it was to discover him sliding his swim shorts down his thighs.

Eagerly Laura closed her fingers around his erection, stunned anew at how incredible it was, formidably rigid and powerful yet sheathed in softest flesh.

'Look at me, Laura *mou*.'

He tipped her chin up and her heart gave an almighty jump as she met his eyes.

His expression was more than hungry for sex. His features seemed lit from within, revealing something complex and wonderful that she could spend hours trying to read. Her throat clogged on a wave of emotion.

She opened her mouth to ask what he was thinking, when he surged forward in her hand and the head of his erection probed the flesh between her open thighs.

Questions fled.

Laura breathed deep, trying to recapture the moment, because it seemed vital that she diagnose what she'd read in his expression. But Vassili dipped his head, lips brushing hers in a barely there slide that fragmented her thoughts. She sat straighter, seeking more from him as her nipples puckered needily.

It had been mere minutes since her orgasm yet, as she guided him to her beneath the water, she knew this wasn't just for Vassili. She wanted him as much as ever. More.

They slid together, their easy joining belying the tremendous jolt of energy that made them both stiffen. Laura hooked her legs around his hips, holding him close, her hands lifting to his head where she scraped her fingers through his wet hair. She *needed* to hold him, as if he were the only secure, real thing in the world now.

Vassili pulled her in so close it was a wonder she could breathe, and when one large hand cupped her buttocks, tilting her as he moved inside her, she forgot all about the need for oxygen.

They rocked together, slowly but with a primal force more profound than anything she'd known. Laura closed her eyes, drinking in the sound of rough breathing, the caress of the sea and the sensation of Vassili's powerful body, moving slowly yet perfectly towards a distant, incredible peak greater than any she'd scaled.

She lost track of whose body was which. Of everything but the dark, potent magic they made together. Their movements were fiercely controlled, yet beneath that control, something primitive and all-consuming surged.

Her man. Her mate.

The words repeated in her head with each thrust of their bodies.

Vassili...

Finally the wild energy they'd sought to tame burst free. Laura clung to Vassili, eyes locked on his as the edges of her vision blurred and a tsunami of sensation hurtled through them. It blasted away everything but their shared bliss and, through it, their indefinable connection.

She heard herself scream his name. Then a throbbing groan that sounded like a prayer or a promise, so husky that it took long seconds to discover it was her own name, spilled by Vassili in the throes of ecstasy.

Later that afternoon Vassili emerged from his office and headed to the kitchen. There'd been work he hadn't been able to avoid any longer, and Laura had taken her notebook and sunhat into the garden, saying she had a date with a hammock.

She needed her rest, which was another reason he'd shut himself in his study. Their sex life left him energised, but Laura needed plenty of sleep, especially after this morning.

What had begun as a short snorkelling tour of Aphrodite's temple ruins had ended with an erotic conflagration that he'd swear had left scorch marks.

Sex with Laura had always been phenomenal but this morning… He shook his head, trying to quantify the unquantifiable. The extra element that transformed a physical act into something that reverberated through his very soul.

A suspicion circled in his brain, an unformed idea that he didn't want to pursue.

You've climbed some of the world's most treacherous peaks, pursued danger on five continents, almost lost your life several times. Since when have you been so easily scared?

The answer to that was simple.

When emotion was involved.

From the day Theo had died, Vassili had fought to keep his life uncluttered by difficult feelings. It wasn't that he didn't feel, but that he preferred to keep a lid screwed down tight on his emotions, rather than feel too strongly. A taxing schedule made that easier. He wasn't usually in one place long enough to get involved.

But you want to get involved now. You want to take on a wife and two children.

Strange how he hadn't thought twice about that. It was the right thing to do. He *wanted* to do it.

It was going to complicate his life enormously.

But, complicated or not, he intended to make it happen.

Enough to curtail your adventures? You made a promise to Theo to live the life he couldn't. How will you do that, tied to domesticity?

Vassili paused in the act of filling a tray with cold drinks.

For more than a month the most adventurous thing he'd done was snorkel in the shallow waters off the point this morning.

If he didn't count tangling with Laura, the most indomitable woman he knew.

He stood still, working that through, waiting for the feeling of itchy feet he knew so well. The eagerness to move on, try something different, tackle a new challenge.

It didn't come.

Vassili groped for the benchtop, staring through the window at the view he knew as well as the back of his hand.

He'd changed. She'd changed him.

Would it last? Was it the novelty of this situation, and his sense of duty, that kept him tethered here?

He'd learned to be strong, first for Theo, then for his mother after his father died. Now he'd be strong for Laura and their babies. Yet this didn't feel like duty. It felt like a choice, one he was happy to make.

He rubbed the heel of his hand across his sternum, easing the ache inside his ribs.

How much of your globetrotting adventures were really about your promise to Theo? And how much was purely selfish, about not keeping still long enough to deal with his loss?

Vassili stiffened.

No wonder he wasn't into self-analysis. It led down wormholes to places he didn't want to be.

But there was one place he absolutely wanted to be. With an urgency he refused to analyse, he grabbed the tray and walked into the sunshine to find Laura.

She'd fallen asleep in the hammock, her hat half across her face and her big notebook open on her lap. Vassili put down the drinks, noticing as he did so that her notebook wasn't the one she showed him with her detailed business plan and related notes.

That had been impressive enough. She had sound business sense and a mix of pragmatism and inspiration that boded well for her business. She planned to start small but had big ideas and a coherent scheme to achieve them. He'd been ready to offer financial assistance to get her started, but held back, sensing she'd suspect, rightly, he was trying to create more ties between them.

What he saw now on those open pages impressed him too.

Laura had said she wanted to design clothes as well as sell them. Her plans included an option for fabric printing, but he'd assumed she'd commission a designer for that.

Now he saw the full extent of her ambition, and her talent.

From time to time he'd seen her sketching, most often in the garden, but she hadn't offered to show him and he hadn't wanted to pry. Now he learned she intended to design both the fashions she sold and the fabrics she used.

One of the open pages had a detailed, coloured sketch of an olive branch. It was good, so good it looked as though he could reach out and feel the leaves.

On the opposite page was something more fascinating. A stylised design, unmistakably olive leaves and fruit, scattered across the page in variations on a repeating pattern, as if on fabric.

'What you think?' Her soft voice made him turn to find sleepy green and gold eyes surveying him. 'Too naff?'

'Not at all. I like it very much. You capture the essence of it with a simplicity that appeals. I assume you mean to print it on fabric?'

It wasn't much of a guess since she'd made notes at the bottom of the page about cottons and what he assumed were other fabrics.

Laura sat up a little, making the hammock swing. 'Maybe. If I come up with something good enough.'

Vassili was about to assure her this was excellent, but he was no expert. 'Do you mind if I have a look?'

After a momentary hesitation she shook her head and he felt a rush of pleasure. She trusted him enough to show him her business plans but this felt different, even more personal. It didn't take the slight wariness in her expression to tell him that.

'Here.' He offered her a tall glass of fresh juice. 'Shall we swap?'

Laura took the glass and passed him the sketchbook. He sat at the base of the gnarled tree and opened it.

Immediately he was absorbed in the world of colour and entrancing forms. Near the front were aquamarines, sea green and the pale gold of an Australian beach. The designs were of waves, shells, seahorses and starfish. There were repeating patterns like the one she'd done of the olive branch and others seemed to be borders.

There were pages of what he guessed were Australian flowers, colourful and unusual, rendered with a deft delicacy.

There was another series in shades of dark blue and silver, inspired by the night sky. Another section that looked like shimmering sunrises and glowing sunsets. And one that began with yachts in the sunshine and ended with abstract geometric patterns that caught and held the eye.

He turned a page and there were the bright red geraniums that grew so prolifically in the villa's garden. Once again she'd started with a realistic scene then spent pages riffing on the theme, coming up with a range of options inspired by the original. After that were Greek wildflowers and finally the olives.

His hand hovered over the page.

'It's okay to say you don't like them. They won't be to everyone's taste.'

'I don't like them, I love them.' He raised his head and met her gaze. 'These are excellent. You have great talent.'

For a moment she didn't reply, then she shook her head. 'You're good for my ego, Vassili.'

She didn't believe him? Surely she knew how good these were, or she wouldn't persist with them. Or did she think he was telling her what he thought she wanted to hear?

'You don't believe me?' He closed the book, annoyed. 'I

thought you knew me by now, Laura. I've always been straight with you. These are outstanding. If it weren't for the fact that you'd probably accuse me of interfering, I'd put you in touch with someone here in Greece who knows about this sort of thing. She started as an interior designer and has branched out into producing her own soft furnishings.'

Laura's eyes widened. 'You're serious!'

Vassili shrugged and put the book down. It was a small thing but the way she brushed off his response rankled. He felt that for all their closeness in other ways, he was no nearer winning her trust.

He couldn't blame her because he *did* have an agenda— persuading her to stay with him permanently.

But today his emotions felt too close to the surface. The morning had been fantastic, but something, maybe being back in that cave he and Theo had haunted as kids, had unsettled him.

He sensed movement then she sat beside him. Light fingers stroked the back of his hand.

'I'm sorry, Vassili. Sometimes I'm too wary.'

He guessed with her learning problems she hadn't received many accolades in her early years. Maybe that was why.

'Don't apologise.' He'd acted like a tetchy kid, ready to take offence. 'I'm just...' Out of sorts? That was no excuse. 'How's your juice?'

'Lovely, thank you. Just what I needed.' She paused. 'And for the record, I'd love to talk to your designer friend if she's interested.'

Vassili nodded, inordinately pleased. 'You'd take a favour from a selfish billionaire?'

'I'll take any reasonable help to get my business off the ground. And I don't think you're selfish. Anything but.' Her fingers curled around his. 'I was thinking about what you said earlier about this place bringing back upsetting memories of your brother. You don't need to stay here with me. I could—'

He lifted his index finger to her mouth, a shiver trailing under his skin at the touch of her velvet-soft lips. 'Absolutely not. I *want* to be here with you, despite what happened in the past.'

Vassili read curiosity in her expression but she said nothing, and suddenly he wanted to explain. Not because he needed to unburden himself, but because it felt right to break down the barriers between them, to prove he trusted her.

He dropped his hand to cover hers, looking at the pile they made, one on top of the other, each comforting the other. How long since he'd accepted comfort?

'Theo and I were close, being twins. We spent most of our time together and were best friends.'

He raised his head, taking in the old olive grove and the sea beyond. 'We spent every summer here and it was the venue for every big family celebration, including our eighteenth birthday party. I knew something was wrong with Theo then, but not how wrong. He'd been away on a sailing trip with friends and when he got here he was unwell.'

Vassili's mouth flattened as he remembered that last weekend. 'He took a turn for the worse the night of a party and ended up in hospital. He was diagnosed with an aggressive blood cancer and was gone in a couple of weeks.'

Darkness edged his vision as memories crowded. Then Laura's other hand completed the pile between them and the brittle weight within him eased a little.

'For years I didn't come here, but now—'

'Now you feel you need to be here because of me.' She leaned close. 'But I can go somewhere else, *we* can go somewhere else. It needn't be here.'

We can go somewhere else.

Vassili liked that *we*. Liked her thinking of them as a pair.

'There's no need. Yes, sometimes I think about Theo here. But that's not a bad thing, in fact I've been remembering the good times more and more.' That was new, for in avoiding the past he'd blocked out the good with the bad. 'Besides, we've been making new memories to counter the sad ones.'

He allowed a little of the ever-present desire he felt for Laura to show in his smile and saw its reflection in her gaze.

But lust wasn't his primary emotion. It was gratitude for this woman who'd inadvertently helped him face the pain of the past.

Gratitude and something deeper. Something that he sensed would change him for ever.

Suspicion hit with the force of lightning from a clear blue sky.

Was he falling in love with Laura?

CHAPTER TWELVE

'MY RECEPTIONIST WILL book you in for a follow-up appointment. But if you've got concerns at any stage I'm just a phone call away.' The obstetrician looked from Laura to Vassili. 'At any time, if it's urgent.'

Laura couldn't imagine any doctor she'd seen in Australia offering to be available any time of the day or night. But she'd never attended a consultation with a billionaire at her side. Money talked.

The doctor turned back to Laura, eyes twinkling. 'Not that I anticipate the need for that. As I said, everything seems to be progressing very well.'

Laura returned his smile, relieved.

She'd been full of questions she'd forgotten to ask the doctor in Sydney yet worried about the language barrier. She needn't have worried. Her new obstetrician in Athens was fluent in English. More, she trusted him. He took his time not only with her physical examination but talking with her, listening carefully and answering questions. Not once had he brushed off any query and, while he was courteous to Vassili, he made it clear he was *her* doctor.

'Thank you, Doctor. It's a relief to know things are going well.'

She shot a look at Vassili, who smiled before leaning across to shake the doctor's hand.

She studied her lover's profile, trying to work out what was different about him. He'd changed. She'd sensed it a few days ago, the day they'd snorkelled around the submerged temple ruins then made love on the shore.

But she couldn't put her finger on the difference in him. He wasn't withdrawn. That was too strong a word. He was as attentive and his lovemaking as wonderful as ever. But there was something...different. A preoccupation. A sense that something weighed on his mind.

When she'd asked, he denied it, and how could she push the point when she had no real evidence that anything was wrong?

Perhaps, she decided as he ushered her out, he'd just been nervous, waiting to hear how the pregnancy was going. He'd had plenty of his own questions for the doctor and had clearly been thinking carefully about her health and that of the twins.

He'll make a great father. But will he make a good husband?

Laura didn't have anything against marriage. But she had reason not to marry unless she was sure there was equal commitment, loyalty and love on both sides.

The wreck of her parents' marriage had been a grim lesson about what could go wrong when that was lacking.

She refused to marry a man simply to make more convenient arrangements for raising their children. Without love...

Laura shivered as they paused by the receptionist's desk and Vassili stroked the small of her back. Even through her clothes that feathering caress sparked a host of reactions.

They were purely physical, she assured herself. The result of a month of amazing sensual intimacy.

Not just sensual intimacy, she amended. Their relationship had reached a new plane where companionship, respect, shared humour and a heightened level of understanding had brought them far closer than mere sexual partners. In fact—

'How does that date suit you, Laura?'

Vassili's question dragged her from her musings to find him and the receptionist regarding her.

'That sounds good, thanks.'

She had no idea what date the receptionist had suggested for the next appointment, but she had nothing in her schedule. Which was a reminder, she realised with a plunging in her stomach, that she should be making concrete plans. She couldn't keep living her idyllic island life, pretending decisions didn't need to be made. About herself and Vassili.

He turned to her. There it was again, that hint of distance in his eyes and in the lines bracketing his mouth. Something bothered him.

But then he smiled, the hint of reserve vanishing in a blaze of what looked like pure pleasure that made her heart give a great leap.

Vassili took her hand, leading her towards the exit, and she couldn't help but grin back at him.

'So.' He leaned in and whispered in her ear. 'Who's a clever mother-to-be? Perfect blood pressure, perfect health, perfect everything!'

'I hardly think clever is right. Lucky, more like.'

It struck her fully then how much good her chance to relax and be pampered in utter privacy had done her. She threaded her fingers through his, drawing him to a stop in the building's foyer.

'Thank you, Vassili. For everything. The way you've taken care of me has made such a difference. If I'd been in Sydney I suspect my blood pressure would be sky-high and the doctor wouldn't be pleased.'

Whatever else was on his mind, Laura couldn't doubt Vassili's warmth as he looked down at her. 'Don't thank me for that. I like taking care of you.' His voice dropped low. 'You know I want to do it permanently.'

Before she could protest that *permanently*, he brushed his mouth across hers. Fleeting the kiss might be, yet it left her breathless and clinging.

Gleaming eyes met hers as he pulled back. His voice was

a husky whisper for her ears alone. 'Let's continue this in privacy.'

Dazzled by the full force of her feelings for him, Laura let him lead her from the building, her mind already on the possibilities offered by the privacy of his Athens penthouse.

Dimly she was aware of a hubbub on the edge of the pavement, a voice calling Vassili's name. Then his arm clamped tight around her, drawing her quickly away in the other direction. A hurried glance revealed a stranger trying to photograph them between the shoulders of two men in dark suits. He called to catch their attention.

'Don't turn around. Keep walking.' Vassili's voice was firm and unhurried. 'Ah, here's the car.'

He didn't rush her but in no time at all the limousine's back door was open and he'd ushered her in, following her inside, his body shielding hers from the guy on the pavement. A second later the vehicle drew away into the busy traffic, leaving the photographer and Vassili's security team behind.

Laura's heart thumped hard and fast and her stomach squirmed sickeningly.

She'd forgotten the press. She'd been so wrapped up in her feelings for Vassili and her excitement over the doctor's news that all was well with the babies, she'd been taken completely unawares.

Now she dropped to harsh reality with a thud.

Vassili looked annoyed. 'I'm sorry. That shouldn't have happened. Only my most trusted staff knew about the appointment.'

He looked so concerned, Laura reached out to cover his clenched fist.

Funny how the connection eased her own tension too. In Australia she'd felt so alone, despite the support of her friends. The last month had shown her that, despite their differences about what the future should hold, Vassili really wanted to help and care for her.

Because you're carrying his babies.

Laura ignored the little jab of pain beneath her ribs. She wasn't blind enough to believe she was his prime focus. There was a growing bond between them that included liking and a strong sexual attraction. But his real interest was his children. Not her. He'd made that clear from the first and she'd never expected anything different.

It wasn't as if he'd ever professed love. That would only have raised her suspicions, knowing how easy it was for men to talk of romance to get what they wanted.

At least Vassili was honest, not pretending theirs was some great romantic union.

'Your staff did their best,' she said slowly. 'And they did stop him following us.'

Still Vassili didn't look happy. Laura wasn't either—she hated being the centre of press speculation—but Vassili looked as close as she'd ever seen to losing his temper.

'Maybe it was an accident that he was there at the wrong moment,' she suggested. 'I'm sure no one on your staff was responsible.'

Vassili raked his hand through his hair. 'You're right. But I don't believe it was an accident. Someone tipped him off.'

Laura shrugged, trying to project unconcern despite the jittery feeling inside and the icy cascade of fear down her spine.

It wasn't being photographed that she disliked, it was being part of scandal, the sort the public loved to drool over. The sort that hounded you, tainting everything...

She rubbed her hands up her arms, trying to warm chilled flesh. Trying not to think about the media storm that was about to hit. She'd cope. Of course she would. 'Maybe someone working in the building saw us arrive. If they happened to know a journalist...'

'Yes, it was probably as simple as that.' Vassili sighed. 'If my knowledge of the press is anything to go by, the stories will start within the next hour or so. They're bound to put two and two together, once it's confirmed we've been to an obstetrician together.'

He threaded his long fingers through hers and, despite everything she knew about the nasty public stories to come, she felt her tension ease a little. 'I'm sorry, Laura. I was sure we'd be able to sneak under the radar for this appointment and then disappear again, no harm done.'

'You did your best.'

She looked at their joined hands, wondering how she was going to cope if she followed through with her determination not to marry him. She'd miss him terribly, when the time came to leave. Almost enough to make her question whether, after all, she could settle for a convenient wedding.

That realisation made her hurry on, focusing on the current problem, not the future one. 'Eudora. You'll have to warn her.'

Vassili showed her his phone, already in his other hand. 'At least she'll get the sympathy vote when the circus starts. I'm more concerned about you.'

His gaze held hers with an intensity that rivalled his lovemaking.

He does care, see?

But not enough. Laura wanted, *needed*, the genuine article in a life partner. Love, true and deep.

'I have no intention of reading the articles. You and I know the truth and so do my friends. As long as you can protect me from being harassed in the street until the furore dies down, we'll get through it.'

Admiration glowed in his eyes. 'I applaud your pragmatism, Laura. We'll get through this, don't worry.'

But instead of cuddling her close and lending her the comfort of his big body, he hit speed dial. It was the decent thing to do, warning his cousin about the media frenzy about to engulf them all. She'd have been disappointed if he hadn't warned Eudora.

Yet, as Laura heard him say 'Eudora' and switch to Greek, she felt unaccountably bereft.

Vassili had taken her at her word. She'd said she'd be okay and she would be. *She* was the one who insisted they shouldn't marry for the sake of the children. She respected him for not pestering her about that.

Only she knew that, deep inside, a part of her that wasn't strong, the part that yearned for more, had wanted him to hold her close and whisper nonsensical words of love and reassurance, as if he really had the power to make everything turn out all right.

Back in his apartment, Vassili couldn't resist any more. He tugged Laura into his arms and onto his lap as he sank onto a sofa.

There. That felt better, so much better.

She leaned into him, head tucked beneath his chin, palm to his chest as he cradled her. His heart slowed.

In the street when that paparazzo had confronted them his pulse had been a manic thud, his instinct to sweep Laura into his arms. Which would have been like throwing kerosene on an already blazing fire, a gift for the snoop who'd waited like a hovering vulture for them to appear.

Then in the car, reading the conflict between the determined tilt of Laura's chin and her too-pale features, between her sensible words and the shock in her eyes, Vassili had wanted desperately to hold her close, whispering words of reassurance. Except he couldn't risk photos of them kissing on the back seat hitting the press. Not for his sake but hers. For the first time he wished his car had tinted windows.

He should have insisted to Eudora that they publicly end this farce of an engagement the moment he discovered Laura's pregnancy. Except that would seriously threaten his cousin's chance of being with the man she loved. And Laura had understood and applauded the decision not to go public.

Now it was too late. What sickened him was that Laura would bear the brunt of the scandal. He'd be cast as a playboy but it was *she* he worried about. The press would trash her reputation, labelling her the other woman.

Fury throbbed. He'd never felt so impotent. She deserved better from him. He was the one who'd convinced her to trust him and come to Greece.

'Your heart's racing,' she murmured, her hand sliding across his chest as she looked up, 'and if you clench your jaw any harder you'll crack a molar.'

'I'm sorry. I let you down.'

That was what he couldn't bear.

'It wasn't your fault a photographer found us.'

Did she have to be so sensible? Vassili wanted to rant and rave, something he never did, or get his hands on that photographer. Today, because it was Laura who'd be hurt, his anger knew no bounds.

'It's more than that.' He slid his hand through the silk of her hair, tugging it down and combing it around her shoulders with his fingers. 'I should have scotched the story about an engagement to Eudora immediately.'

'And possibly wrecked her chance to marry the man she loves? You couldn't do that to her.'

Vassili shook his head, knowing Laura was right. Eudora was dear to him, as dear as a sister. But when it came to a choice between her and Laura, there was no choice.

'I'll do anything I can to help Eudora and her partner. But not at your expense. She and I are announcing the end of our engagement today. We'll say it was a mutual decision because our affections are engaged elsewhere.'

The trouble was that, until Eudora publicly revealed her marriage plans, Laura would be seen as a relationship wrecker.

'Eudora's willing to do that?'

He hadn't given her a choice, but to be fair his cousin hadn't objected. 'She is.'

He paused, planting his hand at the back of Laura's neck and taking hope from her expression of trust and tenderness.

'Laura. I've given you a month to consider. Surely you see now how good we are together. That we could make a fine life for our children, and ourselves, if we're together.' He cleared his scratchy throat. 'I want to marry you.'

He watched her throat move as if she, too, found swallowing difficult. She considered him with serious eyes and he felt that smack of tenderness, of affection and desire, right in the middle of his chest. Surely she felt it too, or something like it.

'This month together has been special, don't you think?' He firmed his mouth, realising he sounded almost needy.

Because he was. He needed Laura in his life. He couldn't imagine returning to an existence without her. The idea sent a shudder along his bones.

'You're asking because you want to include this as part of your press release?'

Vassili frowned. She didn't sound like a woman overcome by excitement or delight.

'I'm asking because I want us to be together.' He moved one hand to her now definite baby bump, feeling that familiar mix of awe, excitement and possessiveness. 'All of us. I'm sure I can make you happy. I'll support you with your business aims and anything else you want to do.'

Other words hovered on his tongue. Persuasive, romantic words, words of love. But he didn't trust them, didn't know for sure if that was what this feeling was. In truth he didn't *want* it to be that.

For thirteen years he'd run from anything that might lead to love, knowing the harrowing depths of despair that love followed by grief could inflict. Being truly close to someone, as he'd been to Theo, was a blessing until their loss turned it into damnation. Every instinct shied from going there again.

Laura's hand covered his on her abdomen and her expression melted something inside him. His breath disintegrated, anticipation stirring. She was going to agree!

'You're a good man, Vassili. I know you'll make a great father. But marriage between us...' She shook her head, her mouth dragging down at the corners. 'It may be sensible but I can't, not even for the children.'

'But you—'

'*Please*, not now.' She shrugged free of his hold and struggled to her feet, looking even paler than before. 'It's been an eventful morning and I need some quiet to take it in. I'll go and have a long soak in the tub.'

Torn between disbelief and annoyance, Vassili was about to demand she stay and talk things through, when he noticed her unsteady progress. He shot to his feet ready to help, but she waved him away.

Reluctantly he held back. This wasn't the time for an argument or to demand her reasons for rejecting him. Even if biting back his words felt like the hardest thing in the world.

He'd bide his time because this wasn't over.

'One thing,' he said as she reached the doorway. A lead weight sank inside him as he watched her stiffen at the sound of his voice. A short time ago she'd been pliant, nestling against him. He'd swear she'd found comfort in his touch as he had in hers.

'Yes?' She didn't even turn her head.

'Eudora and I discussed an evening out tonight at a favourite restaurant with a group of friends. No doubt the press will be outside and it will be a chance to show there are no hard feelings between us and her.' It was part of his strategy to redress any negative reports about Laura. 'But I'll cancel it if you're not up to it.'

He didn't feel up to it.

He felt winded as if someone had delivered a knockout punch and he was still coming around. How could she reject him after all they'd shared?

'No, don't cancel.' Laura turned her head and almost, but not quite, met his eyes. 'It's a good idea.'

Then she was gone, leaving Vassili stunned and alone.

What did he have to do to convince Laura to stay?

For one of the few times in his life, he felt truly powerless, adrift on dark tides of despair.

Then he came back to himself. Death had snatched Theo, and Vassili hadn't been able to change that. But Laura was here, sharing his apartment, about to share parenthood with him. He hadn't lost her yet and he'd do whatever it took to keep her.

All he had to do was discover why she'd rejected him and fix it.

CHAPTER THIRTEEN

LAURA FELT SO strung out, she almost wished her morning sickness would return so she'd have a reason not to spend the evening with Vassili and his friends.

Where was a bit of nausea when you needed it?

Her silent huff of laughter lasted less than a second. This was no laughing matter. In fact, she realised as her mouth set in a grimace, she felt like crying.

She hadn't cried since she was twelve, not even when her mother died. Because by then she'd learned the need to carry on and be strong, not give in to desolation, no matter how deeply felt.

Avoiding her prickling eyes in the mirror, she slicked on lipstick. The trouble was that her lips trembled too much and so did her hand. She wiped off the blurred colour and dropped the lipstick onto the polished surface before her.

She needed a minute, that was all.

A minute! It's going to take more than a minute to get control of yourself.

She sank back in the chair before the mirror and focused on her breathing, measured and slow. But try as she might, calm was elusive. The best she could hope for was an appearance of composure. Surely, after years of modelling, she could manage that.

Except that mere hours ago, Vassili had asked her to marry him.

And she'd almost said yes.

Excitement flickered at the thought of going out there and saying she'd changed her mind. That she'd be his wife.

Laura pressed her hand to her thrumming heart as if, by force of will, she could conquer that rogue thrill.

She *did* want to be Vassili's wife.

She *did* want that life he'd painted for her, of them living happily with their children. He as a supportive husband and doting father.

It *would* be a fine life, as he'd said. What they'd shared on his island had been special and it had almost undone her to hear him put that into words.

For a moment she'd believed it proof he felt the same way as she did.

Until she realised he'd said that to persuade her. Because he wanted the situation neatly wrapped up, for himself, his family and the public.

She yearned to believe he thought her special enough to *want* to marry her, not for their babies but for herself. Yet there'd been no mention of love, not even a hint.

She'd never been that special to anyone. Her dad had felt no qualms at leaving her, his affections elsewhere. Even her mother, with whom she'd been close, hadn't loved her enough to stay with her but had given into a broken heart, losing the will to live and leaving Laura alone.

Was that why Laura wanted to be loved so badly? Because she'd always been second-best? Only willpower and a determination not to give up like her mother had kept Laura strong.

Too late, she realised a month of blissful relaxation and sex with Vassili hadn't been a wonderful perk but another chain binding her to him. Physically she yearned for him and couldn't imagine life without his lovemaking. But worse than that were the mental and emotional ties binding her to him.

She lifted her gaze to her reflection, scared of what she'd see. Her eyes looked febrile, too bright and big for a face that even with make-up looked pale.

Was that how love looked?

She didn't know, had never been in love.

Before.

Laura feared she'd done the unthinkable and given her heart to a man who saw her as a convenience, useful, maybe even admirable, but not essential to his happiness.

Her heart gave an almighty leap, fighting hard and fast as if trying to break free of her ribcage.

Again Laura put her hand over her breastbone, trying to ease her rapid heartbeat. Her palm covered the beautiful gold filigree pendant Vassili had given her to wear tonight.

When he'd offered it to her, she'd almost believed she was wrong and that it was a token of feelings far stronger than duty. She'd seen the delicately wrought gold and hope had blossomed. For it wasn't the sort of blatant, obviously expensive piece she imagined a billionaire ordering with a click of his fingers. It was pretty, charming and intriguing.

Stunned, she'd looked from it to him, searching for tenderness in those dark eyes. But the shutters were down, Vassili's expression blank and he'd merely said he thought the dress needed something extra.

Laura's mouth twisted painfully. Just as well he didn't know the extra she craved was his love.

Setting her shoulders, she grabbed the lipstick and put it on with a steady hand. She slipped her feet into delicate high-heeled sandals the same colour as her dress and stood, surveying herself critically.

The dress, one of several that had been delivered for her to choose from, was a perfect fit. Copper-coloured silk, it flowed, gleaming like molten metal, over her curves. From thin shoulder straps it scooped to a low, but not too low V above her breasts then moulded her body, flaring from her hips and falling in delicate folds around her legs. The soft material glowed, highlighting curves and hollows, including her four-month baby bump.

There was no point trying to hide her pregnancy now. Besides, she didn't want to. She was tired of hiding.

Laura took a step back and the silk caressed her body, making her think of Vassili's hands on her.

A sob caught in her throat.

Could she really withstand the temptation to say yes? She imagined them as a family, summers on the island, winters maybe in Athens. Their children growing, secure in their parents' love.

Was it selfish of her to want, for once in her life, to be the most important person to someone? She should put her babies first, because the more she thought about it, the more she believed they'd blossom having Vassili as a full-time father.

Her stomach churned and she pressed her palm to it.

Then all her doubts and fears swirled away on a tide of elation. It wasn't nerves making her stomach unsettled. It was the twins. She could feel her babies moving!

For a week or so she'd felt strange fluttering sensations but hadn't been sure what they were. But now... She placed both hands on her abdomen. She was almost halfway through the pregnancy. Surely...

Yes! It was. The strangest, most wonderful sensation ever. Her baby or babies moving under her hands.

Laura turned on her heel and hurried to the door. She had to tell Vassili.

Excitement must have fogged her senses because Laura was on the threshold of the big living room before she realised Vassili had visitors. The fine hairs stood up on her arms and at her nape as the tension in the room, fierce and electric, engulfed her.

Three people stood in the centre of the room, the sound of rapid, furious Greek filling the air. Laura didn't have to know the language to understand the tone.

It was the older man who spoke. He was half a head shorter than Vassili and heavy-set, yet there was something about the shape of his head that hinted at a family connection. He wore his grey suit with the aplomb of someone used to wielding power, gesticulating decisively.

Not that he intimidated Vassili, debonair and apparently at ease in a dark jacket and trousers. His attention kept turning to the middle-aged woman beside him.

She looked immaculate from her navy-and-white dress that screamed 'designer original' to the smooth upsweep of her thick hair. Even the streaks of grey there amongst the black only heightened the elegance of her features. But her hands gave her away, restlessly knotting and unknotting as she listened to her companion's tirade.

Laura could guess, too easily, who they were. She was debating whether to disappear to her room when Vassili abruptly turned. Unerringly his gaze locked on hers, in that way he had as if sensing her exact location.

'Laura.'

The strangers' heads snapped around and she felt the pin prickle of their scrutiny. No, not a prickle, the scrape of sharpened blades.

She pushed her shoulders back, elongating her neck to hold her head high and resisting the urge to run her hands down the liquid silk of her dress. She was grateful to be dressed to the nines, not wearing old yoga pants and a T-shirt.

Then Vassili was before her, his face once more that unreadable mask she'd once believed signalled disinterest. Now she knew it was his way of holding powerful emotions in check. Something turned over inside her. Not the babies. Not nerves.

He reached for her and her hand was already there waiting for his. Laura didn't know whether the tirade of Greek had stopped or whether she didn't hear it because, in this moment, all that mattered was her and Vassili, united.

She hated that he'd faced that spew of anger because of her, because of them. Whether they married or not, she *cared* for him, *deeply*. He might not love her but her own feelings—

'I'm sorry,' he murmured, threading their fingers together. Warmth enfolded her as his expression gentled. 'This isn't how I wanted it, but now they're here—'

She nodded. 'Let's get it over.'

His mouth crooked up in an echo of his devastating smile. 'I should have known they wouldn't daunt you.'

Laura wasn't sure of that, but she let him lead her across the room.

'Mamá, I'd like you to meet Laura Bettany from Australia. Laura, this is my mother.'

'How do you do, Kyria Thanos?' Laura pulled her hand free of his and offered it to his mother. She saw something spark in the other woman's dark eyes before warm fingers met hers.

'Ms Bettany.' Her tone, like her handshake, was cautious. 'Welcome to Athens.'

'Welcome to Athens!' came another voice. It was a roar of outrage followed by a baritone spill of words that made Laura glad she didn't speak Greek.

Vassili watched the two women in his life shake hands, their locked gazes assessing, and something shifted hard inside him.

He didn't need his mother's approval but, he discovered, he wanted them to like each other.

His gaze swept Laura as he tried to see her through his mother's eyes. But it was impossible. His gaze was that of a man, a lover. To him Laura was perfection. Her beauty not just in her features and body but in the proud way she held herself and the friendly way she'd offered her hand despite the tension and Constantine's tirade.

From the crown of her upswept hair to the tips of her toes, Laura exuded class. And a sexy allure Vassili felt as a tightening in his groin. That dress, like burnished copper draping her curves, moulded her full breasts and ripening belly, making him wish the visitors were anywhere but here.

He saw his mother's eyes widen on the pendant Laura wore,

reading its significance. It was an heirloom passed by generations of his father's family to each new bride.

Before his mother could comment, Constantine broke the silence with a string of outrage.

Instantly Vassili stepped forward, between his woman and his uncle. 'That's enough!' He didn't raise his voice yet easily cut through the older man's vitriol. 'If you can't be civil, you'll leave. If you decide to stay, speak English, Laura doesn't understand Greek.' Fortunately.

He paused. 'Laura, this is my mother's brother, my uncle, Constantine Pappas.'

Laura moved closer but before she could greet his uncle or offer to shake hands, Constantine stepped back.

'You expect me to welcome your little...?' He stopped, reading Vassili's ire. 'She has no place here, Vassili. This is a family matter.'

Vassili wanted to blurt out that she was family in every way that counted, and not only because she carried his babies. He wanted to announce they were about to marry. But how could he when she'd rejected him? *Again.*

He folded his arms, jaw aching from the tension there. 'Laura stays. This situation concerns her far more than it concerns you.'

Constantine drew herself up. 'Why is that? You can't really intend to marry her?' His uncle's words tumbled over each other. 'Where is your family loyalty, Vassili? How can you bring this disgrace upon the family?'

Letting Constantine stay had been a grave mistake. Vassili moved to propel him from the room, but before he could Laura stepped between them.

Vassili pulled up short. His instinct was to protect her, but she didn't look like a woman who needed protection. Far from being cowed by his uncle, her upright stance, hands on hips, was eloquent with scorn.

'You ask about loyalty?'

Laura's voice was even and low. Anyone who didn't know her would believe her unaffected, but to Vassili that husky edge spoke of abundant emotion. Admiration vied with astonishment, and a spreading warmth that she should try to fight his battles.

Could she care about him after all?

He moved closer, torn between wanting to put her safely behind him so he could deal with his uncle, and respecting her right to speak for herself.

Before Constantine could answer she went on, her voice steady and words clipped. 'Where was your loyalty to Vassili when you announced his engagement without even consulting him? He's a man, not a boy. Yet you don't respect him enough to know he makes his own decisions. Even *then* he remained loyal to you, advising you on commercial matters, despite you betraying his trust by putting him in this appalling situation.'

'Now, see here—'

'I see, all right. You were serving your own interests, not his. You didn't even talk to your stepdaughter.'

'Leave her out of this!' Constantine thrust his head forward like an angry bull and Vassili stepped forward, hand out, but Laura didn't flinch. 'You know nothing about Eudora—'

'Actually,' Laura said in a conversational tone Vassili couldn't help but admire, 'I've spoken with Eudora. Neither she nor Vassili want the engagement.'

Vassili closed his hands around her upper arms. Much as he enjoyed her championing him, he couldn't let her bear the brunt of Constantine's temper. 'It's okay, Laura. I'll handle this.'

'Just as well,' his uncle blustered, adding something offensive under his breath.

A second later Vassili had his hand on Constantine's throat, frogmarching him backwards until he came up hard against the wall, gobbling and gasping for breath. Vassili crowded close, his pulse hammering in his ears, every cell in his body demanding retribution.

'Vassili, no!'

Firm hands pried at his fingers but it was only when he read the dismay in Laura's golden-green eyes that he released Constantine.

He pulled back, flexing his hands. He couldn't remember using physical violence against anyone. Even at school with the usual adolescent skirmishes, it had been Theo getting physical and Vassili playing peacemaker.

'That's not helping, Vassili.'

Laura was right. Even so he took the precaution of shoving his hands deep in his trouser pockets as he fought to manage his fury.

From behind him his mother spoke. 'Constantine! Such gutter language!'

Sullenly he surveyed them. 'Sorry,' he finally murmured. 'But she *is* a gold-digger. Even if that's his child she's carrying, she probably got pregnant to trap him into marriage. She wants his money.'

Vassili wrapped his arm around Laura, holding her close, as if he could prevent Constantine's words hurting her. The feel of her softness against him was a reminder that he couldn't commit violence before her, no matter how attractive it seemed.

Yet his voice was harsh as he responded. 'That shows you're a woeful judge of character, Constantine. Laura has rejected my marriage proposal. Several times.'

He heard his mother's gasp as Constantine goggled at them. 'That can't be right. It's some sort of trick.'

'No trick, Mr Pappas.' Laura spoke with a dignity Vassili envied. She was magnificent! He guessed that only he, holding her as she drew a shuddering breath, knew how much her calm cost her. 'I'm not interested in your nephew's money. And if you stopped to think about it, you'd realise how much you insult him as well as me by suggesting that's why I'm here.'

'But—'

'No more!' Vassili refused to listen to any more. He'd

had enough of this man's interference. 'There's nothing to be gained by prolonging this conversation. One more word from you and I'll see you off the company board. You might be CEO but you know I have the power to do it.'

His uncle looked as if he might choke, so great was his amazement.

Vassili turned to his mother and found her attention not on him or her brother but Laura. She stepped forward, and, to Vassili's surprise, took his hand and Laura's.

'I apologise. I'd hoped to talk, not have a confrontation.' She shot a glare at her brother before turning back. 'It seems the pair of you have a lot to discuss. We'll leave you in privacy to do that.' She paused, leaning in to Laura. 'I wish you well, Ms Bettany. I hope we meet again.'

With those remarkable words, she withdrew and bustled up to Constantine, chivvying him towards the door. Her brother's mouth opened and closed with an audible snap, eyes bulging as if he'd never seen his younger sister take charge before now.

Suddenly Vassili was reminded of the woman he'd known years ago, before the tragedies of her son's and her husband's deaths. A kind, sensible woman who'd given her boys unending loving kindness and instilled in them a strong sense of right and wrong. In these last years his mother had seemed a shadow of her old self. But how much time had Vassili spent with her?

Shame filled him as he realised how rarely he visited Athens. But he could correct that. Theo's death had terrified him into trying to live an isolated life. But, he realised, distancing himself from those he truly cared for was no solution.

'Mamá.' She turned from the doorway. 'I'll call you.'

Her eyes glowed. 'I'll look forward to it, my son.'

'Well,' Laura whispered when the door closed behind them, 'that was…interesting.'

Vassili snorted in grim amusement. 'I admire your restraint. Interesting isn't the word I'd use.'

He guided her to a lounge, sinking onto it with her, aware

of her shivering and berating himself for what he'd put her through.

'I've never been ashamed of my family in my life, until now. My uncle's behaviour was unforgivable. I'm sorry, Laura. I shouldn't have let him in.'

'It's not your fault.'

How wrong she was.

'Unfortunately, it is. For too long I've abrogated my responsibilities and he stepped into the vacuum. I thought it was a good solution but it had consequences. He's grown too full of his own opinions. He's not the man he was when my father was alive.'

'I don't understand. How can you blame yourself? You don't ignore your responsibilities. I know how much time you put into the family business.'

'From a distance. I should have been more hands-on, not just in the company but in the family, taking my father's place.'

'Nonsense. You can't do everything.'

Her hand covered his and he looked down to discover her gaze on him, her expression both indignant and reassuring. As if he were the one who'd borne the brunt of tonight's poison.

Laura's loyalty humbled him. She was the vulnerable one, in a foreign country, pregnant and under pressure. Maybe that was why the truth he'd never spoken tumbled free. Or maybe he wanted her to know because with each day his dissatisfaction with the life he'd built grew.

'I could do a lot more than I have done. I chose not to engage.'

Vassili looked at their joined hands. How often they'd sat like this, linked physically and emotionally. It seemed so natural, as if Laura were an intrinsic part of his life.

An ache opened inside as he remembered how swiftly she'd rejected his suggestion of marriage today. As if their recent closeness meant nothing to her. Whereas to him it meant everything.

'My uncle became company CEO because I couldn't be bothered. It didn't fit my lifestyle. That's the reason I don't see my family so often these days either.'

'Because of your travelling.'

'That's right. Or partly right.' He dragged in a deep breath. 'In the beginning I thought I was doing the right thing, because I'd made a promise. Now I realise it wasn't necessarily a noble gesture on my part.'

'What sort of promise?'

'My brother, Theo, and I were alike in many ways. Strangers couldn't tell us apart. But we had different personalities. I was serious, studious.' He read her surprise. 'Oh, I enjoyed sport and spending the summer outdoors, but I took study seriously. I liked maths and economics and saw myself following my father into the family business.' He paused. 'Theo was different. He hated being still, disliked school. If there was any hair-raising adventure he'd be in the thick of it. He wanted to be a polar explorer, a mountaineer, a rally driver, you name it.'

'And you didn't.'

'Until that last summer.' Vassili swallowed. 'I was with him to the end and I made him a promise that I'd live the life he couldn't, have the adventures he'd never have.'

Laura's eyes glistened. 'All these years you've been fulfilling a promise to your brother?'

Vassili nodded.

'And your uncle dared to lecture you on family loyalty,' she whispered.

'He didn't know. No one did, though perhaps my parents wondered.' He paused. 'And I enjoyed myself, don't think I was making a sacrifice. But in making that my priority, it became easier to find reasons not to be in Greece, to distance myself from family and friends.' He shrugged. 'Oh, I saw them, but I was never around for long. I see now I could have done more in the business, rather than leave the management to my uncle. And in the family...'

His throat closed as he thought of his mother's expression when he'd said he'd call her soon. As if he'd given her a wonderful gift. Vassili felt ashamed. Was it any wonder she'd wanted to see him married and settling down rather than travelling the globe?

'You were grieving. You were doing your best.' Laura shook his hand insistently until he looked at her. 'You didn't give up, Vassili. You acted out of love for your brother. There's nothing shameful in that.'

'Except I let other things slide. If I'd been more actively involved in the family and in the business Constantine wouldn't have—'

'What? He wouldn't have concocted this farcical engagement? He wouldn't have grown bumptious? You can't know that. It seems to me that you've been trying very hard to support *all* your family. You could have announced that the engagement wasn't real but you chose not to because you care about your cousin. You care about your mother too, that's obvious. And about the family company.' She paused. 'And you care about our twins, don't you?'

'More than anything.' He lifted her hands to his mouth, kissing her knuckles as he met her sparking eyes. 'You're a feisty, remarkable woman, Laura.'

'You're pretty special yourself.'

Yet still she wouldn't marry him.

The words *I love you* tingled on his tongue but he pushed them down. He wouldn't court two rejections in one day.

But tomorrow, he vowed. Tomorrow he'd lay himself bare. There would be no more barriers between them. She deserved the truth and he refused to make the same mistakes again, scared to commit himself.

Tomorrow he'd offer her his heart as well as his protection.

CHAPTER FOURTEEN

LAURA LAUGHED, head tilted back, eyes alight with merriment, and heat suffused Vassili. He should be used to it now, that punch of delight at her delight, but it never grew stale.

Perhaps it never would. His feelings for her had deepened, grown stronger every day, and he knew with fundamental certainty deep in his bones that nothing would change that.

He imagined himself, grey-haired and creaky in the joints, still feeling this punch of pleasure when Laura smiled.

'Careful, cousin,' Eudora whispered in his ear. 'If the paps snap a photo of you looking like that, all the world will know you're in love.'

Vassili was about to respond that he didn't give a damn, except he wanted Laura to be the first to know his feelings. Surely, when she understood how he felt she'd agree to stay with him. She *had* to.

He met Eudora's teasing smile and shrugged, saying merely, 'You're in love so you think you see it everywhere.'

He looked at her partner on her other side, talking with friends at the other end of the table. Eudora had judged it safe for the pair of them to be seen in public since she and her lover were part of a larger group, with nothing to show they were dating.

Vassili had almost cancelled tonight's dinner. After the stress of the confrontation with Constantine it had seemed advisable. But Laura had insisted they attend, scoffing at his concern she'd be tired.

He was glad now that she'd insisted. Not because it was a chance to show publicly that they were on friendly terms with Eudora, but because Laura was having such a good time.

It pleased him to see her connect with his friends. After today's upsets, hearing that carefree laugh and basking in her warm smile made him feel he'd done one thing right, at least.

Laura turned, eyes shining as they met his across the table, and he felt that pulse of connection between them, as tangible as if she'd touched him. He grinned back and reached for her hand.

'You're right.' Eudora's whisper was brimful of laughter. 'I'm clearly imagining things and you're not at all bowled over by her. I like her, by the way, very much.'

The evening ended soon after. Despite Laura's insistence that she was fine, Greek dining hours were much later than in Australia and it had been a stressful day. Seeing her eyelids droop as she leaned back in her seat, he announced it was time to go. There were protests from his friends but Laura nodded and reached for her bag. Even then the farewells took time, with promises of calls to arrange coffee dates and other catch-ups.

By the time they turned to leave the restaurant, Vassili was feeling pleased. His joint press release with Eudora had been issued, the evening had gone well and Laura was relaxed, snuggling close against him.

The click of cameras and the clamour of voices as they stepped out onto the street came as a shock. For a while he'd forgotten the press, the initial reason for this dinner.

He tightened his grip around Laura's waist and put his mouth to her ear. 'It will be over soon. Remember, you don't have to say anything.'

'Good.' She shrank against him. 'I hate this.'

They were almost at the limo when one voice called out, more strident than the rest. Instead of shouting Vassili's name, or Laura's, the voice used an unfamiliar one. 'Ms Paige! It is Ms Paige, isn't it? Tell us how you feel about…'

Vassili heard no more, Laura's loud gasp drawing his attention. She jerked around, looking over her shoulder towards the source of the voice, her body stiffening and stumbling mid-step so that only his arm around her kept her upright. He heard her breathing, rushed and panicky, and felt a powerful shudder rack her.

Not waiting to hear more, doubting her inability to move, he half carried her the few steps to the waiting limo's open door and lifted her inside. She was shaking, one hand to her chest, the other to her mouth, as he slid in beside her and the car moved off.

'Laura, what is it? Who's Ms Paige?'

She said something he couldn't make out and he wondered if she even heard him. Her lips moved almost soundlessly and she stared ahead, shoulders curving forward, arms crossing her body as if trying to protect herself or their babies.

He put his arm around her, holding her close, but she didn't seem to notice. A shred of fear skirled around him.

It was as if that unfamiliar name, shouted across the street, had dragged her elsewhere, somewhere he couldn't reach her.

Now wasn't the time for questions. He had to get her someplace she'd feel safe. Heart thudding, Vassili held her close and waited.

Twenty minutes later they were in his apartment, Laura ensconced on the lounge, the lighting low. She still hadn't spoken except to thank him as he helped her from the car. She'd clung to his arm like an old lady, her movements stiff and slow. Anxiety took a tighter grip of his vitals at the change in her.

'Here.' He held out a ceramic mug, waiting till she wrapped her hands around it. 'You'll feel better for some tea.'

He'd learned it was her favourite night-time tipple, one he teased her about. Tonight she didn't smile, merely nodded and took the mug. He watched the surface of the liquid tremble but she held on firmly and sipped.

'Thank you.' She darted him a look that held none of tonight's earlier vibrancy.

A short time ago she'd been laughing with his friends. Before that she'd faced down his uncle's spluttering tirade with firm dignity and a courageous determination to stand up for him, Vassili, that had ground all his doubts and fears to dust and left him glowing with pride.

Now he saw a shadow of that woman and his heart bled.

'I suppose I should explain.'

'Only if you feel up to it.' His curiosity raged. How had that name effected such a change in her? It wasn't one she'd mentioned. 'My prime concern is you and the babies. I don't want you upset.'

Laura's mouth twisted in a grimace. 'Too late for that.' She paused, looking at the milky tea in her hands. 'I'm sorry. I overreacted. I knew it would be difficult facing the press but I hadn't realised it would be so bad, even worse than before. And when he called out...'

'Before? You mean that photo of you in Sydney trying to get away from a photographer?'

'That too.'

Too? When else had she been hounded by the press?

'You've nothing to apologise for. Facing a barrage of attention is tough. I shouldn't have put you in that situation.'

'You weren't to know. *I* didn't know.' She shrugged. 'I wasn't looking forward to it. I *hate* media attention, always have, but I thought that by now I could cope, that all that was in the past. Your idea of being seen with Eudora was a good one.'

Vassili didn't care about Eudora. All his concern was for Laura, still too pale and clearly shaken.

'What can I do?'

She turned, her gaze locking on his, and he thought he read surprise there. 'No questions about what happened?'

'I told you. My prime concern is—'

'The babies and me. Yes, you said.'

Her voice was flat as if that fact didn't cheer her. Anxiety stirred.

'I'd suggest turning in so you can rest but I think you're too wired to sleep. How about I run you a bath?'

The shadow of a smile ghosted across her lips and she reached out to touch the back of his hand. 'You really are serious about taking care of me.' But before he could clasp her hand she moved it back to her tea. 'Thank you, you're very kind.'

Kind! Such a tepid word to describe his feelings. He'd move mountains for her sake. He'd do whatever it took to shift the burden he saw weighing her down.

He moistened his lips, determined to make a clean breast of his feelings. 'Laura—'

'I owe you an explanation, Vassili. Not just because the story will be in the press tomorrow, but because I want you to know.' This time her smile, small as it was, reached her eyes and he felt his knotted muscles ease a little. 'You've shared so much with me and that means a lot. It's time I was completely straight with you.'

She made it sound as if she had some terrible secret. The only one he could think of was a husband she hadn't divorced, but he couldn't believe that of her.

'I'd like there to be no secrets between us.'

He wanted a whole lot more but now wasn't the time to press. If Laura wanted to unburden herself that was what mattered. Everything else could wait.

She put down the mug. But instead of turning to him she looked straight ahead, across the room to the distant, floodlit heights of the Acropolis, visible through the picture windows.

'I told you my mother and I moved to Sydney when I was twelve. We moved from the other side of the country to get away from my father and from the scandal.'

The hairs rose on his nape at her dull, metallic tone, as if all her vibrancy had been extinguished.

'You needed to escape him? Was he violent?'

'Nothing like that. He was just an ordinary man, but he

wasn't around much. His work took him away and most weekends it was just me and Mum. Looking back now I realise how rarely he was there. He never took me to sports practices or helped me with homework. But at the time it didn't seem unusual.' She flashed him a sideways look. 'Kids adjust to most things, don't they?

'It wasn't until I was twelve and attending a big athletics carnival out of town that it all came out. I was so excited to qualify but I was there alone except for one other person from my school. Mum had to work that day and my father was away.'

Vassili wondered how something like an athletic contest could lead to the trauma he saw etched in her face.

Laura looked at her clasped hands. 'There was a girl in the same race as me. She looked familiar but I didn't know why. We got talking. She lived a few hours away from me and our birthdays were only a month apart, in the same year. It was only when her family collected her at the end of the day that I realised why she looked familiar. Her father was my father.'

Vassili digested that, telling himself he'd misheard. 'Your father?' he repeated finally.

She nodded, her expression unutterably bleak. 'I was thrilled when I saw him. I thought he was so proud of me getting into the competition that he'd actually taken time off work to collect *me*. But then my new acquaintance, Caitlin her name was, called out to him.'

Laura snorted. 'I still remember the look on his face. Pure horror. He actually turned to go back to his car but his wife was following with their boys, so he couldn't run away.'

She shut her eyes and Vassili closed the space between them, wrapping his arm around her, feeling the tremors running through her body.

He struggled to grasp what she'd said, even though the scene was vivid in his mind. Too vivid. Pain seared through him as he imagined how twelve-year-old Laura had felt, alone on the field, discovering her father had another family.

'I'm sorry,' he said eventually, knowing how futile the words sounded.

'Thanks. It was…tough. Especially as it happened in public. There was enough fuss that people around us began to understand something was badly wrong. News spread. My mother got a call from a friend before I could tell her.'

It was on the tip of Vassili's tongue to ask how Laura had got home that day. He hoped someone kind had taken her under their wing.

He imagined the trauma of discovering her father was a bigamist, playing out before curious eyes. Then it struck him. 'It made it into the press? That's why you reacted to the name Paige?'

'That was *his* name. We discovered he hadn't legally married my mother. We reverted to her maiden name, Bettany, when we moved away.' Laura rocked forward as if seeking comfort from the movement. 'We were devastated. Our whole lives were a lie. He'd never really loved us, despite what he said. He couldn't have and do that to us. That was bad enough, but being the centre of gossip and speculation made it worse. I couldn't face school, or even walking down the street, and the press kept trying to doorstop us.'

Fury such as he'd never known poured through Vassili's veins. 'They harassed an underage girl?'

'They were trying to interview Mum but she refused. And it got worse when they discovered there was a third wife in another state. Every current affairs programme and commentator wanted to talk about it, about *us*.'

'*Psihi mou*, I don't know what to say.'

He rubbed her back, wishing he could excise her pain. He felt sick to the stomach, thinking of what she'd been through.

She drew a shaky breath and turned to him. Her eyes were dry but haunted and the ache in his chest intensified. He wanted to help her, ease her pain, protect her.

But now he understood what he hadn't before. That trusting

any man would be difficult for Laura. She'd trusted and believed in her father, only to discover he'd lied to and betrayed her and her mother. Laura's early life had been a travesty of affection from a man who didn't know the meaning of true love or loyalty.

Was it any wonder Laura had been ready to distrust Vassili? That she'd scotched any talk of a permanent relationship? That she could give her body to him, enjoy his companionship, yet still not trust him enough to believe he'd always be there for him?

And the words he'd longed to tell her, the news that he loved her, would count as nothing. Presumably her father had said that to her mother and her. Hearing yet another man profess to care for her...

Despair swamped Vassili. For the woman he loved and for himself.

'There's nothing you can say to make it better. At least it's in the past. Or it was. Now...' She shivered. 'The press will dredge it up. I've never been newsworthy enough for anyone to dig into my past. But now they'll never let it go, will they? It will always be there, a juicy scandal to help sell their stories. Even juicier if I'm with you.'

He could stand it no longer, he wrapped his arms fully around her, intending to cradle her on his lap.

Except Laura wriggled from his hold to stand before him, resplendent as a goddess in coppery silk. But she was no untouchable immortal. Her hair fell around her face and her throat worked as if she found it hard to swallow. His heart cramped at the sight of her beauty and her pain.

'I know you mean well, Vassili, but I need time alone. I'll take that bath then head to bed.'

She turned and walked from the room, leaving his heart shredded and his soul in torment.

CHAPTER FIFTEEN

LAURA WOKE FEELING heavy-headed and unrested. It took only seconds for memory to hit with devastating clarity. Her stomach squeezed, her pulse instantly quickening.

The paparazzi. The man calling her name, the name she'd left behind when her world shattered. Word would be spreading now, not only about her pregnancy and her relationship with Vassili, but about her sordid past.

Bile rose but it had nothing to do with morning sickness. She'd done nothing to be ashamed of, yet she felt tainted and she'd brought that taint to her lover and their unborn twins.

Laura rolled over, arm outstretched, seeking Vassili, but the bed was cold, his side unslept in.

Then she remembered. Every time she'd woken from her fitful sleep in the night she'd been alone. Had he slept in a guest bedroom? Or had he left the apartment?

'I need time alone.'

That was what she'd said and he'd taken her at her word. Her spirits plummeted further.

She remembered the concern etched in his features last night, his tender touch, the sympathy in his voice. But instead of turning to him for succour like any normal person, Laura had done what she'd learned to do at the age of twelve, when her mother had withdrawn into herself and there'd been no one for Laura to confide in. She, too, had turned inward, burying her fear, hurt and anger and learning to rely only on herself.

You've reaped what you sowed. You've made Vassili turn from you.

That was no consolation to a woman who felt vulnerable and needy. Yet it was more than that. She didn't simply want a shoulder to cry on or someone to fix things for her.

She wanted Vassili. Needed him. Missed him.

She could fight her own battles, she didn't need a champion. Yet at the same time she wanted him at her side.

She loved him.

For so long she'd suspected, feared it even. But now she faced her feelings it was excitement she felt.

Laura stared, unseeing, across the room. In her mind, images of Vassili vied for precedence. Vassili concentrating on her business plan, giving helpful advice as well as invaluable contacts, but never trying to take charge. Vassili frowning down at her, reverence in his touch as he stroked her swollen abdomen and spoke tenderly of their twins. Vassili teasing her, his gaze glinting with delight. Vassili in the throes of ecstasy, sharing his essence with her as those velvet-dark eyes held hers.

Then last night, Vassili looking sick with dismay yet caressing her soothingly, murmuring reassurance.

He deserved better treatment from her. He'd done everything she'd asked and more, yet when a crisis hit she'd turned from him.

Laura flung back the bedding and reached for her robe. She needed to talk to him straight away.

She found him pacing the terrace, talking on the phone. Against the brilliance of the Greek sunshine his proud profile and athletic body made her heart thump faster.

He ended the call when he saw her. 'How are you, Laura? Do you feel rested?'

Instead of doing what he usually did, closing the space between them, he remained where he was, his expression guarded.

You can't blame him for that. You pushed him away last night.

Yet her heart scrunched up. She missed their easy intimacy.

'I feel better for a sleep, thanks. How about you?' Unusually he wore a suit and tie and, she saw now, the lines around his mouth seemed etched more deeply. 'Has something happened?'

'Nothing unexpected.' He put his phone away. 'The press reports are as we expected but that's manageable.'

Still he didn't approach so Laura moved towards him.

He stiffened, his expression strained. 'We need to talk. Why don't you take a seat?' He gestured to a chair.

She faltered, looking at the lounge beside him. He didn't want to sit together?

'About last night, I'm sorry. I overreacted—'

'You'd had a terrible shock. Your reaction was totally understandable.' Yet his expression was guarded and he stood stiffly. 'Please, sit.'

Laura sank down, grasping the armrests and watching him pace away then back. 'Something's wrong,' she murmured. It was there in the way he held himself and his restlessness.

She realised that in the time they'd been together he'd never seemed to yearn for the adventures that had taken him all around the world. He'd seemed so…comfortable, so content.

He stopped pacing and shoved his hands in his trouser pockets. Feet wide, shoulders back, he looked the epitome of masculine power, ready to take charge in the boardroom and handle the press with ease.

Finally he answered. 'I realised last night how unfair I've been to you.'

'Sorry?' Vassili had been more than reasonable, he'd been kind. He'd accepted the twins as his without demanding a paternity test. He wanted to marry her yet had been so patient, waiting for her to come around to the idea. 'Vassili, I've been thinking—'

'So have I. Now I know your background and how badly it affected you, I've reassessed everything.'

Her ribs tightened around her lungs. Was her history too sordid for him to associate with her any longer? Would it stain his family name? 'You have?'

He nodded. 'You're right. We don't need to marry in order to look after our children. We're both reasonable people and, with goodwill on both sides, there's no reason we can't raise happy, well-adjusted children.'

Laura swallowed, pain piercing her throat at the jerky movement. 'You don't want to marry me any more?'

His gaze met hers and for an instant she felt that flash of heat and connection. Then something shifted in his expression and it was gone as if it had never been.

Perhaps it *had* never been.

Her fingers clawed the armrests.

'I've come to realise that simple solutions aren't always best. I see now that while marriage seemed a perfect solution to me, I didn't take your concerns seriously enough.' He lifted his shoulders. 'I believed what I wanted to believe but I didn't have the full picture. Last night I saw how traumatic it was for you dealing with the press.'

He hunched his shoulders and frowned out at the view of Athens sprawling beyond them.

As if that were easier than meeting her eye?

'I'm used to media interest,' he continued. 'It's annoying but doesn't faze me. But I saw last night how terribly it affected you. It must've been a nightmare, having intrusive press attention when your family imploded. Last night brought it all back and that would never have happened but for who I am.' He paused. 'While you're with me that press interest will be constant. Neither of us wants that.'

He took one hand from his pocket and raked it through his hair, his expression grim. 'But if you go back to your own world, eventually the press interest in you will drop to manageable levels, especially if we're careful to maintain privacy when the children are with me. Naturally I'll ensure you have staff to protect your privacy.'

Laura couldn't seem to get her breath. 'You're sending me back to Australia?' He couldn't!

'It's the best option. You have your friends there and I'll provide every support for you and the children. You won't have to worry about anything. Later we'll work out arrangements for shared parenting in a way that keeps you as much as possible away from the public eye.'

Laura heard the words but couldn't quite take them in.

Did he really believe them separating would save her from public scrutiny?

Or had her wrangle with his family, followed by the revelations of her murky past, finally convinced Vassili that he was better off without her?

After all, it was the twins that had brought them together. The twins he wanted. He'd been kind and thoughtful, a wonderful lover and companion. But he'd never spoken of love or anything like it. Vassili's interest in her was as the mother of his children. He felt he had a duty to her.

Laura pressed her lips together, suppressing the sob she feared might escape if she weren't careful. All this time he'd wanted to marry her and she'd refused. Now, when she finally understood he was the one man in the world for her, the one she couldn't imagine being without, the offer was off the table.

Tell him. Tell him how you feel.

But his next words, so reasonable and unemotional, told her it would make no difference. All she'd achieve would be to make him feel sorry for her. She didn't want his pity.

'It's for the best, Laura. I want what's best for the babies and you. This is it. I have to stay in Athens for a while, but I can have you back in Australia by tomorrow. Or, if you prefer, you could stay on the island as long as you like. You'll be well looked after there.'

Well looked after. By his efficient staff. Would he miss her, even a little?

His phone rang, an urgent jangle of sound that cut across her stretched nerves. She rose, unsure what she was going to say but knowing she needed to say something, do something to turn this around. But Vassili did something that stopped her in her tracks. Something he'd never done before.

He retrieved his phone, muttered that he needed to take the call, then turned his back, dismissing her.

Finally Vassili pocketed his phone. Despite the work he'd already put in, the news about his broken engagement, about Laura and her pregnancy, took some managing. He'd do everything he could to ensure she wasn't painted as a villainess.

That was what made him furious, that because of him Laura was a media target.

That was why he had to let her go. Because keeping her with him was purely selfish. Keeping her with him would only hold her in the public gaze, day after day and year after year. He'd seen last night how traumatic that was for her. He couldn't, mustn't force that upon her again.

Even if it meant giving up the one thing he believed would make him truly happy, a life with Laura.

He rubbed his chest with the heel of his hand, telling himself any amount of personal pain was worth it to spare her. Slowly he turned, an apology on his lips, only to find she'd gone.

His blood froze. Gone completely?

No, the call had taken minutes not hours. He'd see her again before she returned to Australia.

Even though he knew it would be easier if he didn't. That was why he'd scheduled a meeting in the company headquarters this morning. Not because it was necessary but because he needed a reason to be away from Laura. In case his resolve crumbled and he asked her to stay.

That's not an option. If you truly care about her you'll put her needs first. Which means letting her go.

A choking sensation tightened his throat. A sensation he'd felt only twice before, when he'd said goodbye to Theo then, later, his father. Grief so deep it threatened to unman him.

That had him striding across the terrace and through the apartment, only to pull up near the front door.

Because there was Laura, her back to the massive door, hands spread against the wood as if for support.

She'd changed out of her robe and into the elegant outfit she'd worn last night. But she wasn't quite the polished goddess she'd appeared then. Her hair hung around her shoulders, she wore no make-up and she'd forgotten a bra, her nipples hard points against the rich fabric.

A shudder racked him.

She'd never looked more beautiful, more alluring.

And he'd never had to fight so hard to deny himself.

'I need to go—'

'No.'

Vassili stared, then silently cursed as his gaze lingered on the bounty that was the woman he loved. He breathed out hard through his nostrils, trying to force the deep-seated craving from his body. Trying to be the man he needed to be, strong enough to let her go.

Laura read his surprise, then a poignant moment of clear masculine appreciation, his gaze travelling down her body, that made hope bloom. Then a shutter came down, his shoulders stiffened and his gaze grew distant.

Despair was a silent wail, freezing her larynx. She sought for words to stop him leaving and found none so she lurched forward.

Strong hands grabbed her arms, supporting her, but she refused to let him hold her at a distance. She kept going until she was pressed against him, fingers splayed on that dark suit, breasts flattened against his torso, the fine wool of his trousers against her shins.

'Laura, I need to—'

'Listen. You need to listen.' Her voice was thick and slurred. 'Please. It's the last thing I'll ask of you.'

A judder passed through him as if the floor moved beneath his feet. She thought she saw something in his eyes that matched the bleakness she felt. Could it be? She didn't dare hope.

Silently he nodded.

'You're right. Last night was appalling. It brought the past smashing back.'

It had reminded her of being dumped by a violent wave as a child, rolled over and over, unable to find her feet or raise her head because of the force propelling her along. 'For a while I felt like that twelve-year-old again, betrayed and stunned.'

Vassili nodded gravely. 'I understand.'

'You don't. That's what I'm trying to say. Last night was a nasty surprise and it undid me. Even now I'm surprised by how much. But I'm not that twelve-year-old any more. I'm not going to fall apart every time a camera flashes or someone prints rumours about me. I'm much stronger than that.'

He was already shaking his head. 'You shouldn't have to face that because of me.'

'Even if I want to?'

Vassili's eyes widened. 'Sorry?'

His gaze bored into hers. Laura felt seen in a way that left her stripped vulnerable. She could tell the truth and leave herself wide open to rejection. Because maybe, after all, it wasn't the situation with the press that had made him want to send her away. Maybe he'd changed his mind.

Laura wrestled with that fear. But she couldn't, wouldn't let it stop her.

'I want to be with you, Vassili. I want to be your wife and live with you for the rest of our lives.' Amazingly, the words were clear and even, despite her hammering heart and the turmoil she felt.

Yet instead of bestowing one of his breath-stealing smiles, Vassili frowned, no, scowled down at her. 'How can that be? Only yesterday you rejected me. Then last night…' He shook his head.

'I rejected you the first time because, after my experience with a bigamous father, I'd vowed only to marry for love. I wanted a man who loved me, heart and soul. You suggested marriage as a convenient way to raise children.'

Vassili opened his mouth but she shook her head and went on. 'Please, let me finish.'

This time it was she who paused, not used to baring her feelings. 'All the time we were together what I felt for you grew and grew. I saw you weren't like my father. I liked being with you, *loved* being with you.'

His dark eyes glowed like hot coals, making her wonder and hope.

'I began to realise my feelings for you were strong. But I didn't admit it because at the back of my mind was that old fear of betrayal, of not being important enough to hold your loyalty.'

Vassili's arms tightened around her. 'Laura, you have no idea how much—'

'Please, Vassili. Let me finish.' Another shallow breath. 'I told myself I couldn't fall in love with you because you clearly didn't love me. You wanted me because of our babies. And without love, there was no guarantee you'd stick by me. Until I realised how much I'd misjudged you. You've spent years living the life your brother wanted, to keep your promise to him. You could have ended this sham engagement to make things easier for yourself but you didn't because you're loyal to your cousin, and even to your uncle. And you've looked after me and our babies despite me cutting up rough, because it's the decent thing to do. You're the most loyal, trustworthy man I know.'

Laura couldn't hold his gaze any longer. Instead she focused on the perfect knot in his silk tie, her hands firm against his solid chest.

'So even though you don't love me the way I love you, I want to marry you. I know you'll be loyal. I know you care and you'll try to make me happy. I'd rather be with you than alone, on the other side of the world.' She paused then forced herself to continue. 'If you still want me, I'll try hard to fit into your world.'

Silence descended, punctured only by the rush of her pulse in her ears.

'Have you finished?'

Laura nodded and warm fingers brushed her chin, tilting it up till she met that fathomless black gaze. Except it wasn't black but glowing. Dazzling.

'*Psihi mou...*' His voice was rough-cut velvet, caressing her. 'If only I'd known. I've wanted to share my feelings but held back because I didn't want to scare you off.' A smile transformed his taut features. 'I'm in love with you, Laura. That's why I was determined to let you go. Because I love you so much I can't bear to have you hurt any more because of me.'

She clutched at his lapels. 'Except nothing would hurt me as much as you pushing me away.'

'Laura *mou, s'agapo. S'agapo.*'

Then the words ended as his lips met hers, tender but sure, possessive yet inviting her to stake her own claim. Laura needed no second invitation. Arms around his neck, on tiptoes she leaned in, kissing him with all the pent-up longing she hadn't dared reveal before.

Finally they broke part enough to look into each other's eyes. She was on his lap and he was sitting on the sofa and she had no recollection of them moving.

'Don't cry, *psihi mou*.' Gentle thumbs stroked her cheeks, brushing away wetness.

'They're tears of happiness.' The first she'd ever shed. 'I can't believe you love me.'

'Believe it. I've been in love with you since Queensland. It drove me crazy when you wouldn't let me back into your life afterwards. I couldn't settle to anything and was on the point of returning to Australia when I discovered you might be pregnant. And,' he said forcefully, 'while I'm thrilled about our babies, I want you in my life because I love *you*.'

Laura read the truth in his gaze. Her heart sang as he leaned in, whispering in Greek as he kissed her mouth, cheeks and throat with all the fervour she could wish.

'What is that you call me? *Psihi mou?*'

'My soul.' The devastating simplicity of it made her eyes well all over again. 'That's what you are, Laura. You've helped me become a better, stronger man. You make me feel whole.' He kissed her tears away. 'What do you say to a life together filled with love?'

'I say yes. A thousand times yes.' Then for the first time she spoke the most important words she'd ever use in his language. '*S'agapo*, Vassili.'

I love you.

EPILOGUE

VASSILI PUT LILY into her cot. Sleepy golden-green eyes surveyed him, widening as if objecting to being removed from her favourite place in his arms.

'Go,' his *mamá* whispered as she placed a hand on her granddaughter's tummy. 'You know she'll fight sleep if she thinks there's a chance to be with you. She'll settle in no time with me and Anna.'

He nodded and stepped back, letting his mother and the nanny take over. But Vassili wasn't in a hurry to leave. He might be as soft-hearted as everyone said, but he didn't care. His family was so precious he found it hard to part from them.

He looked across at little Theo, long eyelashes resting on his cheeks, already asleep. Of the twins, he was the more relaxed. Lily had her mother's feistiness. Or perhaps, he smiled, her uncle's.

A half-hearted wail sounded from the cot.

'Stop hovering and go,' his mother ordered. 'She's over-tired from excitement.'

'It's okay, Mamá,' said a soft voice behind him. 'I've come to take him back to the party.'

He turned to meet his wife's twinkling gaze.

'They're going to cut the cake but won't start without us.' She looked past him, her gaze tender as she surveyed the cots. 'They need their rest, poor darlings. It's tiring, being the centre of so much adulation.'

'I know,' he whispered back. 'There'll be hell to pay tomorrow morning.' He let her lead him out.

'And you'll enjoy every minute of it, my big, brave twin tamer.'

He grinned. 'You know I love danger and adventure.'

He was still fulfilling his promise to his brother. Not through hair-raising physical feats, but by living a full, satisfying, challenging life with his beloved family. He knew Theo would have been happy for him, embracing the future with an open heart.

In the hall Vassili pulled Laura into his arms. She'd changed his life completely, giving him hope and such steadfast love. 'You're looking particularly gorgeous, Kyria Thanos.'

'It's the new dress.'

He leaned back, surveying the sexy emerald dress she wore with such elegance. The gold filigree pendant just above the tantalising upper slopes of her breasts. The love in her eyes.

His heart beat faster as joy filled him. 'The dress is delightful but not as gorgeous as you, *psihi mou*. You'll always be the most beautiful woman in the world to me.'

He lifted his hand to her cheek, cupping her soft skin and brushing her lips with his.

'We can't,' she whispered, though her mouth clung and her hands crept around his neck. 'Eudora and her new husband are waiting.'

He kissed her more deeply.

'And Constantine is eager to make his speech.'

To his surprise his uncle had re-evaluated his priorities. He'd stopped protesting long enough to get to know Eudora's new husband and admire him. Constantine still worked in the family company, but in tandem with Vassili, sharing the burdens.

Vassili sighed. 'And we don't want to keep them waiting.'

'Well, the wedding is on *our* island.' Laura smoothed her hair but her face was flushed. 'We need to be there.'

Vassili scooped her close and headed towards the sound of music and voices. 'Naturally. But when they're gone...'

'When they're gone, my darling, I'm all yours.' Her glowing look spoke of love and tenderness and that excitement he always felt when they were together.

'I couldn't ask for anything better.'

He swept her close and they went out hand in hand.

* * * * *

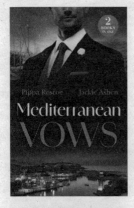

COMING SOON!

We really hope you enjoyed reading this book.
If you're looking for more romance
be sure to head to the shops when
new books are available on

Thursday 23rd May

To see which titles are coming soon, please visit
millsandboon.co.uk/nextmonth

MILLS & BOON

MILLS & BOON ®

Coming next month

TWINS TO TAME HIM
Tara Pammi

Sebastian rubbed a hand over his face. Any momentary hesitation he'd felt about having two little boys to care for, to nurture and protect, dissipated, leaving behind a crystal-clear clarity he had never known in his life.

Whatever instinct had propelled him to demand Laila marry him…it carried the weight of his deepest, most secret desire within it.

For his sons to be happy and well-adjusted and thriving, they needed their mother and he needed them. Ergo, his primary goal now was to do anything to keep Laila in his life.

And while he'd never have admitted it openly to his brute of a father, Sebastian had always known he could be just as ruthless as his twin.

He was keeping his sons and he was keeping their mother in his life, even if it meant he had to seduce every inch of logic and rationale out of Dr. Jaafri. And he would make sure she not only enjoyed the seduction but that she had everything she'd ever wanted. He would make all her wishes and dreams come true. It was only a matter of getting her to admit them.

Continue reading
TWINS TO TAME HIM
Tara Pammi

Available next month
millsandboon.co.uk

afterglow BOOKS

From showing up to glowing up, Afterglow Books features authentic and relatable stories, characters you can't help but fall in love with and plenty of spice!

OUT NOW

To discover more visit:
Afterglowbooks.co.uk

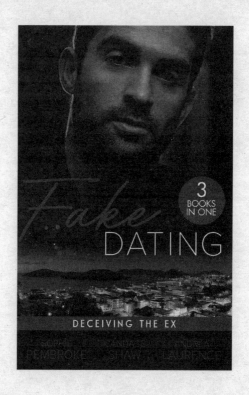

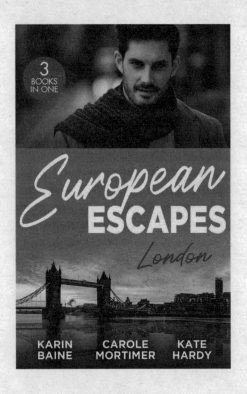

OUT NOW!

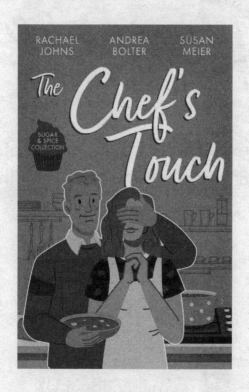

Available at
millsandboon.co.uk

MILLS & BOON

LET'S TALK
Romance

For exclusive extracts, competitions and special offers, find us online:

- **f** MillsandBoon
- **X** @MillsandBoon
- **○** @MillsandBoonUK
- **♪** @MillsandBoonUK

Get in touch on 01413 063 232